MW01196389

Black Dog Short Stories I & II

RACHEL NEUMEIER

CONTENTS

ACKNOWLEDGMENTS

Particular thanks are due to my brother Craig Neumeier and to Laura Florand, who both provided feedback and advice on the rough drafts of these stories; and to Maureen Eichner, who helped me get the details right when I decided Justin's grandmother was Eastern Orthodox. Any errors are definitely mine and no one else's.

CHRISTMAS SHOPPING

Grayson leaned back in his chair, tapping his pen gently on the table, looking exactly like what he was: a busy man hounded beyond endurance by the petty concerns of children. At least, it was easy to feel like a *niña*, when Grayson considered you that way. It was the way he raised his heavy eyebrows. Sort of a pained, faintly astonished expression, as though you'd managed despite yourself to pull off a dubious surprise.

Which wasn't fair at *all*, because even if Grayson really was overworked—which he was, Natividad wasn't denying that, especially short-handed as Dimilioc was these days—but her request was *perfectly reasonable*.

"It's not like I can go shopping with Alejandro," she pointed out. "It wouldn't be right for him to see what I get him."

Grayson set down his pen, exactly aligned with the edge of the table. That kind of precision seemed out of place in so harsh-featured a man, until you knew Grayson a little better and understood the unbreakable control he exercised in every single aspect of his life.

"You can buy anything you like online—" he began.

"Yes, but that's not the same! Anyway, I don't *know* what to get Alejandro, or Miguel either. And you can't look properly at things online, you know. It's not the same as walking down streets and into stores and things. Anyway, my *first* Christmas in America! With a real town only an hour away! It's not fair to say I can't go shopping! And Newport has to be safe. Nobody would dare cause trouble so close to Dimilioc, right? Well, *isn't* that right?"

Though she couldn't help but remember those strays that had attacked her the only other time she had been in

Newport. Had either of her brothers ever happened to tell Grayson about that? She didn't think she had ever mentioned it herself. She decided she really didn't need to mention it now, since those strays had almost certainly been part of Vonhausel's shadow pack. Nothing like that would be a problem now. She said again, firmly, "Newport would be *perfectly* safe."

"Perhaps," Grayson conceded. "Probably. But *probably* is not adequate when it's a question of your safety, Natividad. I think you must acknowledge that these are unsettled days. We hardly know what may happen—even in Newport. Also," he added, his deep, gritty voice coming down on every word with heavy finality, "though Newport is hardly a city, I am certainly not going to approve you driving yourself into or around any town."

Natividad hesitated, because that was a point. She didn't have the kind of license you were supposed to have to drive, but besides that, she had never really learned to drive at all. Only one or two people in Potosi had even owned a car, and unlike her twin she hadn't been interested in learning. And here in Vermont, there were all those rules and signs and things, most of which she didn't know, either. She hadn't exactly thought about that. Now that she did think about it, she really didn't want to try to drive in Newport. Or anywhere else. She said at last, "Maybe DeAnn would like to go shopping. She probably wants to get things for Conway and Thaddeus. If she drove, that wouldn't be a problem."

"Natividad. Do you expect me to risk *both* of Dimilioc's Pure women without a proper guard, in order for you to indulge yourself with shopping you could perfectly well do here, online? I imagine Thaddeus might have one or two things to say to me if I approved any such notion."

Well, when he put it that way . . . but still. It *wasn't* fair. "You let Miguel—" she began.

"Miguel has considerably more experience with cars than you do, Natividad."

"Yes, but—"

"Also," continued Grayson, raising his voice slightly,

"Your brother is not Pure. If he should be so unfortunate as to encounter an unexpected stray black dog, there is no reason it should notice him." There was a slight pause. Then Grayson picked the pen up again, turning it over in his powerful fingers. "However, I agree that it is unjust to cage you here. As you say . . . this *is* your first Christmas here at Dimilioc. Of course you wish to mark the occasion, where your year—and your life—turns from the past to the present."

Natividad blinked in surprise. "You *do* understand!"

The grim line of Grayson's mouth eased. "I believe I do. Yes." He tapped the pen on the desk again. Tap, tap, tap. But this time she thought the tapping seemed more thoughtful than impatient.

"You may go shopping," he conceded at last. "But a black dog must go with you. I understand why you do not wish this to be Alejandro. Very well. Keziah can go with you."

"Keziah! No!"

"Yes," Grayson said inflexibly. "A little trip together will be good for both of you, I believe. You will have your opportunity to escape the confines of Dimilioc for the day. Keziah will have an opportunity to engage in a bit of harmless frivolity—I doubt she is much accustomed to frivolity. She may even enjoy it. And in the unlikely chance that you should encounter any difficulties, Keziah is perfectly capable of protecting you."

Natividad wanted to say, *Yes, but who will protect me from Keziah?* But she had to admit that Keziah was very, very unlikely to actually hurt her. Just . . . she probably wouldn't be very *nice*, either. She muttered, "I could wait till Ezekiel's back. *He* wouldn't mind taking me to Newport."

Ezekiel would be delighted to be asked, she was sure, since he was sort of half courting her. And half certain he'd already claimed her. Black dogs were so exasperatingly territorial. On second thought, she wasn't entirely certain she wanted to ask Ezekiel after all. It was hard to decide whether she wanted to encourage him or try to get him to give her a little more space.

But she didn't have to decide right this minute. Because Grayson only said, "I fear Ezekiel is unlikely to return in time for such an excursion. Keziah. Or—" he tapped his computer's monitor with the pen—"online shopping remains an option."

Natividad sighed. It was plain that now she'd put the idea in his head, Grayson was determined to force her to spend a whole day together with Keziah. Maybe . . . maybe it wouldn't be *so* bad. They could just . . . go to shops and things. They didn't actually have to *talk* to each other.

But if she was going to have to go shopping with *Keziah,* she'd better be able to find something for her brothers. Something just right. If she had to spend *a whole day* with Keziah and didn't even find anything, she would . . . she would put salt and cayenne instead of sugar and cinnamon in Grayson's cinnamon rolls. And he would *deserve* it.

"*Christmas* shopping," Keziah said, tilting her head and gazing at Natividad through her lashes in a way that implied she had never heard of anything so ridiculous. But then she shrugged. "I do not care about Christmas. But I do not mind to go shopping." *Even with you,* her tone implied. "But Newport is certainly not the place to go. It is not so much farther to real cities. Burlington is not so far. An hour and a half, two hours. We will go there."

Natividad blinked, startled. Going farther than Newport hadn't even occurred to her. She knew Newport was not really a city, but it was a lot bigger than Lewis or Brighton. It had seemed big enough to her. She had only thought of how claustrophobic Dimilioc could get, of how she couldn't even walk in the woods because it was too cold and the snow made it hard to walk. It just seemed so . . . stifling, sometimes. So escaping to Newport for a day had seemed enough. Especially since she really did need to go Christmas shopping. But even if she'd thought Newport too small, she wouldn't have had any idea where else to go.

Keziah plainly knew all about where *she* wanted to go.

That made Natividad feel young and stupid, because it had never occurred to her to look at maps and learn what places were near Dimilioc, what cities might be close and what each was like. Keziah obviously had looked at all those things. She was used to real cities, big cities, and used to coming and going as she liked, and taking care of herself.

Natividad said meekly, "Burlington would be wonderful. If Grayson doesn't mind."

"Grayson spoils you so. I am sure he will not want you shopping for Christmas in *Newport*. We will leave tomorrow early and come back in the night. Then we will not need to shop quickly and I can look for what I want. Maybe a bracelet with moonstones." She touched her moonstone earrings, gave Natividad a swift, amused glance, and added, "*You* could get a better coat. You Pure are so delicate. You could get a pink coat that is all puffy with feathers."

She strolled away before Natividad could think of an answer.

Even with Keziah, getting away from Dimilioc for a day was wonderful. They left as the sun rose behind the mountains, the pearl-gray dawn giving way to rose and peach, lavender and gold shining around the edges of the clouds. In this light, the mountains were beautiful, too. The leafless forest still looked stark and forbidding, but wherever it was open, the snow had melted a little on top and then frozen again, white and shiny and smooth, so that it glowed with the colors of the dawn. The trip would have been worth it just for the drive. Natividad rolled her window down just a little to let in the light. She even enjoyed the sharp cold.

Keziah slanted a sideways look at Natividad, but said nothing about the window. Black dogs did not feel the cold, and she was not one of Natividad's brothers, to worry that perhaps Natividad might feel the cold too much. Keziah was very good at driving cars, though she drove faster and more aggressively than Natividad liked—but that was a black dog. It was foolish to expect one to drive gently. Natividad gazed at the mountains unrolling beyond her window and watched the light of the brilliant winter day fill the world and let Keziah drive as she chose.

Hardly more than an hour and a half later, in the heart of Burlington, Keziah tucked the big car into the single available parking space near a big church. The parking space seemed too small, but Keziah parked exactly the same way that she drove: with smooth, elegant skill and a complete disregard for what anyone else thought of her. She hadn't hesitated to steal that space from another driver who had obviously been waiting for it, slipping neatly around his SUV and into the place she wanted. The other driver looked mad, until he got a good look at Keziah. Then he just looked stunned.

Keziah, emerging from the driver's side with lithe grace, seemed oblivious to both his annoyance and his admiration. Natividad was sure the older girl was acutely aware of both. Keziah liked to be admired. She wanted people to look at her. For this trip to Burlington, she was wearing smooth black leggings and high-heeled knee-high black boots and a silk tunic, sapphire-blue but with jagged streaks of black across the blue. Her moonstone-and-crystal earrings glittered, half hidden by the thick fall of her black, black hair. Lavender powder dusted her wide-set eyes, making them seem even larger in her elegant, triangular face.

Next to her, Natividad knew she looked very young. Like a cute girl, maybe, but just a girl. If the other driver had noticed her at all, he probably took her for Keziah's younger sister. They didn't look anything alike, but their coloring was almost the same. She had already found that most *Norteamericanos* noticed only the color of hair and skin and eyes and not the shape of the mouth or eyes or anything, and so thought she and Keziah looked like sisters.

Keziah put her hands on her hips, glancing up and down the street. "Well, it will do, I suppose. That is the shopping area, just there." She nodded toward the area she meant.

"I think it's nice," Natividad protested. All these red brick buildings so neat and well-kept, the park around the big church pretty even in winter. She liked the church, all red brick except for the white bell tower. She might have liked to go look at it, but probably that would not be high on Keziah's list of things to do.

Keziah rolled her eyes. "It is hardly a city. There are real cities in California. New York is a real city. This . . . well, it is better than Newport."

"New York would be a little far to go for Christmas shopping, never mind Los Angeles!" Natividad wondered if the Saudi girl missed Los Angeles. Or, for that matter, whether she ever missed wherever she was really from, Riyadh or wherever. But she couldn't imagine asking anything so personal.

Even though there were a lot of cars, the street was not so very crowded with people, not even with Christmas approaching: summer was tourist season here in this cold country. In the summer, lots of people came to Burlington to go boating on Lake Champlain—the website Natividad had found said so. Boating sounded like fun. She had found herself wondering if maybe Ezekiel might like to go boating with her on Lake Memphremagog. Lake Memphremagog was near Newport, so close to Dimilioc that maybe Grayson would not mind letting Ezekiel free for long enough. Even Ezekiel could not go off on assignments and kill strays *all* the time. Especially not in the spring, when the leaves came back and flowers bloomed and the air smelled of damp earth rather than snow . . . maybe Ezekiel would like to take a little holiday, in the spring.

The thought of going out on a lake, just herself with Ezekiel, alone in a little boat, with the sun finally warm and the air soft instead of bitter—Natividad thought that sounded like a really promising idea. Maybe. If Ezekiel was so determined to claim her, if she had only a few months to decide if she would agree, then she needed to figure out whether he really liked *her*, or just liked the idea of a girl who was Pure. Maybe she *would* ask him to go boating with her. Maybe she would find out he would rather go on missions for Grayson and kill strays. It was hard to guess.

She wasn't sure she wanted to think about how little she

still knew Ezekiel, even after these weeks in Dimilioc. She looked around at Burlington instead, all the long streets that stretched out as far as she could see, paved with red bricks to show where people were supposed to walk and cars were not supposed to drive. That was where lots of the shops were. She looked west to see if Lake Champlain was visible, but couldn't even catch a glimpse of water. Maybe Keziah wouldn't mind walking to the lake later, after they looked at the shops. Jewelry places, like she wanted to see. Probably there were shops that sold jewelry here.

There were indeed jewelry shops. Also shops for books and candles and pretty wooden picture frames. One place sold paper things, cards and books with blank pages, which Natividad had never seen before. Keziah said those were for photos and papers you wanted to keep to remind you of the past, and Natividad really wanted one with all kinds of flowers embossed on its leather cover, gold and brown and very pretty. But she had no papers or pictures to help her remember her past. She didn't want to think about that, about how few pieces of the past she could still touch and lift in her hands. How much she had lost entirely.

They went on to other places that sold fancy chairs and tables and big ornate cabinets for outrageous prices, or toys for children—that one was fun, and Natividad wanted to linger, but Keziah looked bored. There was a shop that sold many kinds of fancy chocolates, with little squiggles on the top so you could tell which kind was which. Keziah bought a dozen tiny little chocolates, and made Natividad buy a dozen for herself, and they walked down the street eating them. Natividad exclaimed at the flavors, which she mostly didn't recognize, and Keziah laughed at her, but not in an unfriendly way.

After that there was another shop that sold things for pets, including sweaters for dogs. Natividad had never imagined putting a *sweater* on a *dog*, but she actually saw two people with little dogs dressed in sweaters. Imagine, a country so cold even the *dogs* needed sweaters! She craned her neck, trying not to be obvious as she stared. The dogs were cute, though. So small she could have held either one cupped in her hands. No wonder they needed sweaters.

In the middle of the whole big shopping area stood a beautiful enormous Christmas tree, and beyond that were more shops, and a fountain to mark the boundary between the shopping area and the ordinary street, though the fountain was turned off because of the cold and Natividad did not even know what it was until Keziah told her.

Keziah found a moonstone bracelet at one place, but the bracelet had a silver chain, so she couldn't try it on. She asked for platinum, but they didn't have one like that. Keziah frowned so fiercely at the girl in the shop that the girl actually took a step backward, so Natividad touched the back of Keziah's hand and wished she would be calm. She whispered that if she wanted the bracelet, Natividad could blood the silver for her. Then she hesitated because on second thought, if Keziah wore a silver bracelet, blooded or not, it would make every other black dog in Dimilioc uncomfortable. On third thought, though, Keziah might like that idea.

Keziah transferred her frown to Natividad, who couldn't quite figure out what was in the older girl's mind. It would have been much easier to go shopping with Alejandro, really.

The girl in the shop said maybe they could make a bracelet to order. So Keziah said that she would think about it, in an abrupt tone that meant she was still angry and stalked out of the shop, with Natividad hurrying to keep up.

After that Natividad thought maybe she had better pick the shops for a while. So she insisted on visiting a place that sold old books, but though she bought Miguel a book about European history and also a book about Japanese art, she couldn't find anything she was sure her twin would really think was special. Nor anything at all for Alejandro.

"But maybe Amira would like a book of fairy tales?" she suggested. "This one is pretty. Look at the pictures. I like this one with all the *cisnes*. I don't know the word in English . . ."

Keziah said scornfully, refusing to look, "A book?

Black dog children do not like books."

Natividad nodded, not arguing. "I know, but sometimes Alejandro used to like to listen to Mamá read stories."

But it was a mistake to say this because even after so long it was painful to think about Mamá, about the evenings when their whole family had gathered to listen to her read aloud. Keziah looked like she might be remembering painful things, too. Natividad quickly led the way out of the shop.

She found a place that sold the most amazing kinds of soap. She lingered over a kind that was supposed to smell of chocolate, and it really did, too. She loved it, but she wasn't sure she really wanted to use soap that smelled of chocolate. She bought a nice smooth bar of soap that smelled of roses instead.

After that there was a place that sold the most amazing, complicated puzzles, made of all these cut-out pieces of stiff paper that you put together to make a picture or build a castle. She lingered over one on display, already put together to make a great cathedral. Maybe Miguel would like this kind of puzzle? She longed to get him one, but was not sure. Her twin was obviously *aburrió* these days; he was restless, he didn't have anything to *do* now that they had joined Dimilioc, when before he had spent a lot of time helping Papá keep track of what was going on with the war. It was hard for him now. Maybe a puzzle would make him happier.

"A tedious exercise in pointlessness," Keziah said dismissively. "When you finish, what do you have? A paper artwork that would be far more beautiful if it had never been cut to pieces in the first place." She insisted on moving on to a shop that sold clothing. She made Natividad wait while she tried on a loose-knit sweater, and a blouse with swirls of glitter on it, and a skirt cut on a sharp diagonal. That shop was more crowded, and many of the people seemed impatient. When Keziah reached for another skirt, the last one on the rack, a young woman older than she was tried to bump her out of the way and get it first. Keziah didn't give way, of course. Not only did she not move, she caught the other woman's wrist and forced her back a step. From the woman's expression, which changed from outraged to shocked, Keziah's grip was probably just short of crushing.

"Careful!" Natividad said, and amended that quickly to, "You don't want to drop that skirt!" so it wouldn't seem like she was trying to give Keziah orders.

Keziah's gave Natividad a look and deliberately opened her hand, letting the skirt crumple to the floor. Then she stepped on it. The young woman gasped, maybe in surprise and maybe just in pain from her wrist. She looked like she was about to make up her mind to scream or shout or something, any minute.

Natividad said hastily, "Let's go somewhere else, okay? I'm hungry, aren't you?"

So Keziah let the woman go, fortunately without dropping *her* on the floor and stepping on her, and strolled out like she'd meant to leave right then anyway. Then they walked a few blocks west because Natividad wanted to see the lake. They ate Thai food at a place overlooking the lake.

Natividad had never eaten Thai food before. Keziah ordered quickly for them both, coconut shrimp, and a noodle dish called pad thai, and a chicken curry. The shrimp were wonderful, and the noodles were made of rice which gave them a very different texture from the spaghetti they sometimes had at Dimilioc with tomato sauce, and there was coconut milk in the curry, along with things like lemongrass that Natividad had never heard of. She discovered all this by asking the waitress many questions. The waitress was very nice. Her name was Joan and she was going to school at the University of Vermont and studying horticulture, and she had three younger siblings, and her mother loved complicated jigsaw puzzles—but Keziah made Natividad leave before she found out if the waitress's mother liked the kind of puzzle that made a sculpture of a cathedral.

So then they walked back to the shopping area. Keziah said she had decided to get the moonstone bracelet after all. She told Natividad, as though this was a brand-new idea and also as though she was doing her a favor, that Natividad could blood the silver for her so she could wear it. So they went back toward the end of the pedestrian walking area, which was where the jewelry shop was, and got the bracelet, and then came out again, and that was when a big green car jumped over the curb and rushed across the red brick pavers right at them. Keziah caught Natividad around the waist and leaped out of the car's path so that instead of hitting them, the car ran straight across the street and smashed into a shop on the other side with a great shattering crash of broken glass and wood and a high-pitched squeal of tearing metal. Someone started screaming, and someone else said, "Oh my God—oh my God—" over and over, and a somewhere a child was crying, great gasping wails that sounded frightened rather than hurt.

Natividad stared at the accident in shock. It was the shop that sold chocolates. The fragrance of chocolate rolled out into the cold air, mingling with the sudden acrid smell of burning plastic and something else underneath that, something even less pleasant, sharp and chemical.

By this time, Keziah had shoved Natividad back into the doorway of the nearest shop and stepped in front of her, which was fine, she was supposed to protect Natividad after all, but it was also infuriating because Natividad couldn't *see*. She stood on her toes, which didn't help because Keziah was too much taller than she was, so then she ducked and tried to squeeze around Keziah, back onto the sidewalk. But Keziah wouldn't let her. She said furiously, "Stupid girl! Stay back! Did you not see that car was aimed straight at you?"

"Aimed!" said Natividad.

"There was no driver!" said Keziah. "Someone pointed it at you and jammed the accelerator down." She was not shouting now. She still sounded furious, though. She was scanning the street, both ways but mostly the way the car had come. Natividad could hardly believe Keziah could be right, but she stayed behind the black dog girl anyway. She ducked down so she could see past her, though.

The child was still wailing, but the screaming had stopped. Someone, a man, was giving urgent orders to *Move that damn car* and *Get that table up off there*, but as far as

Natividad could see, though lots of people were edging close to the disaster, no one was listening. Fire was crawling over the rear of the car and up the shattered remnants of the front of the shop. She could see everyone was afraid of the fire. That made sense: didn't cars explode when they caught on fire?

But Natividad could see a little now, though Keziah still blocked most of her view. She could see that a man, a big man with a beard and a leather jacket, didn't seem afraid that the car might explode. Or maybe he was just desperate—he was shouting—now he was pulling on the car all by himself, trying to lift it, ignoring the fire. Of course he couldn't move it, an ordinary human man like that. Natividad didn't understand why he was trying. A woman was holding back a little girl who was trying to go help him, or maybe trying to pull him away –

Then she understood. She said urgently, "Keziah! There's someone trapped under that car! Or pinned in front of it, or something!"

"Yes," said Keziah. She didn't look at Natividad. She was staring at the accident, then around at the street, then back at the accident. "A girl. She was sitting there. She was twelve, perhaps." She went on after a second, "She looked nothing like Amira."

"Well, she's *somebody's* sister!" Natividad said.

"Yes," said Keziah again. But she added, "I am supposed to protect *you*."

"I don't care!" Natividad said energetically. "I think it *was* an accident! No stray would use a *car* to attack me, you know that. If a stray was out there, he'd already have attacked! In two seconds I'm going to go help that man move that car, and you can come protect me if you want me to stay safe!"

Keziah made a sharp, angry gesture with both hands. "This is impossible! This is all impossible!"

"It was an accident," Natividad insisted. "Or some random thing, not aimed at me especially, we just got in the way! Keziah, that car is going to explode! Think of that girl—Amira's age, you said! It wouldn't take you a second to move that car!"

"Grayson would be very angry if you were injured." But Keziah clearly wanted to go help the girl—that surprised Natividad, but she wasn't going to question it.

Keziah paused for one more instant, to stare down at Natividad and say sternly, "Draw a mandala. Then stay in it. Do not leave it. Do not watch me. Watch for enemies. If you see *anything* that looks wrong, call me. You promise this? Because if you promise, then I will step away from you and pretend to be very distracted over there where the car is. *Then* we will find out if you have an enemy—but you must call me at once if you see anything dangerous, because I truly will be a little bit distracted if I must move that car."

"Yes, yes!" That was clever, using Natividad as bait—that would let Keziah do exactly what she wanted, rescue that girl and also make any enemy come out into the open. But Keziah *was* very clever, always thinking, which wasn't usual for a black dog, but Keziah was unusual in lots of ways.

Natividad didn't have a silver knife or anything with which to draw a proper mandala. She dropped to her knees and drew it with her finger as fast as she could, a tight little circle with just room for her inside, anchored with nothing but smaller mandalas at the cardinal directions. It was a terrible mandala, though she did have a silver coin to set right at the center, which was better than nothing. She felt it spark to life, the cross and then the circle, and tucked her arms around her knees, careful not to break the outer circle.

Keziah waited just long enough to be sure Natividad had finished her mandala. Then she strode across the street, shoved between two bystanders, stepped easily beneath and around burning rubble, grabbed the desperate, straining man by the arm, and tossed him quite casually away from the car, back toward the safety of the street. Reaching down, she curled her own hands around the burning edge of the undercarriage. Then she straightened, tipping the car up and back on its side, swinging it to the side and flinging it at last, with a grimace of effort, to roll upside down. Flames rose up around her, but she ignored the fire, kicking aside the wreckage of several chairs, bending to lift the girl she found beneath the twisted metal of the table. Natividad tried to watch, but everyone was in the way and she couldn't see very well, and anyway she wasn't supposed to watch Keziah—she was supposed to watch for enemies. Which truly made no sense, except that what if there was a *callejero* after all? Or what if there was a black dog with discipline and control, not a stray at all, but a strong black dog who was an enemy of Dimilioc?

But it wasn't a black dog that came for her. Natividad shouldn't have been surprised. She had known no black dog would use a car to attack anybody. She had *known* that. So she shouldn't have been surprised it wasn't a black dog.

But she was shocked to see it was one of the blood kin.

No blood kin should have been here—certainly not *here*, in Vermont, so close to Dimilioc. Blood kin were made by vampires, and all the vampires were gone. Once their masters had lost the power to hide themselves and their servants beneath the miasma, the blood kin had at last been recognized for the monsters they were, and ordinary people everywhere had destroyed them. Silver was good against the blood kin, and cutting off their heads—there were ways, even for ordinary people, so now all the blood kin were gone, along with the vampires.

Except plainly a few had hidden, because this one was *right here*, right out in *broad daylight* in the middle of the public street, even though blood kin hated sunlight and hated being seen clearly. It must have known it would die if it let itself be recognized, but it had come out anyway.

Natividad had always known that blood kin *could* do things on their own, even if they also had to obey the vampire that had made them. They had to be able to make decisions and run things, or they couldn't have become mayors and school superintendents and so on, the way so many had. Blood kin had always sought positions of power and public trust, because they could corrupt and destroy a city better from the inside, and corrupting and destroying cities was what vampires loved best.

But she had always thought that the blood kin would just die without their vampires to rule them. She had not guessed that any of the blood kin, surviving their masters, could own enough independent will to seek revenge. Maybe this one had even been trying to get to Dimilioc—maybe it had sensed Natividad and decided she was an easier target. Blood kin *were* smart, just as smart as the people they'd been before the vampire got them; that was why so many had been able to pass for human for so long.

It was horrible. As soon as it came out in the open, all the people who had been staring at the wreckage of the car and the shop, and most of all at Keziah, turned around and stared at it instead. Something about the blood kin, some instinct bred into people by thousands of years of living with vampires even if they hadn't known it, pulled all their combined attention toward it. Then the screaming started in earnest, people scrambling back and away in all directions. Except the girl's father, who ran to get his daughter from Keziah—but Natividad already knew he was very brave.

Vampires had always made blood kin out of normal people, and for a while after they were made, blood kin looked almost like the people they had been. But there was nothing of that person left in this one. It had been made a long time ago. It was skeletally gaunt, with yellowish papery skin tight across its bones and long yellow fingernails that were like claws. Its eyes were crimson; its teeth, set in a jaw that hinged oddly, were black and pointed. And it moved in a strange disjointed rush, all fits and starts, wanting Natividad but wary of the mandala that surrounded her.

Natividad ducked her face against her knees and closed her eyes, because if she looked she knew she would try to run, and if she ran it would be on her instantly. Keziah had been right to make her draw a mandala. She was Pure, and for her, safety was something she won by defending her ground. Only she wished she'd had time to make a much, much bigger mandala, and anchor it much, much more strongly into the earth.

Then Keziah hit the blood kin. She was almost all the way in her black dog form, which was a very fast change for a black dog; only Ezekiel could shift between one step and the next; usually it took minutes for a black dog to change. But Keziah was fast. Only the blood kin was fast, too. It wheeled to meet her, vicious and quick and a lot stronger than anything so emaciated should have been, hissing in a voice like a snake and raking with its yellow claws—Natividad had never heard that blood kin had poisoned claws, but those nasty yellow claws *looked* poisoned. It was *horrible*, and Keziah wasn't used to fighting blood kin, certainly not all by herself. She already had a nasty long gash all across her face and neck and shoulder. Natividad jumped to her feet and snatched Keziah's new moonstone bracelet out of the little pouch it had come in, wove a memory of moonlight into its stones and around its silver chain, and threw it as hard as she could right at the blood kin.

The bracelet turned over and over, sunlight and the memory of moonlight tangling in its stones and turning them a strange milky golden color. It hit the blood kin on the back, and the monster whirled around, hissing with fury and pain, and Keziah snarled and lunged forward, and the blood kin made a terrible sound, and there was a savage, fast, tumbling blur of shaggy black and gaunt yellow, and then a horrible crimson-eyed head with a narrow vicious jaw flew right at Natividad, who squeaked and ducked, but the head bounced off her mandala and burst into white flames. Black ichor spattered the brick pavers where it rolled, each little drop burning away in its own brief pyre. The smoke smelled like sulfur and rot and hatred.

"Oh, *ugh*," Natividad said, heartfelt.

Keziah was now fully in her black dog form. She wasn't as huge as most black dogs, nothing like as big as Alejandro, but she was still more than three times Natividad's size, and she looked very, very dangerous—which she was. Natividad didn't blame everyone left in the street from flinching and cowering, even the man with the little girl, who had backed away but hadn't yet gotten all the way out of the street. He was staring, his eyes wide and horrified.

Not wanting to see the man's horror, Natividad looked away, focusing again on Keziah. She had that long, nasty gash across her face and neck and shoulder, but that wound wasn't serious enough to drive her back into her human form. She didn't look like she was planning to shift back any time soon. Too angry, too outraged by finding one of the blood kin here where there weren't supposed to be any—too scared, maybe, because what if there was a *vampire* somewhere nearby, what if that was why the blood kin had been here? There wasn't, there couldn't be, all the vampires were dead—but Keziah was probably thinking that maybe one might be left, because blood kin didn't usually come just by themselves.

Natividad certainly understood just how Keziah must feel and what she must be afraid of, because she felt angry and outraged and scared herself and she wasn't even a black dog.

She stepped warily out of the remnants of her mandala. It really hadn't been a very good mandala; just being hit one time by the torn-off head of the blood kin had all but ruined it, but even so Natividad hated to leave its protection. But Keziah was pacing and snarling and staring around, looking for more blood kin and scaring all the human people absolutely out of their minds. Natividad would have put her arms around Alejandro's neck, but all she dared with Keziah was a touch. But she did dare that, and whispered that it was all right, there weren't any more blood kin, she would know—she wasn't sure she would, actually—but she told Keziah firmly that she could change back, that she *ought* to change back, that everything was fine.

Keziah actually listened. Maybe not to her words, because black dogs often lost language when they changed. But at least to Natividad's tone. She turned her head toward Natividad and then finally straightened and dwindled, letting her shadow sink away, reclaiming her human form. She didn't look quite her normal cool, scornful self, but she gave a little shiver and ran her hands through her hair and came very close.

Across the street, the man whose daughter Keziah had saved took a step forward.

"We'd better not stay," Natividad said urgently.

"No," Keziah said vaguely.

"You're a werewolf," said the man. He didn't come closer, but he didn't run away, either.

Keziah gave him a haughty stare, but Natividad said, "Yes, but the good kind!"

More than a little to her surprise the man laughed a little and answered, "Yes, I can see she must be, and is there anything I can do to help? She's your sister, isn't she? Is she all right? That monster hit her—and the car was on fire when she picked it up—"

Keziah turned around. She was so surprised she actually *looked* surprised instead of sarcastic or offended. She opened her mouth and closed it again and said finally, "I am not hurt."

"Werewolves heal fast!" Natividad said quickly. "She's fine. But thanks, though. Is your little girl all right?"

"I think so," said the man. "Yeah, I think so, thanks to you." He was speaking to Keziah now, sounding a little hesitant but not afraid. "You got her out—and you killed that monster. So fast! I saw one of those things kill a dozen people once, the news showed it, armed cops tried to take it down but it tore them up. But you ripped its head right off!" He was looking at Keziah in admiration that didn't have anything to do with Keziah's beauty or style.

Keziah shook her head, looking confused.

"She was glad to help. But I think we better go," said Natividad. "Um, Keziah, are those sirens?"

Keziah blinked and seemed to come back to herself. Then she said sharply, "Yes. Come," and caught Natividad's wrist and dragged her away toward their car, which wasn't fair since Natividad certainly hadn't been trying to dawdle, but she didn't protest. It was better not to argue with black dogs. Especially when they were already doing what you wanted.

Keziah was very silent on the drive home. Eventually she said, “You did not find a gift for your brothers. I am sorry.”

“It wasn’t your fault!” said Natividad.

“No. But I am sorry for it.”

There was another little silence, and then Natividad said, “You didn’t get anything for Amira, either.”

“No,” said Keziah. Then she said, her gaze on the road, not glancing at Natividad, “I know what I wish to give Amira for a Christmas gift. No one has ever given her a Christmas present before, but this is America. Christmas is important here. Amira should have a Christmas present. I thought of one I would like to give her.”

“You did?” Natividad asked, cautiously, because Keziah’s tone seemed a little strange.

Yes,” said Keziah, and paused again. Then she said at last, “Amira does not wish to have a book. She is a black dog, after all. But I think . . . I think she would like to be told stories. At bedtime. The way you said your mother used to tell you stories.”

“I think that’s a wonderful idea—” Natividad began.

“I think she would like *you* to tell her stories at bedtime,” said Keziah. She still was not looking at Natividad.

“Oh,” said Natividad. Then she said, “Not you?”

“She would like *you* to tell her stories, I think,” Keziah said firmly. And then added more softly, “If you will. I know it is another thing to do. And Amira is not *your* sister.”

“I would love to read her stories!” Natividad declared. She was starting to smile. “I would love to be Amira’s Christmas present. And you’ve given me the perfect idea for what to give Miguel, too. I’m going to ask Grayson to give him a job!”

“A . . . job?”

“Yes! You know we’re all supposed to earn our Dimilioc allowances! Miguel may be just my age, but he knows a lot, he knows everything, really! He could do—” she hesitated, then finished more softly, “He could do the same exact job Harrison used to do. Collecting and collating information from all over the country, using news reports to track black dogs and—and blood kin, because that one we found can't have been the only one left. Maybe there are even a few vampires left and we don't even know it!" Horrifying as the idea was, she could see now that it must be possible. She said, "If somebody had been tracking the news like we're supposed to, like Harrison used to, if Miguel had been doing that, I bet that blood kin wouldn't have been able to take us by surprise. Because there's no way it's from Vermont originally, and there's no way it hasn't left a trail! Blood kin, you know!"

Keziah made a skeptical noise, but Natividad was pretty sure it was just habit. Her frown was only thoughtful, not scornful. "And your brother would like this gift?"

"Oh, yes! He would love it!" Natividad hesitated. "I still don't know what I could give Alejandro, though."

"You will think of the right gift," Keziah said confidently. "Not a book."

"No," said Natividad. Then she bounced in her seat in sudden excitement and said, "Or maybe the right kind of book! Oh! That *is* a good idea! One of those blank ones that you said was for pictures and memories? Because I bet Dimilioc has lots of old pictures and—and things, I don't know, but things that would go in a book like that."

"And your brother would like this?"

"Well," said Natividad. "I was thinking . . ." she looked cautiously at the other girl. "I was thinking, pictures of our *papá*. That kind of memory."

"Ah," said Keziah.

"If . . ." said Natividad. "If he would like a handful of memories." She hesitated, uncertain now. "Maybe not. It's hard to remember, sometimes, now that . . ." she couldn't bring herself to complete that sentence.

Keziah glanced at Natividad, an unreadable glance. "No," she said. "Your father was a black dog of the Dimilioc house, yes? He cared for your brother. They were allies, your brother and your father? Then your brother would like that kind of book very much, I think. Even if he is sad. It is good for a black dog to remember to be sad. If you had someone who taught you and protected you, it is good to remember that person." She added after a second, more tentatively, "I will give *you* something, if you wish. I will teach you to drive a car."

"Oh!" Natividad stared at her. "Oh, would you? That would be perfect!"

"You would like this?"

"It would be *perfect*! No one else will want to—Alejandro, you know how protective he is, and Grayson is worse! And Ezekiel is too busy. But you're busy, too," she added in sudden doubt. "You're sure you don't mind?"

"This I would like to do," Keziah said firmly. "Yes. I will teach you to drive a car, and you will tell stories to Amira. This will be better than books and puzzles and soaps that smell of chocolate." She gave Natividad a sidelong glance. "Then, when we come back to Burlington to shop for bracelets and pink coats stuffed with feathers, you can drive. But I will come with you, though I am sure we will never again see blood kin anywhere in the world."

"Perfect!" Natividad said happily. And it was. Keziah was right about everything. They would never, ever run into blood kin again; they couldn't be that unlucky twice. So that *would* be perfect—except maybe not a pink coat. Maybe something elegant. Something nice, something grown up. Something not for a little girl, but for the kind of girl who might learn to drive and maybe, in the spring, go boating on the lake with Ezekiel Korte.

LIBRARY WORK

Étienne Lumondière really was a bastard. Miguel had figured that one out in just about no time, which did nothing to help when he happened to run into the man at the wrong moment. Which was any moment, actually.

Étienne Lumondière thought that ordinary humans were just about fit to wipe the mud off black dog boots. That was the basic issue. It said a lot about Lumondière attitudes. Or maybe it was just Étienne. Scrub the floors, polish the crystal, inventory the pantries and freezers, sweep cobwebs out of the corners. Dust the books in the library.

There were a lot of books in the library. Miguel had the impression that none of them had even been picked up for at least a year, much less dusted. Maybe for a decade. He slid one leather-covered volume—Donne, which seemed a weird choice for a black dog library—off its shelf, blew a cloud of dust off its upper edge, swept a dampish cloth across its gold-embossed cover, and set it aside. About twenty books per shelf, poetry on this one and the two below, Donne to Swinburne. Swinburne seemed a more black dog kind of poet. All that about death lying dead, wasn't that Swinburne? Miguel could stop when he got that far and flip through the book and find out, but if he took a break, that would probably be the moment Étienne Lumondière happened to come around to check up on him. Miguel wasn't afraid of Étienne, exactly. But that would lead to an uncomfortable moment at best. At worst, it would mean another couple of days of ridiculous makework chores.

Eight shelves per block, about four blocks along each wall, except the wall with the windows. Miguel tried to estimate about how many vacuum cleaner bags that much dust would fill, if a vacuum cleaner would get the books really clean. Which, unfortunately it wouldn't. He had tried that. There was just no substitute for taking each book off its shelf and dusting it by hand.

He should have tried harder to stay out of Étienne Lumondière's way. But even in a house as big as this one, it wasn't so easy, staying out of some particular person's way, and unfortunately Étienne seemed unreasonably fond of books and libraries, for a black dog who ought to have been all about running around out of doors killing things. Though only deer and bunnies and so on. Nothing worse, at least one might say that for Étienne, because Lumondière had always been one of the civilized houses.

In the spring, Dimilioc was supposed to hire more people to help with the housework. Miguel didn't see why they should wait for spring. But apparently after all that vicious business before Christmas, there was some kind of black dog insecurity or territoriality or something that made Grayson Lanning put off hiring staff. Trust black dogs to make everything a huge emotional deal.

Or maybe, after all that, everyone from Lewis and wherever else Dimilioc usually hired staff was simply tired of monsters. Maybe it would take a few more months just to get anyone to even think about working in this house. That, at least, Miguel could certainly understand.

"Ah, Miguel!" Étienne had said that morning, finding Miguel carefully stretching from the top of a stepladder to lift one of the massive Dimilioc histories down off the highest shelf. "You have nothing to do today but read a little in the personal histories?" And he had smiled, the kind of smile that made it clear what he thought of some outbred human looking through Dimilioc's private histories. Because Étienne Lumondière might be civilized, but in his case that meant he was a snobbish, stuck-up, condescending *cabrón*.

Unfortunately, he was the kind of snobbish, stuck-up, condescending *cabrón* that an ordinary human couldn't very well tell to go take a flying leap. Étienne had been somebody, in the Lumondière house, Miguel knew that, though not exactly what Étienne's precise rank or position had been. *And* he never let you forget he was French, either. He was a tall, lean man with long, narrow hands and sharp-cut elegant features, and he thought he was far too good to be just another Dimilioc wolf. Also, far, far better than any of Dimilioc's mere human kin.

Dealing with him was going to take subtlety, and patience, and plausible deniability every step of the way. Just at the moment, Miguel had only the most bare-bones outline of an idea in that direction. At least dusting all the books in the entire world was giving him a lot of time to think about it. Not to mention a strong incentive to work out an actual plan.

On the other side of the room, Cassie opened the door and came in with a light, quick step, and paused, catching sight of Miguel kneeling beside a stack of books nearly as tall as he was, with the dust cloth in his hand. Probably with dust streaked across his face, too. He suppressed an urge to rub his face, since he definitely had dust on his hands. Looking stupid was bad enough any time, but looking stupid in front of Cassie Pearson would be worse.

Cassie Pearson was a pretty girl, fine boned and delicate. She was a few months older than Miguel, but looked younger. She had blond hair, cut very short and feathery around her head. Also high cheekbones, tiny ears, a long graceful neck, and big eyes an ambiguous shade between blue and gray. She looked exactly like the kind of winter fairy that ought to flit through the forest here in this cold country, a spirit of the woodlands and winter, darting across the snow without leaving a trace, her fingertips trailing frost through the air with every movement. She dressed the part, too; right now she was wearing an artistically ragged dress of blue and silver and pewter-gray, and silver leggings tucked into low-heeled gray boots. Miguel could just *see* her flitting through the woods in that.

Luckily for Cassie, she was not nearly as delicate as she looked, because she might not be any kind of fairy or elf or spirit, but she wasn't just an ordinary girl anymore, either. One of Vonhausel's black dogs had bitten her, had made her a *cambiador*, a moon-bound shifter. That was nothing Miguel would wish on his worst enemy. He certainly wouldn't wish it for himself, and took half a minute to quickly review the stage of the moon.

He hadn't thought he'd recoiled visibly, but he could see Cassie knew exactly what he was thinking. Her mouth twisted. "Relax. Not till tomorrow," she told him. "I came up early because of the snow."

"Ah—right. Good idea." Yes, there was supposed to be a lot of snow tonight. There never seemed to be anything *but* snow in this country; way more than any sensible winter ought to be able to hold. "Sensible" was not any way to describe a Vermont winter, that was for sure.

"Yeah," said Cassie. Her mouth twisted slightly. "Who knows? Maybe I'll be snowed in here till spring. I don't dare go home unless I'm sure I can get back here—or unless I can start holding *it* off better. Grayson's going to help me." Her voice was the kind that ought to belong to a woodland spirit: light and pretty and slightly breathless.

"Um," said Miguel. "Right. Good luck with that. So, uh, you want something to read?" He couldn't quite keep the incredulity out of his tone.

"No," said Cassie. "I just came to the library to get a dozen cream cakes and a raw steak. Of course something to read, what do you think?"

". . . right."

"For *afterward*, of course," Cassie said impatiently. "You know they won't let me out till the moon's two nights past full. That last day is totally boring. If I change back earlier, it'll be even more boring."

"Oh! Right! Of course." Miguel felt ridiculous. He rubbed his face and got to his feet, looking around uncertainly. "Um, what do you like to read?" There weren't a lot of modern novels in this library, though he knew some people had a shelf or two of personal favorites in their private rooms. He started to say that he thought he'd seen a couple shelves of romances in one of the rooms along the hall past the suite he shared with his brother and twin sister.

Before he could, Cassie said briskly, "I thought I'd go

on with *The Decline and Fall of the Roman Empire.* Gibbon, you know," she added, at Miguel's astonished stare. "It's up there." She pointed helpfully to a high shelf.

"Um," said Miguel.

"So I need the stepladder to get it. The very same stepladder you've got all those books piled on?" She looked critically at the stacks of books on the ladder and floor, then even more critically at Miguel. "Dusting? You couldn't think of anything better to do this morning?"

Miguel cleared his throat. "Étienne thought I looked like I needed something to do."

Cassie rolled her eyes, gratifyingly sympathetic. "Oh, him. He's useful, I guess, but honestly it's almost too bad no one tore his throat out when we had the chance. I guess it's too late now."

Miguel blinked. He hadn't thought that *cambiadors* were especially bloodthirsty until the full moon drew up their corrupted shadows, but she sounded perfectly serious.

"Ladder?" she reminded him. "Oh, never mind, I'll just stand on one of those chairs."

Miguel had a strong suspicion that if she scuffed the cushion on that chair, he'd somehow be the one who wound up explaining why to Étienne. Or, worse, Grayson. He hastily began clearing books off the stepladder. "Gibbon, huh?"

"I've got a copy, but this edition's nicer. Besides, it's got all the footnotes in the original Latin. I need volume two."

"You read Latin?"

"Doesn't everybody?" Cassie stepped out of the way, allowing Miguel to position the ladder.

He was sure that last bit must have been a joke, though she was perfectly deadpan. He gave her a long look, but she still didn't smile. She only lifted her eyebrows expectantly. So he obediently climbed up and handed down volume two. It was a beautiful cloth-bound book with gilt edges. "Um, you don't just keep this in the cage when you change, do you?"

"Of course not." She flipped the book open and turned

a couple pages, then nodded and shut the book again. She turned to go, but said over her shoulder, "Be careful with Étienne

Lumondière. He's going to be trouble one of these days. Though I guess Grayson will come up with a way to deal with him. Or, you know, Ezekiel will."

". . . right," said Miguel, to her back. Just a little bit bloodthirsty, that girl. Though she wasn't wrong. He stood for several minutes after she was gone, gazing after her. Three months since that horror with Vonhausel and his shadow pack. She must have come here twice before, at each full moon, so she—and everyone else—could be kept safe from her shadow when it rose. He'd known that, vaguely. He'd known, equally vaguely, that his sister Natividad was working with Grayson to try to find a way to help moon-bound *cambiadors* gain more control over their shadows, starting with Cassie Pearson.

But he'd known all that and yet he'd only actually *met* that girl now? What a . . . what a *waste of time*.

It didn't take very long at all to decide the rest of the dusting could wait. It was close to noon anyway; not even Étienne Lumondière could expect anybody to spend the *whole day* dusting in the library, surely.

Sandwiches were easy. *Molotes con chorizo y papa* would have been better, and the chorizo filling was actually already made, but Miguel wasn't very good at shaping masa dough and Natividad was nowhere handy. Actually, she was probably already downstairs, working on something to help Cassie. Which was fine, since that'd give Miguel a really good reason to venture downstairs himself.

Probably Cassie would like American-style sandwiches better than *moletes* anyway. There were big rolls in the freezer. Miguel thawed them in the microwave, fifteen seconds each, and piled them with ham and cheese, or turkey with cheese and tomato, or roast beef with cheese and tomato and those mild pickled chilies you got in a jar. The tomatoes were those terrible ones that were all you could get in

American markets in the winter; Miguel wouldn't have bothered with slicing them except he knew Grayson liked even symbolic tomatoes better than no tomatoes at all. Grayson was very likely downstairs already, too, so that was potentially two birds with one stone. So, sandwiches, different kinds because he didn't know what Cassie liked. And apples. Vermont did have good apples. And cream cakes, also out of the freezer. They would thaw quickly. Miguel piled everything on a platter and carried it carefully down the hall to the stairs.

Cassie was in the cage already, but its door was standing open. That was fine, of course, even though Natividad was right there in the cage with her. The moon wasn't yet dangerously near full, and anyway, Miguel had been right. Grayson Lanning was there, too. Even if Cassie changed early, Grayson would be able to control her, as any black dog could dominate and control any mere *cambiador*. It was perfectly safe, and never mind Miguel's little involuntary flinch to see his twin sister so near a moon-bound shifter this close to the full moon.

Cassie, her legs drawn up and her fingers linked around her knees, was sitting in the middle of a circle Natividad had just drawn on the cement floor, The circle wasn't really visible, not to Miguel; it was more a lingering impression of a circle that might have been there a minute ago, kind of like seeing the fading ripple from a pebble tossed into a pond after the pebble itself had vanished. Even that was more than Miguel would have been able to see, except that Natividad must have only just finished that circle. His twin was kneeling on the floor, a hand mirror face-up beside her, unselfconsciously rubbing her nose as she frowned at something invisible in the air between herself and Cassie.

Grayson was not, of course, sitting on the floor with the girls. The Master of Dimilioc was far too dignified to sit on the floor. He was sitting in a chair outside the cage, a big, fancy chair someone had brought down from the house above. His broad hands gripped the arms of the chair, not hard, but with a power that implied he could crush the heavy wood like balsa. He probably could, if he got annoyed. Not that he would do anything of the kind, because he was also far too dignified to get in a temper and wreck the furniture.

A fancy table that matched the chair stood between it and the silver-wrapped bars of the cage; the fat volume of Gibbon Cassie had brought downstairs lay on the table. A human hand could reach between the bars and pick up that book, but as long as Cassie got it back on the table before she shifted, her other form wouldn't be able to touch it. Especially with the silver on the bars. Miguel wondered if the silver would burn her in her human form, now that her shadow had been contaminated. It had never occurred to him to wonder about that before. Civilized black dogs killed *cambiadors* when they caught them, so what did it matter what shifters could and couldn't do?

Natividad hadn't looked around when Miguel came down the stairs, but Cassie glanced up sharply and looked first surprised and then annoyed. Grayson glanced at him and the tray of sandwiches and lifted heavy eyebrows. Miguel hoped he wasn't flushing. The Master didn't miss much, but hey, it really was lunchtime. Miguel held up the tray illustratively and said easily, "Always harder to fight evil on an empty stomach, right?" He was satisfied with his own easy tone. Growing up around black dogs would teach anybody to sound casual, relaxed, friendly, cheerful. It was all part of learning how to slide right on by a black dog's uncertain temper.

Grayson started to say something, probably something terse, but before he could, Natividad glanced up and said, "Oh, food, great! Thanks! Is there one with turkey and lettuce and mayonnaise and not those awful tomatoes?" "Just for you," Miguel told her, turning the tray and indicating the sandwich he'd made for his twin. "And cream cakes for Cassie, so don't eat them all." He put the tray down on the table, glancing sidelong at the Master. "This one's for you, sir."

"How very thoughtful of you, Miguel," Grayson said. His heavy, gritty voice wasn't the only thing that made him sound suspicious, Miguel was fairly certain. The Master was no fool.

"Cream cakes, huh?" said Cassie. The corners of her mouth had tucked upward and she was looking at Miguel now with some interest and, he hoped, appreciation.

"You're on your own as far as the raw steak goes, though."

"Huh. I guess that's all right, as long as you've got the cakes. Pass 'em here, then." She started to get up.

"Don't reach through the circle! Just let me finish this first," Natividad ordered, and added to Miguel, "It's kind of a variant on the *Aplacando*, see, only if I did it right it'll tighten as the moon waxes and ease off again as it wanes. Only I'm not sure if it'll work. It's kind of a new thing." She looked doubtfully at the invisible magic in the air or set into the cement or whatever.

"You should sound more confident," Cassie told her. "You should say, 'This'll definitely do the job. Yeah, once I've got this done, you won't have any trouble with your shadow.' Like the placebo effect, right?"

Natividad murmured wordlessly, plainly not paying attention. She was doing something with her hands, as though she was braiding invisible threads or light or something.

Cassie shrugged and said to Miguel instead, "Planning to leave the rest of the dusting till tomorrow, are you?"

"I thought maybe I'd take a break to read the first volume of Gibbon," Miguel explained. "Maybe I should learn Latin first, though." She'd offered him a pretty good straight line in more than one way, though, so he also added, watching Grayson covertly from the corner of his eye, "Though Étienne might be pissed off if I don't get more done today, I guess." To his surprise and pleasure, Cassie picked this up.

It wasn't anything obvious, just a slight widening of her eyes. But she said smoothly, "Oh, yeah, we wouldn't want Étienne to get pissed off," with only the slightest emphasis on the name and without looking at Grayson at all.

The Master, who had gathered up his sandwich neatly in

a napkin, paused, regarding Miguel with narrow curiosity. "Dusting?"

"I'm sure someone has to dust," Miguel said easily. "I guess Étienne was used to having things polished up all neat and clean when he was Master of Lumondière."

Grayson's gaze became more intent. "Étienne was never Master of Lumondière. His cousin was Master. Before that, his uncle."

"Oh, really?" said Miguel, as though slightly surprised but not very interested. "I figured he'd been Master. You ready for a sandwich, *gemela*?"

His twin had sighed and sat back on her heels, rubbing her face with both hands. She looked up, though, smiling, when he offered her the platter. "*Sí.* Yes. Thank you. It's fine, you can move now," she added to Cassie. "I don't know—" then she stopped and said instead, firmly, "This will help you very much. It will make it much easier for you to reach past your shadow even when the moon is all the way full."

"That's the way," Cassie said approvingly. She added casually, "I thought he'd been Master, too. He sure thinks he's his own gift to the world."

"He knows his own strength," Grayson said, his voice lowering toward a growl. "He is an asset to Dimilioc."

That could be a warning to a mere human not to criticize a strong black dog—or more likely a warning to a human kid not to criticize someone so much older, or so much more senior in Dimilioc. But Miguel hoped that tone also implied dislike of Étienne Lumondière. Who, yes, was undeniably an asset to Dimilioc. It was just that he was also a pain in the ass.

"Sure," Miguel said easily. "It's just a pity he can't be an asset to Dimilioc from somewhere else. France would be perfect."

"I doubt the French would have him back," said Cassie. "Not that there was ever anything wrong with Lumondière. But, well, France, right?"

"France?" Natividad said, innocently providing another

straight line.

Miguel was all set to take that opening, but before he could, Cassie answered, "Sure. That business with the forêt des Landes? That's the biggest forest in France, you know, and almost all of it deliberately planted by a house called Èvanouir so their black dogs would have a proper forest to hunt people in."

Natividad paused. "Oh, no. Seriously?"

"They sold it as a way to deswampify this huge region, but yeah, Èvanouir was really into it as a hunting preserve."

Natividad was looking more and more upset. Miguel wouldn't have raked up all that old history, if he'd been the one to explain. He said quickly, "Lumondière put a stop to that, though! They were already getting strong by then. They tore up Èvanouir and took over France almost before the trees had all been planted."

"Sure," agreed Cassie. "But not before Landes had already become a hunting ground. Finding out about Landes gave pretty much all of France a permanent hate-on for all black dogs. Èvanouir or Lumondière, the French mostly don't care, and I don't blame 'em."

Natividad shook her head, wordlessly.

Unable to help himself, Miguel demanded, "How do *you* know all that?"

Cassie gave him an amused little tip of her head. "I paid attention in school."

"Oh." That . . . actually made a lot of sense. Miguel should have been able to figure that out without asking. The whole town of Lewis was almost part of Dimilioc, after all. Lots of human kin must have settled there, over the years. It made sense the people in the town would know a lot about black dog history. Plus, Cassie's *papá* was just the sort of guy who would want to know *all* about black dogs, and she'd probably picked it up from him. Yeah, that was obvious, now that he'd let himself look like an idiot in front of her. But who'd have guessed she would have cared about learning all that stuff?

"It seems unlikely there are enough black wolves of the

Lumondière bloodlines left to re-establish their house in any case," Grayson said. If he was annoyed by this little tour down memory lane, or for that matter entertained by Cassie showing up Miguel, he didn't show it.

"Yeah, too bad," Miguel said, absently, as though he wasn't that interested. He wasn't sure the hook was set. But slow and subtle was good. Plausible deniability and never, ever making any kind of real suggestion about anything. You had to lead black dogs very, very gently. Especially Grayson Lanning.

And on that thought, Miguel began gathering up the debris from lunch. No good overstaying his welcome, especially since he hadn't actually been invited to this party. "Well, good luck, then," he said vaguely. "I'll come back down when the moon's started to wane and see if you're ready for the third volume, okay?"

But Miguel actually came back down the second full-moon day. Three full-moon nights, that was the rule, and two days—but you had to be careful because some of the moon-bound shifters would change for as much as five nights and four days, not three and two. That was what Grayson and Natividad were helping Cassie with, of course: learning to control her shadow well enough to minimize the time of its rising. Intellectually, that was an interesting question: whether someone who'd become moon-bound could learn things like that, or whether it all depended on the strength of their corrupted shadows and not at all on their own will and determination.

It was the sort of question Miguel preferred to keep at an intellectual level. It was pretty awful to let himself imagine what it would be like, if will and determination turned out to count for nothing, if everything instead turned out to depend on luck—the strength of the black dog that bit you, the invasiveness of the demonic influence, the length of time you'd been moon-bound, whatever. Things you couldn't control.

He really didn't want to believe that could be true. He

supposed he was going to find out if it was, though. They were all going to find out. Because of Cassie. Who read Gibbon with the footnotes in Latin—unless she'd made that up to impress him—and who knew a lot about the history of black dogs in Europe. She couldn't have made *that* up. Probably she really did read Latin.

So he went downstairs on the second full-moon day, just to look in on her and see how she was doing. Whether her shadow still held control. It would, of course. It was too early for her to fight it back, no matter what magic Natividad had worked on her. But he went downstairs anyway.

He'd almost finished the dusting by then, though not quite; he'd left some of the highest shelves for later. He'd also left some artistic piles of books on the floor to make it clear that he'd been terribly busy, just in case Étienne came to see how he was getting on. He seriously did not want the Lumondière black dog pissed off at him. At least, not yet.

Cassie was indeed still in her shifted form. Of course. Shifters were called moon-bound for a reason, and they just could not learn control the way a true black dog could.

Though Miguel wondered now whether that necessarily had to be the case. A black dog, at least a Dimilioc black dog, worked on control almost from birth, and since the shadow was weak at first, that gave a black dog *niño* a chance to learn how to control it before it got strong. A *cambiador*, a shifter . . . the shadow was strong right from the beginning, and the person had no practice dealing with demonic corruption. But maybe . . . maybe time and practice could do the same job, if a shifter could only depend on other people to help keep her from killing everyone she loved while she learned.

That Cassie in her shifted form would have been delighted to kill Miguel was extremely plain, not that he hadn't known that already. Moon-bound *cambiadors* were like that. Their shadows wanted to kill, but wanted even more to cause pain: left free during the full moon, a shifter always went first for family and friends. Then, driven back and down by the moon's waning, the shadow would subside until the next full moon—leaving its horrified, grieving host to bear the guilt.

Miguel had never really wanted to know how much a shifter remembered of what its shadow had done, after the moon finally let him go. Or her.

He said to Cassie, "Hey, you in there?

She stared back at him, her fiery eyes burning with contempt and hatred. Though he tried, Miguel could see nothing human in those eyes.

She was a lot smaller than a real black dog. A whole lot less massive. She was built for speed, not for crushing her enemies with her sheer bulk. Her head was not as broad, her shoulders not as a powerful as those of a black dog. She might be bigger than a wolf, but she probably didn't weigh as much as, say, a mastiff. The overall impression was quite different. A shifter really did look more like a wolf than the bear-dog-monster that was a black dog. Her eyes were not like a wolf's eyes, though. They were fiery yellow, though as far as Miguel knew, a shifter couldn't call up *actual* fire the way some black dogs could.

Miguel held up the book he held. "I thought about reading you some of the Gibbon, only I don't read Latin, so I wasn't sure that would work. So I brought this. It's not Gibbon, but I thought maybe you'd like it. It's *The Hunting of the Snark*. Completely frivolous and silly, so you probably won't like it, but you can't read things like Gibbon all the time, your brain would melt and dribble out your ears, very messy—"

Cassie—or the shadow that had taken her for the duration of the full moon—snarled. It was a slow, rising sound, barely audible but filled with knife-sharp fury and hatred.

"Yeah," said Miguel. "But I figure you might be awake in there, though. I don't think anybody ever told me if you shifters stay awake and, well. Anyway. I figure it's not much to just read for you for a little while. If you don't remember anything about it afterward, hey, next month I'll know better, right?"

Cassie snarled again.

"Right, then," said Miguel. He pulled the chair around so he wouldn't quite be facing the cage and opened the book.

The Hunting of the Snark might be completely frivolous and silly, but it was fun to read. Miguel had to pay just enough attention to it that he didn't have to pay attention to Cassie, who gave up snarling and lay still instead, staring intently at Miguel. Though he tried not to look at her, he couldn't help but glance over now and then, and after a while, he had the impression she wasn't even blinking. Maybe she didn't have to. Maybe black dogs didn't need to blink either, and he'd just never noticed because no black dog had ever stared at him with such intensity and hatred. He could have done without Cassie staring at him like that now. Not that the monster was really Cassie. That was the whole point.

Miguel read the whole poem. He didn't let himself read too fast. Just the right pace for the poem. It was a fun poem, complete nonsense with its Barrister and Baker and Beaver, and its five signs of a Snark, and seeking it with thimbles and forks and soap and everything. And finding out it was a Boojum, of course, at the end. But every line flowed right off the tongue. He'd always liked it, but he thought he might never be able to read it again without thinking of this surreal scene: himself sitting outside a cage with bars wrapped in silver wire, with an unblinking monster on the other side waiting for its chance to kill him.

It was a weird afternoon.

"I'll come back tomorrow," he said at the end. "Maybe you'll be able to shift back tomorrow, huh? What should I bring to read? Probably not *Alice in Wonderland*." He paused.

Cassie didn't answer, of course. She just stared, her fiery gaze so filled with animosity Miguel was a little surprised it didn't blister his skin. He pretended not to notice. "Well, I'll think of something. Something not too long. One of Shakespeare's histories, maybe. All those power politics and things, it's just like reading black dog history, you probably love the histories, huh? Or, hey, I could read you *The Taming of the Shrew*."

Cassie snarled, a slow, rising sound.

"Just kidding. *Richard III*, then. At least Act I." Miguel sauntered out. He didn't let himself sag and shudder until he was up the stairs with the door shut firmly behind him.

It had been worse than he'd expected, seeing her like that. Being hated like that. He had kind of expected to see something of Cassie in that monster, at least glimpses, at least now and then. But he had seen nothing.

Probably the real girl had not even known he was there.

But he knew he would go back anyway, the next afternoon.

He rearranged some of the piles of books in the morning, though, before he went back downstairs. But though he finished dusting, he didn't actually put all the books back on the shelves. Sometimes books were more useful in stacks. Disorderly stacks that didn't quite keep to alphabetical order.

He also found himself thinking, as he stacked up books, about what Cassie might like. Short stories by O. Henry? "The Ransom of Red Chief" was funny. "A Retrieved Reformation" had a nice ending. Maybe she would like short stories better than Shakespeare.

Maybe he should ask her what she liked before the next full moon.

He took both O. Henry and Shakespeare with him when he went downstairs. But as it turned out, he didn't need to choose which to read to her. Cassie was already back in human form, a full night and half a day before he might have expected her to manage it.

She had plainly just changed. She was curled into a ball on the cement floor, her arms drawn in and her face tucked down. She obviously hadn't been wearing her winter-fairy dress when she'd shifted, and the reason was obvious, because she looked cold even in the ragged jeans and oversized white sweater she was wearing. She looked terrible, washed out and pale, and even thinner, as though weight had burned off her just over the three nights of the full moon. But she looked completely human. There was no trace of the monster left, to Miguel's eyes, though no doubt a black dog would have still recognized her as a shifter.

At first Miguel thought she didn't even know he was there. Then she said, still not looking up, "Go away."

"Right," he said. He was obscurely embarrassed, as though he'd walked in on a girl in the shower or something. He said, rattled enough fall back into his mother's Spanish—he, who'd been reading and speaking colloquial English since he could remember— *"Lo siento."* Then he said, "Sorry," and started to back away again, up the stairs, clumsy because he was backing up—but that wasn't why he *felt* clumsy.

"Wait!" Cassie said, and uncurled suddenly.

She looked even thinner and more desperate once she sat up. The wild look in her eyes might have belonged to a creature of frost and winter, a fairy, a woodland elf—but it was Cassie, herself, and not her shadow. Miguel wanted to say something, but what could he say? *He* wasn't moon-bound. She wasn't going to want sympathy from *him*.

"I heard you," she said. Her tone was fierce and angry. "I was there."

She didn't say she was glad he'd come down to read to her. From her fury, she might hate him for it. Miguel nodded, awkwardly. "Right . . ."

"You want to get rid of Étienne Lumondière."

Miguel hadn't expected that at all, and stared at her, speechless.

Cassie told him, "We need black dogs right now. We need numbers. But Étienne isn't the kind we need. He's trouble. No human is going to want to be here as long as he is. He's not worth that kind of problem."

"That's what I thought," admitted Miguel. "But I'm pretty sure Grayson isn't going to see it that way."

"Yeah, not unless you plant the idea in his mind. You've already started, I know, but you could do better—and he mustn't catch you at it."

"Yeah, working that out is the hard part—"

"I know how. But not now. Come back in an hour."

It was easy, actually, in principle. Tricky in practice, though.

It was all about getting Grayson to see Étienne Lumondière as a threat to Dimilioc, as well as an asset. The Master had to decide he was an asset better used elsewhere, not kept close to Dimilioc's central territory. And the Master had to be annoyed enough to get rid of him, but not so much so as to kill him—a fine line with a black dog. Plus Miguel and Cassie had to arrange everything without letting anyone, not Grayson nor Étienne nor anyone else, see they were doing anything at all on purpose.

Yeah, in practice it was tricky. Without Cassie's help, Miguel wasn't sure how he would have arranged to get Grayson in the right spot at just the right moment. That had always been the key. Setting the hook was one thing, but landing the fish was the thing. It was more like hooking a shark. A shark was not what you wanted to catch unless you had very strong fishing line. And preferably a harpoon. Miguel had only words. And Cassie Pearson's help, now. Miguel didn't know exactly how she got Grayson to the library at just the right moment: she sure hadn't asked the Master of Dimilioc for his personal help in finding just the right book. Or maybe she had; maybe she could actually pull off something like that.

Miguel had been the one to get Étienne Lumondière to the library on schedule, though. That part had been simple. He had just announced he was finished dusting, and of course Étienne had said, *Are you?* in that sarcastic, superior way of his and had come to check. No actual white gloves, but all the attitude. And of course Miguel had made sure to be pretty casual about alphabetizing the whole last section when he put the books back on the shelves, and of course Étienne was just the perfectionist to notice.

"Careless," he said severely to Miguel, who made sure to duck his head, all properly meek and apologetic. "Slovenly. What is this, all these books out of order?"

"Anybody can find Wodehouse, once they get to the W's," Miguel pointed out. But meekly and apologetically.

"It's not like those got mixed in with Gibbon or anything. Anyway, they're dusted—"

Étienne ran the tip of one finger along the top shelf and looked at Miguel even more severely.

"Well, *you* could dust," Miguel suggested. He could hear someone approaching, out in the hallway. Just a second more . . . he straightened his shoulders, met Étienne's eyes, and said, not meekly at all, "Since you're taller than me and can see up that high, maybe you should take over *all* the high shelves, if you care about dust so much."

Combined with that look, it was enough to make Étienne hit him. Miguel had been almost sure he would. Proud, Étienne Lumondière. Proud and vain and very sure of his prerogatives. And not so concerned with Dimilioc custom or law, because he was so certain Lumondière's ways were superior.

Étienne did not mean to hit him very hard. He only hit him with the back of his hand, with no claws or anything. It was more difficult than Miguel had expected to step into the blow instead of jumping back—he'd argued with Cassie about that; she'd said anything would do, it wasn't necessary for Étienne to leave a mark. Miguel had insisted he needed to show at least a bruise. But when it came right to the moment, he tried to flinch in both directions at once and had to grab the back of a chair to stop himself stumbling. Which looked perfect, of course, so that worked out, though he hadn't done it on purpose.

He yelled, too, just a little, not enough to be embarrassing, just a small sound of shock, timed to coincide with the arrival of Grayson Lanning in the doorway, Cassie hovering behind him. Cassie looked hugely entertained, which was okay, since he was the only one paying any attention to her. Miguel's face hurt, his cheek and eye both, but he had to suppress an urge to laugh—that would be insanely stupid, after all this trouble, but Étienne's expression *was* funny. Grayson didn't say a word, not then. He just gave Étienne a long, measured stare. Then he nodded to the door.

Étienne didn't exactly slink out of the room, but his

attitude sure had changed.

"Are you hurt?" Grayson asked Miguel.

Miguel touched his cheek, carefully. That whole side of his face ached. He'd cut the inside of his mouth against his teeth. But he said, "No, sir. I don't think so. I shouldn't have been rude to him—"

"True," Grayson said, and walked out.

"There you go," Cassie said, pleased with herself and with him. "That should do it." She came over to look closely at Miguel's face. "Ow. You're going to have a black eye."

"Yeah? Good." He touched the inside of his cheek gingerly with his tongue. It hurt. "If we need to do this again, maybe he can hit you next time."

"Not very chivalrous," she mocked him. "Black eyes are your business." She glanced at the shelves. "Yeah, mixing Wodehouse up with Tennessee Williams, I bet that made Étienne mad."

"Seemed to," agreed Miguel, satisfied.

Étienne Lumondière left Dimilioc four days later. In a way. Grayson sent him to Denver along with five other recently recruited black dogs to re-establish Dimilioc's western sept. Once that whole region had been held by Dimilioc black wolves, mostly of the Hammond and Toland bloodlines, but over the course of the war between black dogs and vampires, the whole western sept had been destroyed. Every black wolf and Pure woman had been killed, their human kin scattered, except for a couple who had pulled back to Dimilioc proper, and even those had died later. But now, with the vampires gone, of course it was important to re-establish Dimilioc's presence in the west. So in a way, you could consider that Étienne Lumondière had only been sent to another part of Dimilioc. In a way, it was even a promotion: in Denver, Étienne would be Master because none of the black dogs that went with him approached his combination of strength and control. Miguel was okay with that. A Lumondière black wolf, even a bastard like Étienne, would know how to run a civilized house, even if he would want to put a Lumondière stamp on it. Working on that would keep him busy and occupied and out of everyone's hair. Yeah, really, it was perfect.

The day after Étienne left, Miguel came back from helping his sister and Cassie move furniture around in the guest room Cassie had picked—she wanted every single thing over ten pounds moved, and then moved again—and found Ezekiel Korte waiting for him in his room.

Ezekiel was sitting in Miguel's best chair—his only chair actually—playing solitaire on his computer. He glanced up when Miguel came in, though, and one corner of his mouth crooked upward. He looked faintly bored, faintly amused, and just a little bit scary because Ezekiel always looked a little bit scary.

"What do you . . . uh, can I do something for you?" asked Miguel.

"You've got some interesting files here. Very broad-ranging. That big compilation of black dog activity out west is especially impressive."

"I'm supposed to collate that. For Grayson."

"Of course. I know he values the work you do for him." Ezekiel stood up, a smooth, effortless motion, like a spring uncoiling. "He wants to see you. Now."

"Uh . . ." said Miguel. "Right." He didn't say, *So why'd he send you?* He didn't ask, *So why didn't he pick up a house phone and call me?* Sometimes a question was better left unanswered. Besides, maybe the answer was, *No reason*, and why borrow trouble?

Grayson was in the conference room he used as a study. He was working on something, some kind of spreadsheet or something, Miguel could glimpse the open file. There were papers, maps and lists and things, all over his desk and half the long table. The door was open. He looked up when Ezekiel tapped on the door frame, gave a short nod, set down the pencil he held in one hand, and leaned back in his chair. He looked tired, Miguel thought. And impatient. And not amused at all. But that might have just been him. Grayson Lanning was not a man who often looked amused.

Ezekiel slid into the room and leaned his hip against the edge of the table, perfectly relaxed and comfortable. Miguel thought about taking a chair to show that he was also relaxed and comfortable. Then he thought better of it. He said, "Sir?" in his most innocent tone.

Grayson said without preliminary, "I had intended to send Étienne Lumondière to Denver in six months. Or a year. I intended to send him with ten black dogs to support him, not five. Now I've been forced to send him early, with far less support than he needs and yet more than I could afford to give him. If he fails to establish control in the west, he will be embarrassed, but Dimilioc will be weakened."

Miguel said nothing. It seemed the wisest course.

"I do not care to see my options constrained because of the self-indulgent tantrums of a clever boy who thinks he knows Dimilioc's necessities better than I do," Grayson added.

"If you didn't *want* to send him to Denver—" Miguel began.

"You shamed him in front of me. I was forced to punish him. Now I am required both to demonstrate my continuing trust in his strength and ability, and to offer him a chance to win back my personal regard. Do you think he would be satisfied by some meaningless gesture?"

This seemed like another good opportunity for Miguel to keep his mouth shut.

Grayson said, even more grimly, "Thos Korte always considered a riding crop appropriate for human kin he wished to punish. Whatever else one may say for the method, it was certainly effective. And even humans rarely sustain any permanent injury from such punishment. They were nearly always back on their feet within a week or so, as I recall."

Miguel found himself glancing involuntarily at Ezekiel, who smiled. It was a scary smile. Miguel wrenched his attention back to Grayson. "I—" he began, and then stopped and made himself think. He said after a moment, "I didn't mean to do anything to put Dimilioc at a disadvantage. I knew you would want to get Étienne Lumondière out of the house eventually. I figured now would be as good a time as any." He hesitated, then shook his head. "You wouldn't have sent him now if you thought he couldn't succeed. Or that his absence would put us in a real bind. But I'm sorry if I—if I misjudged."

Grayson leaned forward, folding his big hands on his desk. "I don't like being led, Miguel. I don't like being handled. I most particularly do not like to be considered *stupid*."

No, Miguel bet he didn't. He tried not to look at Ezekiel. He said, "No, sir." It was surprisingly easy to sound humble, this time.

Grayson leaned back in his chair again. He said, his tone very level, "I notice the W's in the library are out of order."

Miguel stared at him.

"I think you had better put that section in order. In fact, I think you may take all the books back off the shelves, re-dust them, and put them back on the shelves, this time in perfect order. You had better start with the A's in order to be sure every single volume is precisely in its proper place."

Miguel found his mouth was open, and closed it.

"I notice this task took you several days when you did it for Étienne. You will not need to hurry when you do it for me. I will expect the job to take you a month."

"A month!" Miguel exclaimed, and shut his mouth again.

"If you work at it for, oh, six hours a day. You may start today. I am sure the books will be the better for being thoroughly dusted. And the shelves can be polished properly. I don't believe you attended to that adequately for Étienne. Three or four coats of that pleasant lemon polish should be adequate. You may put the books back on the shelves after each coat, so that people may find what they wish to read without searching through stacks on the floor. This will, of course, require you to take all the books off the shelves and put them back on repeatedly. I'm sure you will prove equal to the task."

"But—" said Miguel. "My work—the reports I'm

supposed to collect for you—you said—I thought—"

Grayson raised his heavy eyebrows "That work is indeed important to me and to Dimilioc. I'm perfectly certain you will manage to complete *all* your duties satisfactorily. Yes?"

"Right," muttered Miguel. "Yes, sir."

"Cassandra Pearson likes to read, I know. I think she will be joining you in this little task."

Miguel was surprised again, this time in a good way.

"You may wish to work in silence, however. If you distract each other, then you will find yourselves working in the library on alternate days. If that occurs, I imagine the job will take twice as long to complete."

Ah. That wasn't so good. Miguel took a deep breath. "Yes, sir."

"Then we will not need to impose on Ezekiel's time."

Miguel glanced that way again, involuntarily. Ezekiel was still smiling. "No," Miguel said. "Sir."

"Good." Grayson paused. "Next time you have a concern, Miguel, perhaps you will discuss it with me openly."

Miguel swallowed, nodded, and retreated from the field, not in very good order. In fact, *routed comprehensively* was about right. Who would ever have expected a black dog, even *Grayson*, to *notice* every little thing?

But it wasn't all bad. Cassie Pearson turned out to know sign language. Miguel figured that in a month, he would know it pretty well, too.

A LEARNING EXPERIENCE

Thaddeus knew exactly why the Master of Dimilioc had picked him, just him and no one else, to help clean the worst of the cur black dogs out of Chicago. It sure wasn't because Thaddeus knew the city. At the moment, they were hunting just east of Chinatown, an area he didn't even know well. He had lived most of his life down near Joliet, and exploring other black dogs' territories definitely hadn't been a thing. Besides, before the war, all of downtown had belonged to the vampires and their blood kin and no black dog would dare venture anywhere near vampire territory.

Then Dimilioc had started the war, and finished it, too, if just barely. Now here Thaddeus was, back in Illinois, with the Dimilioc Master at his back, and everything was different.

Dimilioc had rules. Thaddeus was still figuring them out. He had grown up with rules, sure, but those rules had been simple. Easy to understand. Keep to yourself; defend your territory; don't kill too many people; most important of all, don't let vicious young black dog curs draw Dimilioc attention. Those had been the rules Thaddeus had learned from his father. Those had been the rules for any black dog born outside Dimilioc who wanted to live to get old.

Now Thaddeus was part of Dimilioc himself, and all the rules were different.

Not the first time he'd had the rules change on him, though. Except before, it hadn't been Dimilioc who set all his rules tumbling. The first time, it had been DeAnn.

Thaddeus first met DeAnn when he was twelve and she was nine. His dad had taken him hunting way outside their normal territory, tracking down a pair of black dogs who were just too noisy and too brutal to leave alone. Usually Dan

Williams didn't take his son hunting above Bolingbrook, that was pretty close to the northern edge of their territory, but this was a bad situation, black dogs in no-man's-land drawing way too much notice.

Regular people weren't the problem. Normal people didn't know, couldn't know, regular people didn't see bad stuff right out plain. The news was all about dog packs and pit bulls on the one hand and an especially violent serial rapist on the other. But all of it was really these black dogs, and Thaddeus's father said if they let it go on, eventually someone from Dimilioc, maybe the Dimilioc executioner his own damn self, would come down from the east and take care of the problem personally. And if that happened, most likely he would take his time about it, track down and kill every single black dog in Chicago and for fifty miles around. They could do that, the black wolves of Dimilioc. They *would* do it, if the curs got too noisy. It was impossible to hide from them because they had ways of tracking you down, even if you were very quiet.

So Dan Williams took his son hunting.

Downtown was vampire territory, had always been vampire territory. The blood kin would get any black dog who ventured there. North, past Waukegan and all the way up to Milwaukee, was the territory of a black dog, a man named Conrad, who, along with a handful of curs he held tight under his thumb, kept down the noise in that region. Way out west toward DeKalb, a black dog woman named Schoen—no one ever called her anything else and Thaddeus didn't know her first name—held a small territory all by herself and killed anyone who tried her borders.

But these damned stupid black dogs, by luck or some kind of basic cunning, kept to a region bounded on the east by La Grange, in the north by Arlington Heights, in the south by Bolingbrook, and in the west by Aurora, so that they weren't properly anybody's problem. But they made trouble, and made trouble, until it was plain someone had to take care of them. And Dan had Thaddeus, who was already, at twelve, big and tough and good in a fight. So his father told Thaddeus they'd do it and get it done, and waited for a good waxing moon that would probably bring out the strays, but that wouldn't draw the Beasts too hard for Thaddeus to handle his.

Dan Williams had known just where to hunt, too. "See there, them morons, they let theirselves get predictable," he told his son. "Never get predictable, kid. Anybody who wants to can track you down, see?"

Thaddeus had nodded. The two cur black dogs were skulking down Bailey toward a big forest preserve. Probably they wanted to find someone they could chase into the woods and hunt there. Thaddeus would've liked to do that himself. Maybe those two curs would get that far and they could have a real hunt. His Beast pressed forward, wanting that. He wanted to let it up and roar forward, but his dad laid a restraining hand on his arm to keep him still.

"Wait for it," Dan Williams said. "Wait for it, kid. Let them get past us and focus on that dim old cow over on at the corner of Modaff—see, there?"

Thaddeus had seen exactly how his dad had used that careless woman as bait for their enemies. That was smart. He told himself he would remember. Let your enemies get past you, let them get distracted by something else. Then they'd be stupid and you could hit them from behind. That was best, hitting your enemies from behind so they couldn't fight back. He hadn't had to be taught that part. It was obvious. Maybe they could get just one on their first rush and take their time with the other . . .

The simple plan worked, too, at first. Thaddeus and his father hit one of the black dogs from either side and tore him up and left him in pieces, but the other one fled, not west into the woods like he was supposed to, but north. Plus he was fast, that bastard, and it took almost two miles to catch him, and they only got him in the end because he suddenly broke stride and twisted around to the west, across the dark suburban yards, and then they could cut across the angle of his flight, and they caught him all right, and that was that.

Except that there was something else just a little farther

away to the west. Thaddeus realized that the minute he and his dad had made their kill. Something close, very close, way more dangerous than any stupid back dog cur. Not blood kin—Dan Williams and Conrad and that Schoen woman, they all hunted blood kin when they found them out of their own territory, so vampire influence was mostly limited to downtown. Anyway, he knew what blood kin smelled like, felt like. This wasn't like that. This was something else. Something that just *needed* to be killed, destroyed, wiped right out of the world, crushed so hard no one would ever find even a smear of its blood.

No wonder their quarry had turned like that, once he caught this scent. Thaddeus dropped the cur's head, human now the cur was dead, and turned straight west, toward this new thing. It was something terrible. Something very dangerous to black dogs, to him personally, he knew it, he could *feel* it. And he hated it. Hated, hated, *hated* . . .

His father's hand closed on the back of his neck, hard, claws out just enough to prick through the shaggy pelt. Thaddeus flinched, startled and angry: he hadn't even noticed his dad had shifted back to human form. He was big even in that form, not nearly as heavy as Thaddeus's Beast, but taller, with the black dog's fire lingering in his eyes. He shook Thaddeus lightly, warning and threat, a reminder of his own strength and authority. "Shift," he ordered. "Now."

Thaddeus swung his head to stare west, then glared at his father. Couldn't he *tell* about the monster?

"*Shift*, Thad. *Now*."

It took several tries and some minutes. Thaddeus wouldn't have managed it without that grip on the back of his neck, without his father's insistence and that naked threat. Getting a leash on his Beast wasn't usually so hard, but the Beast longed to run west and kill whatever that was. It fought him, worse than it had in years. But he managed the change at last, and knelt panting on the hard pavement, surrounded by the torn pieces of their enemy, with the smell of ash and blood thick in the air and his dad still looming over him. Everyone said Thaddeus would probably be even bigger than his father one day, but right now Dan Williams could still do a pretty good job looming. Thaddeus kept his eyes down and his human hands flat on the hot pavement and tried to steady his breathing, expecting any minute for his father to hit him, to yell at him, *Don't I teach you better than that? Fuck, kid, you some stupid lazy cur? Might as well be an* animal *if you can't get your Beast chained up!*

Thaddeus knew he would deserve it. He was having trouble just holding his human shape even now that he'd got it back. His Beast pushed and snarled right below the surface of his skin, wanting out, wanting to kill . . . he bit his lip and clenched his hands into fists and pushed it back as hard as he could.

"Come on," his dad said abruptly, and hauled him up by the back of the neck and shoved him forward. West, after all. Thaddeus hadn't expected that, and stumbled, and his dad pulled him up again and said harshly, "Shift back and I'll beat you bloody, you hear me, Thad? You stay human and you keep your Beast *way* the fuck underneath. We're gonna find this woman and you're not going to kill her, you're not even gonna to try, you hear me? You keep human and you keep close to me or I'll chain you up and beat you senseless every day for a week, you hear me?"

Only that continual mutter of low-voiced threats let Thaddeus keep his Beast under while they closed the distance between themselves and this new thing, this monster-woman that his father obviously knew about even though Thaddeus had never scented anything like her. He knew his father meant every word. His Beast knew it, too, and was just wary enough of the threatened punishment that Thaddeus could manage to keep it back and under. He tried to concentrate on the unfamiliar streets, on the suburbs that stretched out all around them, but it was impossible. Mostly he was just aware of the woman they were tracking.

She was in the street, out in the moonlight. She looked like an ordinary woman, but Thaddeus could tell she wasn't. She wasn't a black dog either. She was something else, some other kind of person. He hated her, but he wasn't sure why—

he could tell by now that it was mostly his Beast that hated her, but he couldn't tell if it was *just* his Beast or if part of it was also him. He blinked, and blinked again, trying to look at her better, without the Beast looking through his eyes.

She looked so ordinary. She was black, though not as dark as Thaddeus or his father. Old, at least thirty. Not pretty, or he thought she wasn't pretty, it was hard to tell with his Beast hating her and hating her and *hating* her. He was scared of her—or his Beast was, he couldn't really tell which. The Beast wanted to roar up and lunge across the little remaining distance and tear her in half. But his father still held him; that dangerous, threatening grip on the back of his neck, so Thaddeus was able to keep it under.

The woman was doing something, walking in a slow circle around her house and its small yard and part of her neighbor's yard. It was slow, because she was stooping as she went, dragging a knife across the lawn and the sidewalk and the pavement. She bent and cut the line with her knife and edged forward again, moving wearily as though every step took an effort.

A little kid, a girl with skin half a shade lighter than her mother's and her hair in tight braids against her head, stood on the porch, watching. The girl's hands were filled with a tangle of light. Thaddeus hated her, too. He wanted to rush at her and tear her apart, except that his father still held him and anyway he kept losing sight of the girl when he blinked. Something about the light she had in her hands confused his eye and made it hard to keep track of her even though she was standing still.

"Two of 'em. New here," grunted Thaddeus's father. "Yeah. No wonder they're so damned loud. Anybody can find 'em till she gets that circle laid down. Fucking lucky there ain't no blood kin way out here. 'Cept she could probably tell, I guess, so it's not all luck. Us putting that damn cur dog down before it could get her, *that* was luck."

Thaddeus barely heard his dad and didn't understand what he meant. His blood was full of the Beast's fire. The fire thundered in his veins, wanting out, wanting the hunt and the kill. Nearly all his concentration had to go to keeping his Beast inside, not letting it out.

"Come on," said Dan Williams. "Don't you *dare* shift." He pulled his son forward.

The woman saw them. She flinched hard and started to step back, then looked quickly along the circle she'd been drawing, and then glanced at the girl on the porch and the open door behind the kid, and then flung another desperate look at Thaddeus's dad. It was plain even to Thaddeus that she was thinking maybe she had time to finish her circle but that she knew really she didn't, that she knew how fast a black dog could move and that it was too late for her to do anything, she knew she couldn't finish her circle or reach her kid or do *anything*—but she didn't scream or run, she straightened her back and held out her hands, looking straight at Thaddeus's dad. Moonlight pooled in her hands, so maybe she wasn't completely harmless, but Thaddeus couldn't imagine what she meant to do.

She said, her voice even and surprisingly deep for a woman, "You haven't shifted. Who are you?"

Thaddeus hadn't exactly realized this, although it was very, very obvious and very, very strange. His father *was* still in human form, except for claws that pricked the skin of Thaddeus's neck. If *his* Beast was pushing him toward killing fury, it didn't show at all.

Dan Williams didn't let Thaddeus go, but he held his other hand out toward the woman, open and empty, human right down to the fingernails. "Yeah," he said. "No, listen. I'm calm. I'm good. A woman like you, she did it for me a long time ago. I want you to do it for my boy. I want him calm. Lot safer from those Dimilioc bastards that way—safer from vampires, too—safer from his own damn Beast. He's got a strong one, it'll get stronger, he's got to get one hell of a chain on it or pretty soon it'll eat him."

Thaddeus blinked at that, startled even through the hatred and the consuming effort to keep his Beast down. It would get stronger, yeah, they did, yeah it seemed plenty strong now, but his father had never said *someday soon it will eat you.* That would scare him, he thought, once he got a chance to think about it, but right now he had no room for anything but hating the woman and the girl—yeah, definitely her, too, she was just the same as her mother—

"You can do that," Dan Williams said. "That's what you are, that's what you do, isn't that right." It wasn't a question.

The woman didn't step away from her mostly-completed circle, but she looked carefully across the street at Thaddeus. He shuddered with the need to kill her, but his dad shook him hard and muttered threats, and he didn't dare fight. He glared at the woman, but he didn't move.

"Yeah," said the woman. "I need to finish my circle first. It's almost done."

"No," said Thaddeus's father. "You'll close me out, us out, no way. First you get my boy Calm."

This time Thaddeus heard the capital letter. He almost did try to fight then, because what the fuck was his father planning to let this woman *do* to him, except it was his *dad*, who might beat the shit out of him if he didn't obey, but who also taught him and protected him and made sure he was better than those black dog curs on the street—it was his *dad*, and though his Beast was sure this was a kind of death and they had to fight, had to get away, had to kill the woman, Thaddeus wouldn't listen, he fought the Beast back and locked his hands—human hands, still, despite his Beast pushing him—into fists and crammed them in his jean pockets and wouldn't fight. He wouldn't, he didn't, he wouldn't, it was his *dad* and he didn't *care* what his Beast thought about *anything*.

"She won't close you out," said the girl on the porch. Not pretty, Thaddeus could see that, her face was too broad to be pretty, her mouth too wide, but she stood up straight and looked directly at Thaddeus and his father, steady and confident. Her voice had a burr to it, not exactly an accent, but different somehow. Thaddeus hated her just as much as he hated her mother, but she met his eyes and then said again, to Thaddeus father, "She won't close you out. She wouldn't. She won't. Anyway, if she does, *I'll* do the Calming for you."

The woman made a wordless sound of surprised protest, and the girl looked at her, and smiled, and shrugged. "You wouldn't leave them out in the cold," she said to her mother. And then said again to Thaddeus's father, "But if she does, I won't. I promise."

"Don't make promises!" said the woman. "Damn, girl, you know better!"

"Sometimes you have to," said the girl. "*You* taught me that. Sometimes you have to make a promise, even when it's dangerous." She ran down the steps, two at a time, ignoring her mother's shout, and came confidently to stand almost within arm's length of Thaddeus and his father. "I'll wait out here with you while my mother finishes her circle," she said. "That way you can be sure, all right?"

And that was DeAnn.

Yeah, meeting DeAnn had changed everything. Thaddeus could even see how meeting DeAnn had brought him, by a very strange route, back here to this city, hunting strays again, full circle. Only this time, with the Dimilioc Master rather than his father—

"Pay attention," growled Grayson Lanning, the Dimilioc Master, from behind him. "Daydreaming about old times, Williams? You've missed the trail."

He had. There was nothing he could say. He'd gone right past it, that subtle breath of sulfur and ash and old blood they'd been following: it had faded suddenly as the stray shifted to his human form—that spoke well for his control—and ducked away west down a little alley that ran between the ass-ends of crowded businesses, restaurants and who knew what, right into the heart of Chinatown where he might hope to hide his scent in the cluttered smells of spices and cooking, fish and herbs and who knew what.

And, yeah, Thaddeus had missed it, gone right past. Angry and embarrassed, he wanted to snarl back at Grayson, but that would be stupid, a kid's temper. He took a deep breath instead to fix the weaker, less distinctive scent, and turned west to follow the trail. What all *did* lie over in this direction, anyway, once you got past the restaurants but before you got to the river? Apartments, warehouses, both, maybe. He wasn't sure. But the kid hadn't gotten too much of a lead even with his little dodge; they'd catch him before he'd got two blocks, probably. Then there'd be one less cur in Chicago.

Hunting strays was the point, but only on the surface. Thaddeus wasn't a fool. Sure, lots of strays were making trouble these days. Sure, yeah, too many for that scary-ass young punk Ezekiel to deal with all by his own damn self. But no one had to explain to Thaddeus why Grayson had decided to take this particular mission himself, and why he'd decided to bring Thaddeus—and no one else—as backup and support. This was a test. Thaddeus could have counted on his fingers all the different ways it was a test, and even then he might have missed a couple unless he took off his shoes.

It was a test of Thaddeus's temper, because Grayson wasn't making any damn effort to be nice. It was a test of Thaddeus's control of his Beast, what in Dimilioc they called his shadow, a stupid name for something that could explode up out of a man and take on real substance. A man cast his *own* shadow. The Beast was something else, something outside a man, though it clung close, yeah, okay, close as a shadow, that part was right. It was something that came straight from Hell, just like they said; that part he believed.

So, yeah, this whole damn mission was a test of Thaddeus's control, because here he was, way out here alone with Grayson Lanning, just the two of them, no one else for miles, no hostages, no witnesses, and if they fought, neither of them knew who would prove stronger.

But Thaddeus kept his Beast down, with a continual effort. It wanted to rise, wanted to fight: ambitious and furious and crazy, what else was new. He'd had lots of practice. He kept it down and he kept his mouth shut and he did what he was told. That was maybe another part of the test. Or maybe it was a test of his commitment to DeAnn and Conway, left behind in Dimilioc. Or a test of his trust in Dimilioc, to obey the Master and leave his wife and little son behind. Who knew what the hell the Dimilioc Master had in his head?

And, so, yeah, what could make any test worse? Why, making yourself look like a moron by getting lost in your own head and missing a trail, that was what.

The stray had been in black dog form when they'd caught his scent. Thaddeus didn't know whether he'd caught that sulfur-stink first, or if Grayson had just waited to see how long he'd take to catch it—another test, maybe, it could of been. But the kid had some kind of control or he wouldn't have been able to try to hide his scent by shifting to human form. He wouldn't be able to keep his Beast down long, though, not now when he was scared, when he knew he had way meaner black dogs on his tail. No, he'd let his Beast back up, or lose control of it and it would come back up on its own. It wouldn't make any difference. A single ordinary cur black dog wasn't going to last even half a minute once they caught him—

Then Thaddeus caught a sharp, acrid stink and a heavy blood scent, and swung around. A seafood place on one side, the smell of spices and shrimp blurred the ash-and-sulfur scents of black dogs, but the blood smell was strong and sweet. Nothing could hide that. Another alley led off south between two hulking dark buildings, toward 22nd and who knew what, except that someone was dead there, and a black dog—no, two black dogs—by the scent, stronger than the stray Grayson and Thaddeus had been tracking. Though maybe without as much control.

Grayson lifted his head, breathing deeply, sorting the scents. "Full moon," he growled in disgust, meaning all the strays in the city were out tonight.

Thaddeus felt the pull of the moon himself, and his control was much, much better than any stupid kid's. Except around Grayson. Around the Dimilioc Master, he felt like a stupid kid himself, which didn't help his control any. Made it hard to talk, too. But Thaddeus jerked his head the way they'd been going, then toward the alley and gritted out, "Which?"

Their original target plainly wasn't completely stupid. If they didn't catch him soon, he might be able to hide, and DeAnn had stayed with Con at Dimilioc, which was fine, but now they had no Pure woman with them to help them track a stray if they lost him. So maybe it would be better to chase that one down now, before he got too far ahead. If they caught him quick, they might still have time to circle back and track these others by the scent of the lingering blood and rage. But if they lost these, they'd lose two and only have caught the one. Thaddeus thought they should take the two, but he wasn't calling the shots, not tonight.

Grayson thought it over.

The Dimilioc Master showed no sign of being affected by the moon. He was a big man, not as big as Thaddeus, but broad-boned and heavy, with powerful shoulders and big hands, a strong jaw and deep-set eyes beneath heavy brows. But he wouldn't have intimidated Thaddeus at all except for his Beast. The Master's Beast was very, very strong. Grayson hadn't let it up, there was no trace of its distortion in his hands or face. But Thaddeus could see it, gathered right below his skin or maybe hovering right over it, so dense it was almost palpable. The Master was not much older than Thaddeus, but the strength of his Beast made him seem a *lot* older. Just having Grayson Lanning walk into the same city as them ought to have made all these stupid strays flatten out—but ignorant, crazy curs, yeah, what did they know? Kids with no sense and no experience and no idea their noise might draw the wrong kind of attention. They probably thought they needed to watch out for ordinary humans armed with silver, and had no idea at all they should worry a whole lot more about Dimilioc black wolves.

"You, go after that one," Grayson ordered, stabbing a finger down the alley the way they had been going. "When you've dealt with him, go back to the hotel. Don't argue—go."

Thaddeus *had* been about to object. Splitting up was stupid and unnecessary, because finding yourself facing a whole pack of enemies out here wasn't likely, but it could happen—or, much more likely, there might be men with guns and silver bullets. Murderous strays would draw that kind of reaction in a hurry these days, and these days even in Chicago a lot of people went armed and never mind moronic laws that told them they were supposed to let themselves be the prey of monsters in the dark

If Thaddeus let Grayson Lanning get killed on this mission, Ezekiel would hunt him down and make him a fucking example for the ages. Thaddeus didn't need Dimilioc's young executioner to actually stroll up and say so in person. He knew it was true.

But it was also obvious that the Dimilioc Master wasn't going to take *Fuck, no* for an answer. Sooner done, sooner home picking your teeth, as Thaddeus's father used to say. Thaddeus turned without a word and loped after their original target.

His target was a young stray, not very strong yet, probably he'd never be very strong. But he wasn't as stupid as most. Everything pointed to that, and Thaddeus thought so again now, tracking the kid down the last block and right through a restaurant, in the back door and out the front, a little hole-in-the-wall place meant for Chinese people rather than tourists, violent with chilies and Sichuan pepper, steamed fish and black mushrooms, hot oil and sizzling pork. Clever kid, scared kid, he should have tucked himself in at a table in the back and stayed right here in this place. If he'd done that, Thaddeus might of lost him in the confusion of scents, or would at least have been forced to lie low and wait rather than taking him out in the middle of a public restaurant, because the place wasn't crowded, but it wasn't empty either. But he'd gone through, the scent was clear outside the front door . . . and disappeared three steps down the street.

Thaddeus paused, nostrils flaring. No one challenged him. No one had said anything when he'd come in the back way and strode through the restaurant, no one said anything now, though he had stopped dead, forcing people out here on the sidewalk to go around him. He turned in a circle, taking deep breaths, sorting out what must of happened.

Not a stupid kid, no. He'd come out the front door and turned around and gone straight back in, and he was probably out the back again by now and running for safety. No one from the restaurant had showed a thing, not by so much as a glance. Known here, maybe, that kid. And of course Thaddeus was a stranger. Not that it would make any difference, in the end.

Turning, he took a long step back toward the restaurant's front door.

No one tried to stop him, but two of the staff got in his way, like it was accidental. He shoved past them, ignoring their sullen, wary looks. The back door was now locked. Yeah, like that was a coincidence, right? He broke the lock and flung the door open, and was back out in the alley, casting back and forth. Yes. The kid's scent was here, stronger now. He was in black dog form again. The moon or just plain fear had driven him to shift, but he was still heading west—yes, one small street and then parking lots, empty in the dark.

And then the bulk of some large building, not a little shop but something big. There was a green banner in the front, right up the face of the building above the front door, three stories if it was an inch, but Thaddeus couldn't read the Chinese characters on the banner. He didn't care what building it was, anyway. All that he cared about was the hunt, the hunt with his quarry running before him, yeah, the kid knew he was back here, knew he hadn't managed to throw him off the trail. Maybe he'd hidden and waited, watching the back of the restaurant. Maybe he'd seen Thaddeus come back out. He was scared, Thaddeus could smell it. Any stray would know right away, seeing Thaddeus, that there could be no way to fight. That Thaddeus was the hunter tonight, and the kid was just prey.

The kid hadn't gone in the front door of the building. Around the side, and away toward the river—toward the river, really? Thaddeus cast one way and the other, circled wide around the building and then more closely, and found, as he'd half-expected, his quarry's scent on a rear wall and a balcony one story up. Yes. The same exact trick again, fake trail and doubling back, but it was a good trick and the kid hadn't had a lot of options once he'd got this far. This time he'd laid down a lot more of a trail to draw Thaddeus away toward the river before he doubled back. And jumping up to the balcony, that was clever, if Thaddeus had been a little more careless, that break in the scent trail might have thrown him off. Maybe it was even another false trail . . . but no. The scent was strong here. He was sure the stray had gone in through the balcony door.

The door wasn't ajar, but it was unlocked. A black dog could slide it open, but only a human hand could work the little lock, and his quarry was too scared now to manage the shift back to human form. Thaddeus had never yet let his Beast up; he had no need to. If he ran into ordinary human people, better to do it in his human form and not as the Beast. Grayson had laid down that rule, but it was true. No need to change, not yet, plenty of time for that once he caught up with the stray at last. So he had no trouble sliding the balcony door open and then shutting it behind him.

An apartment. A bedroom, and beyond that another room, and across the room a door, closed, but probably leading out to the main hall. Dark and empty; this apartment even smelled empty. No one lived here. The scent trail led straight through each room, detoured to one side and the other, and then led out through the interior door. Thaddeus had his hand actually on the doorknob before a breath or a sound or, hell, maybe a half-conscious thought about kids who doubled back and doubled back again, made him turn.

He was shifting as he turned, and he ducked, too, hit the floor and rolled, or he might have bought it right there, ambushed by a kid a third his age and less than a third his size. DeAnn would never have let him hear the end of it. That was the thought that made him move so fast, that brought his Beast roaring up. In that form he was close to half a ton of jet-black shaggy monster, all muscled bulk and hot breath and fiery eyes and knife-sharp claws. And the kid was only a kid, hardly bigger than a big dog. It was not an even contest.

Thaddeus's Beast loved the younger black dog's fear and despair. It didn't want a *contest.* It wanted a hunt and a leisurely slaughter, preferably not too fast. That wasn't what a decent man would want: if killing had to happen, a decent man would make it quick. But it was hard; harder than it should of been; he'd been scared by that ambush and now he was angry—or his Beast was angry, it was always angry, but this was a hotter, more vicious rage, feeding his own anger. Thaddeus had intended to make it quick, but instead he only tore five shallow gouges along the stray's shoulder and side and threw him against the far wall. Then, embarrassed by the self-indulgence, he lunged to finish the stray, but the young black dog rolled and tucked himself down and fled before Thaddeus caught him, out the door and gone down the hallway. Thaddeus wanted to curse. It came out as a low, grating snarl.

There were no screams, that was something; apparently no one was out there just at the moment. Thaddeus tore his own way through the doorway, wrecking a good chunk of the doorframe and wall, and followed. The trail was so clear it might have been lit by burning fire; there was no missing it now. The door at the end of the hall—that was a stair, and the stray had fled upward, very nice, the kid would run out of *up* soon enough—a chase, a hunt, a victim who had no hope of getting away . . . he tried not to savor it, but it was hard.

Out on the highest floor, and here at last someone was out in the hall, an elderly Chinese woman who pressed back against the wall, her hands over her mouth. The Beast wanted to tear her intestines out in passing. Thaddeus blocked the impulse, barely noticing the familiar effort, and slammed his weight against the door through which the scent trail led.

The stray flung himself at Thaddeus as he came through the door, one last desperate effort, but Thaddeus turned his shoulder to that rush, blocked the first frantic slashing blow and the second, and someone shot him.

It wasn't silver. He knew that first. It wasn't a killing shot, obviously, or he'd never have known anything about it.

A handgun, something small caliber, it hadn't made much noise. It hadn't made much of a wound, either: he'd been shot in the chest, but his heavy bones had deflected the bullet and in this form he was very hard to kill. But it hurt. His anger roared up, vast and burning. The stray was in front of him again. Thaddeus knocked him down and aside, crushed his ribs and tore through his belly, flung him aside and turned on the man with the gun . . . who was an old man, old, old, ninety years old, a hundred maybe, a little old Chinese man with a thin face and wispy white hair and a pissant gun gripped in his shaking hands. Hands shaking like that, it was a miracle he'd hit Thaddeus at all, even if Thaddeus in his black dog form was a target hardly smaller than the broad side of a barn.

Then the kid was there. Thaddeus had hurt him, hurt him bad, he'd done it deliberately, forcing him to shift back to human form to shed those injuries, getting one enemy down so he could figure out this new threat. That had worked fine, because of course the kid didn't have the control to shift back to his black dog form, not right away, not when it counted most. But he flung himself in front of Thaddeus in his fragile human form. Like a toy terrier pup facing down a wolf. Just like that. It was a surprise, a black dog cur facing Thaddeus like that, protecting an old human man—his father, no, too old: maybe his grandfather. That was . . . actually, that was kind of something, a black dog kid acting like that.

The kid was shouting, quick and angry, but at the old man, not at Thaddeus. Thaddeus couldn't understand him and thought at first he'd lost language after all, though he hadn't in years, but it wasn't that, of course: the kid was shouting in Chinese, cussing up a storm by the tone, but the old man wasn't budging. He was trying to get around the kid, shoot Thaddeus again. So the kid grabbed the gun out of his hands and *threw it away*, smart kid, even right now, right this minute, even with everything else. That was *seriously* astonishing. Hard to believe he was an ordinary stray's kid—but then, Thaddeus knew better than most, better than any stuck-up Dimilioc wolf, that some black dogs actually did do their best to train up their kids.

The gun skidded all the way across the room and under a threadbare old couch, gone, out of easy reach. Not that it had been much of a gun anyway. The kid was pushing the old man back bodily, away from Thaddeus, down an interior hallway. The kid shoved the old man away and then blocked the hallway with his own body, like his skinny ass would slow anybody down for more than half a second. Not that the old man went, he was pushing at the kid's back, yelling something loud and angry in Chinese.

Thaddeus caught his Beast by the tail and dragged it back and down, forced it down when it didn't want to yield, stomped his foot down on it and braced himself good against it getting free. Then he crossed his arms over his chest and glowered at both the black dog kid and the old man. "What the hell?" he demanded. "Kid wants to save your sorry ass, what's your problem, old man?"

"Don't hurt him," the kid said, quick and urgent. Thirteen, fourteen. No way he was as much as fifteen, skinny little kid like that, all knees and elbows. "Don't hurt him," he said again. "He's not one of us, he's nothing, you don't have to kill him, people know him, everyone knows him, killing him'll only make trouble, people with guns—"

"Yeah?" said Thaddeus.

"*Real* guns, man," insisted the kid. "Not like that one." He said something else, something violent, in Chinese, and the old man stopped pushing at him and glared over the kid's shoulder at Thaddeus.

The kid took an urgent step forward. "I'll go with you. Listen, not here, but I'll go *with* you, wherever you want, the river, the park, you want a fight? I'll fight you—"

Thaddeus snorted. "You? Fight me?"

"I will!" snapped the kid, jerking his head up in affront. "That's what you want, right? That'd make it more fun for you, wouldn't it? But not here. Lots better down by the river. Lots more space." And he stood up real straight and glared right into Thaddeus's face in deliberate challenge.

Brave kid. Smart kid, decent control. Yet he'd been out

there in the city. Hunting. A stray. Dimilioc put down strays like ordinary people put down mad dogs. Kind of the same thing, except black dogs that got out of control were a lot worse than rabid dogs. A lot smarter, a lot more deliberately vicious. Killing mostly when the moon rose full and their control dropped into the pit, but violent all the time, even when the moon was dark, raping girls and beating up anybody who looked like a target, yeah, that was a black dog cur. But this kid . . . Thaddeus looked him up and down. The kid managed not to back up. The effort was visible.

"Come on," Thaddeus said abruptly. "Come with me." He caught the kid by one skinny wrist and dragged him back through the apartment toward the door. After the first involuntary jerk to get free, the kid didn't fight him. He shoved his grandfather back when the old man tried to catch at his other wrist and then came willingly, fast, pulling Thaddeus, even, instead of the other way around, into the hall and right past the old woman and two other old people who'd come out to see what was going on. One had a gun, a .38. Even a black dog would feel that, even though it wasn't loaded with silver. Thaddeus slapped it out of the man's hands and strode down the stairs. The kid stayed right with him, no problems at all.

Then he did balk suddenly. "Not that way—this way, fire exit, quicker, the alarm doesn't work, it's the best way out."

Thaddeus shrugged and went the way the kid indicated. "You're awful damn eager to get out, for a damn fool who led me straight here."

A sullen look, scared and resentful. "I thought I'd got away. I thought you'd lose me for sure—nobody ever—and I needed Grandfather. The monster, it was hard to keep it down—it wanted up so bad—the moon—" he stopped.

"Yeah," said Thaddeus. That made sense. Especially if you were an inexperienced kid and you didn't have a clue what you'd run into when Dimilioc came after you.

Out of the building then, and, yes, down toward the river. Quieter down this way, a couple big buildings, warehouses or offices or whatever, deserted at this hour, surrounded by empty parking lots and lit by streetlights and the full moon. Sirens, not too far away. But not here. Thaddeus let the kid go, straightened to his full height, and stared at him.

The kid looked away at once, took a sharp breath, and looked back. Then away again. Another breath. He pressed his hands together, rubbed his hands up his arms, glanced warily at Thaddeus once more. But he didn't shift. He didn't try to run.

"Full moon tonight," Thaddeus observed, ignoring the part of him that wanted to snarl and *make* the kid run. He said instead, "A kid like you, out in the city for a little fun, seeing what turns up? Didn't get so far away from home, did you, huh? You always hunt in your own backyard? Didn't your daddy teach you better? He didn't teach you to get clear of your own neighborhood before you hunt, huh?"

The kid was shaking his head. "Not like that. *Not* like that. Stray cats, man, it's all about stray cats, there're some big-ass rats behind the restaurants, maybe a dog or two, no people, man, really!"

"Yeah?"

"Grandfather wouldn't like it!" The kid sounded young and desperate. Thaddeus could hear his Beast's vicious snarl behind his human voice. But the human voice was in front. The human kid was in front.

Thaddeus paused. How often had he faced off against the Beast, determined not to let it pull him along with what it wanted *because DeAnn wouldn't like it?*

After that first meeting, after DeAnn's momma had done the Calming on him and the whole world had changed, Thaddeus had been fascinated by the Pure. To hate them so much! And then see them change right in front of him to something beautiful! *Beauty* wasn't something a black dog noticed, much. But after the Calming, he suddenly seemed to have attention left over for noticing all kinds of things. The fragrance of a flower became something to enjoy, along with the scent of blood. Watching a mom with her kid on a playground became something more than, better than, just watching potential prey. His Beast was still there, still in him every minute, but it was like it had been shoved more toward the side, like suddenly there was more room for his own thoughts and feelings.

The Calming made it so much easier to be a real person as well as the Beast.

Thaddeus's father had not wanted to expand his territory west. Fighting Schoen wasn't a good idea. She was in her fifties, older than any other black dog Thaddeus had ever heard of. She lived alone and hunted alone and fought alone, but she'd lasted so long because she was just that tough. Nobody wanted to fight her. Besides, they needed her out there. Chicagoland was so big, it took several strong black dogs to keep down the curs and avoid Dimilioc attention.

So DeAnn and her mother eventually moved south instead, into the heart of Thaddeus's father's territory. The move got them a little farther from the vampires and blood kin downtown, too, which was even more important. This time the move was easy and almost safe, because Dan Williams and his son made damn sure of it, hunting curs and moon-bound shifters with dedicated fury for a week beforehand and then making sure the move took place at the new moon.

That was how DeAnn got to go to a real school. It wasn't a great school, but it was safe, because Thaddeus went with her. There were gangs, but that wasn't the danger. Not for DeAnn. Just having her around seemed to calm trouble down, make people a little nicer to each other.

No, the problem was the constant worry that a vicious young black dog might suddenly catch her scent. Thaddeus remembered vividly how that had felt. He knew any normal black dog would go straight for her, no matter what. Of course she had the protection of her magic, but the school was a big place and she was just a kid, she couldn't make the school and grounds and whole *neighborhood* safe.

But Thaddeus could make it safe for her. He loved that

he could make it safe for her, that he could give her something she really wanted.

He'd never gone to school before. He'd never wanted to, but DeAnn did. She was smart, and she liked people. Thaddeus wasn't so smart and he didn't like anybody, but school was kind of fun if you didn't take it seriously. Even in his human form, Thaddeus was way too big and fast and ruthless to have trouble with gang members or bullies or anyone—and with his Beast waiting just beneath his skin, less trouble still.

He liked watching the human kids. They were so soft and vulnerable. They didn't know how to protect themselves at all. Soft, clumsy . . . he liked to watch them, especially in groups. He could have killed a dozen of them any time he wanted. Two dozen. Just rip into them with claws and rage . . . but DeAnn wouldn't like it, of course. So he wasn't really tempted. Even if mass slaughter like that hadn't been against the rules.

No one watched him in return. Not openly. Some unacknowledged instinct made not only the other students but also the teachers avoid Thaddeus's gaze and give him a whole lot of extra space. So he hung out in the classrooms and the halls and kept an eye out for DeAnn and watched the show, and every now and then read a book because DeAnn wanted him to. Some of them were even kind of okay. He sort of liked the story about the bear. He liked the dog in the story, the dog named Lion. Even though Lion was a stupid name for a dog. He even wrote a paper about that dog. DeAnn wanted him to, and explained about commas and how to quote things, and he wouldn't of wanted to bother with things like that every day, but it was okay. The teacher gave it back to him, with a B and a little smiley face next to the grade, and told him he should turn in more papers, that he could certainly pass the class. Thaddeus was surprised to discover that he kind of liked the teacher saying that, even though he didn't care about passing anything.

"See? Mr. Theodore's a good guy," DeAnn told him, smiling. "He likes you."

“He does not,” Thaddeus scoffed.

“He likes anybody who can write a decent paper—even big, scary dudes like you. Hey, I memorized a real long poem. Want to hear? It’s about bells. It’s got great words. The part about iron bells rolling on the human heart a stone is all grim and scary—you’ll like it.”

So that was a taste of real life. It was almost like being an ordinary person. DeAnn did that for him, made him into someone who could seem, more or less, most of the time, like a normal person. She could give him enough room in his own head and heart to *want* to seem like a normal person, when for years he’d seemed to have less and less room all the time—he could look back on his life and see that, now. He loved her for it, and made a new set of rules for himself based on what she wanted him to be.

Because DeAnn wouldn’t like it. That was the line between what he would do and what he would refuse to let the Beast do. That was the leash he had on his monster.

And now here he stood, decades later, and this kid had the nerve to face him straight up and claim a leash like that one?

“Your granddad’s gonna die,” he said at last.

“No!” the kid said instantly. He squared off, straightening his shoulders and glaring at Thaddeus. Not quite attacking, no—his black dog instincts must be telling him *exactly* how far out of his league he was. He said instead, desperate and sharp, arguing because all he had was words even though words were never a black dog’s best thing, “They’ll *all* have guns by the time you get back there. Silver bullets, some of ’em! You won’t—”

Thaddeus held up one hand. “Not me. The old man with the scythe. *Old age*, kid! How old’s your granddad? Ninety years older’n God, he looked to me.”

The kid took a breath, watching Thaddeus warily. He said at last, “Doesn’t matter. Won’t matter. How you think Qingming would work for me if I been killing people? My grandfather wouldn’t like it any better just ’cause he was dead!”

“Yeah?” said Thaddeus. “What’s your name, kid?”

Another wary look. “Lee.”

“Lee, sure. You ever hear of Dimilioc, Lee?”

A wary headshake.

“Yeah, you don’t know much. Damn good thing you got that granddad of yours. You been listenin’ to him and that’s good. But now you listen to me, kid. Dimilioc don’t like strays making trouble, understand? But strays who keep the rules, sometimes Dimilioc looks the other way. You know the rules, kid? *Keep a low profile*, that mean anything to you? Don’t kill people, above all don’t let any stupid black dogs kill people or rape girls or whatever shit like that, because any Dimilioc black wolf who comes to deal with them, he might just deal with you, too. You hear me?”

A slight nod. Thaddeus couldn’t tell whether the kid was actually listening or not. He said, “Dimilioc’s got more room in it than it used to. A lot more room. You think about what I’m tellin’ you. When your granddad’s gone, Lee, you gonna find your Beast pushing you hard. They get stronger anyway, and then you get into trouble, you hear me? *Before* that happens, you come to Vermont—”

“Vermont!”

“Shut up and listen. You come to Vermont if you find your Beast pushing you too hard, getting out of control. You come to Newport and then once you’re there, you ask around for Dimilioc till a black dog turns up and wants to know who’s asking. And then you tell him you’re looking for me. Thaddeus. You got that?”

A nod, which didn’t mean the kid agreed. That kind of submission was just meant to appease a stronger black dog. Thaddeus knew all about that. But he thought the kid would remember. Maybe he wouldn’t take that advice. But time would pass and his granddad would die and his Beast would get stronger . . . and at that point, maybe he would.

And at that point, maybe Thaddeus would be able to give him a hand. If Grayson Lanning didn’t kill him in the meantime, for disobeying orders, or disrespect, or whatever the fuck.

"Yeah," Thaddeus said to the kid. "Well, remember. And in the meantime, you listen to me: you don't hunt people and you lay off dogs, hear me? Rats are fine, but people don't like monsters killin' their dogs. You do what your granddad says and you keep your Beast leashed tight. And you meet a Pure woman, kid—you know the Pure?"

A headshake.

"If you do, you'll hate her on sight. That's how you'll know her. But it's your Beast that'll hate her, not you yourself. You listening to me?"

Another tight little nod. "Yeah."

"You kill a Pure woman, nothing can save you. But you stay smart and keep that leash tight and don't hurt her and she can save *you,* hear me? You ask her to do the Calming on you, you hear me, kid? That'll change your whole fucking life. You hear me?"

Another, "Yeah," and who knew what the kid was thinking, but it was the best Thaddeus could do.

"Then get," said Thaddeus, and jerked his head back the way they'd come.

No questions. The kid took a wary step away, not really believing it, Thaddeus could tell. Expecting to get just so far and then Thaddeus would let his Beast up and come right after him, the chase, the hunt, the brief savage fight at the end, with its outcome never in doubt. Yeah, the Beast wanted that. Thaddeus held it on a tight leash while the kid turned at last and walked away, not running—running would draw pursuit, the kid knew it, and Thaddeus wondered again about the kid's father and who'd taught him anything about being what he was.

No telling. No dad in the picture at this point, that was clear. Just the granddad. Who seemed to be enough, at least for now. Thaddeus stood in the dark and watched till the kid was out of sight and cursed himself for a soft touch and a sentimental fool, but he held his Beast and didn't take a single step in pursuit.

Instead, once the kid was out of sight, he turned and

strode back east, back toward the hotel where they were staying. Right downtown, right where the vampires had once ruled; that was a kind of statement there, too.

Grayson Lanning was already at the hotel, settled in his half of the suite, with the curtains pulled open to let the moonlight in and only one dim lamp turned on, in the corner. He'd been back long enough to shed the anger and intensity of the hunt and seemed now like a bank manager or something

Well, okay, maybe the guy who managed a bank for the mob or something, nothing could mask that kind of aura.

Grayson had his laptop open on one of the small hotel tables, but he was standing in the middle of the suite's common room, facing the door, when Thaddeus opened it. He looked him up and down, his expression unreadable. Thaddeus had, as always, the strong sense that the Dimilioc Master could look straight into him and see not only him, but also his hidden Beast.

"Well?" said the Master.

"Yeah," said Thaddeus. He wanted a shower and something to eat, chips or something like a normal person would want, something to make himself feel normal. Or else he wanted a hard run in the forest, a hunt with blood at the end. Most of all he wanted time to get himself ready for this. But he'd had time, all the time to walk back to the hotel from Chinatown, and it hadn't helped at all. More time wouldn't help, either.

He said, to delay the moment, "How about you, you have any trouble?"

Grayson gave him a long look, but then lifted his shoulders in a minimal shrug. "The strays were fairly strong, but stupid. There was no difficulty." He paused, then added, "I trust the stray you pursued gave you very little trouble as well?"

At this point Thaddeus just wanted it over, so he said, as quick and blunt as he could, "I caught him, yeah. He was just a kid, with a grandfather—a human grandfather. He's trying hard to be decent 'cause of wanting to keep the old man happy. I told him stay out of trouble, keep quiet, don't kill people, when his grandfather passes he should come to Dimilioc—" at that point, Grayson's raised eyebrows brought him to a halt. Though that was fine. Thaddeus didn't have much idea what else he could say.

"Indeed," said Grayson, in his most unreadable tone. "I don't recall specifying an exception for young strays with grandfathers."

"Yeah," said Thaddeus. "No." He waited. He didn't look down, though black dog instinct pushed him to flinch. Grayson scared him. Only two people in the world scared him, and Grayson Lanning was one of them. He didn't know whether the Dimilioc Master was stronger than he was, didn't know who would win a one-on-one fight. It didn't matter. Even if Thaddeus had been sure he could take him, Grayson Lanning was a scary dude—and he had Ezekiel Korte at his back, even if the young Dimilioc executioner wasn't physically present in this very room right at this exact moment. If Thaddeus did kill Grayson, there was no way Ezekiel would just let it go. That was always something anyone had to have in the back of his mind when he thought of challenging the Dimilioc Master.

"You let this young stray live. Was that your decision to make?"

Thaddeus moved his shoulders, not knowing what he should say, what the Master wanted to hear. "I . . . didn't want to kill him."

"I see." Grayson looked at him thoughtfully. "You tracked this pup to his home, I gather. Good. Tell me where he lives."

A direct order. That wasn't good. Yeah, no, that was bad. Thaddeus didn't look away, but he wanted to. He let his breath out slowly and shook his head, deliberately, once, back and forth.

"Indeed," said Grayson. "Defiance, Williams?"

Thaddeus didn't answer. It didn't seem necessary. Silence was answer enough.

The Master walked forward. He hadn't shifted, not yet, but his shadow gathered tightly around and below him, so heavy Thaddeus could almost see it as a separate presence.

Thaddeus took a step back before he even knew he'd moved. Then he caught himself and stopped. Then he asked himself what the hell he was trying to prove, and just how stupid he had to be. He knew exactly what DeAnn would say, if she was here—he could almost hear her: *Thad, you idiot, what the* hell *are you trying to prove?* If he got himself killed because he was too proud to submit to the Master of Dimilioc, she would be *pissed.*

So then he dropped to one knee and turned his face aside, and the Master came close and set one hand on his shoulder, close by his neck—a threat; razor-edged claws tipping suddenly blunt fingers, *deadly* threat, he could tear out Thaddeus's throat and there was nothing Thaddeus could do to stop him. The Master lifted his other hand toward Thaddeus's face, toward his eyes, and Thaddeus found his Beast surging furiously upward, pressing hard, sure the Master was going to kill him right here and now, and for something so *stupid*—

"No," said the Master. Somehow that one quiet word echoed with more force than a shout; it seemed to strike Thaddeus like a physical blow. The Master was watching Thaddeus intently, but with very little of the furious heat of the black dog in his dark eyes. He said, still quietly, "Don't let it rise. Hear me?"

Thaddeus set his jaw and fought his Beast. It was like wrapping your arms around a great big old grizzly and trying to haul it backward while it snarled and shoved forward—it was like trying to drag that big old grizzly back while you were *drowning*—not in water, but in heat and fury—his grip was slipping, and if the Beast got loose now, either he was going to kill Grayson or else the Dimilioc Master was going to kill him—better than just cowering down like a beaten pup and letting the Master tear out his throat without even a fight—no, that was the Beast, that hot rage, but he couldn't hold it—

The Master's shadow rolled forward, heavy but fast, smothering, irresistible.

Thaddeus found himself breathing hard, his Beast flattened beneath the Master's power. He could think again. He could understand just how close he had come to losing control. And just how disastrous that would have been for him, maybe for DeAnn—maybe for Conway, too. He made an effort to steady his breathing and looked up, warily, trying to gauge Grayson Lanning's temper and guess what the Master might do.

Grayson said calmly, "Again. This time, I want you to get your shadow down without my help."

Thaddeus started to say that now he *had* control, that his Beast wasn't going to get away from him a second time, that if Grayson hadn't pushed him so hard he wouldn't have lost control of it in the first place. But the Master gripped his shoulder again, held him hard, and ripped claws unexpectedly across his chest, right through muscle and bone.

That brought the Beast. It roared up, terrified and enraged, taking the injury almost before Thaddeus was aware of the brutal pain. He found himself almost fully shifted, on the other side of the room, shaking blood and ichor from his pelt, a heavy bass growl vibrating in his chest.

Grayson had not shifted. He stood still, in human form, studying Thaddeus with a calm detachment that would have made even the stupidest black dog wary. He said, "Yes. Now put it back down."

Thaddeus glared at him, trying to make sense of this command.

"Put it *down*," snapped Grayson impatiently.

Down. The Beast should go down, because letting it up was bad. Letting it up to fight Grayson Lanning was very bad, though for a long moment Thaddeus did not remember why. DeAnn. Yes. Conway, who needed his father. Yes. He knew that.

But it would be so much easier to tear Grayson Lanning into little pieces. The Master still had not shifted. Little and human and vulnerable . . . except he was the Dimilioc Master.

Not vulnerable at all.

He could roll Thaddeus's Beast down and under. He could do that. But he wouldn't. Because Thaddeus was supposed to force his beast down by himself. Some kind of fucking test or something, who knew what, some damn thing that seemed like a good idea to Grayson. Sadistic bastard. Thaddeus was furious, a fury that fed on and from his Beast's rage. He snarled, low and grating, longing to frighten Grayson, but the Master's eyes only narrowed slightly; he didn't look at all frightened. Not even concerned, damn him. Except it was also something to cling to, that lack of fear. Because no black dog wanted to attack another who looked that fearless.

Thaddeus dragged at his Beast. Dragged at it, struck up through it like a drowning man striking up from the depths of a rolling sea, pulled it down and began to shake himself free of it. He got partway shifted, but Grayson took one step toward him, and Thaddeus stuck right there. Scared. *Damn* Grayson. Thaddeus snarled again and found the Beast's snarl rising underneath his fury, and fought it. He had never been unable to control his Beast, not since the Calming. But then Grayson just stood there and looked at him with that grim patience—it was like when Ezekiel had first come to get him, just like that, and Thaddeus was upset and furious and all right, yes, scared, and he *couldn't shift*, not if the Dimilioc Master killed him right here for his failure. Grayson might do it; kill a black dog of his who turned out to be disobedient and defiant and now completely unable to control his own Beast.

So he tried. He caught his Beast and pulled it under with him, but it fought him furiously, completely at odds with his equally furious attempts to force it down, until its fury burned up through him and he began to slip back toward the fully shifted form.

"*Thaddeus*," Grayson said, like the crack of a whip.

Thaddeus flinched, and made it back once more to his half-shifted form. And stuck, panting.

The Dimilioc Master rolled his shadow once more. Then

he crossed his arms over his chest and stood there watching Thaddeus, just as calm and impenetrable as ever. Thaddeus wanted to snarl at him, curse him, maybe both. He fixed his gaze on the floor instead and thought hard about just how easily Grayson had forced his Beast down. Attacking the Dimilioc Master would be very, very stupid. He was shaking, and tried to stop, and couldn't.

"Again," said the Master. He stepped forward.

Thaddeus flinched back. "You want me to tell you where you can find that stupid kid? Because you haven't even asked me again, so if that's what you want, tell me!"

Grayson stopped. For a long moment, Thaddeus thought he wasn't going to answer at all. But he said eventually, "You're upset and angry, and the moon is full. It's important to seize the chance to work on your control at such times, if you mean to gain full command of your shadow. I don't need to *force* you to tell me what I want to know. You'll tell me when you've had time to think it through." He paused, regarding Thaddeus thoughtfully. Then he ordered, "Tell me where that stray can be found. When you're ready. Take your time." He waited.

Thaddeus wasn't sure he could manage to think about anything yet. He stared at the floor between his hands. The carpet was one of those neutral colors between blue and gray. His claws had scored right through it, and there was a charred patch where his hands had rested. Somebody would have to pay for that. Probably Dimilioc could afford it, though.

The shaking had passed. Thinking about the stupid carpet had helped. Thinking about anything else that had just happened . . . that didn't help at all. Upset and angry and pushed toward the monster by the full moon, yeah, all of that. But he had proved himself unable to manage his Beast. And Grayson Lanning had done this to him on purpose. For training. For *practice*.

And now he pushed again, damn him, to make Thaddeus answer the question he'd already refused to answer once.

Except that wasn't right. Because he didn't push, did he? *Take your time.* Right. Time to recover, to steady himself. He'd said he would force Thaddeus's Beast up again. But he hadn't. He didn't. He was waiting. He wasn't even watching Thaddeus now. He had crossed the room and stood by the window, gazing out at the night. The light of the full moon poured over him, silver and seductive, enough to pull any black dog toward the hunt and the kill. But it wasn't only a hunter's moon, a black dog's moon. It was also the kind of moon the Pure loved and could use best.

What would DeAnn say? What would she do? What would she think he should do?

He remembered what she had said to him right after they had been brought by force, along with their little son, to Dimilioc. Thaddeus had been given the choice of joining or death.

"Some choice," Thaddeus had growled to her. "Grayson Lanning wants us under his eye and under his thumb. You and me both. He'll never let us go. The minute I don't toe his line, he'll kill me and do whatever he wants with you and Con. He'd kill me as soon as blink, you can see it, can't you, and that young Korte bastard is worse."

And DeAnn had said, "Yeah, it's not a choice at all, but what it is, is a chance, the best chance we've ever had. Because the part you're not seeing, the part you don't understand, Thad, is once we're on the inside, once we're his, Grayson Lanning won't want to kill you. He'll work hard to make sure he never has to. He'll do everything in his power to make us all strong and keep us all safe."

Thaddeus hadn't believed her. He hadn't believed she could be right.

"Trust me on this," DeAnn had said. "That's how he is. I can tell."

So he had trusted her, and she had been right after all. Right about Grayson Lanning, and right that Thaddeus hadn't been able to see it. Not till they'd stepped inside Dimilioc. Then everything had changed. Eventually Thaddeus had understood that he'd been right, too: Grayson would never let them go. But *not letting go* was a lot more complicated than he'd ever imagined. Now he understood it included things like taking the chance of this night to push Thaddeus to gain better control over his Beast.

And even so, when Thaddeus had protested, he'd eased back. He'd even stopped to explain. There was also this about Grayson Lanning: he was a hard bastard, and he would never let go of what was his, but he never, ever lost control of his Beast and he was not pointlessly cruel.

Thaddeus said, not really knowing he was going to say this till the words were out, "Just west of where we separated. Big apartment building. Green banner with three Chinese characters up the front of the building. Third floor apartment. He said his name was Lee, but probably he was lying about that."

Grayson had turned and stood now with the moon at his back, his face in shadow, utterly unreadable. "No doubt. But I imagine that would be enough to find him. Why did you tell me?"

Thaddeus bowed his head. "Because you're the Dimilioc Master."

"I'm the Dimilioc Master, and I'll punish you if you defy me?"

"No," said Thaddeus. "You're the Dimilioc Master, so I tell you I let the kid go, and you decide what you want to do about that." He waited.

"Good," said Grayson. "What led to this epiphany?"

Thaddeus glared at him, grabbed hard hold of his temper, and lowered his gaze. "You said think it through. I thought it through."

To Thaddeus's relief, Grayson gave a small nod to this. He said, "Very well. Good. You're far less upset. That should make it easier to control your shadow. So. Are you ready to try this again?"

Thaddeus let out a slow breath. "Yeah. Wait. What about the kid?"

Grayson, who had moved forward a step, stopped. "The matter does not seem urgent. In a year or two, if your young stray proves annoying, we can kill him then. Or if he remembers your invitation and appears at Dimilioc's doorstep, we can consider whether he might prove an asset."

This was a lot better than Thaddeus had expected. And yet in another way, it didn't surprise him at all. He nodded, and rubbed a hand across his mouth, and then got slowly to his feet. "We're going to . . . go another round?"

"Yes."

"But . . . this isn't punishment."

Grayson tilted his head slightly. "The customary understanding of the matter is that the appropriate punishment for a job well done is another job. In one month, when the moon again approaches full, I believe I will send you to Columbus on an assignment very similar to this one. With Ethan."

Thaddeus stared at him, taken utterly by surprise. "A job *well* done? Me and *Ethan*?"

"As my nephew, Ethan understands in his blood and bones that he has the right to decide his own course when operating independently. He can teach you that. But he'll never match your strength. He needs to learn to accept that. Which he will find far easier without witnesses. So: you and he together can clear Columbus. You can work that entire circuit: Columbus to Indianapolis to Nashville, then back around through North Carolina and Virginia. I'll have Ezekiel meet you in D.C. and direct operations there; D.C.'s always a mess and hardly less so even without the vampires and their blood kin. I will expect a complete report following that tour. Including the full disclosure of any unexpected impulses you experience along the way to spare random black dogs."

Thaddeus didn't know what to say.

"Also, Ethan is a good choice to help you with your control. He won't lose his. His temper, possibly. But you will find it easier to train for better control with fewer witnesses, I imagine. Thus, an independent mission fills that requirement as well." Grayson looked Thaddeus up and down, thoughtfully. "You have far better control than an ordinary stray. But that's primarily to your wife's credit, not to yours. Your control is inadequate when your shadow is strong and you are upset. You must do better. So. We will draw your shadow up again now. This time, I expect you to put it down without my help. If you fail, I will indeed punish you. Do you understand?"

Thaddeus understood. That threat was meant to scare him and make him angry, so that he would have to work hard to control his Beast. But it felt too familiar to be very effective. It was a lot like the way his father had trained him. Training, Thaddeus could handle. He was determined that this time, he would succeed.

Thaddeus could handle his Beast. He could handle Ethan Lanning, too. He could handle anything the Dimilioc Master handed him and come back for more, and he was going to prove it. "Yeah," he said. "Yeah, I'm ready."

Ezekiel knelt amid overgrown forsythia and shadows, watching the girl on the bench. Her name was Melanie Manteufel. She was pretty, if not beautiful. She had a broad forehead and wide-set gray eyes, a slightly snub nose and a generous mouth. She was also the sort of girl who lit up with genuine pleasure when she met a friend or a stranger, which gave her a different and rarer kind of beauty.

Ezekiel did not remember a time when he had not desired her. But at the turning of the year, Melanie had announced—blushing and shy and delighted with herself—that she and Daniel Hammond would marry in the coming spring. This spring. In June, now just a few short months away.

Daniel Hammond.

Ezekiel had always known that Melanie was more important to him than he was to her. Everyone loved Melanie. For him it was different. Everyone but Melanie was afraid of him.

He had known he was too young for her. But a year, two years, that difference in ages became less important as people got older. He had been willing to wait. He had been willing to wait, and hope no one else won her in the meantime. He had intended to begun courting her this spring. He'd had it all planned out: flowers and little attentions and the surety that no one else could protect her as well as he could.

And then, Daniel.

It had never crossed Ezekiel's mind that Melanie might choose a man like Daniel Hammond—a cousin from the town, an ordinary human with neither strength of his own nor position within Dimilioc, and besides that seven years older than her. Ezekiel had known he had many rivals, but he had never guessed *Daniel* might be among them.

When she'd made the announcement, he'd known that if he said anything, he would say too much, and so he'd said nothing at all. But he thought of the coming wedding whenever he looked at Melanie, and could not entirely keep away from her.

Now they were both in Madison, alone together for the first time since her proud announcement, and Ezekiel was not entirely certain he knew how to handle this. Dimilioc law was clear: it was her choice. But did the law mean he wasn't allowed to court her a little anyway, maybe try to get her to change her mind?

This was Melanie's first visit to Madison. Ezekiel's, as well, but he was accustomed to travel and she was not. They had arrived only two days before, on the same plane, at four in the afternoon, with an east wind spitting icy drizzle from the overcast sky. Ezekiel had followed her off the plane, and he had continued to follow her since: sometimes closely and sometimes at a greater distance, but always taking care to stay unobtrusive. He was good at that, but then he was good at many things.

Yesterday the skies had been clearing, but the wind that had driven out the clouds had been bitter. Even so, Melanie had walked for some time along the city streets with evidently no consciousness of potential hazard, though most of the neighborhoods she visited were dangerous. Today was much more pleasant, so perhaps it was not surprising she should stroll around the city from dawn until dusk, until at last she alighted on that park bench where daffodils and pink tulips bloomed between the clump of forsythia. This was not in fact a very safe area, but the park was pretty, and a girl who was a recent arrival in the city might not know that.

Ezekiel knew it very well. To him, the very air smelled of anger and dry ash, burnt clay and desperation. The earth of the little park was permeated by the metallic tang of fear and blood, scents that were growing stronger as the sun began to dip down below the jagged horizon of the city. Ezekiel breathed slowly and deeply, appreciating the exciting aromas.

Before him, Melanie sighed, glancing at the lowering sun. For a moment she gazed at the moon, near full, which was already visible in the sky, though pale and nearly transparent in the lingering light. She tucked a foot up under her other thigh, and reached for her sketchpad.

The first black dog burst from a narrow alleyway on the other side of the street and hurled himself toward the woman, closely followed by a second. They were huge, not actually much like dogs: far too big even for mastiffs, black claws too long and too sharp for any dog—to experienced eyes, they didn't look like any natural animal at all. Their skulls was broad, their muzzles blunt and set with savage fangs as black as their claws; their eyes blazed with red fire. They separated as they rushed forward, coming at Melanie from two directions at once—more teamwork than one expected from stray black dogs. One lunged up and over a parked car, leaving gouges and slashes not just in the paintwork, but in the metal itself.

Melanie tucked herself down against the arm of the bench, her arms wrapped tight around her legs, her face pressed against her knees. She didn't make a sound.

Ezekiel was moving almost before the first black dog had lunged into the open. His shadow moved with him and around him, wanting to rise. He let it come, let the change take him, hot and furious; the new grasses charred and smoked where his feet fell. His claws tore the earth.

Both black dogs had stopped in the middle of the street, rearing up on their hind legs, snarling, trying to frighten Melanie and make her run. They knew she was Pure; any black dog would smell her Purity. They hated her and longed to kill her, but they also wanted the helpless flight of doomed prey to sweeten the blood. Melanie still did not move, but the black dogs were not experienced enough to wonder why. They were far too focused on their prey to sense Ezekiel.

He took the first with one blow, his claws tearing through shaggy pelt and muscle and ripping across the spine: the surest blow for an instant kill. The black dog screamed, black ichor and then red blood spraying as his body twisted into human form, one limb and then another, half his face and then the rest, grotesquely piecemeal. The great, smoky cloud of his shadow rose free, struggling to cling to the dying human body but unable to retain purchase, dispersing in the air. The human who had hosted it within his soul, of course, was simply dead.

The second black dog swung around, slashing. He was fast and strong, but Ezekiel simply ducked, folding himself down into his much smaller human form, letting the black dog's blow whip over his head, then letting his shadow rise again. The black dog had not expected to miss his strike and found himself seriously overextended.

Ezekiel would have liked to play with his prey for a little while—he, too, relished the chase and the hunt and the kill—but Melanie would not like to watch such sport. So he tore out the black dog's throat and three of his cervical vertebrae with one economical blow. Then he dismissed his own shadow and stood back as this black dog, dying, writhed and twisted into his human form.

"You let them get too close," Melanie said, not looking up. Her voice didn't shake, but her body trembled with reaction.

Ezekiel was amused. "How would you know? You didn't watch. You never watch."

"I felt them." The woman cautiously lifted her head, flinching from the bodies that lay contorted and human in the street. "Oh, God. Just kids. Poor boys."

Ezekiel lifted a contemptuous eyebrow. "Strays. Savages. They don't deserve your pity."

"They do. They never had training, never had the Calming, never even knew their shadows *could* be controlled. Born to the wrong mothers—"

"Whom they probably killed."

"Probably. Poor things." She might have meant the mothers or the dead black dogs. She likely meant both. She got to her feet, stiffly. She rubbed her eyes hard, then dropped her hands and looked up at the red-streaked sky. To Ezekiel, the red looked like blood. He had no idea what the sky looked like to Melanie.

She said again, "You let them get way too close to me."

Ezekiel wanted to go to her, touch her shoulder. More than her shoulder—killing put him in the mood. But she wouldn't welcome even a friend's touch from him now, and certainly not more. She'd made her choice, and it hadn't been him. He stood still. But he said, "I let them get exactly close enough. I would never have let them touch you. But I'm sorry if you were frightened."

"I wasn't frightened," Melanie said, though she must know Ezekiel could tell she lied. She didn't look at him. "I want to go home."

"Soon. One more."

"We should forget the last stray," she protested, though she followed obediently when he turned and walked away. "That one's been quiet enough. Who cares about him, as long as he doesn't kill a lot of people, make headlines, stir things up? We could just go straight to the airport, be home by morning . . ." her tone was wistful.

Ezekiel said, not quite politely, "And will *you* explain to Thos why we left a stray roaming free in this city, or would you leave that to me?" He tried to smother his annoyance. She was Pure. Her hesitancy wasn't her fault. But she knew they couldn't leave Madison with the job unfinished. He wanted to snap at her. He wanted to grab her, shake her, shout at her. He moved a step farther away from her instead.

"I know," Melanie said, not quite coherently. "I *know*, all right?"

"Only one more. We'll do him tonight, go to the airport right after. We can still be home tomorrow." He couldn't quite stop himself from adding, "Daniel will be glad to see you, I'm sure."

Melanie didn't exactly flinch, but she darted a glance at his face and away.

Ezekiel wasn't quite sure how to read that glance. He looked away. In the near distance, sirens wailed. He put out a hand, not quite touching Melanie's arm, gesturing her toward a parked car.

"That belongs to someone," she said, not very firmly.

Ezekiel lifted an eyebrow. "Not even you care. Whoever owns it, we need it more. You're too tired to walk any farther tonight." Ezekiel cut through the lock with a delicately elongated claw of sharp-edged shadow, reached across to unlock the passenger-side door, and went around to lift the hood and hotwire the ignition. The sirens approached, but several streets over: not an immediate concern. He got in behind the wheel and glanced sidelong at Melanie. "You have our direction?"

"Yes, yes . . . I will. Just a minute . . ." she had taken a small hand mirror out of her back pocket, the glass shimmering with silvery light. A *trouvez*. She'd done the finding magic the same night they'd arrived in Madison; it was still halfway in place. She passed her hand across the mirror and peered into it. "Left up there at the light."

"Left?" Ezekiel was surprised: left would take them toward one of the decent parts of Madison, not the dismal mostly-deserted streets in which he'd have expected to find a stray black dog. But Melanie gave him an impatient shrug, so he said nothing more, but turned left and left the sirens behind.

Madison's remaining stray proved to be very little like the brutes who had attacked Melanie. He was a little older: thirty at least. That was surprising. They died young, these wild black dogs who had never learned control and had no idea of Dimilioc law. Until they broke it too egregiously, of course, and found the Dimilioc executioner suddenly behind them.

This black dog was not only older than the other strays, he actually looked more or less civilized. He was a tall man with a bony, angular face. He wore good jeans and a plain white tee-shirt. He could have passed both for nearly human and nearly respectable in almost any company. And he was in human form, despite the nearly full moon, which explained why he'd never come to Dimilioc's attention: he plainly had a good deal more control than most strays.

The black dog plainly knew what Melanie was as soon as he opened his front door and caught her scent, but though she backed away fast to draw him out, he didn't let his shadow up and he didn't attack her. Instead, he looked past her immediately, nostrils flaring, obviously looking for Ezekiel. He found him, too, amid the ordinary shadows of the night, though Ezekiel had expected to strike unseen as the black dog came out into the night after Melanie.

Since he'd been spotted, however, Ezekiel met the black dog's eyes and smiled.

The black dog's hand closed so hard on the edge of his door that the wood cracked. He'd had a black dog father to teach him, Ezekiel surmised—unusual, but sometimes a stray black dog actually raised a son rather than abandoning him. Whatever the story might have been, this man plainly knew who Ezekiel was: the Dimilioc executioner, who showed no mercy to Dimilioc's enemies. Ezekiel Korte, who for three years now had been Thos Korte's killer.

This black dog had sense enough not to fight and control enough not to run. He backed up instead, wordlessly yielding his place in the doorway as Ezekiel walked forward. He backed farther, down the hallway and into a dimly lit living room with a carpet that was old but clean, a single leather recliner, a small table holding a sweating bottle of beer, and, to one side, an ancient black-and-white television, the picture flickering. The sound was on, but turned very low. A paperback book lay open, face down on the arm of the chair. Ezekiel couldn't read the title.

Ezekiel looked around, still smiling. He said, "How nice."

The man flinched, but Melanie said, "Ezekiel!"

"Don't you think it's nice? So very . . . ordinary."

The man ducked his head, avoiding Ezekiel's gaze. He said, in a deep, harsh voice, his diction surprisingly precise, "I don't make noise—I don't hunt in the city—those God-damned black pups, I knew they'd draw Dimilioc attention—"

"Then you should have run, shouldn't you?" Ezekiel

took a step forward, hoping the man would let his shadow up, that he would at least try to fight.

Instead, the black dog took another step back. He opened his mouth, but closed it again without speaking. He was beginning to lose language, clearly. Many black dogs did, when the change took them. This one was still trying to cling to his human shape, but his face was beginning to distort, lips peeling back from lengthening black fangs; his shoulders shifting and broadening. But he neither lunged forward nor flung himself wildly away. Still mostly a man, then, and still fighting hard for control of his shadow. As though his paltry control would help him—

Melanie suddenly moved, catching Ezekiel's arm, dragging at him. No one else in the world would have dared get between Dimilioc's executioner and his prey, or would have dared lay a hand on him without invitation. Ezekiel tilted his head, his eyebrows rising, making no move to shake her hand off his arm.

"I can do the *Beschwichtigung,"* Melanie said quickly. "Ezekiel, look how good his control is already, you don't have to kill him, I can do the Calming for him, *that* would finish the job here, wouldn't it? Thos wouldn't have to know the details, would he? What difference would it make? Except to me, you know it would make a difference to *me*—"

Ezekiel glanced from the girl to the black dog and back again, still smiling. "Is there something in this for me? Would Daniel approve, do you think?"

Melanie let him go, punched him hard on the arm—the only person in the world who would dare. "*God*, Ezekiel—"

"Ah. You're presuming on my better nature. You think I have one?"

Melanie didn't hit him again, but she looked like she wanted to. "Don't be an ass!"

Ezekiel laughed. He said impatiently to the black dog, "Get your shadow down, cur. Show me some control. Change now and I *will* kill you, understand?" He waited while the man fought his shadow down and back, while his face and hands and body slowly recovered their purely human shape.

Ezekiel waited with something approaching patience until he could see the man had his shadow in hand. Then he asked, "You're willing to take the *Beschwichtigung?* You know what that is?"

"The Calming," whispered the other man, his voice thick and his words clumsy. "My father, he told me . . ."

"But he couldn't find a Pure woman to work the spell for you?" Melanie said sympathetically. "Well, I can do it now."

"Let me just add," Ezekiel put in, staring hard at the black dog, "if you say yes, you don't get to change your mind halfway through. You hurt her, I won't just kill you, I'll make you into an example for the ages. Do you understand?"

The black dog understood. He held very still while Melanie opened the window to let in the night air and the moonlight, and drew her pentagram in silver light on the kitchen floor around him. He shuddered with the effort of forcing his shadow to submit, but he did not move out of the pentagram. Ezekiel helped by leaning against the doorjamb, looking as threatening as possible; and Melanie, occupied with braiding moonlight into a silver cord to bind the darkness in the black dog's soul, never noticed the potential danger at all.

And when she was finished with the Calming, once she'd reopened the pentagram, Ezekiel said harshly, "Well, cur?"

The black dog bowed his head, glancing covertly at Ezekiel through his lashes, avoiding the direct look that might be taken as a challenge. But his voice was clearer and more human now, and he looked at Melanie with dawning astonishment—the first time in his life, Ezekiel presumed, that he'd ever seen a Pure woman without wanting to kill her. This was not a change he remembered in himself: Dimilioc black wolves had the *Beschwichtigung* done when they were infants and never experienced that visceral hatred of the Pure.

Melanie met the man's eyes and smiled. She smiled at Ezekiel, too. For that alone, he supposed the trouble and time spent here, even the risk of trouble with Thos, had been worthwhile.

"Don't draw Dimilioc attention," Ezekiel warned the black dog. "Keep clear of stray black dogs who might draw our attention. I don't have to tell you that if I find you again, I'll kill you."

"Yes," whispered the man. "No. I understand."

"Get out of Madison. Go south, or west. Or both. There's room here and there for a quiet black dog. So stay quiet. Understand?"

The black dog met his eyes for an instant before looking down again. "Believe me," he said, his deep voice husky, "putting a great deal more space between me and Dimilioc is my new ambition."

"Good," said Ezekiel, and beckoned to Melanie. "Home by noon tomorrow," he reminded her. "Unless we get stopped for speeding on the way to the airport."

"You could let me drive," Melanie said, though with resignation because she knew he wouldn't. She smiled at the black dog once more, nodded, and headed for the door. "*Much* better than just slaughtering everyone," she said to Ezekiel, over her shoulder.

"Not for me," Ezekiel said, but the black dog didn't attack him when he turned his back, so he regretfully gave up any chance of a fight and followed Melanie out of the house.

Dimilioc was set amid the Vermont mountains, in the part of the state sometimes called the Northeast Kingdom, though the humans who called it by that name had no idea how apt a name it was. At this time of year, the maples were still dormant, the firs and spruce black-green against the barren hardwoods.

The Dimilioc house stood alone on a rise amid the forest, the trees cleared back around it to open up all the approaches. It was a huge structure with two wings and three stories, large enough to house nearly a hundred humans if they were friendly, or perhaps half so many black wolves, who seldom were.

Ezekiel swung the big SUV around the long curve of the

drive and parked in front of the generous porch. The plane flight had been fine, but the drive from Newport had been unpleasant: sleet and freezing rain all the way, every road worse than the one before, until he'd been genuinely tempted to abandon the SUV and run the rest of the way to Dimilioc in his other form. But Melanie couldn't run across country and he could hardly leave her in a Newport hotel. So he had cursed the weather and had driven ever more slowly and carefully because if he wrecked the SUV, he would have to kill the first fool who laughed. Which was fine, but Melanie wouldn't like it.

Stupid to care, when she cared only for Daniel. But he drove carefully anyway, and was absurdly relieved when he could finally take his foot off the gas and coast gently to a halt directly before the wide porch.

"Mind the steps," he warned her.

She rolled her eyes, cheerfully scornful. "Do you want to hold my hand while I brave the treacherous ascent?" Then, as his crooked smile told her how that had sounded, she added hastily, "Too bad!" She leaped out of the car and fled up the steps without assistance, laughing. Happy. Happy to be home, happy because, of course, Daniel was waiting for her.

Ezekiel left the SUV for someone else to put away in the garage and followed more slowly.

But Daniel wasn't waiting for Melanie in the atrium, though Ezekiel had called ahead from Newport. Nor was he waiting in the hallway beyond, nor in the kitchen. Melanie, enthusiasm undimmed, turned toward the stairs that led up to the private apartments on the second floor, but one of the Lanning cousins caught them before she could run up the stairs. The cousin was human, a boy barely out of his teens. He flinched away from Ezekiel, but that was nothing unusual. But then his eyes slid away from Melanie's as well, and that was strange. Ezekiel frowned. Melanie said, questioningly, "Matt?"

"Thos wants you," the cousin muttered. "As soon as you came in, he said."

Ezekiel sighed.

"Poor Ezekiel!" Melanie said, laughing, but she meant it, too. "I'll put some hot chocolate on for you, shall I, as soon as I find Daniel—"

"I meant, you," Matt said. "Both of you." He ducked his head at Ezekiel's sudden sharp glance. "Don't know anything about it," he protested, and backed clumsily through the door, tripping over nothing in his hurry to escape.

"What do you suppose?" Melanie said. She had gone pale. She looked at Ezekiel. "Thos found out we didn't kill that last stray? But—"

"He hasn't had time to find out. But if he has, it was my decision, not yours."

Melanie took a quick breath and nodded. It was like her to say *we*, to claim part ownership in that defiance of Thos Korte's order. It was a measure of her fear of the Dimilioc Master that she was willing to let Ezekiel take the blame for it now.

"Thos won't punish *you* for anything," Ezekiel said flatly. He meant that *he* was Dimilioc's executioner and he wouldn't carry out any such order. He meant more than that: he wouldn't permit anyone else to punish her either. Not even Thos Korte himself. He touched her hand: not a black dog gesture, but the kind of gesture a human might use to reassure a friend—a gesture he'd learned from Melanie, in fact.

And she *was* reassured. She understood what he had not quite said, or else the gesture was the right one. Her heartbeat, which had picked up, slowed nearly to normal. She laid a hand on his arm, drawing reassurance from that touch—the only woman in the world who would. "All right," she said. "All right. Into the black wolf's den, I guess . . ."

But Thos hadn't heard or didn't care about the details of the Madison run. He listened without changing expression as Ezekiel reported, briefly, that the black dog problem in that city had been dealt with.

"Good," he said, without much apparent interest. "Four cities cleaned up this month. We shall assume the stray population properly cowed for the present. Write a report for Zachariah." Zachariah was Ezekiel's uncle, Thos Korte's brother, and the man responsible for tracking blood kin and black dog strays.

"Now," said Thos. "Sit down. We shall discuss an unrelated matter of possibly greater immediate importance." He paused.

"Master?" Ezekiel asked politely, in case Thos was waiting for that acknowledgment. The disinterested tone was not reassuring. Thos sounded like that when he expected trouble. It was impossible to guess, now, what kind of trouble the Master expected, or why.

The Master of Dimilioc was a tall, thin, colorless man who sounded exactly the same whether he was barely paying attention or about to tear out someone's throat. He did that, sometimes, to a black wolf who defied him. Sometimes he did it himself and sometimes he ordered his executioner to do it. Thos liked to have the world fear his executioner. The Master was a great believer in Machiavelli's dictum about love and fear. Ordinarily Ezekiel approved. But Ezekiel knew Melanie was afraid, too, now. That, he did not like at all.

"Where's Daniel?" Melanie asked abruptly. She was perched on the edge of her chair.

Ezekiel glanced at her, surprised. It had not occurred to him to wonder.

Thos did not seem surprised at all. Nor did he seem disturbed by Melanie's sharpness, though he would never have permitted any Dimilioc wolf to speak to him in that tone. He said briefly, "Downstairs. Be quiet. Sit down and listen."

Melanie, who had jumped to her feet and opened her mouth, sank back again. She darted a look at Ezekiel: appeal and something else. Fear. Not for herself. For Daniel. Because if her fiancé had somehow offended Thos Korte, then whatever he had done and whatever punishment Thos had decreed, it was very likely Ezekiel who would punish him.

"I don't care for disturbance in the house," Thos said,

which was even true. He didn't like disturbance and he didn't allow it. He simply demanded total, unquestioning compliance from everyone, black wolf or human or Pure. He said to Melanie, "Daniel is not being punished. He is simply a guarantor of your cooperation. A match with a human man is, of course, an absolute waste of a Pure woman."

He had said this before, when Melanie had announced that she would marry Daniel. But Ezekiel had believed the Master of Dimilioc had accepted her choice, as Dimilioc law required. Now he didn't know what to believe.

"Your children by Ezekiel would be far more valuable," Thos said, his tone flat. "You may marry Daniel: I don't care. But first you will bear a black dog son and a Pure daughter to Ezekiel. So that there will be no confusion as to the parentage of your children, I will release Daniel only when we are certain you are carrying. If you want him free, I suggest a certain alacrity about your duty."

Melanie stared at the Master, white and still, utterly wordless.

Thos said to Ezekiel, "You have her until she's bearing. Then Daniel can have her until she delivers the child, do you understand? I will not have any trouble over that, is that clear? You may take her again once she bears the first child, until she gives you at least one black dog son and at least one Pure daughter. Is that clear?"

It was very clear. Ezekiel looked at Melanie.

She stared back. Then she jumped to her feet. "No!"

"Be quiet," Thos ordered her, without emphasis. He gestured to Ezekiel, a small movement of one finger, disinterested command. "Take her away before she has hysterics. Get her pregnant. Tonight, preferably. Don't forget that report, however. Go."

Ezekiel closed a hand around Melanie's wrist, hard enough to stop the flooding outrage in her eyes before she could give it voice. The outrage turned to fear when he touched her. He did not let go.

She did not have hysterics. She didn't shout or scream

or fight him. He was grateful for that. Fear was so seductive; a struggle far more so. Melanie's furious calm made it much easier to let her go once they were clear of the Master's office.

"Go see Daniel," Ezekiel told her.

Melanie took several steps backward, bumped into the wall, stopped, and glared at him. "I won't do it! He has no right!"

"He's the Master of Dimilioc—"

"I'll leave—I'll *never* come back, I'll tell Carolyn and Hannah and Beth, see how he likes losing *all* of Dimilioc's Pure women—"

"And Daniel?"

She stopped dead. *A guarantor of your cooperation*, Thos Korte had said. They both knew exactly what that meant. Melanie opened her mouth, and closed it again.

Ezekiel knew exactly what she had meant to say, and exactly why she had stopped. She had started to demand—ask—beg, that he let Daniel out of the cage downstairs. She had stopped because he was the Master's executioner. If she defied Thos, it was *Ezekiel* whom Thos would order to punish Daniel. And she thought he would do it, because she knew, she had to know, that Ezekiel wanted her. She thought Ezekiel would be glad to punish Daniel just for that, if once Thos gave him the excuse. She might even be right: Ezekiel wasn't entirely certain himself. She stared at him in helpless silence.

"Go see Daniel," Ezekiel repeated. "I'll write that report. I'll expect you, later. I'll order a late supper for two. For eight o'clock. And you'll join me for it. Won't you?"

"Yes," she whispered. She had lowered her eyes, which might be merely caution, but from her probably meant that she was trying to hide her fury and fear. She couldn't, of course. Both were as evident to a black dog as though she had shouted aloud.

"This is not worth risking the Master's anger," he told her sharply. "You know I won't hurt you." But he wasn't even sure himself whether he meant that as reassurance or as a plea for her understanding.

She backed away, one step and another; then turned and fled.

Ezekiel wrote the Madison report quickly and casually. He was mostly thinking about Melanie, and about Thos Korte, and a little about Daniel. He had little patience for reports. But he wrote it because Thos had ordered him to write it.

Six double-spaced pages of dry facts: arrived on such-and-such a date, used recent newspaper headlines to locate the hunting territories of the uncontrolled black dogs, narrowed the searches with Melanie's *trouvez*. Confirmed there would be no need to trespass on blood kin territory to take out the black dogs—not a surprise, that last, because if a black dog was stupid enough to make a nuisance of himself in blood kin territory, there wasn't likely to be any need to send the Dimilioc executioner after him. Dates and numbers of black dogs killed, names where Ezekiel had been able to make a reasonable guess. *Trouvez* confirmation that the city had been cleared out.

Then he glanced over the report once more to make sure it looked quick and casual throughout, and also to make sure he hadn't been so distracted as to include any hint that he'd hidden an extra black dog stray between the lines.

Then Ezekiel printed and stapled the report, found a folder to give it official heft, and went to find Zachariah. He could have emailed it, of course. Ordinarily he would have emailed it. He wasn't even sure why he had printed a hard copy, except that he discovered he longed for an excuse to leave his apartment. He wanted to move, to run, to fight; at least he could walk from one wing of the house to the other, climb two flights of stairs, and hand-deliver the damned report.

And then, possibly he wanted to leave his rooms because he looked forward to Melanie being there when he got back.

Zachariah Korte possessed a generous apartment on the

third floor of the house. Ezekiel took the stairs two at a time and strode down the wide hallway that led to that apartment, paying very little attention to his surroundings. He was still thinking about Melanie. He was angry—any black dog was often angry, but he did not know why he was angry this time, or at whom. He had wanted her, and he would have her. No one could argue that Thos was wrong about the waste of a Pure woman bearing her children to a mere human man . . .

". . . problem is Ezekiel," said Zachariah's voice, clearly audible to black dog ears even through a closed door.

Hearing his own name caught Ezekiel's attention, and that *problem is Ezekiel* was certainly fraught. He stopped dead in the hallway, listening.

"I can't take him," Zachariah said to someone unseen. His voice was light, cool, sardonic, unmoved. He might have been chatting about the weather, about the menu for supper, about whether the servants dusted thoroughly enough. But what he said was, "None of us can take Ezekiel. Not one on one; not two on one; possibly not even all of us together. But if it came to a serious fight, I think he might hesitate to kill me. I might be able to slow him down."

"Well, that's fine then, as long as you can *slow him down*," growled a rougher, deeper voice. Harrison Lanning, sounding thoroughly exasperated.

In the privacy of the hallway, Ezekiel lifted an ironic eyebrow. But then a woman's voice exclaimed, "I don't want anybody killing anybody!" and Ezekiel, startled to realize Melanie was also there, eased forward a soundless step before he even realized he had moved.

A third man spoke: a deep, gritty voice, but not quite so heavy as Harrison's. "A killing battle is coming, whether or not any of us wants it. The question is, who will do the dying? If it comes now, most likely that will be us."

Grayson Lanning, of course. Grayson and Harrison Lanning and Zachariah Korte: a triumvirate of powerful black wolves; the only Dimilioc wolves who might possibly challenge Thos Korte. Ezekiel didn't know whether he felt like laughing or swearing. Of course Melanie had gone to

Grayson Lanning. Who else would anybody in Dimilioc go to, when they found themselves in trouble with Thos?

That had started years ago, when Ezekiel had been just a kid and Grayson not much over twenty. Grayson had interceded for a stupid black pup who'd lost his head and accidentally killed a townsman. He'd gotten Thos to let him teach the youngster proper control rather than simply killing him. Then Grayson had taken over the broader duty of teaching the pups rather than leaving the job, as tradition dictated, to their fathers. No one had objected, especially after it became obvious that the youngsters he trained almost always did develop excellent control.

Ezekiel, fatherless, only ten years old at the time, had been one of the youngsters who had benefited most from Grayson's teaching—one of the few to surpass his teacher's control. Soon he had surpassed anyone's level of control. Very soon after that he had realized what a tremendous advantage this gave him. Then Thos Korte had realized it. Ezekiel had become Dimilioc's executioner while still in his teens, unprecedented for such a young black wolf, but no one had objected. No one had dared object.

Grayson Lanning held no such formal position, but eventually Ezekiel had realized that a new take-your-problems-to-Grayson tradition had appeared within Dimilioc at about the same time. It made sense. Grayson had trained so many of the younger black wolves. They knew he would be fair, and calm, and would never lose his temper unless you deserved it. Besides, no one in his right mind would take a problem to Thos. So Ezekiel dealt mostly with problems only after they became too serious for the Dimilioc Master to ignore, and Grayson Lanning mostly kept problems from becoming that serious, and Thos Korte either didn't notice Grayson's increasing influence or else was too confident of his own strength to care.

Then Grayson killed a female black dog.

She was from Germany, one of three Gehorsam cousins who had come to Dimilioc to discuss some kind of high level business with Thos Korte. But Ursula Gehorsam had, it seemed, an unfortunate inclination to indulge her shadow's natural sadism, and she liked to use the human servants for that indulgence. Of course that was forbidden, but Thos did not want to offend Gehorsam. He refused to notice the problem. Grayson had not ignored it. Ursula Gehorsam had paid no attention to Grayson's first warning, or his second. She had not grown up in Dimilioc and did not know Grayson, but Ezekiel thought even so she should have known better.

Thos had punished Grayson, of course, for usurping the Master's prerogatives when he'd killed the woman, and for creating a problem between Gehorsam and Dimilioc.

More precisely, Thos had ordered Ezekiel to punish Grayson.

And Ezekiel had done it, of course. But he had not realized how strong an impression that incident had left in Grayson's mind until this moment, when he heard the other man say to Melanie, "I don't think you understand how seriously overmatched we are."

"But you—" Melanie began.

"No," said Grayson, his deep voice flat. "Ezekiel has fought several times as many killing battles as the three of us put together, and Thos can force even my shadow down. I can't do the same to him: he's too strong for me. Together, they are far too strong for us."

Harrison added, "If we act together, we might take either Thos or Ezekiel. Not both. But if we tackle one alone, we'd lose surprise with the other. Then there'd be another fight—one we'd probably just lose. Ezekiel isn't the Master's only partisan, unfortunately."

"But—" said Melanie, and then, more strongly, "It's not just what Thos is doing to me. You get that, right? It's not about *me*. Thos is a terrible Master! You know that! He's cruel and hateful and he's made Dimilioc cruel and hateful. You know it, I know it, but everybody's too scared of him to *do* anything—"

Ezekiel blinked, almost physically staggered. It had never occurred to him to wonder whether Thos was a good Master or a bad one; it had never occurred to him to consider what Dimilioc might be like under a different Master. Clearly others had considered these questions. He had had no idea.

"Well, fine, but if nobody does anything, nothing will get done!" said Melanie, not quite shouting. She lowered her voice, gaining in intensity what she lost in volume. "Grayson, people would follow you, you *know* they would—you'd be a much better Master than Thos—"

"Someday," said Grayson. "Not now."

"And not with my vicious nephew on Thos Korte's shortest chain," put in Zachariah.

"He's not vicious!" protested Melanie, just as Grayson himself said in a deceptively mild rumble, "He's not as sadistic as he pretends."

There was a startled silence. In the hallway, Ezekiel, at least as surprised as anyone else, raised an eyebrow a second time. He might have expected Melanie's defense, but Grayson's astonished him. Ezekiel had, in fact, apologized to him for the punishment over Ursula Gerhorsam. He had meant that apology. He had known he should have stopped the woman himself. He had made certain, afterward, that no similar situation ever occurred again. But he had not expected Grayson to remember that, or to care.

"Good to know," Zachariah said, his tone sardonic, plainly unconvinced. "Does it make a practical difference?"

"Not today," said Grayson, and, to Melanie, "I'm sorry. I'll do what I can. I'll talk to Daniel. Then I'll see what I can do with Thos. It will be easier if you don't openly defy him. Understand?"

"Yes," whispered Melanie. "Yes, all right." She sounded sick. She sounded like she had given up. She sounded afraid, and black dogs loved fear, but Ezekiel had never wanted *her* to fear him.

Ezekiel did not wait for her to come out of Zachariah's apartment and find him listening. He retreated soundlessly.

The servants had brought up the cold supper he'd ordered. The candles, too, and the pretty tablecloth. Everything was arranged beautifully on a small side table in his living room.

Ezekiel stood in the middle of the room, studying the effect. He had planned it out so carefully. He had meant to try to seduce Melanie away from Daniel—whatever she thought she wanted, he had hardly believed she could really prefer a human man to him.

Now the whole scene revolted him, though he hardly understood why.

Everything was the same. Grayson wouldn't challenge Thos, no one would challenge Ezekiel, even Melanie would obey the Dimilioc Master.

And yet everything had changed. Ezekiel stood perfectly still, waiting for the silent waves of fury and grief and shock to crest and ebb. He was used to fury; but he did not understand the grief or the shock, and he was distantly aware there was no time now to sort out what he felt or why.

Melanie flung open his door without knocking, stalked in, saw the supper table, and glared at Ezekiel. "I suppose you think—"

Ezekiel took the few necessary steps, caught her arm, and pulled her hard against his chest. He set his other hand behind her neck, stopping her attempt to wrench herself away. Her heart leaped and raced. Ezekiel met her eyes from a distance of mere inches. She seemed so small. Vulnerable.

Ezekiel smiled, his lazy executioner's smile, the way he smiled when he wanted to terrify someone. Then he kissed her, brutally hard, and the intoxicating scent of fear suddenly filled the room, far more vivid than the scents of food and hot candlewax.

Her eyes were wide with disbelief as well as fear. The fear was what he needed; the disbelief was dangerous. When she tried to speak, he put a hand hard over her mouth, refusing to allow it. Leaning forward, he whispered to her what he wanted to do to her. He told her explicitly what he intended to do to her, how much he hoped she would not get pregnant right away, how much he planned to enjoy the weeks before a pregnancy could be confirmed. She believed him. She fought, twisting to get away . . . utterly hopeless;

she could not possibly match his strength. She knew it, but she fought anyway. She was panting, short hard breaths like an animal run to exhaustion. Like prey. Utterly seductive.

"I want you forever," he told her. He held her still, met her eyes, and smiled with black-dog savagery and with the special savagery that was all his own. "I won't give you up to Daniel," he whispered. "And you'll smile for me no matter what I do, or I'll make Daniel an example for the ages. Thos won't object. Shall we make sure?" He caught her wrist again and hauled her toward the door.

She was weeping by the time they had reached Thos Korte's private apartment. She was trying not to, but she was terrified and couldn't hide it. Ezekiel had left bruises on her arms, on her throat. He had let his shadow claws tear bloody tracks in her wrist; he had hit her once when she had persisted in trying to fight him, a slap that had bloodied her lip as well. She was no longer trying to fight him. The scents of blood and terror were intense, provocative.

Thos opened his door. He surveyed the scene. One pale eyebrow rose, and he stepped back, inviting Ezekiel to enter with a brief tip of his head.

"She went to Grayson," Ezekiel told him, with savage scorn. "Grayson and his brother and Zachariah. I overheard part of their little chat. Why don't you send for them, ask them about the rest of it?" He shoved Melanie hard, so that she stumbled across the room, catching at a heavy chair to stop herself falling to the floor.

The other eyebrow rose. Thos picked up a house phone and murmured into it.

"I want her without strings," Ezekiel told the Master. "I don't care about Daniel, he could even be useful, but I'm not having him touch her. That's the order I want you to give."

Thos was beginning to look amused. "We can discuss it."

"I've earned her," Ezekiel began, but stopped, swinging around aggressively, as Grayson appeared in the doorway. Harrison and Zachariah were at his back.

Grayson's eyes flicked from Melanie, still clinging to

the chair, to Ezekiel, to Thos. The expression in his eyes went bleak and hard. A lesser black wolf might have broken and run, however hopeless that flight. Grayson had far too much control for that. When Thos beckoned to him, he came, grimly. Harrison and Zachariah glanced at each other. Harrison's expression was as grim as his brother's. Zachariah showed nothing at all. Both of them followed Grayson, one on his left and the other on his right, making no attempt to disguise their allegiance. Not that any such attempt could have succeeded.

"And I'll earn her again tonight," Ezekiel said to Thos. He added to Zachariah, smiling his savage, deadly smile, "Well, uncle, do you think you might slow me down? Do you think I might hesitate to kill you?"

Zachariah's mouth tightened. He said nothing.

"Grayson's the cornerstone," Ezekiel said to Thos. "Kill him, and the other two will fall into line."

"Yes," the Master said, in that faintly impatient tone that was sometimes the only warning he gave of rising temper.

"Well, then?" Ezekiel shifted forward half a step, his attention on Grayson, watching with predatory alertness for any sign that the other man might try to fight, might try to run. Grayson might even attack Thos. If he did, things might get very complicated and very dangerous.

Grayson shifted his weight, measuring both Ezekiel and Thos—his face and hands began to distort with the change as his shadow rose—everyone balanced for that instant on the knife-edge of violence—

Then Thos Korte lifted a hand. His shadow rose, heavy, so dense it seemed to have actual physical heft. It rolled forward with irresistible power, pressing Grayson's shadow down and back. Grayson tried to fight that smothering weight, but he had told Melanie he did not have the Master's strength and he had been right. He lowered his eyes suddenly, like a fencer casting down his weapon, and went heavily to his knees.

"Well?" said Thos.

"Ezekiel's right," Grayson said, his tone flat. "Without

me, neither Harrison nor Zachariah will threaten you."

"With or without you, neither of them can threaten me. But it's clear enough one treacherous conspiracy after another is going to form around you, if you live." There was still nothing stronger in the Master's tone than that trace of impatience. He glanced at Ezekiel. "Do it," he ordered. "Don't draw it out."

Ezekiel smiled. He let his black-dog shadow burn through his body like fire. His bones twisted and thickened. Black claws extended from his fingertips. He stepped toward Grayson. Harrison turned his head away; Melanie sank to her knees, pressing her hands to her mouth. No one else moved. Grayson met Ezekiel's eyes. He did not move or speak.

Ezekiel stared back at Grayson. He didn't glance aside. But, as he passed close to Thos, he drove his claws straight across the Master's back, tearing through his spine in one swift blow. Ezekiel did not wait to see what violent defense Thos might wring out of the last second of his life, but instantly following the first blow with another slashing cut across the Master's belly and side, and then, almost before his body twisted around and began to fall, a third across his neck, a brutal blow that again tore across the spine.

Thos did not even have time to look surprised. His dense shadow roiled and twisted, abruptly freed, and his body hit the floor almost before the blood sprayed across the room.

Ezekiel took two precise steps back, away from Grayson, shifting from human to black dog and back again as he moved, letting his shadow carry away both the drenching blood and the hot rage between one step and the next—a blatant display of control no other Dimilioc wolf could match. He turned his shoulder to the three older Dimilioc wolves, holding a hand down toward Melanie instead. He was not smiling now. He was not trying to frighten anyone: he had let that go. He let everything go. He looked into Melanie's face. She stared back, appearing stunned.

He said quietly, ignoring the other black wolves, "I'm sorry. I needed your fear and anger and blood. As a distraction, do you understand? I couldn't let Thos realize *I* was afraid. But I am sorry."

Melanie continued to stare at him, her eyes wide. Her gaze slid toward Thos' body and jerked away as though the sight burned her.

"You saved yourself," Ezekiel told her. "You said Thos was a terrible Master. I heard you. I asked myself, was that true? I had never . . . do you understand, I had never wondered that before?"

Melanie said nothing. She shook her head a little, not in denial, Ezekiel thought, but in disbelief of . . . just everything.

"You said people would follow Grayson. I could see that was true. I asked myself, would Dimilioc be different if Grayson were Master? And I could see it would be different. Better."

Still no response.

Ezekiel backed away a step to give her a little more room. He said, even more quietly, "I saw there was this chance, tonight, if I chose to take it. So I did. But it was cruel for you. I am truly sorry."

After another moment, Melanie uncurled slowly from her tucked-down self-protective posture. Reaching out, she let Ezekiel take her hand and lift her to her feet. He put a hand under her elbow to steady her. She seemed to need the support. "You're all right," he told her, hoping it was true.

"I . . ."

"Go let Daniel out. He'll be glad to see you. Tell him—" he stopped. Then he said, and heard the weariness in his own voice, "Tell him no one will step between you and him now."

The mention of Daniel gave her new strength and assurance, and a new direction, as he had intended. She nodded firmly, pressed his arm once in wordless gratitude—he thought it was gratitude, though she might have just needed to catch her balance. Then she was gone.

Ezekiel turned to face Grayson. Zachariah and Harrison had spread out, one to either side, aware, as Melanie had not been, that the evening was not over. They were ready to attack or defend. So was Grayson. He had gotten to his feet at some point after Thos' death and now stood regarding

Ezekiel, his expression unreadable.

"Do you think you can take me?" Ezekiel asked him. "Even all of you together? Shall we find out?" He shifted his weight forward in subtle threat. Harrison immediately eased around to get behind him on the left, Zachariah moving to the right. Ezekiel's shadow wanted to answer that implicit threat. It wanted the change and then the fight, blood and fire and death. It did not care who died as long as it wasn't him.

Grayson's eyes narrowed. His shadow rose, dark and powerful. As Thos had done, he let his shadow roll forward to flatten and smother Ezekiel's shadow. Except, as they had both known, Grayson was not as strong as Thos Korte had been.

Ezekiel took a step forward. Another. His black-dog shadow rose around him. Not as smoothly or as fast as usual. But it rose. Grayson might hobble it, but he could not force it down. Ezekiel said softly, "It's like walking through molasses. But I think I could still take you, even now, one on one. Possibly even all of you together."

Grayson tilted his head. "What does that mean to you?"

Ezekiel met his eyes. "It means I'm too dangerous. You can't trust me at your back."

Heavy brows rose. "*Thos* certainly couldn't trust you at his back, and he was much stronger than I. But I am not Thos."

Ezekiel nodded slightly, acknowledging this. He said slowly, "I don't want to fight you. I don't want to kill you."

"Then don't."

Grayson made it sound simple. There was nothing simple about it. Ezekiel glanced over his shoulder at his uncle. Zachariah met his gaze, wordless. Waiting. For a signal from Grayson, for a sign from Ezekiel himself? Ezekiel couldn't tell. He said, though he didn't know why it seemed important that he say it, "You were right, you know. I don't want to kill you either, uncle. If it came to a fight, you could slow me down."

"That's good to know," said Zachariah, without detectable irony.

Ezekiel turned back to Grayson, took a step forward. Another. His black-dog shadow pressed him hard, wanting to rise, wanting to force the change. It drove him more fiercely than usual because the moment was so stiff with tension and the threat of violence. But Ezekiel held his shadow flat almost without effort, although Grayson was no longer trying to use his own power to smother it. He had learned to do that from Grayson, of course.

He dropped to his knees.

Showing no surprise, Grayson came forward the remaining small distance and set a hand on Ezekiel's shoulder, closing his other hand around Ezekiel's throat. His hands were nearly human, but blunter and broader than human hands, every finger tipped with a curved black claw.

Ezekiel did not move to evade Grayson's grip. His heartbeat had picked up: he couldn't help that, though he knew they could all hear it. Yet, though he was afraid of what Grayson would do, he found himself oddly unafraid of Grayson himself. He realized now—he had not understood it before—that he had *always* been afraid of Thos Korte.

He said, "Melanie was right. You'll be a good Master for Dimilioc." Then he waited.

But the pause lengthened, and Grayson did not tear out Ezekiel's throat. He said, his deep voice unreadable, "I don't want to kill you. Can I trust you at my back? I think I can. I think I might."

"I *killed* Thos."

Grayson's heavy eyebrows rose. "I'm not Thos. Besides, Melanie trusts you."

"Not anymore—"

"Of course she does." Grayson gazed down at Ezekiel for a long moment. "I thought Thos had ruined you. Now . . . now I think not. Or I think you can choose not. I think you've chosen that now."

Ezekiel turned this over in his mind. He said at last, "I don't know about trust, or choice. I don't know. But if you take Dimilioc, if you don't kill me, we'll both find out."

Grayson continued to stare down at him for the space

of a long breath. Then he lifted his hands and stepped back. He said, “Dimilioc is mine.”

Ezekiel got to his feet. No one tried to stop him. “It will never be the same,” he said, with just the faintest edge to his tone. He had meant to sound sarcastic. But as he made it, the statement sounded like a warning and a promise, and he knew it was true.

GENETICS IN THE WORLD OF BLACK DOG

First, a quick (very quick) look at the basics of genetics in the real world, to introduce the relevant vocabulary. Plus, I admit, a bit of this and that, some of which may not be entirely relevant, but I threw it in because it's interesting. If you'd rather just skip straight down to the bit where I lay out exactly how this all applies to black dogs, no problem – that's clearly marked a few pages on.

Humans, as you probably know, have 23 pairs of chromosomes, 46 chromosomes total. Chromosomes consist of long strands of DNA and associated proteins. Genes are sections of DNA that are found at specific locations (loci) on particular chromosomes. You get half of your chromosomes (and thus half your genes) from your father and half from your mother, which is why chromosomes come in pairs. It's different for, say, daylilies, but for humans, every genetically normal individual has *two and only two* copies of each gene, because chromosomes come in *pairs*. Each member of a pair possesses the same genes.

There's nothing special about the human chromosomal number, by the way. Gorillas have 48 chromosomes, horses have 64, dogs have 78, cats have 38, koalas have 16, lampreys have 174, and fruit flies have 4. Always in pairs. Anyway, we all have about the same amount of chromosomal material, it's just divided up differently. Not that this is particularly relevant to black dog genetics, but isn't it interesting? I had no idea lampreys had so many chromosomes until I looked it up for this essay.

Even though it's true that you have two copies of each gene, these copies are not always identical. Many genes occur in various distinct forms, each a little bit different, which are called *alleles*. Different alleles arise because of changes in the DNA (mutations). A specific gene may have one, two, three, four, or more alleles, all occurring at different frequencies in the population. Thus, the *agouti* gene in dogs has at least three different alleles, for red sable, black-and-tan, and black. Or in humans, we see A, B, and O blood types. Because chromosomes come in pairs, any genetically normal individual can have no more than two different alleles for one gene, no matter how many different alleles occur in the population.

Genes don't work by magic (well, not in the real world). Instead, each allele codes for a particular protein, which goes on to play a role in some part of overall metabolism. Or an allele may fail to code correctly for a protein, in which case its particular metabolic pathway misses a step. Altering a metabolic pathway creates the visible expression of a mutation. Mutations can be harmful, neutral, or helpful. Often a particular mutation will be harmful in some environments and helpful in others.

The X and Y chromosomes determine sex; the other 22 pairs of chromosomes are called *autosomal* chromosomes. Genes located on the X chromosome are said to be *x-linked.* In mammals, females have two X chromosomes, so they always have two alleles for each x-linked gene. Because males have one X and one Y, they cannot have more than one allele for any x-linked gene. This is one reason more boys than girls show the effects of x-linked disorders such as hemophilia A and Duchene's muscular dystrophy. If a boy gets the wrong X-chromosome from one parent, there is no chance of masking it with the right X-chromosome from the other parent – unless he is a genetically abnormal XXY male, and that carries other consequences.

The visible appearance of an individual is called the

phenotype. You cannot tell exactly what alleles are actually present by just looking at an individual. Sometimes specific alleles are carried invisibly (have no effect on the phenotype). Thus, a tabby cat might be carrying black, or a pinto horse might be carrying solid color, or a healthy woman might be carrying hemophilia A. The actual alleles that are present constitute the *genotype*, whether you see them or not.

Individuals who have two matching alleles for a gene are said to be *homozygous* for that gene. Individuals who have two different alleles for any particular gene are said to be *heterozygous* for that gene. Inbreeding increases homozygosity across all loci. We're used to thinking of inbreeding as bad, but actually increasing homozygosity is not in itself either good or bad: it depends on which alleles happen to be passed along to successive generations. Sometimes an inbred line lucks out, the right alleles happen to be collected together, and the line enjoys unusual health, vigor, and longevity. This isn't directly relevant to black dog genetics, except that black dog families are usually a little bit more inbred than the overall human population, in the same way as you'd see in any somewhat isolated community in the real world.

You will recall that genes, and therefore alleles, come in pairs. Now: if one allele by itself is sufficient to fully create a particular phenotype, without needing to be reinforced by the other gene of the pair, then that allele is said to be *dominant*. If an allele needs to be homozygous to create a phenotypic trait, that allele is said to be *recessive*.

Years of teaching and more years of reading have made it clear to me that there are many incorrect definitions of "dominant" out there, so let me add this: Dominant alleles are *not* necessarily common in the overall population, *nor* are they necessarily beneficial, *nor* are they more likely to be passed on to offspring. Recessive alleles can be beneficial or neutral or deleterious, and in any case *can be very common* or even ubiquitous (*fixed*) in a population. For example, 100% of all Golden Retrievers are recessive at the *extension* locus (ee). That's why they're all blond.

Naturally, in the real world, things are a lot more complicated than the dominant/recessive dichotomy implies. For example, often one allele is not able to *fully* create a particular phenotype. In that case, dominance is said to be *partial* or *incomplete*. If a particular gene includes three or more alleles, then some of the alleles may show complete dominance and others may show partial dominance and still others may be entirely recessive. For example, at the *spotting* locus in dogs, there is a series of four alleles that run through solid color (Labrador Retriever) through flashy white markings (Bernese Mountain Dog) and pinto spotting (Cavalier King Charles Spaniel) to extended white (Clumber Spaniel). Solid color is completely dominant to all kinds of spotting patterns and then dominance is partial as you go down the list, which is why you get such a wide range of spotting patterns in dogs.

Though we're always hearing about "the gene" for this and "the gene" for that, in fact, it's relatively rare for a particular phenotypic trait to be created by a single gene. More often, traits are created by the interactions of two or three or more genes. For example, the trait of "coat color" in dogs is controlled by more than a dozen interacting genes. These traits are often called *polygenic*.

In one type of polygenic interaction, one gene may disable another or change how the first is expressed, in interactions that are referred to as *epistatic* or *hypostatic*. For example, if a horse is chestnut or sorrel (ee at the *extension* locus, the same genotype that gives us Golden Retrievers), then the production of black and brown eumelanin is suppressed and the action of the *agouti* alleles that code for black and brown color are rendered invisible. Because the *extension* gene can hide the *agouti* gene, the former is said to be epistatic to the latter.

In another type of polygenic interaction, one gene may reinforce another, so that several genes act together to add up to one phenotypic trait. Human skin color is created by many interacting genes, each of which might (or might not) add a "dose" of melanin. This is why so many different skin tones are possible for humans.

Traits created by a single gene are said to be *simple.* Traits created by many interacting genes are said to be *complex.* Complex traits are sometimes also strongly influenced by the environment as well as by the genes involved. In that case, they may be referred to as *multifactorial.*

Whew. With all that out of the way, now we can finally talk about black dog genetics! The black dog / Pure / human phenotypes are controlled by a system of three interacting unlinked genes.

First, there is an x-linked allele, the X^e allele, which seems to have appeared as a mutation of the X^E allele possibly tens of thousands of years ago, possibly more than once. (Some mutations occur a lot more frequently than others.) This allele confers natural resistance against all manner of demonic influences – whether the result of black dog influence (in Europe, the Middle East, and the Americas) or witches (Africa, Polynesia) or vampires (until very recently, everywhere except East Asia).

Individuals homozygous for the X^e allele are more resistant to demonic influence than individuals heterozygous for it. No doubt you immediately realize that women may be $X^e X^e$, whereas the best a genetically normal man can hope for is a $X^e Y$ genotype.

Though widespread, this allele is not all that common, although naturally some lucky families or whole populations carry it at a high frequency. You would think that the X^e

allele would tend to increase in all populations, and it probably does, but some kinds of demonic influences tend to target people carrying that allele, so it evens out.

Next, the autosomal *black dog* gene is a simple gene with two alleles. The completely dominant allele, B, always makes an individual into a black dog. Though everyone with even one B allele will be a black dog, homozygous BB individuals have stronger "black dog shadows" than heterozygous Bb individuals. This is not a good thing, since without enhanced control, a stronger shadow means that you are more likely to be "consumed" by your shadow, gradually losing your humanity and becoming a purely demonic monster.

Individuals must be homozygous for the recessive b allele in order to be normal humans. Obviously, b is by far the more common allele in all human populations.

Finally, a mutation to the autosomal *resistance* gene created the Pure. The Pure actually arose in about 750 AD, in Germany, through an apparently miraculous intervention by Saint Walburga, so this appears to have been a directed rather than a spontaneous mutation. (Saint Walburga was a real person; you should look her up; her bio makes fascinating reading. I coopted her into the secret history of the *Black Dog* world because she is really perfect for this miracle.)

Anyway, before the saint intervened, the only allele at this locus was r, "no resistance." The miracle acted to create the partially dominant r^p allele. The r^p allele always confers additional resistance to demonic influence. It cannot create the Pure by itself, but anyone who is homozygous for *both* the r^p allele *and* the X^e allele at the same time is Pure – but only if she would otherwise be a black dog. You see this is a complex trait! A Pure individual must always have the genotype Bb r^pr^p $X^e X^e$ or BB r^pr^p $X^e X^e$. That's why all the Pure are women and why the Pure never appear in an exclusively human family. If black dogs were ever wiped out, the Pure would disappear as well.

The more r^p alleles and X^e alleles a black dog has, the more control he will have over his demonic shadow. Dimilioc has been breeding for both the r^p allele and the X^e allele for hundreds of years, though not with perfect consistency because we're talking about people here, not cows, and people have their own ideas about this kind of thing. Still, Ezekiel's genotype is almost certainly BB r^pr^p X^eY – he is a very strong black dog with a whole lot of control over his demonic shadow, and because of individual variation and unusual determination, both his strength and his control are exceptional even for this genotype.

But there's more! Somewhere around 1110 AD, probably in the flourishing Jewish community in Spain, a second mutation occurred at the r locus, producing the R allele, which is partially dominant to both other alleles at this locus. This mutation almost certainly occurred as a result of another directed, miraculous intervention, but the details are not known. It's clear, though, that the R allele already existed before the Islamic sect Almohades took control in Spain and outlawed both Judaism and Christianity – in the world of *Black Dog*, the Almohades sect was actually established by a black dog family. Anyway, the R mutation spread from Spain along the lines of the Sephardic Jewish migrations into Portugal, Italy, Morocco, Egypt, Tunisia, and later into Turkey during the Ottoman period. Eventually the R allele was carried by continuing population migrations into Eastern and Western Europe and South and North America. It is still most common in families descended from Sephardic Jews.

Dimilioc doesn't know anything about the R allele, though at the present time it's probably more widespread than the r^p allele. Here's the most important part: Unlike the r^p allele, the R allele can interact with the $X^e X^e$ genotype to create the Pure phenotype *even if* one or the other gene occurs in heterozygous form.

Without the R allele, there are only two possible genotypes (out of thirty) that can give rise to the Pure. *With* the R allele, ten out of thirty possible genotypes produce the Pure, and two of those give rise to Pure males. This does not mean that any population anywhere has a third of all children turn out to be Pure. Remember that in all populations, the B allele and both the R and the r^p alleles are relatively rare, and the X^e allele is also far from ubiquitous.

It is worth noting here that demonic influences strongly influence Mendelian ratios – in other words, strict probability does not govern black dog inheritance. When a black dog produces a child with a human, as for example in this cross:

$$Bb\ rr\ X^eYX \quad x \quad bb\ r^pr\ X^EX^E$$

Then there should be a 50% chance of producing a black dog child. But the chance is actually significantly higher. Similarly, there should be a 50% chance of the mother passing on her r^p allele or the father passing on his X^e allele to a child, but in fact the chance of either is significantly lower. All this taken together makes it most likely for this cross to produce a black dog son and least likely for it to produce a human daughter.

Also, in a long-term relationship, a black dog will "corrupt" a human mate, a process which influences the expected Mendelian ratios to an even greater degree: the risk of producing strong black dog sons that lack control and are consumed by their shadows increases with each birth. This is not true if a black dog produces a child with a Pure mate, however. The Pure may not be perfect, but they are incorruptible by direct demonic influence. That's why they're called Pure.

Outside of Dimilioc and other civilized black dog families, most black dog / human offspring result from rape. This is typical of "stray" black dogs, who are usually savage and violent in all their relationships. Around the time of the full moon, they're likely to kill; but when the moon is new, they're more likely to rape a woman than kill her. This is what maintains the black dog gene in the general population – otherwise it would quickly decrease in frequency and there would be few or no "stray" black dogs. Black dogs carrying one or more of the various resistance alleles are more likely to be able to control their vicious tendencies, but only if they are taught that control is desirable, which seldom happens outside the civilized black dog families. The Pure can conduct a permanent Calming magic on a black dog, which is very effective, but of course this, too, is not likely outside of civilized black dog families.

At different times, many areas of the world have suffered from the existence of black dog families that valued strength and control, but hated the Pure. Where black dogs had a lot of influence and hatred of the Pure was particularly strong, this propensity led to the subjugation of women in general. This attitude has tended to infect the surrounding human cultures, with unfortunate results. Thus in the world of *Black Dog*, women are seriously oppressed in, say, Saudi Arabia – where Keziah and Amira are from – but not in Lebanon, Tunisia, or Morocco, all of which had black dog houses that valued the Pure.

Now that the vampire miasma has been removed and humans have become aware of black dogs, human societies may finally begin to reject all kinds of demonically inspired attitudes and hatreds – we can hope! In that way, at least, the world of *Black Dog* may actually face a brighter near-future than seems likely for the real world.

MOTHERS AND SISTERS

Keziah's life changed on a still, hot noon; on a day drenched in heat and light and blood.

She began the day kneeling with her cheek against the curtains that divided the women's quarters, listening as her mother labored to bring forth the child, Keziah's brother, the son that would be her father's heir. Other women of the household had come to help with the birth, but only human women. A *dhi'ba adhameyya,* a black wolf girl, would bring the worst of luck to a birth, so Keziah knelt behind the curtains, present but not present, listening to her mother's panting cries and the low, tense voices of the human women. Waiting for her brother's birth and her mother's triumph.

Her father had other wives, other sons. But it was Keziah's mother, Kalila, who made her father a prince. Hers was the royal line. It was Princess Kalila who must bear him a son of royal blood to be his heir. A *dhi'b adhami* son of royal blood: that was the need and the desire of Keziah's father. For many days before this day, everyone had known the coming child was a black wolf. It would be a son, must be a son, because a son was so ardently desired. Her father had not prayed for a son, for only *abeed*—slaves—begged favors of God. Prayer was for women, and humans, and the weak. But he had commanded the human women of the household to pray five times a day for this child to be male. Keziah's mother had prayed most fervently of all.

Keziah had been Princess Kalila's firstborn, a *dhi'ba,* even more worthless than a human daughter, for a human woman might bear useful sons to the masters of the family, but the children of a black wolf woman were of no value. Her sons were too strong in one way and not strong enough in another. The fury of their hearts was too strong; the man not strong enough to rule the dark shadow. They died young, the sons of such women. Or if they lived, their fathers put them to death when their shadows consumed them and they became uncontrollable.

Or such a woman might bear black wolf daughters, and that was even worse, for what man would want such a difficult, disobedient daughter?

After Keziah, Princess Kalila had borne first one and then another baby, both boys, but she had borne them too early to live. Now at last came this one, still early, but not too early. This child would live. It would be a son. The whole household had prayed for a son, and anyone could tell it was a black wolf child. Black wolves were far more often male than female because men were stronger than women, strong enough to carry heavy shadows and so worthy of power.

This time the baby would be a son, and he would live.

There would be a feast: mutton and eggplant, pigeon pies fragrant with spices, pastries with cheese and dates, wheat cooked with dates and rosewater. Even the women would be allowed their own feast. Keziah's father would send her mother every delicacy, and the women would give her special foods to bring her milk in and to strengthen her blood. Princess Kalila would regain her strength and her health and she would nurse the child until he became too dangerous to put to her breast. Then Keziah would feed the baby from a bottle because even the fiercest black wolf child couldn't hurt her. And she would have a brother. She knew just how it would be. She would feed him and protect him while he was a crawling infant; she would make him a friend. Thus when he grew up, her brother would protect her from their father and uncles.

The air behind the curtains was very still and hot. The curtains smelled of dust and sunlight. There was not much blood; not then. The birth was easy enough, the child small and well-positioned.

The blood came later, after the child was born, and turned out to be another black wolf girl after all.

Aunt Sofia brought the baby to Keziah after her father was gone from the women's quarters. Princess Kalila was finally dead. After all the screams and then the weak, pathetic whimpers, the silence had been deafening. Keziah's ears rang with it until she heard nothing else. But once her father had gone, the girl-infant at last began screaming angrily, and Keziah stirred and scrambled to her feet and went out into the cooler places of the women's quarters to find the child. She could not tell whether she was bitterly angry or actually curious; whether she mourned or was merely afraid. It was often difficult to sort out what she herself felt and thought from the darker impulses of her shadow.

The child had not cried until her father departed. Even the youngest black wolf infant knew when to be silent. Now she was screaming more and more loudly, a passionate demand for life, because Aunt Sofia was only human and could not frighten a black wolf baby into silence.

But Keziah's sister quieted when she felt Keziah come near. She was still angry, as a black wolf baby was always angry, but even mere hours old, she knew that Keziah was also a black wolf, and stronger. Keziah could not remember whether she had felt such things when she was as little as this. She could not remember her father coming to beat her mother after her own birth, though she could guess now just how angry he must have been to have been given such a worthless daughter.

And here now was this other even more worthless daughter, tiny and wrinkled, still smeared with the fluids of the birth. But her infant eyes tracked Keziah's approach with more than human attentiveness, and the way she grew quiet and still in the crook of Aunt Sofia's arm made it clear she knew she was in the presence of a stronger black wolf.

"She is yours, if you will have her," Aunt Sofia told Keziah. "Or if you will not, then she will die."

Keziah nodded. She knew that.

One of the women, Zara, had plenty of milk. Her son—human, and thus almost as worthless as the new baby—was only three months old. But Zara was human, and no human woman would nurse a black wolf infant unless Keziah's father or one of her uncles commanded it. A black wolf woman might more easily rear this child, this disaster of a girl-child, if her father permitted. But the only black wolf woman in all Riyadh was Aunt Ayesha, who lived in the tower in the middle of the city, not in the villa here at the northern edge of the city. Keziah knew Aunt Ayesha would not care if the child lived or died. Or perhaps she would wish her to die, lest someday she become a rival.

Keziah was not certain herself whether she wanted this child to live or die. Part of her, the dark half, wished to kill the baby. That was to be expected. But her mother had taught her to recognize the half of her soul that was her own, and in that part of her soul, maybe she wanted the child to live.

Or perhaps not. This angry baby had killed her mother. Keziah stared down into the small face, screwed up now in anger and fear, orange flecks in her cloudy infant eyes. Keziah could see nothing of their mother in her. But nothing of their father, either. Nor of herself. She was a new person: herself. Aunt Sofia had washed her and wrapped her in swaddling to stop her struggling to bite, but when Keziah touched her cheek, she did not try to bite, but only lay very still.

This was Keziah's sister, this little helpless thing. What use was a black wolf sister younger than Keziah? A girl who would always be younger and weaker than Keziah, who would never have any influence or power in the house, never win their father's favor.

"She did not kill your mother," Aunt Sofa said. She was perceptive, for a human. But human women had to be perceptive to survive in a black wolf's house. Now she nodded softly at Keziah's angry stare and went on, unafraid. "Your father murdered Kalila. That is not the baby's fault. She might live. If she has a sister who wishes her to live. Maybe you will be glad someday if you protect her now. Every *dhi'ba adhameyya* needs an ally at her back. Especially a girl. A brother would someday have turned against you or ignored you or dismissed you, for such are brothers. But a sister would be different. You will have each other, if you teach her and make her your friend. She might learn to be fierce and strong, if she has someone to teach her."

Aunt Sofia did not say, *If you teach her, Keziah, your sister might learn to be more than a slave.* No human woman would say such a thing. Not in this house, where all women were slaves, black wolf and human alike.

But Keziah heard what Aunt Sofia had not quite said. She knew that what her aunt meant was, *She might someday be strong enough to help you kill your father and your uncles.*

Aunt Sofia was her mother's half-sister, neither royal nor valuable, but she was clever, and she had loved Kalila. She had begged to be permitted to leave her father's palace in Madinah so that she might accompany Princess Kalila to this house and bear her company here. And here Aunt Sofia had learned how to hate in the way a woman hated: quietly and for a long, long time.

Humans could not hate like black wolves. Not even Aunt Sofia. But slave women in a black wolf's house learned to hate in their own way. Keziah's father and uncles and brothers and male cousins did not even seem to know that. But Keziah was not so blind.

Keziah took the baby from Aunt Sofia. She tucked the baby into the bend of her elbow and met her aunt's gaze. Sofia, human though she was, she did not flinch.

"My father did not name her," Keziah told her aunt. "He will not. So I will. Her name is Amira. That is what she will be called, for she is a princess, even if no one but the women of my father's household remembers it is so."

Aunt Sophia bowed her head as a human woman must to a black wolf's command, even a girl, even one as young as Keziah. But she smiled, too, because she was not afraid. She said with satisfaction, "You are both princesses. There is not a drop of royal blood in your father's veins, but from your mother you have inherited the blood of kings. That is something his sons will never have."

Keziah smiled, too, because she knew this was true. She knew exactly what Aunt Sofia meant. Aunt Sofia mean that if her father wanted grandsons whose veins ran with the blood of kings, he would have to get them from Keziah herself or from this new baby. That was safety, of a kind, for them both. For a while. She said softly, like a vow, "He will never see a living son of Kalila's blood. Now he will never see a living grandson of her blood. He will die knowing his loins have failed to give him a royal heir."

"A dangerous vow," murmured Aunt Sofia.

"It will be so," Keziah said fiercely. "Never while he lives will I or my sister bear him living grandsons. He will die without his desired heir, he who valued his wife so little he murdered all the possible sons he might have gotten from her."

"Will your sister die, then, to be sure she cannot bear a child?"

Keziah looked down at the tiny, helpless body in her arms. She said, "My sister will live. Tell Zara she need not put her to suck, but she must give me milk for her."

And Aunt Sofia smiled and went away, soft-footed and silent, through the curtains of the women's quarters.

The baby lived, and grew strong. The women called her Amira, as Keziah had commanded, and kept out of the child's way as she learned to crawl and then to toddle and then to run, swift and neat-footed as black wolf children were at an age where human children still staggered clumsily.

The men did not call the child anything, for Keziah kept her sister out of their way. The woman's part of the villa was separate from the men's part; the women's courtyards were so arranged that they were not subject to the view of men. This was so in both of Keziah's father's villas, for he had had them made just alike. He did not like change, so the villa in Riyadh was just like the one in Taif, to which the household retired from June to September in order to escape the dust. Indeed, the only difference was that the slaves had to repaint the villa in Riyadh every year, after the sandstorms turned the snow-white walls to a dimmer ivory, whereas the villa in the cooler mountains of Taif seldom had to be repainted. Both villas were furnished in exactly the same way and decorated with the same rugs and the same paintings. Whenever her father bought anything, he bought it twice and sent one of the things to the other house, so that he need not be troubled because one item or another had been accidentally left behind.

In both villas, Keziah had a room of her own because she was her mother's daughter and a princess, and in both she made room for Amira. Their father might have forgotten Amira had ever been born. The women did not remind him. Certainly Keziah did not remind him.

Keziah fed her sister milk at first, and then, as Amira's teeth came in, lamb minced very fine, and milk sweets, all such delicacies. She stole the meat from the kitchens, for such rich foods were not often given to women or girl-babies. No other girl dared steal the meat intended for the men's table; women waited for the men to finish eating and then divided what was left, if any, among themselves in some way that no doubt made sense to human slaves. Keziah did not care how human women sorted out such matters, so long as she got the best of the food left from the men's table, and so long as she could take what her little sister needed before the finished dishes left the kitchens for the men's side of the house.

The slave women did not dare so much as look at Keziah when she took food from the kitchen. Their fear pleased her. But they were far more afraid of her father, so she took only enough for Amira, lest eventually he might realize his portion had been scanted. In a way she did not completely understand, it pleased her to give her sister meat she might have eaten herself. Her dark shadow wished to eat all the best food, or perhaps all the food so it could laugh at Amira as she starved. But it pleased Keziah herself to give her sister the best meat and the finest sweets, and take for her own the broken meats sent back to the kitchen.

"You are kind to your sister," observed Aunt Sofia, one day when Keziah had just turned twelve and Amira was nearly five.

She had come to see Keziah in the room that Keziah shared with Amira, a room that opened onto the small woman's courtyard. This courtyard was plain, without the lemon trees and pomegranates that leaned over the fountains in the men's courtyard, but for a black wolf toddler, it was better than no courtyard at all. Keziah thought that soon Amira would need broader lands and a wider sky, at least when the swelling moon most strongly urged up the dark half of her soul. She wished she knew how to give her those things. Black wolf girls were not allowed to take their other shape and hunt in the desert...though there were ways to slip out and slip back in without being seen. Especially if one had a human woman who would be sure to keep windows open and sweep the sand off the floors.

It would be harder for two girls together.

But that did not matter yet. Now Keziah watched the child splash in the shallow fountain and chase after the lizard that had been hiding from the sun on the shadowy tiles, and thought that perhaps soon she would like to take her to the desert and teach her to hunt larger game.

Perhaps it was *kind,* to have such thoughts while she watched her sister play. Keziah had never thought of it that way.

Aunt Sofia must have seen her doubt, for she said, "You gave her your tiger's eye bracelet to chew on when her teeth pained her coming in, and now that she is able to eat proper food, you give her the best portions. And she runs in your courtyard and sleeps in your room and is not afraid of you. You are her friend. But I wonder, have you also taught her to be *your* friend? Are you teaching her to be kind?"

Keziah stared at her aunt, puzzled, wondering whether she should be offended. She was a black wolf and a princess, and she did not need kindness from anybody; certainly not from a child such as Amira.

"Ah, well," Aunt Sofia said gently. "Even you may someday find you need a friend, Keziah. A black wolf friend, one who understands you better than we poor humans may ever understand you. Perhaps you will find this is so sooner than you might imagine. You are a woman now, young as you are." She looked Keziah up and down: a close, direct look such as was insolence from a human to a black wolf, but there was no insolence in it. Only worry, and perhaps a shadow of the affection a human woman might bear for another; Keziah was not certain what she saw in her aunt at that moment.

Then Aunt Sofia said, "Your father has sent for you. He wishes to see you. You are to be presented to him before the afternoon meal."

Fear crept on many little feet down Keziah's spine. She raised her chin, refusing to flinch.

"Good," said Aunt Sofia. "Also, not good. You must be brave, but not too brave—well, I am sure I need not explain this to a black wolf girl! Even so, if I may suggest...your hair. You may wish to take it down, to braid it simply, as a child might. Perhaps you may wish to braid it with a single strand of pearls. That is a charming style for a child. Possibly you may wish to change your clothing. I certainly would not suggest an *abaya*, though you are tall. No one will be there except relatives. I have a simple dress that I think will fit you. Very expensive, but also modest. Quite suitable for a girl still a child but nearing womanhood. I have laid it out in my room, if you should wish to consider it."

"You are not very subtle," Keziah said coldly. She spoke coldly because she wished to show she did not care whether her aunt advised her or not, and because she would not admit she was afraid.

Aunt Sofia shrugged, a complicated, graceful movement that began with her shoulders and ended with her fingertips. "Your father is not a subtle man, Keziah."

This was true in some ways. Less true in others, and Keziah was not certain whether her aunt's advice was good or bad, whether making herself look like a younger child was clever or foolish. Though Aunt Sofia had seldom been foolish, in Keziah's experience. And she often gave good advice.

"Very well." Keziah agreed graciously. "You may assist

me to dress, so that I may look well when I present myself to my father and he may be pleased."

"Good," Aunt Sofia said softly, with no trace of irony. She looked Keziah up and down once more. "You are graceful as a willow, as Kalila was graceful; not heavy-figured as Youssef's Russian cow. This is good."

Keziah nodded her understanding. Uncle Youssef was like all the rest of Keziah's father's brothers: old and grim and strong and cruel. Sons he had indeed, one a year older than Keziah and one a year younger, both of whom he defended from the other black wolves of Riyadh with grim efficiency, both borne by a big-breasted yellow-haired Russian woman.

After the Soviet Empire had fallen, a decade or two before Keziah was born, many Russian women had been lured to Riyadh with the promise of work. Others had simply been stolen, taken by the procurers who supplied the sudden market for Slavic women. All of them had been made into slaves. "The very word 'Slav' means slave, for they are born to serve," Aunt Sofia had explained to Keziah, not without pity. "They have always been so. Even the Turks took many Slavic women, and long ago the Persians. It does not matter. In Russia, many of them would have been slaves anyway, subject to The Dacha. Here they will bear strong sons for our men—and better they should be so used than we or our daughters."

Keziah had barely understood any of this. She had never heard of the Russian black wolves of The Dacha; not then. And she knew nothing of Turks or Persians except what everyone knew: that the Turks were savages and the Persians much degenerated from their days of power. But she knew Uncle Youssef had bought one of those Russian women, a big-boned broad-faced woman with heavy breasts and hips made for bearing. This was the mother of his sons. He had not killed her yet, though she had borne him only human girls since: big-boned plain girls much like their mother, but Uncle Youssef protected them as well, though not with any great attention.

In time, of course, Uncle Youssef could barter his daughters for favor from some other, more powerful black wolf. Perhaps even a prince might be pleased to take one or another, big hipped compliant girls who ought to be able to bear easily. Then Youssef's grandsons would carry royal blood. Keziah hoped so. She would enjoy seeing her father's jealousy if that should be so.

"At least your father has waited for your twelfth year to come upon you," observed Aunt Sofia. "You are young, but you are becoming a woman, that is plain. You are early to it, but I think it is often so for black wolf girls." She paused and added more distantly, "My father gave my sister to our uncle when she was nine."

Keziah was uncertain what response her aunt wished. "That is permitted under the law," she said, though she knew her aunt knew this.

Aunt Sofia agreed without changing her soft tone. "Of course the law permits such a marriage, for the law was made by black wolf men and not for women. But it was not kind of my father to agree to my uncle's request. Though we were not surprised that he did. Black wolves so rarely care for kindness. Certainly not in Riyadh. Certainly my father did not. Nor my uncle. My little sister did not quite live to be your age, Keziah."

Keziah said nothing. The child Aunt Sofia remembered must have been another of Princess Kalila's half-sisters, by one of her mother's father's other wives. Part of Keziah delighted in the thought of the terror and suffering of that child, her own half-aunt, who had died in misery—she had no doubt of the misery—before she quite turned twelve. But Keziah herself flinched from a sudden vivid image of her own little Amira being given to a brutal black wolf uncle. Her eyes went to the child hunting the lizard around the fountain, and she found she could after all find pity in her heart for the child who had been given to such a marriage.

In her mind and in her heart, Keziah deliberately turned her back on the part of her soul that reveled in the pain and fear of others. She shut a door between the two halves of her soul; not quite solid, that door, but enough of a barrier to help her distinguish her own self from her heavy shadow when its darkness became too invasive. She had discovered that trick for herself. It occurred to her now, for the first time, that she had not taught this to Amira, and that perhaps she should.

Aunt Sofia was watching her closely. "It takes a different manner of strength for a black wolf to be kind. It takes the strength that comes from the right-hand side of your soul rather than the left. You have that strength from your mother. Your father, being what he is, does not value kindness or generosity or compassion. Neither in himself, nor in his brothers, nor in his sons. It is a kind of strength he does not even see." She meant, *Because like my father, like all black wolf men, he is a monster.* She did not say so, of course. She said instead, "Perhaps only a human mother can teach that kind of strength to her daughters. Perhaps it is too difficult for a black wolf girl to teach it to her sister."

Keziah tilted her head. "You surely do not believe you are being subtle. Indeed, Aunt, you are not very subtle in anything today."

Aunt Sofia only bowed her head meekly and murmured, "I don't wish to speak where it is my place to keep silent. I know that for a black wolf, to be kind requires a strict and terrible discipline. It is different for other black wolves elsewhere, perhaps. One hears tales of Nurullah in Lebanon, of black wolf houses in Israel...perhaps it is different for them. But for us..."

"Kindness is no use for a black wolf," Keziah said, interrupting. But though she made certain her tone was sharp, she was actually uncertain. She was trying to remember whether her mother had ever tried to teach her to be kind. It was hard to imagine. Surely no one would have formed any such ambition for a black wolf child.

Maybe Keziah had missed some point her aunt had meant to make. It was a woman's art, to speak tangentially, around the edges of meaning, so that no one could truthfully claim to have heard her say anything disrespectful or disloyal. But sometimes that woman's opacity was difficult for a girl to unravel. Even a black wolf girl carrying a heavy shadow.

But she did not ask. She said only, regally, "You may assist me to dress, Aunt, if you wish. But I will not wear white pearls, but black, as suits my mother's daughter."

"As you wish, of course," murmured Aunt Sofia.

Keziah's father did not comment about the color of the pearls. Nor did he ask after the younger of his daughters. Keziah had feared he might, but once she had come before him, he only studied her in silence for a few minutes without speaking a word. She did not look at him directly, but knelt before him with her head bowed—partly because she could tell he was much stronger than she and partly so that he would not see the hatred in her eyes. He would know she hated him, of course, for all black wolves hated those more powerful than they. But he would not care, so long as she came at his summons and knelt obediently at his feet.

Her father was not alone in his office. Her uncles were there also: Youssef and Rayan, Ahmed and Hamsa. This frightened Keziah, though she made sure she did not show her fear. Youssef was grim, Rayan smiling, Ahmed bored. And Hamsa, thin, half-ruined Hamsa, with his bitter eyes and scarred, twisted arm, was impossible to read at all through the density of his powerful shadow. If her father hadn't used treacherous silver to destroy his right shoulder and arm, Hamsa would be master of this household, of the villa in Riyadh and the identical one in Taif where the household went to escape the heat of summer. If that had been so, Princess Kalila's father would have given his daughter to Hamsa and everything would be...different. Better, worse, those words meant nothing. But different.

Except then whatever children Princess Kalila had borne to Hamsa, one of them would not have been Keziah and the other would not have been Amira.

But even then, those ghost-children, those might-have-been girls, they would have hated their father, just as Keziah hated hers.

All her uncles were all old, powerful, cruel, dangerous. Even Hamsa, especially Hamsa, who must give way to all his brothers and many of their sons. In his weakness, he was the cruelest of all.

If Keziah's mother had borne a boy-child, would he someday have become like this? Kalila's son would have been strong. Perhaps a rival would have driven a silver knife into his shoulder and cut the tendons of his arm, and then he would surely have become another such as Hamsa. Keziah had been certain she could make a little brother into a friend, but she found now that she was glad she had a little sister instead.

She wore the modest child's dress, as Aunt Sofia had suggested. It fell straight from shoulder to ankle, with no suggestion of a woman's shape. Aunt Sofia had made sure of that by binding Keziah's small breasts and carefully padding her narrow waist to hide the recent swelling off her hips. Her hair fell across one shoulder in a single thick plait, reaching almost to the floor when she knelt and bowed her head.

"Pretty," said Uncle Youssef, his tone bored.

"Young," said Uncle Ahmed more judiciously. "Is she not twelve? It's late for this bud to open."

"Some men like to open a tight little bud," said Uncle Rayan, his smile widening.

Uncle Hamsa did not speak at all, but Keziah could feel his eyes on her, hating her for her youth and sound limbs, despising her for being weaker than he. Someday she would be stronger, even though she was a girl, because she had the use of all her limbs. But even then Uncle Hamsa would be a master in this house and Keziah would be a slave. She did not meet his gaze.

Her father rose to his feet, and came forward, and took hold of Keziah's braid to pull her head back. He looked into her face and she stared back, her dark shadow shuddering and trying to rise. She checked it, held it, her own heart wiser; she knew her father would kill her right now if she let her shadow up. It would try to fight him and he would kill her. She could not turn her face aside, not with his grip on her hair. All she could do was close her eyes and hope he let go before her control failed.

Her father grunted, released her hair, and turned away. "She'll do," he said. "If she were human, she'd do better. But she'll do. If she's bred to one of ibn Abdel's human sons, my grandsons might be worth something after all."

"A human is a good choice for her, *sidi,"* agreed Uncle Rayan. As the youngest brother, he was carefully respectful of the eldest. "So many human sons is ill luck. They can do nothing for a man but give him black wolf grandsons. But I fear ibn Abdel may not be so pleased if she guts one of his sons."

Uncle Youssef laughed. "I'm sure any of the black wolves of ibn Abdel's household would be pleased to help a human son tame her."

"Or we could send her to ibn Abdel's son already taught to yield to any man's hand, even the hand of a human," suggested Uncle Rayan. "He might even prefer that. Humans are such cowards."

"Unacceptable," her father snapped. "A human man might prefer it so, but we will not offend a man who may be an ally by offering a human son of his used goods. If you want a toy, buy one in the Evening Market."

"Ah, *sidi,* that is too expensive," objected Uncle Rayan. "They don't last long enough. Not like this girl." His gaze ran up and down Keziah's kneeling form while she trembled with rage and fought for control over her shadow.

"A human woman can last for many years, if you're careful," Uncle Youssef told Uncle Rayan.

"Who wishes to be *careful?"*

Uncle Ahmed warned them both, "I'm not advancing anyone anything on his allowance because he uses up a girl and can't afford another." Uncle Ahmed kept the family accounts. He was stingy with the women's requests. Evidently with the men's requests as well.

"I will propose the match to ibn Abdel and see whether the idea pleases him. If it does, she will be sent to her husband untouched, and not until she has become more womanly," said Keziah's father flatly. "Keziah, you may go."

Keziah rose gracefully, not wishing to shame herself by letting them see she was afraid. She could feel all their eyes on her: her father possessive and Uncle Rayan greedy; Uncle Youssef scornful and Uncle Ahmed indifferent. She kept her own gaze on the floor, mostly. But when she couldn't restrain a covert glance from beneath lowered lashes, it was Uncle Hansa's eyes that caught hers. He was looking at her, really *looking*. His gaze flickered to her bound breasts and padded waist, and Keziah guessed he knew all of Aunt Sofia's tricks, and hers.

She was terrified he would reveal her deceit to her father, to her other uncles. But he said nothing at all.

Instead, he came that night through the women's courtyard to find Keziah in the room she shared with little Amira.

Keziah fought him. She was not strong enough to kill him; not strong enough to even mark him. He was more than forty and she was only twelve, but even so she would have tried her best to cripple his other arm. But Uncle Hamsa proved to have a power she had never guessed, for part of his strength was to force her dark shadow down deep within her and hold her to her human form.

"My father will *kill* you," she snarled in his face, surrounded by the wreckage of her pallet, while Amira cowered in a corner and Uncle Hamsa pinned both her wrists with his one good hand. "*I* will kill you!"

He laughed at her, his breath stinking of sulfur and ash. The women of the household said he was beautiful, the most beautiful of a handsome family, but his face was like a hawk's face or a knife's edge, beautiful but cruel. His eyes were hot and yellow, the dark shadow riding close behind the man. He said, his voice scraped raw with the bloodlust of his shadow, "If your father discovers what you have done, he will kill *you*, little bud, for what use to him is an opened flower? You had better be careful he does not know anything." Her own threat he ignored, for the threats of girls were less than the whisper of the breeze across the desert.

Keziah tried again to call up her own shadow and again she failed. His shadow pressed hers down and she could not shed her weak girl's form.

Then Amira, no longer cowering, leaped upon Uncle Hamsa from behind.

The little girl had shifted, the first time in her life that her shadow had fully risen up, and so when she struck Uncle Hamsa, it was with a weight and violence impossible for so young a human child. He sprawled, cursing and spitting, losing his grip on Keziah's wrists but not his grip on her shadow—she should have run, should have seized her chance and fled, out into the courtyard or farther still, into the crowded apartments where the human women slept. Someone would have started screaming, and maybe Uncle Hamsa would have changed his mind.

But she could not leave Amira to their uncle's rage. So she caught up a chair and broke it over Uncle Hansa's head instead.

He staggered and fell, but the blow he had aimed at Amira, that would otherwise have torn her in half, only raked across the child's hip. But then he forced Amira into human form, so she cried in shock and fled, baby-chubby and helpless. And then he caught the remnants of the chair with a strength Keziah couldn't match, tore the broken pieces out of Keziah's hands, seized her by the throat, and flung her down.

Then he beat her, and did what he had come to do, and left her bleeding behind him.

Once he was gone, Keziah was finally able to shift. Girls were not allowed to take the other form save when the moon called up their shadows. At other times, they were punished when they were caught in that form. But Keziah shifted. She shook away the pain, the broken bones and the other injuries that might have killed a human girl. The dark shadow took her and she fled into the courtyard and leaped from there onto the roof where it was lowest, and though girls were not allowed to leave the women's quarters and certainly not allowed to leave the house, she ran across the rooftops of the house so lightly that no one below could have heard her and fled into the desert.

She came back because of Amira.

In the desert, Keziah had run down and killed a fox and then, more satisfyingly, a gazelle. She had seen men, but they had not seen her. In her other form, ordinary humans looked away from her and thought she was a dog or a wolf or an ordinary shadow. Their blindness made them weak, made them prey, but Keziah did not kill them even though tonight she would have been glad to kill any man. A fox's death would not be marked; a gazelle's death was nothing. But word of the deaths of men might come to the ears of her father, or to Uncle Hamsa, or to some other of her uncles or cousins. *They* would not be blind.

She had run a long way, through moonlight and shadow, feeling invincible and savage. Then she had glimpsed another black wolf hunting, much bigger and older than she. It might have been Uncle Hansa; she could not tell; it might have been anyone. She knew it was an enemy. She hid amid the natural shadows until the other black wolf was gone and then she shifted back to her human form so she could think better. In that form, she was still wearing the torn and bloody remnants of her nightdress—she should have expected it, but she had not, and was revolted by its touch, by the smell of it. She stripped off the ugly garment, throwing it away into the shadows. Then she sat down on the ground, naked as she was. She wrapped her arms around her drawn-up knees and sat for a long time in the desert, thinking about what she should do.

Before she had quite decided, she smelled a hot wind and knew a sandstorm was coming. She did not know whether the black wolf could breathe the dusty wind or see in that kind of darkness. Besides, there was Amira. So she went back to her father's villa.

Aunt Sofia was waiting for her. She had cleaned up Keziah's room and brought new furniture to replace what had been broken. The room smelled of soap and pomegranates and only a little tiny bit of blood.

The pomegranates were because Aunt Sofia had brought Amira pomegranates to eat in order to keep her quiet. Probably she had told Amira the juice of pomegranates was the blood of those you hated and you should think of the one you hated with every seed you ate, and then every seed you ate laid a curse on that one until eventually he died.

That was what Keziah's mother had told Keziah, long ago, to keep her quiet. It had taken Keziah years to understand it was not true. Otherwise, with all the pomegranates the women consumed, there should have been no men left alive in her father's household. But in her childhood, Keziah had eaten pomegranates with some intensity.

Amira knew she had come back first, of course, and turned quickly, shifting most of the way to her other form and then just as quickly back again. Only then did Aunt Sofia look around, carefully pretending not to see Amira shift and shift again, or Keziah shake off the remnants of her dark shadow. Even then Aunt Sofia kept her eyes carefully lowered.

Once she had shifted back to her human form, Keziah did not say a word to Aunt Sofia, but she make sure to pause and smile at Amira. "Save one for me," she said, flicking a hand at the bowl of pomegranates, and went to take a bath.

When she came back into her room, Aunt Sofia gave her a robe and Amira gave her the last of the pomegranates and Keziah sat down on her new bed and told them both, "I will kill him."

"Hamsa," Aunt Sofia said, not quite a question, and then with faint doubt, "Or Rayam?"

"Hamsa," Keziah told her, keeping her tone cool. She peeled the pomegranate delicately open with the tip of a shadow claw, which was strictly forbidden, and carefully ate one seed. The taste burst over her tongue, completely different from the taste of fresh blood.

"Yes. Hansa is clever, and good at hiding what he does," Aunt Sofia said thoughtfully. "But he does not need to be as good at hiding what he does as you need to be at hiding what you do. If your father finds out what he did to you, he'll punish Hamsa. But you he will kill. Or again, if you kill Hamsa and your father realizes your hand held the knife, he will kill you."

Keziah said nothing. She knew all this was true.

"Once you are married to one of ibn Abdel's human sons, you would be safe from Hamsa," Aunt Sofia added. Her eyes were calm, her mouth secretive.

"If I go to ibn Abdel's palace, Hamsa will be safe from me," Keziah said. "And I will not leave Amira."

"Well, it would not serve anyway. The black wolves of ibn Abdel's household will be no better and may be worse, and of course a human son could not protect you . . ."

"I will protect myself," Keziah said softly, savagely. "I will kill them all."

"Yes!" Amira agreed, coming to her feet with a grace no five-year-old human could have owned. "I will help!"

Keziah smiled at her sister, surprised to find an odd, soft feeling underlying her savage satisfaction at this declaration. "Good, good," she crooned softly. "Yes, little sister, you will help me. Together we will kill them all."

"Ambitious," murmured Aunt Sofia. "Dangerous."

"We are not strong," agreed Keziah. "We are too young." Amira made a tiny sound of protest, and she smiled at her sister. "As we are not as strong, we must be clever. We *will* be very clever, and so when Uncle Hamsa dies, no one will know it was us." She turned then to Aunt Sofia, expectantly. "*You* are clever," she said to her, knowing it was true. "*You* will think of a way."

Aunt Sofia smiled at her, looking daringly into Keziah's face. "When you were born, I alone was not dismayed that you were a girl. I was pleased, for I knew then that if your father let you live, you would grow to be as a knife pointed at his heart. When he murdered Kalila, I mourned my sister, but I knew you would someday avenge her. When you took Amira, I was glad, for a girl needs allies and none are better than sisters. Listen, then, heart-child, knife-child, sister-daughter. I will teach you to think of a way yourself. Cleverness is a woman's weapon. Your father and your uncles are so strong they do not believe they need to be clever. But a woman must be clever if she will defeat a man. I will teach you to think."

"And Uncle Hamsa?" Keziah said impatiently. "I will not have him to touch me again."

"Sometimes a woman must be patient with suffering. You are a black wolf, daughter of my sister. Nothing he does to you will leave a mark on your body. That is a great thing for a woman, for you may hate him and hate what he does, but you need not *fear* him. To achieve your vengeance, are you willing to suffer and be patient? You must decide, for if you are careless or hasty, he will surely kill you and you will win nothing. And Amira will die as well, as your father will not want any black wolf daughter once he understands you could be dangerous to him."

Keziah studied her aunt. A human woman had no weapons of her own, no way to protect herself against anything, no shadow to carry away pain and injury. Keziah had known human women suffered, but she had not cared. Now she thought of Uncle Youssef's Russian woman, of the other women who were used for the pleasure of her uncles and her father. The women who conceived in pain and bore their sons in pain, and whose daughters would be slaves like their mothers and live without even hope of vengeance. She found a part of herself could pity them after all. Nor did she blame Aunt Sofia for wanting to use Keziah to take vengeance of her own on this household. That part made perfect sense.

She turned her own hands over, studying her fingers, bringing out her shadow claws and then causing them to subside once more. She thought of Uncle Hamsa's face, carved open by those claws...but he was so much stronger. She could see no way to touch him.

But Aunt Sofia would teach her to find a way.

"I will be patient," she said at last. Patience was not an easy thing for a black wolf, and harder still when she thought again of Uncle Hamsa. Of his breath and weight and his fists, of the way he had forced her to keep to her weak human form while he did as he wished to her. She refused to think of him, yet she could not think of anything else. She said fiercely, "But I will not be *too* patient."

Aunt Sofia smiled. "Do not be afraid. Hamsa will not dare kill you, and anything else you can endure. Endurance is a woman's strength and her weapon. You will think of a way. You will think: 'What will he do? And if I act in this way, or that way, what will he do then?' You will learn to understand him. You will learn to make him think what you wish him to think, and when you kill him, he will know that you were his enemy after all and not his prey, and he will be astonished."

"Yes," Keziah said fiercely. "Yes."

That was the end of her childhood, that night and the dawn that followed. That was the end of her slavery, though neither her father nor her uncles knew it.

The marriage to one of ibn Abdel's human sons did not occur. The negotiations lasted almost a year, but in the end ibn Abdel could not come to an agreement with Keziah's father.

Keziah knew this because she had learned to slip into the men's part of the house so she could listen to what they said when they thought no woman listened. It was very important to be careful, to remain unseen. She learned to move gently and breath softly, how to give her weight to her shadow so her footsteps were utterly silent, how to pull the lesser shadows around her greater shadow so that she always moved concealed. Fear taught her all these things. Necessity taught her. So she knew that any of ibn Abdel's human sons would have liked to take a princess for a wife, but even when pressed by their father, none of them dared take a black wolf girl.

They were thus proven cowards and Keziah despised them, but she was glad the negotiations failed. If she had gone into ibn Abdel's household it would have been more difficult to kill Uncle Hamsa. Besides, she did not think her husband would have allowed Amira to accompany her, except perhaps as a second wife, and Amira, now six, was still three years away from marriageable age.

And besides that, she did not want to lose Aunt Sofia's counsel. By the end of the year of negotiations, Keziah had come to truly understand how wise Aunt Sofia was in the ways of men and women, how wise in the ways of masters and slaves, and how subtle in her long designs. By then, Keziah had also realized that Aunt Sofia had *always* intended to wield Princess Kalila's daughters as the weapons of her own vengeance. That long intention was a thing of humans and not of black wolves. But Keziah learned it of Aunt Sofia.

Long intention was something she needed to learn, for Uncle Hamsa came to her room whenever he thought he could do so unobserved. He disgusted and frightened and repulsed Keziah, but Aunt Sofia taught her to hide what she felt, how to pretend to be witless and then how to pretend to be dead. How to pretend she was resigned and then that she did not care. How to think of the empty desert where she would go afterward to run and hunt and tear down prey of her own. Aunt Sofia helped her get out of the house and then back in unseen, and Keziah learned to bury her rage beneath the endless sand and rock and wind. Once she had learned all these lessons well, Uncle Hamsa gradually stopped forcing himself on her because he thought she did not care enough to suffer as he wanted.

Truly, Uncle Hamsa was very stupid. Like any man, he saw in a woman only what he wished to see: a poor wit and a weak will and a broken spirit.

So finally Keziah found the means and the moment to lay out her trap for him, like a snare laid out for a cruel and dangerous desert eagle. Aunt Sofia helped her think of it. Aunt Sofia asked questions, and taught Keziah to ask questions, too. What did Uncle Hamsa fear? What did any man fear? What did he want? What did any man want?

"He fears those more powerful than he, like your father, but that is not what he fears most," Aunt Sofia explained to Keziah. "A black wolf man need not think of what slaves or women think or feel. But a woman must be able to think as a man thinks, see the world as he sees it. Look through Hamsa's eyes and you will know what he fears most."

As she learned to follow this advice, Keziah came eventually to understand what Uncle Hamsa feared. He feared *women.* He feared any hint of a crack in the mastery he held over the women of the household. Maimed as he was, he was nearly least among the men. All black wolf men wanted to be feared by women, but this was Hamsa's weakness: that he cared also whether he was respected. He feared the *scorn* of women.

And he particularly feared the disdain of black wolf women, because human slaves were less than nothing, but a black wolf woman was almost a person. That was why, when he'd realized Keziah was becoming a woman, he had wanted to make her less even than a slave. That was why he had lost interest in her once he believed he had succeeded

"He is *weak,"* Keziah said to Aunt Sofia in astonishment once she realized this. "He is afraid not only of my father, but of *me."*

Aunt Sofia nodded. "He is strong," she corrected Keziah. "But his strength is brittle, like a knife made of flawed steel. If he is dealt the right blow, like a flawed knife he will shatter."

"How do we do it." Amira asked eagerly. "How do we strike the right kind of blow?"

Keziah smiled, because she knew now the shape of the trap she would lay for her enemy. "But we need a weapon," she said to Aunt Sofia. "He is stronger than we are—and he can force us into human shape. We need a weapon that can make him weak; a weapon that can force *him* into human shape. We need a knife of burning silver."

"I will get you such a knife," Aunt Sofia promised. "A knife with a silver blade and a hilt wrapped in leather and steel wire, that you may told it without danger to your hands." Her dark eyes gleamed. She was never precisely happy. Happiness was not a woman's privilege; not in a black wolf's house in Riyadh. But she was pleased. She was very pleased. Keziah understood this. It was the satisfaction of a woman who had suffered for a long time in patience and now saw the time coming when her enemies would suffer instead.

Never before had Keziah thought of her own newly womanly shape as a weapon. She had seen this only as a problem; a thing that made her father think of how best to sell her and Uncle Hamsa think of her at all. But once she understood Uncle Hamsa, she knew immediately how he would feel if she dressed, not to hide her body, but to accent the swell of her breasts and the curve of her hip. This was the way a helpless human woman might dress because her only safety lay in pleasing a man and making him her protector. All her life she had seen this, but she had never understood.

Now she understood. She knew exactly how Uncle Hamsa would feel if she dressed in that way and then caught his eye and gave him the kind of look a woman gives a man. First the look a woman gives a man she desires. Then the heavy-lidded sideways look she gives a man she scorns.

The slave women had showed her these things. Keziah had paid little heed. She was not one of them. They were not her kind. But all the women were the same in this: they were all hated and desired by men. And now Keziah found she understood the weapons of a woman better than she had guessed, for she had learned from the human women of the household without ever knowing what she learned.

So Keziah dressed herself carefully, accenting her eyes and lips and cheekbones as the slave women did, as Aunt Sofia taught her. But the silver knife she gave to Amira. That part would be her sister's. That part could not belong to Keziah.

"You he will not expect at all," Keziah told her sister. "Even if he realizes you are there, he will not care. Never in life would he expect you to have such a weapon, for you will be behind me, where I cannot see you. What black wolf would let another hold such a weapon at his back?"

Amira grinned fiercely. She was slim and graceful in her human form; small and almost delicate in her shadow form.

But though she was a child, her shadow was strong and she was quick. Though the men of their family held girls in contempt, Amira was born to hunt and kill—and she hated Uncle Hamsa as much as Keziah hated him—and Keziah trusted her. Men could not trust one another, but sisters were different. Keziah had learned that, at least. Aunt Sofia had been right from the beginning. For a woman, a sister was the best ally.

So the end it was not difficult to kill Uncle Hamsa. The difficult part lay in luring him out into the desert, for killing him in the house would have been too dangerous. Even that was not actually difficult. Keziah merely passed by Uncle Hamsa when the women brought out the food for the evening banquet on the holiday of Eid al-Adha. Of course her father and uncles did not care about the holiday itself; such things mattered to humans, not to black wolves. Still, her father made the gesture of providing roasted lamb for anyone who came to their villa's compound before feasting himself, and so the meal was served late and everyone was hungry. Keziah brought the very best platter of roasted lamb to the table herself, but though she served her father first, she served her beautiful cousin Malik, Uncle Ahmed's eldest son, with a special smile—one that she had practiced before Amira and Aunt Sofia. Amira had laughed when Keziah smiled so. Aunt Sofia had not.

Now Keziah turned with swaying hips and gazed over her shoulder with heavy-eyed desire toward Malik. And then she turned as though by chance to catch Uncle Hamsa's eye, and on him she turned a glance of such scorn and contempt as no woman should dare show any man. Only a flickering glance, and only for Uncle Hamsa to see. He did see it. She knew. He hid his anger. Uncle Hamsa never showed his rage to his brothers or their sons for fear of their mockery. But Keziah felt it even across the banquet hall.

He came for her that night. Of course he did. But she fled the way she had prepared, out into the courtyard and up the palm tree, through the window and out, across the rooftops and down into the wild desert. She fled first in black wolf form and then in human form as Uncle Hamsa forced the change on her, but she had known she would have to run this way in her human form. She had practiced for it.

Uncle Hamsa pursued her. But he was too angry to be suspicious; too angry to suspect a trap even when he ought to have wondered at the certainty of her flight. Keziah did not get very far from the house. But she did not have to get very far. Only to the wadi that cut through the earth, and the shadows of the rocks where Amira was waiting.

Then she fell. She fell among the shadows of the rocks. But she turned and lifted herself on her elbow and laughed with scorn, and Uncle Hamsa came after her and bent down and seized her. He was far, far too angry to feel the waiting silver. And when he bent over Keziah, Amira slid delicately out of the shadows where she had been hiding and stabbed the knife into his back, low, to strike for the kidney.

Amira let go of the knife at once as Uncle Hamsa convulsed and screamed. She left it in his back, ripping at him with her claws as he tried to turn and get away, then tried to reach back and grasp the handle of the knife. He tried all of that at once, in a desperate bloody scramble. But freed from his control, Keziah shifted and tore at his belly and he screamed again, his form stuttering between human and black wolf and back again to human as his shadow tried to carry away the injuries. It could not take away the knife wound. Injuries dealt by silver could not be carried away, and the knife still stood in his back. From the moment Amira struck, he was a dead man. Only it took some time for him to die. Time enough for him to understand that this was not chance or happenstance. Time enough for him to understand what Keziah and Amira had done.

"So much blood!" Amira whispered, crouching to withdraw the knife.

Keziah nodded, intensely satisfied. "You did very well, my sister. Take the knife—carefully. Would you like me to take it? Are your hands burned?"

"I am not hurt at all," Amira declared, as though surprised to realize it. "Uncle Hamsa is dead and we aren't hurt at all!"

"So it will be with them all," Keziah declared. "Let the jackals tear his flesh! Let the vultures follow the sunrise down to the desert and find him here! Let nothing remain but the smell of blood and ash! When our father discovers his body, let it be torn and ruined so no one can see how he died. Here, see, I will tear the body so the knife wound does not show so plainly. You have the knife—good! Put it away carefully, *ukhti as-saghira.* Tomorrow we will begin understanding Uncle Youssef, so that we can make a way to kill him, too."

"Not Uncle Youssef next," Amira demurred. "Uncle Ahmed. He is stronger than Uncle Youssef. Or maybe Cousin Malik. Did you see how he looked at you tonight? After you looked at him? He is dangerous, Keziah! Dangerous to you especially!"

"Perhaps," Keziah conceded. She had not thought of that possibility when she had chosen to look with hot desire at her cousin. Now she could see she had been foolish. He was a very young man, yes, but a man, vicious as any man. She already knew their father would not protect her—that no one would protect her. Amira was right: Cousin Malik was dangerous.

But it did not matter. Keziah knew now she would keep the vow she had made on the day of her sister's birth and her mother's death. She would kill them all.

But she looked at her little sister and smiled, because she knew also that she would not face all her enemies alone.

Keziah and Amira waited all through the next day for the news of Uncle Hamsa's death to run through the household. They waited to see what their father would do, what Uncle Ahmed and Uncle Youssef and Uncle Rayan would do. They waited for fury and questions. Keziah told Amira not to be afraid. She explained again why none of the men would suspect girls—even black wolf girls. She explained this not because Amira needed to hear it, but because she needed to hear herself say it.

But nothing happened. All day the household was quiet. The body was found; what was left of it. Much damaged; jackals or wolves had indeed found it. Men went out in grim silence and came back with the torn remains of the body. But whatever they thought had befallen Uncle Hamsa, no one explained anything to women. The news came at last to the woman's side of the house with an unexpected twist.

"The Quiet War," Aunt Sofia murmured when she brought the black wolf girls their supper. "Zara served the meat tonight and that is the word she brought us. The men think this was a move in the Soft War with the *khafash*. Hamsa's body was found close to this house. Too close perhaps for safety, for if enemies dare strike so close, next they may be through the very walls." Smiling, she laid out dishes of chicken in cream, saffron rice with tart barberries, and rounds of tameez bread.

"The Quiet War," Keziah repeated, rolling the words across her tongue. "The Soft War. "The khafash?" This sounded mysterious and exciting. She tried to imagine who the khafash might be. It was not a name she had heard before. Who were these people who might be engaged in a subtle war against her father? Whom might he blame for a death when there was no evidence of anything but jackals and vultures? A prince, perhaps. Some relative of Kalila's, offended by her father's pretense to royalty he did not truly possess. Or someone like ibn Abdel, who constantly strove to surpass other Arabic black wolves in wealth and power.

But Aunt Sofia said, "That is a name for the people of blood. You have heard of the people of blood? They are all shadow where you black wolves are half shadow. They fill the empty bodies of the dead and rise up to hunt the living. It seems the truce between the dark kindreds has been broken." She sounded uncertain herself on this last. "I have heard of the khafash, but not of this truce. But I think that is what your father believes. That the people of blood have begun to hunt black wolves here—black wolves of powerful families, where any blow they strike will be felt most deeply. It is not altogether a foolish notion, perhaps. If the people of blood did move against us here in Riyadh, your father's household probably would be targeted among the first, as he is wealthy and powerful, but not royal."

"The...people of blood?" Amira asked doubtfully. "They are shadow all through?" She looked at Keziah.

Keziah did not know either, so she nodded to Aunt Sofia, a regal nod as though she, Keziah, could answer if she chose but preferred Aunt Sofia to explain.

Aunt Sofia inclined her head. "So it is said. They do not ordinarily come into Saudi Arabia, these blood-drinkers, these khafash. They dwell in Africa, far to the south where the land is less desert and the great trees shade the earth. Or again, many rule in Bulgaria and Romania and such cold lands. They do not come across the Red Sea or the Black Sea or the Mediterranean."

It took a moment for Keziah to remember those names, which Aunt Sofia spoke in English. She knew them better by their Arabic names: the *Al-Bahr Al'Ahmar* and the *Al-Bahr Al'Aswad* and the *Al-Bahr Al'Abyad Almutawassit.* These were the little seas that lay between Saudi Arabia and neighboring lands, and the rest of the world. Keziah said, "Yet perhaps they do cross the water. Or why would my father believe they had killed Uncle Hamsa?"

"The men fear the khafash," Aunt Sofia answered simply. "This I know. When I was a child, my mother told us that the people of blood do not rule, but ruin. They do not wish to have and build power, but to corrupt and spoil. But now Zara says the men spoke of this Quiet War and of the people of blood and the breaking of the long truce. I will listen. We will all listen. If the people of blood are killing black wolf men . . ." her voice trailed off; she would not finish that thought aloud. But she smiled.

So did Keziah. So, after the barest moment, did Amira. "Yes," she whispered. "I see! If the khafash are killing black wolf men, then the khafash may be blamed when any black wolf man dies!"

This was exactly right. Keziah looked proudly at her little sister, and Aunt Sofia nodded and murmured,

"Confusion among one's enemies is as much a weapon as a silver knife. We will all watch and listen, and soon you will lay another trap before one of your uncles, a snare for him to step into while he is looking over his shoulder for enemies behind him. The people of blood kill slowly, taking blood and life from their prey. Knowing this, how will you kill to make it seem certain the death came from the fangs of the khafash?"

When the question was posed that way, the answer was obvious. Blood could be carried away by water, and the readiest place with drains and water was the men's pool, which was without the household compound but separate from the main house; screened behind lattice and surrounded by palms and oleander. Women were not, of course, permitted near the pool. But everyone knew men sometimes took a woman there, late at night when a man could be private. And everyone knew the man most likely to bend the household rules in that way was Uncle Rayan.

That made everything simple.

Uncle Rayan was not clever like Uncle Ahmed; not careful like Uncle Youssef. No. Uncle Rayan was stupid. Also, he was one of those who preferred the youngest girls. Girls too young even for child-marriage, girls of seven or eight. Girls Amira's age.

Uncle Rayan bought such girls at the Evening Market. But he could not do so as often as he wished because Uncle Ahmed thought it a waste of household funds, so sometimes he took a girl from the household. He would not ordinarily have dared touch a daughter of his brother. But a black wolf daughter...the second and even more useless of two black wolf daughters...when such a temptation was presented to him temptingly enough, how could he resist? If the way looked easy and smooth...after all, everyone knew Amira was not a *valuable* daughter. Amira was kept so much out of the way that probably Uncle Rayan did not even know her name. Probably he did not know her by sight at all.

So the time and place were obvious enough, and the lure was simple. The danger to Amira was not great, because any injury Uncle Rayan dealt her could be given to her shadow—indeed, he could not hurt her too much without forcing the change.

Hiding the silver knife so Uncle Rayan wouldn't feel its presence, that seemed at first impossible, but actually turned out to be simple as well. Keziah buried the knife in the grit below the palms, its fire muted by a gold tray she stole for the purpose.

So at first everything was very easy. Keziah was certain Uncle Rayan couldn't resist the bait Amira offered. Men never resisted such lures. Indeed, he did not resist it. Amira put herself in his way twice and again over the course of a day, and once she'd caught his eye, she made sure Uncle Rayan thought he saw her slipping into the pool enclosure for an illicit swim. Of course he followed.

So the ambush started very well. But as soon as Keziah moved to carry out her part of the plan, everything became suddenly very much more complicated.

The trouble came first because of Keziah's mistake. Amira's first cry of uncalculated fear made Keziah move too soon, lest she leave her move too late and allow Amira to come to harm. She *knew* Amira was not so vulnerable as a human child, but still she moved, and, more quickly when her second cry held pain as well as fear. The gravel scattered with a shower of little sounds when Keziah retrieved the silver knife; more gravel gritted underfoot as Keziah hurled herself forward; she was in too much of a hurry to be as quiet as she should have been. Uncle Rayan heard her. He should have been too stupid and too focused on Amira to heed anything, but it turned out he was not quite that stupid. He hurled Amira away and spun around, and fast as she was, Keziah was not quite close enough to stab him.

She feinted and dodged, but she couldn't shift; there wasn't time and besides she would have had to drop the knife. Amira was shifting, but too slowly; Uncle Rayan, snarling furiously, was already half in his black wolf shape. Foolish, foolish, Keziah knew she should have thought of something to do in case the first blow went awry.

She dodged again, and Uncle Rayan roared, and then *Uncle Youssef* charged into the pool enclosure, gravel scattering and steam hissing up from the damp tiles as his great clawed feet touched them.

Both Keziah and Amira should both have died right there, torn to pieces by male fury. But Amira, still mostly in her tiny, vulnerable little-girl form, scrambled sideways to get behind Youssef, and Keziah flung her little sister the knife while she herself leaped straight at Rayan's face, shifting as fast as she could, threatening his eyes to make him focus on her. Youssef reared up, massive and terrible, to destroy Keziah, but then he screamed as Amira sank the knife into his side and tore it across his spine with strength that would have been utterly beyond any truly human girl her size. Black ichor was followed by red blood as Youssef body contorted into human shape—his shadow was trying to take away the injury, but wounds dealt by silver could not be given away.

It was so fast. Before Keziah, half stunned by what had happened, could entirely realize that Youssef was dead, Uncle Rayan struck her. She felt him behind her at the last moment, his massiveness and the wave of heat that came from him, and she *nearly* dodged, but not quite. The blow smashed bones up and down her left side. Keziah couldn't scream; pain stopped her breath; she was forced back into her human form far too quickly as her shadow carried away the crushing injuries.

For a few terrifying seconds, Keziah was blind with lingering pain and the shock of the forced change. Even so, she rolled fast to the side and scrambled to her feet, reaching for the change of body. She couldn't shift. Everyone knew sudden serious injury would force the change, but she hadn't realized it could stop her from shifting back again, didn't know how long that would last. But Uncle Rayan didn't kill her, not yet, which meant he wasn't after her, which probably meant he was after *Amira.* Keziah blinked and shook her head, trying to recover her vision and sense by sheer force of will.

Her sister cried out, a thin sound of fury and terror and pain. Keziah saw Uncle Rayan mainly as a huge black bulk, halfway between human and black wolf, his eyes burning red and his misshapen form wreathed with steam. But his hands were almost human and he held Amira, he held her pinned against the floor though she struggled. In his other hand he held the silver-bladed knife.

He said something to Amira, a low growl, and the knife moved, flashing through the white veils of steam. The little girl shrieked.

Keziah flung herself forward across gravel and tile, at the last second realized Uncle Rayan was using Amira as bait, and barely ducked a raking blow, dodged again, rolled sideways, caught up a handful of gravel to fling at his face, and dropped low to slash at his legs and feet. She doubted she had dealt much injury, but there was gritty ripping sound and a loud splash, and Amira arrowed across the pool in her sleek human form and lunged out on the other side, turned and threw a bar of silver fire that rose up...and arced across the pool...and Keziah lunged, together with Uncle Rayan, but she had understood first and she was faster, and she caught the knife by its burning blade. She bit her lip against a cry of pain as she shifted her grip and whirled and held it out, and Rayan ran heavily onto the blade before he could stop himself, and Keziah jerked the knife upward with all her strength even as his weight knocked her into the pool.

Uncle Rayan was making small sounds when she came up, gasping and tossing her head to get her hair out of her eyes—obviously he was not dead, and Keziah's stomach clenched in case he should come after her again. But then she saw the knife still in him, high up under his ribs where her last effort had forced it. Rayan was on his knees, clawing at his own stomach, blood coming out of his mouth. Blood was everywhere, the blood that was supposed to all be in the pool or rinsed away. Keziah did not know what kinds of bodies the khafash left behind them when they came and went, but nothing in the pool enclosure suggested anything but black wolf violence. Surely they had made enough noise to bring the whole household down on them—they had to get out of this place—if there was still time to get out, and she feared there could not be. She looked for Amira –

– and found her sister in human form, but running toward Uncle Rayan and not away. Half of Amira's face was masked with blood, but her snarl held fury rather than pain and she ducked and seized the knife, tore it free of Rayan's body, and slashed it across his throat, dodging his weak attempt to defend himself with contemptuous ease. Uncle Rayan opened his mouth, but no sound came out. He crumpled forward, and Aunt Sofia ran in.

Aunt Sofia was running with tiny cautious steps, her dress gathered up and her slippers almost silent on the tiles. She cast one comprehensive glance over the whole scene, snatched the knife from Amira, flung it down next to Rayan's body, and pushed Amira into the pool. Amira, too surprised to resist, splashed ineffectually for a few seconds and then swam across to join Keziah, who was just pulling herself from the water on the other side of the pool.

Keziah lifted her little sister out of the pool and put her arm around her, cautiously, in case Amira could not tolerate the touch of another black wolf. But Amira clung to her. So she held her and did not let go. Keziah was furious and afraid and worried about the vicious cut all down Amira's face, from just below one eye to the corner of her mouth. She started to ask Aunt Sofia about that, about what to do for a silver injury, but Aunt Sofia shook her head, lifting a finger to her lips just as, with a roar and a shimmer of furious fire, all the other black wolves of the household arrived.

Or nearly all. It seemed like all of them in that first moment. Keziah's father was at the forefront, and Uncle Ahmed was with him, and Cousin Malik and Cousin Saleh, and also a handful of human men, but they did not matter. Keziah's father was the one that mattered. He had shifted halfway, into a grotesque form larger and stronger than any human man. Keziah had not known it was possible to shift partway and then stop, but he had done it, and held in one hand a weapon like a sword, with a steel hilt and a silver edge.

Uncle Ahmed was in human shape, but not much less frightening for that; huge and wreathed in fire. The cousins were mostly in black wolf form, shouldering forward to stare at the blood with burning eyes that promised violence. But no matter how terrifying they all were, Keziah's father was still the one that mattered.

Keziah shuddered with the effort not to run. Running would not help anything now.

Her father slowly looked from one side of the pool enclosure to the other, taking in Youssef's body near the other door and Rayan's body near the edge of the pool; the silver knife lying by him, the splashes of smoking black ichor and sticky crimson blood, and on the other side of the pool, Keziah and Amira kneeling together, their nightclothes soaking wet and blood still running sluggishly down Amira's face.

Keziah had no idea what to say.

Aunt Sofia turned out to be a much better liar than Keziah had realized. Cleverer, too. Aunt Sofia clasped her hands together in a pose of terrified supplication, fixed her wide dark eyes submissively on the bloody tiles, and swore she had seen everything, every detail of the fight between Uncle Rayan and Uncle Youssef that had left both black wolf men dead. Keziah knelt with her hand resting lightly on Amira's shivering back and listened in amazement.

"Rayan wanted the little one, the one the women call Amira, but she is so little, only recently has she turned seven," whispered Aunt Sofia. "But what could I do? Rayan said I must bring her here. So I brought her, but first I cut her, I borrowed Youssef's knife and cut her so he would not want her. He was so angry. But Youssef found out why I had taken his knife. He came here also. He was very angry also, but not with me. I am only a weak and foolish woman, so what could I do but what I did? He was angry with Rayan. He quarreled with him, and they fought."

"*You* cut the girl?" said Keziah's father. He studied

Amira. He had returned to human form, all the men had, but he looked hardly less dangerous for that. Keziah didn't know whether he had ever looked at his younger daughter before, but he stared at her now. Amira cowered, seeming tiny and even younger than her seven years.

Aunt Sofia looked anxiously from the girls to the black wolf men and wrung her hands, trembling. "I did not know what else to do, *Rayiysi*. Rayan said I must bring her. But it would have been wrong to let him so use your own daughter."

"And then he and Youssef fought?" Keziah's father surveyed the scene again, grimly, this time never quite looking at Amira. He was frowning, angry and perhaps suspicious. "Over the girl?"

"Oh, no, not just because of the child." Aunt Sofia answered as though surprised by the suggestion. "Youssef was angry because he said Rayan was foolish to unsettle the household in times of trouble, and he was angry because it was his knife that had cut your daughter, and the—the smell of black wolf blood, even a girl's, he said it was not wise to shed blood when there might be khafash nearby watching for signs of weakness. And Rayan said the child was not good for anything else and it was all very well for a man who had his own woman, even a heavy pale overblown woman. That is what he said. I knew then they would fight, *Rayiysi,* and so I—I tried to keep the girls away. I pushed them in the pool and—and I *tried* to stop your brothers, truly, but what could I do? I am only a woman."

Keziah found this account perfectly unbelievable, but Aunt Sofia told it with total conviction, just as though it was entirely true. Keziah could see, peering covertly up through her lashes, that the male black wolves believed it. Her father looked back and forth between the two bodies with heavy scorn. Then he stared once more across the pool toward the girls. Then he said to Aunt Sofia, "You should not have cut my daughter with a silver knife. Look at her. That will scar badly. She is completely useless to me now."

"I—I did not know what else to do," whispered Aunt

Sofia. “If he had taken her, she would have been likewise ruined for any proper marriage. What man would want her after Rayan had her?”

“Stupid woman,” Keziah’s father said contemptuously. “Nothing he did to her would have marked her. Now this daughter of mine is marked forever. You should have come to me.”

“I—I didn’t think you—he was your brother—he ordered me –” Aunt Sofia wrung her hands again, sounding for all the world like she was truly devastated over what had happened, and half-witted besides.

Keziah’s father swept the sword he still held up and around and cut off Aunt Sofia’s head. The blow was so fast and so unexpected that at first Keziah didn’t understand what he had done, what she had seen him do. It seemed to take a long time for Aunt Sofia’s head to strike the tiles and roll grotesquely away into the oleander, for her body to crumple, for the blood to pour out. Next to Keziah, Amira stopped shivering, holding perfectly still, and after an instant Keziah understood her little sister was waiting to see whether their father would kill her, too. Aunt Sofia for the crime of marking her, Amira for the crime of bearing a disfiguring scar that would render her not only utterly useless but also unsightly.

For a long moment, their father stared across the pool at them. Then, perhaps judging that it would be too much trouble to stride around the pool to kill Amira, he turned away and began to give orders to other men: to clean up the pool enclosure and to see to his brothers’ bodies. As far as Keziah could tell, he had completely dismissed both his daughters from his attention. If he had ever wondered about her own presence here, utterly ignored by Aunt Sofia, he did not care enough to demand answers. Lest he might yet think of questions to ask, she touched Amira lightly on the arm and drew her little sister after her, away. Out of sight and away.

After that the household seemed different. Quieter. Grimmer. In the women’s quarters, Youssef’s Russian woman wept, and her daughters wept with her. Keziah wanted to command them to be quiet. But she felt oddly like she almost understood them, and even, more strangely, she felt as though she owed those women tolerance. Uncle Youssef had been their protector, as much as any woman had a protector in Riyadh. Now they had no male who cared whether they lived or died, and though neither Keziah's father nor Uncle Ahmed was likely to notice them, neither would trouble to protect them from the male cousins.

Their father sent for Amira and examined her face, so Keziah had to wait in fear to see whether her sister would return to the woman's quarters. Keziah had done everything wrong; she saw this now. She should have forgotten vengeance and vows, she should have taken Amira and fled as soon as her little sister was old enough....Only it would have been impossible. Their father would never have permitted his possessions to escape him.

So then she thought she should have planned to kill their father first of all, before even Uncle Hamsa.

Only then Uncle Ahmed would have been lord of the household, and he was clever and disciplined; more clever and disciplined than her father, the most dangerous of all the uncles.

So then Keziah did not know what else she should have done. Except be cleverer and plan better and not let things go wrong. She saw she had not thought enough about what to do after taking vengeance; about how to flee and survive. Aunt Sofia might have thought more on these things. Now Keziah must think and be clever, or in the end she and Amira would surely both die. If they survived this night.

Their father did not kill Amira. Zara stitched up Amira's wound with black silk, the way a human's wound might be stitched. Aunt Sofia would have done a better job, Keziah was certain. Zara's work was neat enough, but she said the wound would scar. There was nothing any of them could do about that.

Even with the black silk stitches vivid across her face, their father did not kill Amira. Keziah's little sister returned, pale and silent, but safe. As safe as any of them. Keziah touched her hand and wished she could take her little sister hunting in the desert. But with the household wary and upset and without Aunt Sofia to keep watch, even that was impossible.

So Keziah began to spend much time drifting softly through the men's part of the villa, silent and listening. She tried to be very careful, but she knew she had to find things out. Without Aunt Sofia, how would she ever know what the men were thinking and saying and planning? She had not realized before how much information Aunt Sofia had collected and shared, or how much all the women had depended on her to tell them what was happening in the men's part of the villa. So Keziah learned to hide, and sneak, and draw up shadows to hide herself. It was *like* hunting, but different. It pleased her to think of her father and Uncle Ahmed as her prey, though it also frightened her to think of them that way.

The cousins were less frightening and noisier and more foolish, and Keziah listened more to them. Malik and Saad were the leaders among the young men, and Saleh sometimes. Atif was quieter than the others. Keziah thought he would eventually become the master of the household, for all Malik strutted and reminded the others he was the elder son of the eldest brother of her father. But even he did not look closely enough into the shadows to find Keziah listening there.

As her face healed and the blood smell faded, Amira began to follow her on these forays. Keziah taught her little sister all that she had learned. She taught her to give her weight into her shadow so she could walk in total silence; to make herself into a hollow place in the air; to pretend she was emptiness, was dust, was nothing. Amira practiced on the human women until she learned to make even a quick, fearful eye look past her; and then she practiced on Keziah because the senses of a black wolf were harder to confuse than those of a human. Then she began to venture into the men's part of the villa.

"Softly. Softly," Keziah cautioned her little sister. "Patience is hard, I know. But above everything we must rule impatience, for it can kill us as surely as—more surely than—any other foolishness. We have seen now how careful we must be, and how patient. We must practice being quiet, being nothing, for in the end we must cross the empty lands unseen so that we may escape."

Amira listened to her and nodded earnestly. "Where will we go?"

"Oh…France," Keziah said almost at random. She knew that beautiful clothing and jewelry came from France. "We will cross the empty lands and the seas and go to Paris. That is the city that is the heart of France. There is no sand there, no desert. It is a cold land where there are no kings and black wolves must be cautious. That is what the slaves say. Even if our cousins seek us there, they must be cautious. We will be clever and quiet and they will never find us."

"Is Paris very far away?"

Keziah hardly knew. She said, "We will find maps and look. We will plan how to go. We will take jewelry and money so we can buy everything we need." As she said this, she realized how little she had prepared and how much more clever she must be, and the realization almost overwhelmed her. But she said confidently, "We will have time. First we must kill Uncle Ahmed and our father. And Malik as well, and perhaps some of the other cousins. While we plan that, we shall also plan the rest."

Amira listened to her and tried to do everything she said. Keziah tried hard to be right in everything lest she mislead her sister into disaster a second time. She feared discovery for her sister's sake more than for her own, for she could not believe their father would forgive Amira anything now that she was scarred. It dawned on her gradually that this fierce protectiveness must be what a human meant by *fondness*. It was a strange realization. It made her feel a little more familiar with the human slaves of the household; a little more mindful. A little more kind.

In their quiet listening, in their discreet search for maps

and papers, both Keziah and Amira learned more about the Quiet War and about the khafash. The other women heard a word here and there, and they murmured together of what they heard, and to this gossip as well Keziah listened carefully. Keziah began to put together an idea of people of blood and of the Quiet War. She had not managed to blame Rayan's death on the khafash as she had originally planned, but it had not been a stupid idea. A black wolf cartel in Yemen was known to have lost several sons to the people of blood; likewise a cartel in the Emirates. So, closer to home, had a family in Jeddah and a cartel in Medina.

The khafash were a little like black wolves. They did not touch silver. They made ordinary humans into their slaves and their cattle, but worse than black wolves, for they made their slaves into creatures less than human. Keziah did not know exactly what this meant; frustratingly, nothing she heard or read explained it. But she understood that the khafash would not suffer rivals. They killed any that opposed them. They killed by spilling blood; they killed by corrupting flesh; they killed in ways that Keziah did not understand. But she thought about ways to make death look like it came from the hands of the people of blood. She thought about this all the time.

The Quiet War had begun some time before; Keziah could not tell how long, for no one spoke of that. It had not touched Saudi Arabia at all, not for a long time. Neither Saudi Arabia nor Jordan nor Iraq, nor Oman nor Yemen nor Egypt nor any important country. It had been a war far away, on the other side of the world, in America. The black wolves there had begun it. Then the war had spread to Europe, even to France. In a way this was useful, for the black wolves of Europe were in disarray and surely had little attention to spare for hunting two Saudi girls—if she and Amira could get so far. She knew better now how far France was, and how many lands lay between, and she feared the khafash might have very much attention bent toward hunting black wolves. Even girls.

Now the war had come here, too. Only a little so far, but

her father and remaining uncle thought it would get worse. Again Keziah thought that in one way this might be useful and in another way dangerous.

"Dimilioc's war," her father declared in disgust, speaking to Uncle Ahmed, one evening when Keziah was concealed and listening. She did not know the word, *Dimilioc,* and tucked it away to remember. "It's bad for us all. Did the *vampires* trouble us here?" He used an English word Keziah did not know, but plainly he meant the khafash. "No," he continued. "The desert lands have always been ours. Now there is all...*this.*"

Keziah heard the heavy thump as her father struck a table or wall on that last word. She was always listening these days, while Amira guarded the way back into the woman's part of the villa. Or Amira listened and Keziah guarded her little sister's retreat. Sometimes one and sometimes the other. That was fair.

Her father went on, "And now my household has fewer strong black wolves to face any threat. We should all come together for a great hunt, *all* of us together, sweep across the desert and through the cities and force all the vampires who have dared come across the sea into the sun to burn. But the king delays and his sons quarrel and every house is left on its own."

"Ibn Abdel has lost two sons already, and a daughter," agreed Uncle Ahmed. "He might ally with us in such an effort even if the king will not give the command. I have learned something interesting: he has captured one of the Nurullah women, and set her to laying wards around his palace and lands."

"Oh, a Naqi woman!" said Keziah's father with contempt. But then he added, "Still, I cannot say this was unwise. Find out if ibn Abdel will sell her to me when he has done with her. Or if he means to breed her to his black wolf sons, well enough, but perhaps then we might...rent her. Find out what he would demand in return, Ahmed."

"Too much," Uncle Ahmed muttered. "We should get one of our own. Probably not from Lebanon. Nurullah will guard their women all the more closely now they have lost one. Israel is hopeless; the families there are far too well-guarded. But we could set our agents moving in Morocco, perhaps. The black wolves there have been engaged in the Quiet War longer than we. They have lost many of their people. What few remain surely cannot hold their territory secure against a bold move."

"If they are so weak, they will have no Pure women remaining," disagreed Keziah's father. "The vampires hunt those women first among all prey. This woman of ibn Abdel's is the better choice, however expensive she might be. Inquire, Ahmed, and we shall see whether she may be made available to us."

Uncle Ahmed complained about the impoverishment of the household, but he did not protest too loudly. Keziah slipped away to find Zara, wanting to ask about these Pure women, who were so important even Uncle Ahmed was willing to spend money to get one.

"Ah, the Pure," murmured Zara. She was afraid of Keziah in a way Aunt Sofia had never feared her, so she glanced away as she spoke. But she answered willingly enough. "Yes, these Naqi are said to carry magic in their hands so they may curse a black wolf and weaken his shadow. In Lebanon, yes, and Jordan, and Israel, but also in Tunisia and Morocco and all through Europe. They teach a black wolf to go right when the dark half of his soul urges him to go left—so it is said. Who knows whether that is true? They are also said to weaken black wolves too much, so that men lose their mastery over women." She glanced warily at Keziah and away again. "I do not know whether that is true either. I think it cannot be true. If the black wolves of Israel and Lebanon and Jordan were so weak, surely our men would have driven them out and taken their lands and their women long ago. So it cannot be true."

Keziah also thought this was not likely. But she demanded, "Why did no one tell me of these women before?"

Zara flinched at Keziah's aggressive tone. She said softly, "Because it does not matter whether those stories are true in those other lands. Naqi are as weak as any other woman when our men bring them here into the desert." Zara saw Keziah's bewilderment and sighed. "Listen, then, and I will tell you. Kalila's grandmother, your great-grandmother, was of that kind. Your great-grandfather stole her from Lebanon, from the black wolf house called Nurullah, as now ibn Abdel has taken this other woman. Did Sofia not tell you so? Well, it does not matter, because whatever stories women whisper of the Pure, your great-grandmother was no stronger than any other woman. Maybe that is why Sofia did not tell you: because one must seek protection from black wolves and not from the Pure. She died young, your great-grandmother, long before I was born. I remember the old women speaking of her. They said she was wise. If she was, her wisdom did not help her. The black wolves hated her and valued her and got children of her and killed her, as they would do with any woman. She could not protect anyone. Not even herself."

Keziah nodded as though she did not really care. She didn't like to show anyone what she was thinking, certainly not Zara. But what she was thinking, for the first time in her life, was that after she and Amira killed their father, if they wanted to live, they must go somewhere. She was thinking that perhaps Lebanon might not be too far. A country where black wolf men had lost their mastery over women! She could not really imagine this. But now she knew she *wanted* to be able to imagine it.

And if their great-grandmother had carried the blood of Nurullah in her veins, maybe...maybe the black wolves of that family would not be too offended if two black wolf girls came there to look for their distant kin.

So later she stole a map from the library and showed Amira where Lebanon lay, far to the north, on the shores of the Al-Bahr Al'Abyad Almutawassit, the Mediterranean. She did not know how far. The map made it look a long way, but Keziah did not know how to reckon the true distance from the map or how to judge how long it would take a woman on foot or a black wolf running or a person in a car to go so far.

Amira traced the outlines of the countries. “I like to see that the world is larger than our father’s house,” she said softly. “When we run, could we go there, to Lebanon? See, that is one way to go to France. Look here, Jordan is in between. Jordan and then Lebanon and then farther. Perhaps black wolves there guard the territories that lie between, but we could slip by them. We are very good now at being quiet and not being noticed.”

Amira was very brave, Keziah realized. If Keziah has been as brave, she would have left their father’s house long ago. Except that for a long time she had been too little, and then for a long time, Amira had been too little.

Now neither of them was too little. But now they had to wait, because they had not yet found their chance to kill their father and Uncle Ahmed.

Maybe it would be better to forget vows and vengeance and just go.

Except Keziah knew if she said this and persuaded Amira and they fled, even if they got away, she would forever see Aunt Sofia’s blood in the pool enclosure, and hear at the back of her mind her mother screaming as her father killed her.

“It is a long way,” she temporized. “And everywhere black wolves are watching for intrusion because of the Quiet War. But yes, I think we must someday make a chance and try to go there. We must be patient. There will be time.”

“Someday,” Amira echoed, and sighed, but she nodded too. “There will be time,” she agreed. She traced the path north from Riyadh toward Jordan and Lebanon. “I will listen and ask about the way. I will find out how to go and I will remember.”

Keziah knew her little sister would find out and remember. Amira did not seem so young these days. Black wolf children grew up quickly, but pain and caution had made Amira older still. Her face had healed at last, though the mark from the silver knife was still vivid across her cheek and jaw. The scar would fade, Zara promised—but she would not promise that it would fade completely. It drew Amira’s mouth to the side a little; it hurt her when she smiled—but Amira rarely smiled.

"We *will* go," Keziah promised her. "We will find out the best ways and the quiet ways, and when our father is dead, everyone will be confused and no one will look for us. Then we will run very far, to Jordan and Lebanon and farther, until we come to Paris. We will go farther if we must; to the other side of the world. We will find a place where men do not rule women and where we can be free."

And when they *were* free, Keziah thought, they would find those Pure women and learn how to pay attention to the side of their souls that was theirs alone, and how to choose to go to the right when the dark half of the soul wished them go to the left.

This they would do. Because Keziah would never be a slave again; never in life. Not a slave to any man; not a slave to her own dark shadow. She would find those Pure women, and she would be free, and she would forever make her own choices. Amira would be free, and not afraid, and her face would heal better so that she could smile. They would both learn to be happy.

But in the end, there was not enough time to learn more about the Pure or about the black wolves of Nurullah in Lebanon that were supposed to be so different from those of Saudi Arabia. Because very soon after that, when Keziah was sixteen and Amira very nearly nine, the world ended.

It happened because Keziah's father finally managed to persuade two of the Saud princes that all the black wolves who ruled Saudi Arabia had to cooperate against the khafash, and the princes persuaded their uncle the king, and he spoke earnestly to the king of Jordan and the President of Iraq and the mullahs of Iran and the masters of the cartels in the Emirates and Yemen, and they all agreed to put aside their differences for this one time and for this one purpose.

By then the khafash had made their anger felt the length and breadth of the world. The Quiet War was no longer so quiet. In Turkey, where for ages the long truce had held between khafash and black wolves, the truce now failed. Vampires and black wolves hunted one another not only through the empty lands, but through the streets of Ankara and Bursa. The human death toll mounted. Of course the humans, blind to all the darker shadows, could not understand what was happening. But they could not mistake that something was wrong. They made up their own stories to explain the blood and destruction, as they always did; black wolves ordered their own affairs using humans as their servants and slaves and pawns, as they always did. Ankara changed hands twice and then the black wolves eradicated their enemies, and for a brief time it seemed the war might ease away without involving Saudi Arabia.

But beyond Turkey, in Romania and Bulgaria, black wolves were all but exterminated.

Then the vampires and their servants struck out of Bulgaria into Turkey. They took Istanbul, destroying the black wolf family that had ruled there since the Eastern Roman Empire had fallen.

Amira traced the outlines of these countries on a stolen map, pronouncing the names of faraway places carefully. "So far away," Amira said, touching a fingertip to the dot that was Istanbul. "But not so far as Paris. Even Paris would not be far enough, I think."

Keziah agreed. "This is what will force all the black wolves to act at last—or so our father says. Probably he is right. Uncle Ahmed says the same, even when he thinks he is alone with his sons. But they think so much of the war now. I think this may be a good time to catch Uncle Ahmed while he is distracted."

"We shall watch all the time," Amira said softly.

They did watch, but they found no opportunity. And all the time the war became worse and their father and Uncle Ahmed quieter and more dangerous. Israel and Lebanon tightened their common defenses and refused alliance, preferring to depend on their own resources, but all the rest agreed they must act. So the king sent out his orders and all of Saudi Arabia listened.

All through those days, Keziah moved noiselessly through the shadows of the villa, listening. And Amira, the same. The men were busy and important and did not pay attention to the women, which made everything easier in one way. But the men feared khafash spies and watched everywhere, which made everything harder in another way.

It should be easy to blame Uncle Ahmed's death on the vampires now. But it was harder to get anyone alone when the whole household roused at the least alarm.

Still, perhaps it might be possible to lure a man out of the villa and let the actual khafash get him. Or make it seem as though they had.

An idea hovered in the back of Keziah's mind, but it would not come clear. Very well; better to be patient. She could be patient. She had learned that lesson well. She had time. Even though she was already fifteen, even though Amira would soon be nine and marriageable—if anyone's human son would accept a scarred child as a bride—no one now spoke of marriages or such ordinary matters. All the men's attention was on the vampires.

Keziah wished the khafash would kill every male black wolf in Saudi Arabia, starting with her father and Uncle Ahmed and all her cousins. But she listened to the preparations for the war, and knew the vampires would indeed be forced into the sunlight and the sea. There was no other possible outcome, not when every black wolf joined together to fight. Ibn Abdel had his Pure woman, who had that mysterious magic in her hands; some of the princes had magical mirrors or other tools that would let them see through the darkest shadows; some of them had ordinary weapons—rocket launchers and such things—Keziah did not know everything they had, but she was sure the khafash would all be killed, and then life would go back to normal.

She was half right. For on a single bright midsummer day, when the sun was fierce and the wind smelled of fire and heat and bitter ash, all the black wolves rose up and all the vampires who had dared come into Saudi Arabia were killed.

And likewise in the other countries of the Middle East, and likewise in Istanbul, where the black wolves took back their city from the darker monsters that had so briefly held it. All through the land, the khafash were pushed back and destroyed.

Thus the world ended, and there was no more time.

Human people never saw deeply into dark shadows. This was a truth as certain as any Keziah had ever known. Human people were meant to be slaves, for the blind could not rule what they could not see. She had never thought to ask—why should she have thought to ask?—*why* humankind were so blind.

Then the vampires died, many vampires, all through the Middle East; following into the dark all the others of their kind that had died all through the Quiet War. And black wolves everywhere found out that the khafash had all along been responsible for blinding humankind. Without the khafash, human people everywhere could see what had been hidden from them for thousands of years.

And all through the Middle East, what they saw was that their rulers were monsters, and had always been monsters; that when they thought they bowed down to tyrants of their own kind, they had actually been enslaved by heavy-shadowed half-souled creatures. They had believed they had been the subjects of a human king and his sons, when all along they had been *prey*.

This Keziah understood later. What she understood at first was that the city of Riyadh had risen against its masters. She did not guess why, not then. But she saw that with torch and gun and knife and unstoppable fury, the people had risen. All across the city, palaces burned.

"We should go," Amira whispered to Keziah. "Before the mobs come here too."

Keziah nodded.

They had gone up onto the rooftops of the women's quarters so they could see better, and because the lines of retreat were better from the rooftops. Their father's villa had been safe at first, for it lay a little beyond the outskirts of

Riyadh and the enraged humans had not ventured so far in the beginning. The servants were gone...Keziah did not know whether to hide or lead the mobs to this house. Malik and Saad and Atif had gone north with the older men, to fight and kill the vampires and their servants. But Uncle Ahmed's son Saleh and a few of the other young men had been left in Riyadh to represent the interests of the household. They were somewhere below, in the villa. Keziah wondered whether they would be able to turn back the human rabble by themselves. She hoped they would not. She wanted the villa to burn.

The sun was low now. Soon it would be dark. Humans feared the dark, but tonight they would conquer the night with the light of the fires they had set. From where the girls crouched, watching, it seemed that the entire center of the city was aflame.

And not so far away were more bright spots of fire, approaching.

"Men," said Amira. "With torches. Listen. You can hear them. They are angry."

Keziah nodded. She heard this too, beyond the ordinary sounds of the night. It was the sound of many men who had forgotten fear. "They are too angry to be afraid."

"They are coming to burn the villa."

Keziah nodded again. "I wonder whether Saleh will be able to stop them?" The fury of the city beat against her face like fire, but she could not believe their cousin would be caught in the conflagration. No. Saleh and the other young men would crush the human people under their heels...

"We can't just wait here and do nothing! We have to go. Even without killing Uncle Ahmed and Father. All the cousins will be distracted by fire and blood. No one will think to look for us tonight."

Keziah nodded again. Amira was right. Everything her sister said was true. She knew it was true. "We will go north. Maybe Lebanon is different, if the black wolves there are different."

"Maybe we can stay in the desert. Just us, alone in the

desert." Amira's tone was wistful. "I would like that. I think I would feel safe if we were just us, alone in the desert. Do you think there are any vampires out in the desert tonight? Or any black wolves?"

Keziah shook her head. "Even if there are vampires, even if there are wolves, they won't care about us. Not tonight." She looked around once more; at the desert stretching out forever to the north and the city burning just behind them to the south. "Yes," she said at last. "We should go. Just us, in the desert. We will go north and maybe we will go to Lebanon, maybe we will go to Paris. Maybe we will go farther. But for now...just us. But wait. Just a single moment. Let us make certain Saleh cannot defend this house."

And she set her palms flat on the rooftop and called the fire. The black wolf fire, that was made of rage and hatred: boys were taught to call and channel that fire. No one had taught Keziah. But she found the way of it now, in this night already filled with fire, and below her palms the fire blazed up.

Keziah laughed, reveling in the violence of the flames. Then, with her sister beside her, she leaped down from the rooftop and ran into the desert. The gritty earth and the sands that stretched away to the north were lit by the last light of the sun and by the rising flames. From behind them came outraged masculine shouts; from a little farther away human ululations of triumph and the first gunshots. Keziah laughed again. She hoped the human men would shoot Saleh, that they would shoot all the cousins who dared linger. She and Amira were away and would not be caught by anyone.

When the light failed, they would run through the dark. They would follow the stars and the wind, and they would never stop.

Her father might yet live, somewhere. Keziah was sure he would live. That was a vow failed. But this—*this* was a vow she would keep: that she and her sister would never stop until they found a place where they could live as themselves, free, their mother's daughters and no man's slaves.

The detective heading up the kidnapping team was a man named Ayerson. Ezekiel knew that before he stepped through the man's door. John Ayerson. An experienced man. Eight years a homicide detective, with a solid record before that in other units. Methodical, thorough, the sort of man who patiently made his way through tangled cases and who more often than not closed them successfully. Twice wounded in the course of duty, twice commended—not the same events. Reprimanded once, for insubordination. This was all more or less public record.

Slightly more difficult to discover were private details. Ezekiel had tracked down a handful of those, too. Ayerson's wife was a nurse. Her name was Hannah. They had been married for nineteen years. They had twin daughters, both currently attending Colorado State. Ayerson's friends were his colleagues, and his wife's. Every summer, Ayerson went fly fishing with a buddy; every fall he hunted elk or moose with his wife and another couple. All of that was also relatively easy to ascertain, even for Ezekiel, who was no kind of detective. Certainly not in Ayerson's league. That was why he'd come here: because why waste time and effort on a project a professional had undoubtedly already filed a report on?

It had been surprisingly easy to make an appointment with Ayerson. Kidnapping. That horrified the police. It was almost worse when they didn't find bodies, when it was just disappearances straight up. Multiple kidnappings, worse still; that terrified the entire community. Of course the polite police receptionist had wanted to set up Ezekiel with a junior detective, the sort who was assigned to take hotline tips from the public during high-profile cases. But it *was* a high-profile case. He had not had to insist very hard to get this appointment with John Ayerson.

The detective's office was toward the back of the building, maybe a little smaller than some, but with a window that looked out over the parking lot and admitted gritty light despite the overcast day. Ezekiel's guide—a uniformed officer—rapped on the door, swung it briskly open, and announced, "Mr. Grayson," which was the name on Ezekiel's driver's license. The officer stepped aside, tilting his head in laconic invitation for Ezekiel to enter.

Ayerson was a heavy-set man, graying but obviously still strong, built big and broad. He might have been anything from a truck driver to a football coach, but he did not immediately look much like a senior police detective. His jacket, and also his holstered gun, were hanging over the back of a second chair a short distance away. Typing quickly with thick fingers, the detective grunted acknowledgement and muttered, "Be right with you—take a seat," but did not immediately glance up. The uniformed officer gave Ezekiel a wry look and went away. Ezekiel stepped into the office, nudged the door shut with his foot, leaned a shoulder against a heavy bookshelf, crossed his arms over his chest, and waited, half amused and half impatient.

Detective Ayerson paused, glared fixedly at his computer screen for a moment, typed two more words, hit 'save,' and finally shoved his chair back from his desk and looked up. Immediately, though not a muscle moved in his face, something changed. Ezekiel admired the lack of hesitation, the way the man acted even before he could have been certain. Ayerson leaned forward, one hand flat on the desk, weight shifting as he reached for his weapon.

Ezekiel was much faster. He stepped forward, his own hand coming down firmly on top of Ayerson's, pinning it to the desk. By that time Ezekiel's hand was no longer perfectly human. Even in that scant instant, his hand had broadened and thickened, his fingers becoming shorter and blunter. Jet-black claws lightly pricked the skin on the back of Ayerson's wrist. The detective tried to pull away, but found himself held by a strength he could not match. He drew breath for a shout. Ezekiel said quickly, making sure his tone stayed level, "Don't call out."

Resolution hardened Ayerson's eyes and set his jaw: He was going to shout anyway, and damn any threat Ezekiel made.

"I'm here for information," Ezekiel told him. He made every word deliberately matter-of-fact. "An exchange of information, that's all; nothing exciting. A mass slaughter of police officers is not on my schedule for today. You're not in danger. No one here is in danger. Certainly I'm not. Your gun's not loaded with silver. No one out there is loading silver." From this distance, he could tell there was no silver in Ayerson's gun, though the other part was a guess. But it seemed likely. Silver ammunition was very expensive. Even after the war had whittled down the number of vampires in the world until their miasma finally failed, after the whole world had learned at last to recognize the monsters that preyed on them, few police officers had ever been armed with silver. After all, no one had been at war with ordinary humans.

Ezekiel said softly, "Settle down, Detective. Sit down. Let's have a civilized chat."

There was a pause. Detective Ayerson, mouth hard, stared into his face. Ezekiel's black dog shadow wanted to read that attitude as a threat and a challenge. Ezekiel did not allow himself to respond with anything other than amusement. He could hear Ayerson's heartbeat: fast but steady. The detective's breathing was fast as well, but he did not now seem inclined to raise a general alarm. The man was afraid, but far from panic. Ezekiel's shadow would have enjoyed panic, a hopeless struggle, blood. Ezekiel himself approved of the man's steadiness.

"How did you know?" Ezekiel asked him. He asked the question mostly so that Ayerson would have to think about answering, about entering a dialogue; so that the man would settle down. But he was also curious. He lifted his hand, turned it to make the claws glitter, then shifted it back to a fully human hand. *See? No threat here.* Sitting down, he stretched his legs out comfortably, setting a good example. He met the detective's eyes, and smiled; not his executioner's smile, meant to terrify, but a civilized, polite expression.

Ayerson stared at him for a long moment. Then he turned, plucked his gun out of its holster, turned back, laid the weapon down on his desk ready to hand, gave Ezekiel another long look, and dropped into his own chair. Not relaxed, far from it; but the threat of imminent violence had clearly passed. He said curtly, "Saw that interview. Everyone did. Don't know how you walked right through the whole crowd out there –" He broke off, looking Ezekiel up and down.

"That damned news clip," Ezekiel said lightly. "That was months ago and a long way away, and everyone looks different by lamplight, surrounded by blood and death. You'd be surprised how few people recognize me. They don't expect to see me, not walking into their everyday world."

"A cop doesn't have an everyday world," Ayerson said grimly. "Everyone out there should have recognized you." It was plain he was going to remind every cop in this station of that as soon as Ezekiel was gone. For now, he only stared at Ezekiel some more. His heart rate was slowing. He said, inflection not quite making it a question, "Information."

Ezekiel inclined his head. "Your kidnappings. Women; young, but not girls. One married, one in a committed relationship, two single. Mostly students at the university. None of them the kind to walk away and leave their families wondering." Just the sort, in fact, that would make Detective Ayerson think of his own daughters. One more reason for the detective to be grim. One more reason, too, for the man to cooperate, even knowing what Ezekiel was. Perhaps especially knowing what Ezekiel was. He would be desperate to close this case.

"And?" said Ayerson. He did not sound desperate. He sounded wary. He looked Ezekiel up and down once more, eyes half-closed, expression neutral, as though half expecting him to admit to kidnapping those women himself. Perhaps to eating them right down to the bones. Ezekiel doubted the detective believed that, but no doubt the idea was now crossing his mind. But Ayerson didn't touch the gun on his desk. Instead, he said, "Werewolves leave a body. Parts of a body."

"Usually," Ezekiel agreed. "But try plotting those disappearances on a map. Along with any wild animal attacks from the last three months or so, 'werewolf' sightings, slasher murders if you've had any. Unexplained violent homicide. Also any violent stranger rapes. Add those in, too. Any from the last few months. With the dates of each. You can do that? You've got those data?" He paused and then added, "I'll wait."

The detective regarded Ezekiel for another moment. Then he grunted and turned to his computer. Ezekiel rose and moved around the desk so that he had a view of the computer screen. Ayerson's heart rate picked up again as Ezekiel got up, particularly as he stepped around to stand behind him. Ezekiel sat down in the other chair, the one where the now-empty holster hung. He crossed his arms and tilted his head, trying to look young and harmless.

Detective Ayerson gave Ezekiel a sidelong look. He didn't say anything, though. He opened another screen. Little square icons flashed in different colors, three red and a scattering of black. Two blue icons joined the red and black. Ayerson glanced over the information there, then moved the mouse, deleting one and then another of the black icons. Then a third. Ezekiel made an interested sound.

"Explained homicides," Ayerson said, his tone flat. "Boyfriend, mother's boyfriend, woman who drowned her kid. The ones left on the screen, we don't know." He began to add dates to each icon, referring now and then to notes in other files. Though Ezekiel had not suggested adding a phase-of-the-moon notation to each icon, the detective did that, too. Ezekiel's opinion of the man, already high, rose another notch. He leaned forward, considering the pattern of those icons, certain now of what he faced in this town. Then he noted the sudden tension in Ayerson's shoulders and neck, and made himself relax again. “Four,” he observed, his tone carefully neutral. “You always get so many mysterious murders in this town?”

“No,” said Ayerson. “A woman, a woman, a woman, a couple.” He swiveled his chair to face Ezekiel. “The first three were up north, out of our jurisdiction. I don’t know the details. Nothing was specifically identified as a werewolf attack. But that might have been...political pressure. Nobody likes to think we’ve got a serial killer; a werewolf would be worse. But it could have been a werewolf. Though none of them were...eaten.” He pointed at the screen. “The moon was full or near full for all these. This one here, too. If it were my people working that case, I’d have thought about handing out silver ammo.” His hard gaze shifted to examine Ezekiel’s hands, now lying relaxed along the arms of his chair, then rose again to his face. “You a cop? That what you are?” He sounded skeptical, perhaps because of Ezekiel’s youth as much as because of what he was.

The detective’s tone was edged with hostility. But the suggestion was, perhaps, something of a compliment. Ezekiel tried not to sound too sardonic. “In a way. If your killer, or killers, are werewolves, then they are assuredly my business.”

“You don’t let werewolves kill people. That’s your law. You said that, on camera. Was it the truth?”

Ezekiel met his eyes. “It was the truth.”

The detective grunted, thoroughly noncommittal.

“What’s the blue?”

“Rapes. Violent stranger rapes, like you said. This one – ” Ayerson reached to tap the screen with one blunt finger, “This one was cut up. Her tits, her belly. Shallow little cuts, just through the skin.”

“She, ah, couldn’t tell who cut her, or whether he used a knife or claws?”

“It was dark. He was big. She never got a glimpse. Dark or not, I guess she would have noticed if he were –” The detective gestured, unwilling to put some things into words.

“He would have been in human form,” Ezekiel assured him. “At least mostly.” It took a black dog with excellent control to extend shadow claws from human hands. But Ezekiel had already suspected that was the kind of black dog he faced in this city.

The detective gave Ezekiel a long look, then tapped the screen again, forcefully. "Moon's new for the rapes and the disappearances, full for the homicides. That a coincidence?"

"Maybe," said Ezekiel. He knew it wasn't. Even a black dog who usually owned plenty of control might lose some of that control during the full moon. Clever of Ayerson to guess that.

"Huh. You know who this is, doing this?"

"I think I have a general idea."

Ayerson tapped the computer screen. "It's all north of the Foothills campus, town side of the reservoir. All in town, nothing in the park. That we know of. Campus housing all through here." The detective swept a fingertip across the map. "University buildings up through here. You'd think our killer'd be hunting in this area, not many witnesses after dark, but so far, all the action's been farther east. If our killer's hunting tonight . . ." He leaned forward in his chair. "It's a full moon, near enough. A killing moon. This bastard's going to go for the kill tonight or tomorrow. Isn't he? Where? You know where this guy is. Or how to find him. Tell me where he'll be."

Ezekiel studied the map. "Somewhere he can hunt. Somewhere with room to run." The park west of the reservoir should have been perfect. But perhaps not for the kind of hunting these particular black dogs had in mind. He suspected they weren't very interested in isolated hikers. No. They would want to hunt somewhere they could study their prey. Someplace they could cut just the ones they wanted out of the herd.

What *he* wanted was someplace suited to an ambush. Ezekiel wanted a swift kill, several swift kills, so that he would no longer be seriously outnumbered when he found the rest. Ezekiel did not need the numbers to be *equal*, but he suspected he faced more than a couple of black dogs here, and probably all of them decently trained. He did not want to face all of these enemies at once.

But for an ambush, he would indeed need to guess where young black dogs would go to hunt.

He wished he could wave a magic wand, find them instantly, take them before the moon even rose. If Natividad had been here—but he was very glad Natividad wasn't here, that no Pure woman was here. He would have been glad to use Pure magic to find those black dogs. But if the black dogs in this city were what he suspected, this city would be deadly dangerous for any Pure woman. Far better that Natividad was at Dimilioc, and safe.

He said coolly, "I'll put a stop to this, Detective. Tonight, I hope, though I can't promise that. But I suspect I may have a general idea of where to hunt, now. For which I am in your debt. I will repay that debt by suggesting, strongly, that tonight you and your people would do best to stay off the streets and out of my way."

Ayerson snorted.

Ezekiel, smiling, tilted his head. "Well, if you must go out tonight, Detective, then load your gun with silver, if you have any. But don't shoot me by mistake."

"If I shoot you, it won't be by mistake."

Ezekiel suppressed a grin. He stood up, noting the way the man carefully did not flinch. He said, "Why don't you walk me out, Detective? I'll give you my card. If I don't get these guys taken care of tonight, if they're seen elsewhere or if they kill someone else, call me." He met Ayerson's eyes. "I'm your best chance to rid your city of this danger. Keep that in mind, Detective."

From Ayerson's unfriendly stare, the detective wasn't convinced. But Ezekiel thought he might call, if he had to. He wasn't a fool. And he might not trust Ezekiel, but he was probably astute enough to understand that he was not, in this, the enemy.

The evening was hot, sullen, still. Here in this industrial district, the air felt gritty with the scents of asphalt and rust and hot stone, the stink of diesel and truck exhaust that overlay organic smells of rot and clotting algae from a nearby lake. Ezekiel breathed through his mouth. It helped only a little.

There had been nothing so clear on Ayerson's map as a circle of activity surrounding an obvious black dog lair. It might have been exactly that simple, if the black dogs here had been sufficiently ignorant and stupid. Young strays often were abysmally stupid, having never learned to think under the pressure of their shadows. But these black dogs clearly had better control of themselves, more ability to think, to plan. Ezekiel suspected they weren't strays at all. And he was almost certain they were ruled by an experienced black dog, though the group plainly also contained a handful of vicious youngsters; enough youngsters, and strong enough, that the older one could not fully control them. Not when the moon rose full.

It had risen now. Even indoors and hours before dusk, Ezekiel had felt its seductive pull. For a young black dog, for any black dog with poor control, that pull might well prove irresistible. They would slip their leader's control, and hunt. And there was a very good chance they would hunt right here, in these empty streets scattered with industrial buildings shut tight and silent warehouses, with broad parking lots fenced against vandals and vagrants and nothing else but empty countryside and the wide lake. Here, in these unpeopled, little-patrolled streets, they could hunt almost as freely as though they ran in the trackless mountains.

And Ezekiel was almost sure they would hunt here tonight, because tonight they could find prey here. Because tonight, in defiance of good sense and public warnings and the rising moon, half the young people from the university had decided to attend a rave in one great empty warehouse, here in this otherwise all-but-deserted area. The music pounded through the air, heavy as the stench of hot asphalt.

They told themselves, no doubt, that there was safety in numbers. They told themselves that they would stay close to friends, that they would not venture out into the dark alone. That they would be safer at a noisy and crowded rave than ever they would be in their lonely student apartments.

But what young people told themselves while sober and sensible was easily forgotten when they were stupid with drink. Anyone would guess that one or two of these foolish children would stumble out alone into the night. Ezekiel leaned in a shadowed corner of a flat roof, two stories up, where the moonlight falling past concealed him as though he stood behind a sheer curtain. Here he had a good view of the back of the warehouse, the hardly lit parking lot behind it, the street that ran east toward the lake and west toward the mountains. He watched the scene patiently, without paying any particular detail much attention. It was not his eyes he depended on tonight, nor any specific human sense. He was listening to the falling moonlight, waiting for the faint stir of air where something bulky moved, scenting the gritty air for the heavy sulfuric spoor of a black dog. His was the patience of the hunter, and he was aware of the young human people below mainly as prey. Or as bait.

And they came. Three black dogs, young and hot for the chase, sliding through the shadows, angling to get between a pair of young women and the car that was their obvious goal. The women had not seen them, not yet. They were half drunk, supporting one another, laughing too loudly, a little bit afraid of the dark, but not nearly as afraid as they should be. One held a cellphone in her hand, like a talisman. The other clutched a beaded handbag as though it contained a weapon. Ezekiel pictured a panicky girl pulling out pepper spray to use against a black dog, and wanted to laugh...or his black dog wanted to laugh. That was the moon, of course; even *his* shadow became that little bit more ascendant when the moon was full.

One of the black dogs was indeed laughing, vicious soundless black dog laughter, jet-black fangs visible in the fiery gape of his jaw, crimson eyes burning like coals in the dark. The other two came behind that one. Both of those were larger and heavier, but clearly subordinate to the first; they crowded each other, snapping sideways in challenge and half-serious threat, but they did not crowd up against the one in front. Massive shoulders flexed beneath shaggy pelts, asphalt smoked beneath the fall of heavy paws, blunt-muzzled heads dropped low, snaking back and forth on powerful necks as they measured their quarry. They would drive those girls west and north, Ezekiel guessed, toward the mountains, into the empty countryside and away from any hope of help. The hunt and the chase and the red blood...Ezekiel half closed his eyes, setting himself against the pull of the moon, the seduction of the change. He *would* change, of course. But not now, not yet, not simply yielding to the urgent pressure of his shadow.

And not until his prey committed to their hunt and forgot to watch for those who might be hunting *them*.

Below his perch, the smaller black dog in the lead allowed himself to be seen. There was one reverberating instant in which nothing moved: girls and black dogs all equally still and silent.

Then the black dog dropped his lower jaw in a silent, fiery laugh, and the younger of the girls—a vivid teenager with blue glitter dusted across her high, angled cheekbones, with blue eye shadow and blue lipstick and her white-blonde hair buzzed short—caught the other's hand and pulled her back toward the crowded rave. But the other two black dogs loomed suddenly into the glow of the streetlights, blocking that escape. The older girl, taller and prettier but not so striking, jerked to a halt, shrieking. The younger screamed as well, for help that was as far out of reach as though they had been the only souls in all the city. The high voices cut through the pounding rhythm of the music, frightened and desperate.

Within the warehouse, someone yelled. But the black dogs lunged, snapping, their terrible claws gouging the pavement, pressing the girls away from any hope of safety, making them run. They would run them to exhaustion and then tear them down—and in the morning, someone would have to decide whether to proclaim their deaths due to animal attacks, or to a serial killer, or to werewolves. But whatever authorities declared, anyone with sense would know what had happened. And all across this state, people would begin to panic and call for the authorities to do something, anything, so long as the monsters were destroyed and the night made safe for themselves and their children . . .

Ezekiel shook his head fiercely and stepped forward, away from his sheltering corner and off the roof. He let his shadow rise as he fell, burning and dark, and when he struck the pavement, it cracked and smoked under the rush of roaring heat. He flung himself forward, but soundlessly, and the strays did not turn. Young and careless and accustomed to be the hunters; they might be strong, but they would be easy prey. Ezekiel wanted to laugh; he wanted to roar out a challenge and a threat. But his shadow understood about ambushes, about a sudden unanticipated leap out of the dark. He ran in silence, now on the street and now scaling a wall to run along the rooftops.

The strays were loping in pursuit of their prey, their attitude a strange mix of intensity and indolence—they did not want to catch those girls, not yet; they wanted their prey to run, they wanted their terror and hopeless exhaustion. Their whole attention was on their hunt—careless, when they hunted so near a crowded city. Distant sirens pointed up that carelessness.

But there was no hope for these girls in that sound. The girls knew it, too. They had kicked off their shoes and ran now down the middle of the empty street, flinched from a lunging black dog, and sprinted straight ahead, north. Ezekiel saw the moment the younger girl thought of the lake, and caught the older girl's hand, urging her to the east. That was clever, because black dogs did not like to swim. But of course the crimson-eyed one lunged and snapped, forcing the girls to turn. Ezekiel, running along the edge of a warehouse's flat rooftop, could see the awareness of death in the frantic way the younger girl turned at bay, snatching up a broken brick; in the way the older ducked sideways to shake the locked gate that closed off a parking lot.

The three black dogs spread out in a line, heads low, jaws gaping. But they left an opening: west, toward the mountains, away from the lake and from any hope of help. The sirens were still distant, a lonely sound like the wail of wolves. The biggest of the black dogs, a yellow-eyed monster, snapped at the air, a loud chopping sound that echoed through the dark. *Run*, that meant. *Run into the night. Run to your death.*

Ezekiel flowed over the edge of the roof and took the yellow-eyed stray in a silent rush. The black dog was larger and heavier than he was, but he had been too focused on his own hunt to suspect Ezekiel's presence until it was far too late. A fight would have been entertaining, a drawn-out kill; Ezekiel's shadow urged him to let his enemy understand that he was going to die. But that was foolish, of course, when there were three. Ezekiel drove his first blow across the back of the stray's neck, his claws lengthening as he struck. He tore out chunks of the black dog's spine, black ichor spraying into the air, and then red blood as the stray's shadow dispersed and his body contorted in spasmodic, disjointed haste back into his human form. A tall man, his head half-torn free of his body, sprawled on the street: hawk-featured, his hair black as his shadow and his skin amber in the glow of the moon; dead dead dead because his shadow could not possibly carry away that much damage.

Ezekiel had already leaped past him, slashing sideways, slicing the hamstring of the second stray, cutting halfway through the heavy bone of his leg. The stray toppled, roaring. He would shift; he would let his shadow carry away that crippling injury; but shock and pain would challenge his control. Nearly any black dog would take moments to recapture his human form after such an injury, and longer moments to shift back, and for those moments he could be discounted as a threat.

The third stray, the smallest and most vicious, was the threat. He could not be taken by surprise or from behind, not now, and he was an experienced fighter, fast and deadly. Ezekiel ducked a hammering blow that could have caved in his skull and perhaps even killed him, shifting into his human form and rolling beneath the curved slash of the heavy paw, instantly calling up his shadow and rising again as a black dog, lunging—but his opponent had leaped away and was not there. The crimson-eyed black dog guarded himself, his back to the bulk of a solid warehouse wall, heavy shoulders bunching, eyes burning with fury, smoke rising from his jaws and little wisps of flame flickering from the asphalt where he crouched. He snarled, a long wavering sound, not loud, but filled with hatred.

Behind Ezekiel, the injured stray shook himself from vulnerable human to black dog form—that was faster than Ezekiel had expected—and roared.

The girls had ducked low against a wall, out of the way, but now the younger girl caught the other by the hand, and they ran, right past Ezekiel, which was brave and perceptive. They cowered as they passed him, but didn't hesitate, and then they fled down the street the way they had come, back toward the crowded rave and life.

The black dog facing him snarled again, aching with frustrated fury because those girls had been his, they had belonged to him, *his* prey, his to hunt. Ezekiel let his jaw open in a silent, savage laugh and leaped—not forward, but sideways, attacking the black dog he had already injured once, driving that one back, slashing at his face, ducking low in human shape and a step later coming up inside his guard in black dog form; raking his belly and flank and spinning away from a counterattack. The crimson-eyed black dog rushed forward, but Ezekiel gave back mockingly, refusing to face him.

Then he leaped sideways again, with instinct-driven urgency, not quite avoiding the raking blow of another black dog. Ezekiel had not suspected this one's presence—no, nor the other, for there was another behind him—*five* strays, not three, had come to these deserted streets to hunt. The three had driven their prey this way, meaning to drive them into the waiting jaws of these two; he could guess that now. It was too late to wonder whether prudence might have suggested calling for backup rather than facing this particular enemy pack alone, but Ezekiel laughed. Trained and strong and working as a team, these black dogs were a lot more dangerous than ordinary strays, but after all, he'd already killed one. Four at once was a challenge, but he could take them. He had no doubt of it, and laughed, letting them see his confidence. He hoped they would realize who he was, hoped they would be afraid.

His attacker's claws had torn across his flank and hip, a trivial injury because, though deep, none of the cuts were life-threatening. Ezekiel flickered into human form, letting his shadow carry away the wounds, letting his enemies get a good look at his face. He darted forward in human shape, light footed and quick—ducked low under a scything blow that would have crushed all the bones of his vulnerable human chest, skidded and rolled and rose into a powerful lunge as he exploded back into his massive black dog form. He tore through the belly of his nearest opponent; the black dog screamed and twisted away, and while he was off balance, Ezekiel threw his weight against him and flung him down, and tore out his throat with a savage snap and a jerk of his head. Black ichor and red blood fountained. The black dog might have recovered even from that; he jerked himself back into his human form, writhing, the terrible wounds partly healed as his shadow tried to carry them away. But he could not recover his black dog shape as quickly as he had shed it, and Ezekiel snapped his human neck while he was still vulnerable, even as he spun in a tight circle to meet the concerted attack of all three of his remaining enemies.

Dodge and dodge and twist away, shift for half a heartbeat, nearly human for a single breath and then black dog once more, riding the knife-edge of the change—he took a raking blow across his face, just failing to return a strike that would have torn across the neck of one of his enemies—his enemies were even better trained than he'd expected and if his own control had been a fraction less perfect, he would have been dead twice over already.

He did not doubt that he was going to win, of course he would kill them all, his shadow always acceded to his will because it knew they would always win. Doubt would shake his control, so he had no doubt. He flashed from black dog to human and then back to black dog, swift as the strobe lights at that ridiculous rave, and crushed the forelimb of one of his enemies, but it was not a killing blow and he could not press his advantage because the other two forced him back. Ordinary strays almost never worked as a team, but these supported one another with the smoothness of long practice. The leader of his enemies snarled with pride and offense and a confidence that almost matched Ezekiel's. He had the temerity to laugh, crimson eyes burning, and Ezekiel readied himself for a feint that would offer that arrogant young black dog enough of an opening to draw him out, draw him away from the protection of his companions –

Then the *boom* of a shotgun cracked open the night, and the black dog farthest toward the rear of the group screamed, rearing up and then collapsing, flames rising from the gaping wounds the silver shot had torn through his body. The other two black dogs whirled, snapping at the air in astonishment and furious threat, but before they could attack the man who stood there, the shotgun boomed a second time. Another of them fell, his shadow shredding into the air, melting into the dark. His body contorted jerkily back into human form, hawk-fierce features and long limbs emerging piecemeal from the massive form of his black dog.

The remaining black dog fled, the crimson-eyed leader. Detective Ayerson turned, smoothly tracking the path of his flight, his arm and hand tensing as he prepared to shoot. Ezekiel lunged to stop him.

Ayerson, eyes wide with shock and anger, spun back, trying desperately to bring his shotgun to bear. Ezekiel dropped into his human form, nearly deafened by the shotgun blast as Ayerson, unable to correct his aim for his now much smaller target, squeezed the trigger. Ezekiel would have sworn he actually felt the burn of the silver pellets as they slashed over his head. Then he closed one hand hard on Ayerson's wrist, forcing the gun aside and down, and with the other firmly gripped the man's throat, claws out just enough to warn him against struggling.

He ordered, half a growl, "Drop the gun, Detective. Drop it."

Ayerson tried to break away, disregarding the threat of Ezekiel's claws pricking against his skin. He tried again, with all his strength. Ezekiel, half annoyed and half amused, retracted his claws so that he would not cut the man despite himself. He simply allowed Ayerson to discover that he could not begin to find the limits of black dog strength. Ezekiel tightened his grip on the detective's wrist, illustratively. Then a fraction more, until Ayerson, gasping with pain, at last ceased his struggles and opened his hand. The shotgun struck the pavement with a clatter. Ezekiel kicked it away, said shortly, "Don't run. Don't fight. Be still," and let him go.

Ayerson staggered, caught his balance, and straightened. He lifted one hand to rub his throat, realized what he was doing, and hooked his hands in his belt instead. He glared at Ezekiel. But he was not dead. He wasn't even hurt, beyond a few bruises. Ezekiel saw the man's eyes narrow as he realized that.

Ezekiel took a slow breath. The hot air was heavy with the smells of gunpowder and ichor, blood and hot pavement, fear and rage. Ezekiel let his breath trickle out again through his teeth, shrugging to settle his shadow firmly below his human self. He said, his voice taking on its familiar cool tone, "One of them had to run, or I would have nothing to track. He'll go home, that one. He's strong, and he's not stupid, but he's young, and for the moment his shadow is ascendant. He'll run home, and I'll find him there and finish this."

He glanced around. Four enemies. Four corpses. They looked small and ordinary and harmless now. They looked human. All of them with those fierce hawk-features and that amber skin, all with black hair matted with blood, and dark human eyes open and empty. They looked so alike they might be brothers. No doubt they were at least cousins. Saudi, probably. Definitely from a family and not a cartel, or they would never have stayed together when they fled their home territory.

The cartels had splintered in the aftermath of the war, most of their black dogs torn down by internal strife or literally shot to pieces by mobs of the humans they'd ruled for so long. All the cartel black dogs hated the Pure; all of them treated women brutally; any of them might have thought of kidnapping human women in a bid to establish a new, strong family after losing so much in the aftermath of the war. But Ezekiel could not believe enough black dogs from any cartel could have survived to make themselves a problem here in America.

Grayson was fairly certain that the remnants of the North African cartels had been destroyed by the civilized black dog families of Morocco and Tunisia. He and Ezekiel had discussed that part of the world, and Grayson thought that most of the fleeing black dogs had probably been driven entirely out of black dog territory, into West and East Africa. What would become of them there, whether they might be able to carve out new territory or whether they would be overpowered by the strange magic of those regions, was not clear. But they weren't Dimilioc's problem, which was all that mattered to Ezekiel.

No, the Saudi black dogs were surely the likeliest to have made themselves Dimilioc's problem. Ezekiel couldn't imagine the powerful, civilized houses of Israel and Lebanon allowing any black dogs from Saudi Arabia to flee through their territories. But some might have survived the furious aftermath of the vampire war and got out through Kuwait, perhaps. Or the Emirates. After all, Keziah had gotten out somehow. With her sister, too, which couldn't have been easy. He hadn't ever asked her how she'd done it, and it didn't really matter. But he should have realized that some of her cousins might also have fled to America. Especially because the black dog houses of Europe had often drawn much more violent reactions from the surrounding human populations than Dimilioc. Too many of those houses had treated ordinary humans with contempt, and so found themselves hunted with merciless determination once they were exposed to human view. Those were more dangerous lands for black dogs now.

Ezekiel nodded to himself, considering. Saudi or otherwise, he could guess that quite a few black dogs would be waiting for him at their house when he found it. How many? A least one old and canny black dog. Maybe just one. But with so many youngsters, he suspected there might very likely be two or three older black dogs.

And they would know he was coming. He should call Étienne, call for backup. Actually, it was a pity he couldn't call *Keziah*. The corner of his mouth tugged upward in reluctant amusement at the thought of Keziah taking on this particular fight. That would be highly appropriate. She would almost certainly enjoy it.

And he would like to call the main sept of Dimilioc, to hear familiar voices, speak to the Master of Dimilioc. Even to Natividad, though he could not immediately think of a clever excuse to justify that conversation.

But of course there was no time to call anyone. Not even Étienne, who was so much closer. Anyone Étienne sent could be here in half an hour, forty minutes, perhaps an hour. That would be the wisest course: call for help and wait.

But if Ezekiel did that, they would have time to run, these foreign black dogs who had dared intrude in Dimilioc's far-flung territory. They would hide somewhere in the vast reaches of these western states, and by the time he found them again, they might be far more dangerous. No, better to finish it now.

He started to turn toward the trail the young crimson-eyed black dog had left for him.

"You'll finish it, will you?" Ayerson said roughly. "By yourself? They would have killed you! What if that one has more friends than you can cope with?"

Ezekiel lifted an eyebrow. "No, Detective. I would have killed them. However many there prove to be, I assure you that I'll manage."

He infused his tone with confidence, but Ayerson didn't look impressed. "Yeah? And what if you're wrong? If you get killed, I'll have those monsters loose in my city, and what then? You need someone at your back when you find them."

Ezekiel looked at him.

Ayerson turned, strode to his abandoned gun, bent to pick it up. His whole manner defied Ezekiel to stop him. He hefted the weapon, broke it open to check on the loaded shells, didn't even glance over to see if Ezekiel objected.

The man's audacity was amusing, Ezekiel decided. He refused to be offended, refused to allow his shadow to press him. Human allies with silver bullets were something Dimilioc wolves had learned to appreciate, recently. Human enemies so armed were...not as welcome. But Ayerson was not, perhaps, exactly an enemy. Not, at least, at the moment.

And he knew the man was right. These black dogs were not *civilized*, but they were not strays, and he had no idea how many of them he might be facing. He did need backup.

He said, lightly, "I suppose you may as well come along. As long as your report makes Dimilioc's dedication to calm coexistence clear. And as long as you can keep up with me. You have a car nearby, Detective?"

The house was a rambling monstrosity well outside the city, at the end of a mile-long private drive, hard against the sharp rise of the mountains, framed by dark pines and the occasional spreading oak; the sort of place that might have been meant to anchor an upscale resort in the seventies or early eighties, but had never quite managed to thrive. It had been sold and sold again, no doubt, while it gradually fell into disrepair. The silver moonlight picked out its age in merciless detail: the paint on its faux-classical columns that was peeling in strips; the porch floor that sagged askew in the middle; the fallen shingles that left scattered gaps across what should have been a graceful roof. Here and there an upper-story window had broken and been boarded up. The other windows were mostly dark, but the uncertain light of oil lamps glimmered here and there. Several lamps shone in the highest windows.

It would have made a splendid setting for a horror movie; something with violent ghosts or demonic possession.

That last, of course, was not far from the truth.

"I'll go straight in," Ezekiel said quietly. And, as Ayerson opened his mouth to protest, "There's a time for subtlety, but this isn't it, Detective. We came in good time. They're still there. If they see I'm coming in alone, they may not run. I think that would be best: to finish this now, tonight. You will stay out of sight until they are all fully engaged in battle. Then...it would be best if they do not realize your presence until you begin shooting." He turned his head, meeting Ayerson's eyes.

The detective offered only a curt nod.

They had come in quietly, on foot through the woods for the last little distance because a car would have given away the presence of human allies. Whoever was in that house, they would have too much sense to face both Dimilioc's executioner and a man with a shotgun loaded with silver shot. If they knew Ayerson was here, they would run.

"Wait until they're fully engaged with me," he repeated. Then he turned and ran toward the house.

He let his shadow pour up through him with his first step, so that by his second he was fully in his black dog form. All his doubts fell away, for his black dog was long accustomed to savage victory. Its confidence rose through him; more than confidence, a hot-edged arrogance that fed a sensual anticipation of the coming fight. He lowered his head as he ran, his snarl edged with rough black-dog laughter, and shook fire from his shaggy pelt. The spring grasses smoked where his broad paws fell, but he did not want to set fire to that house—for a moment, he did not remember why he did not want to burn it to the ground, but it came to him: yes, the light in the attic window. That was why. It didn't matter; fire would have been satisfying, but blood would be better.

They knew he was here, those lesser black dogs. Three of them—no, five—well, five or six or perhaps seven; it was hard to be certain. Three of them had come out to meet him. At least two more held back, waiting, letting the others run ahead—one of those would be the master here, old and strong and experienced. That was fine. He would kill them all, send their shadows shrieking into the night, spill their red blood upon the earth—he leapt sideways suddenly, not knowing why until the sharp *crack* of a rifle echoed across the face of the mountains. The shot went wide, and now he saw the figure move in one of the darkened windows, the shine of moonlight on the barrel of the rifle, which some part of his mind had glimpsed barely in time.

That was infuriating: both the gun and his failure to think of the possibility. Stray black dogs did not work with human men—but these were not precisely strays. He dodged sideways and away, shifting again and again, human and black dog and human again, ducking in and out of the shadows of the tall pines, angling toward the house because he knew he did not dare stay out in the open, not with that gunman in the window. The rifle cracked again, and once more, and the four black dogs rushed forward to block him from shelter, force him out into the bright moonlight –

Behind him, not very far behind, a shotgun boomed. Of course, a shotgun. Ezekiel had underestimated Ayerson as an ally. He wanted to laugh. The rifle had fallen silent, and now his enemies were far less eager to close—but now it was too late; they were too near to get away, if they ran now he would tear them down one at a time from behind. They knew it, too. The master of the little pack roared, and all of them rushed forward together.

But now both guns were silent, and Ezekiel hurled himself to meet his enemies with no more hesitation. Feint and feint, duck into human shape and lunge back up with all the massive strength of the black dog, and one of his enemies writhed, dwindling abruptly to human form in disorderly death.

He took a blow across the chest that would have killed a black dog with only ordinary control, but he simply flickered into human form to shed the wounds and then brought his shadow up again, so fast that the following blow, intended to crush the fragile bones of a human, only raked harmlessly across his black dog's heavy shoulder. Ezekiel laughed and tore his enemy's throat and side, not killing blows, not yet, but debilitating if the black dog could not rid himself of those injuries by shifting to his human form. And he couldn't, because he was too hard pressed and would never be able to reclaim his black dog shape before Ezekiel killed him. The black dog roared in frustrated fury, setting half a dozen pines ablaze, and tried to retreat, to let the other two carry the fight, but Ezekiel ducked past them in human form, reared up into his black dog shape, and slashed claws across his opponent's face, trying again for his throat.

The shotgun boomed. Ezekiel had once again almost forgotten about it, but he found himself suddenly no longer threatened from the rear. Freed to concentrate on a single enemy, he struck, and contemptuously shrugged aside a return blow, and struck again, finishing his opponent, leaving him to crumple in human form to the torn ground. His enemy's shadow, denser than most, wailed almost audibly as it shredded into the air.

The last of the black dogs fled for the house. Ezekiel was faster, and afterward loped past the torn corpse and leaped up the wide shallow stairs to the sagging porch. He let his shadow carry his weight because the structure was plainly unequal to bearing even the step of an ordinary human, far less the full bulk of a black dog. The door was half open, but even shoved wide, it was not adequate for his size. Silence within suggested no threat. He was certain at last one or two more black dogs had been here, maybe more. He was in particular quite sure that he had not yet killed the young crimson-eyed black dog he had pursued out of the city and tracked to this place. But any remaining enemies had retreated deeper into the house, or fled entirely. Ezekiel didn't mind if they fled into the mountains, but he didn't want them lingering here in this house. He snarled, a deadly scraping warning to any within: *Run!* But there was no sound; no sense of any threat.

He stepped through the doorway in human form, taking in the high cobwebby ceilings and dingy walls, the paucity of furniture. His quiet footsteps echoed. A single oil lamp hung from the chain that should have held a glittering chandelier, its warm light deepening the shadows that lay in the corners. At the far end of the antechamber, a graceful stairway curved up to the floor above. Ezekiel crossed the cracked tiles of the floor and started up, but had not gone five steps before hearing, behind him, the metallic sound of a shotgun being cocked.

He turned, annoyed with himself. He wasn't surprised, precisely. At the same time, he would never have put himself in a stairwell that limited his movements if he had remembered the human, and the gun.

"Two of the monsters ran for the mountains," Ayerson told Ezekiel. "At least two. They're hard to see in the dark, but I might've seen as many as three, even four. The pace they lit out, I don't think they'll stop until they get to California."

The detective's mouth was set, his gaze difficult to read. He held the shotgun steady on Ezekiel's chest. That he hadn't fired yet meant that he was still making up his mind. Ezekiel stood very still. He said, "They'll be dangerous until they're dead, any black dogs from this house. I, or someone of Dimilioc, will track them down eventually. I'm sure you realize how useful we will be for that purpose. Believe me, you do not want to deal with issues of jurisdiction when you pursue such prey." He paused. Ayerson said nothing. Ezekiel added, "If you pull that trigger, don't add that detail to your report. Don't even mention it to your immediate superior. Never whisper it aloud. Let everyone assume my death came from the black dogs here, or their human accomplice."

Ayerson's eyes narrowed.

"It would be a mistake to shoot me, Detective. In so many ways. Among other things, if Dimilioc finds out you killed me, they won't forgive it. The Master of Dimilioc will personally come looking for you. But you're a decent man. A good cop. You don't deserve to die for killing monsters."

There was a little pause, that stretched out. Ayerson didn't move. He was thinking that over, but if he had to think this long, Ezekiel was fairly confident of how the decision would come out. Besides, he heard a muffled sound from above. Gesturing upward, he said casually, "There's one of the reasons you'll be glad you didn't shoot me. You know those women are still alive, don't you? The attic, I think."

Turning, he went up the stairs, lightly, not too fast. Behind him, he heard Ayerson's muttered curse and then the heavier tread as the man followed him. He didn't shoot. Ezekiel had been almost certain he wouldn't.

The stairway led to darkened hallways that stretched away to either side. Ezekiel ignored them, turning on the landing to continue upward. The stairs narrowed after the third floor, and steepened, and lost the graceful curve to run straight up between walls dark with stained paper and smelling of mildew. They ended at last before a locked door. This would be the attic from which the light had shone, if Ezekiel had the plan of the house clear in his head. The lock was new and sturdy, but the door was old. He slammed his hand right through the aged wood, first above and then below the lock, tore it free, and shoved the door wide.

Six narrow beds in a row, and six hard-backed chairs pulled into a tight group before a small iron stove, and a grim smell of stale bread and boiled venison and fear and illness, and five terrified women who cowered at the far end of the long attic room.

Ezekiel liked people to fear him, but he didn't like this. It was too much like something Thos Korte might have done; too much, in fact, like the things Thos had actually tried to do when he had still been Master of Dimilioc. Ezekiel was not generally troubled by a vivid imagination, but it was far too easy to picture that row of cages in Dimilioc's basement, each containing a woman like one of these women. He could all but see Melanie in a cage like that. Even Natividad, if Thos had tracked down her father and killed him and forced Natividad into Dimilioc.

Thos would have done it. For all his Dimilioc blood, he'd been nearly as vicious as any black dog lying dead out there in front of this house.

How to persuade these women that not all black dogs were like that? That Dimilioc was not like that, not under

Grayson; that they were safe, would be safe?

Brutalized, frightened, kept like animals or like slaves...after what had been done to these women, nothing he could say would be right. Especially after they had already watched him smash through their door: inhuman strength was surely not very reassuring, under the circumstances. If Natividad were here...or better still, DeAnn, ten years older than Natividad, older than any of these women, calm and steady, good with wounded creatures. Or even Grayson, whose integrity no one could doubt, even on first meeting. Dimilioc's executioner was hardly the right person to do this. But he was the only one here.

Ezekiel said, without preamble, what in their place he would have wanted most to hear: "All your captors are dead. They died in fear, knowing they would die. You are safe, and free." He ignored the detail that a handful of the black dogs here had fled. They were dead, too, after all. He would track them down eventually. He moved aside and gestured toward Ayerson. "This is Detective Ayerson, who has rescued you all."

"You're one of them," accused one of the women. She was older than the rest, or perhaps captivity in this house had aged her. She was tall and straight-backed, striking even under these conditions. She wore a blue dress that was almost clean, and her dark hair was bound back with a cord that looked like silk and had beads of real lapis braided into its ends. She sounded angry rather than afraid. Ezekiel approved of her. She seemed strong. And she continued to stare at him, not Ayerson, which showed perspicuity. She was also very pregnant. They were all pregnant, he was fairly sure. But with this one, no one could have missed the fact. She stood with her head up and her hands folded across her belly, clearly near her time, but fiercely defiant despite her fear. He was glad of her strength and courage. She would need both, however this came out.

"I'm certainly a black dog," he agreed. "But hardly one of *them*." His lip curled with scorn at the idea. "I'm Dimilioc. We're a civilized house. We cherish our human kin and respect the mothers of our children."

"Oh, the *mothers of your children.* We've seen how you treat the mothers of your children!"

Ezekiel tilted his head, keeping his manner quiet. "In fact, you have not. I hope you will meet my fiancée, who will be the mother of my children. She is as fierce as you, in her way." He couldn't quite shut out an image of Natividad, wounded and desperate as this woman was wounded and desperate. Natividad would be furious and grieved at what had been done here. Thinking of her, how she would feel, helped him keep his tone steady and mild. "I hope you meet DeAnn, who is married to a black dog man. Their son is six years old, a fine boy." He looked deliberately around at the other women and went on carefully, "Every woman of Dimilioc is held within our protection. No one may harm her. The black dogs who brought you here were savages. But they are dead. Dimilioc does not tolerate such barbarity."

The woman tipped her chin up, her expression closed and hard, but Ezekiel thought she was listening. He hoped they all were.

"He killed most of 'em himself," growled Ayerson, unexpectedly. "And brought me here, and told me you all were up here, or I wouldn't have known to look."

"You'd have figured it out, Detective," Ezekiel said drily, though he was pleased by this unexpected testimony. "You're all free," he added, speaking again to all the women. "You are free to do whatever you wish, go wherever you wish. But there are complications. Certainly for you." He paused.

The woman in blue knew what was coming. Her face tightened, and her hands spread protectively across her swollen belly.

"You've guessed, then," said Ezekiel. "Or did they tell you?"

"They told us," said the woman, bitterly. "Breeding little monsters, and God help us if we have a normal child –"

"Yours is a black dog."

"I know! They said that. He did, the one they called

their prince. He gave me a new dress and a necklace and things, and better food, and told me he'd beat me if it were born dead –"

"Savages," Ezekiel acknowledged. "Barbarians. Saudi, were they? Yes, I thought so. They thought they were kings among men, dark lords of the Earth. To them, ordinary humans were slaves. Slaves and prey. Then their slaves realized that their chains had been put on them by monsters, and rose up against them, and found that monsters can be killed if the hands of decent men are set against them."

Ezekiel didn't have a gift for words. His uncle Zachariah had been the storyteller of the family. But they were listening. Ezekiel went on, quietly, "This was some prince who escaped the days of blood. A prince who, driven out of his homeland but finding himself still alive, aspired to greater things. He thought Dimilioc would allow him to build up a house of his own, here. Now he is dead, and all his kindred with him." He let his contempt show in his voice, even though the Saudi prince's plan might have worked, if Ezekiel had not happened to hear of an unusual run of kidnappings in an area where werewolves were thought to be hunting. He had guessed immediately what kind of black dog might kidnap girls, and why.

He said, "We would never have permitted it. They were dead the moment they caught our attention. I'm only sorry I did not discover their intentions before they could do you such harm." He meant this, to his own slight surprise. He glanced from the first woman to the others, meeting each one's eyes, trying to let them see his sincerity. They all seemed healthy, at least. Bruised, but sound enough, and perhaps beginning to believe they might be safe. The youngest of the women, pale and blonde, with dark circles under her eyes and bruises vivid on her upper arms, looked about sixteen but was probably several years older; he thought she was one of Ayerson's more recent kidnap victims, which made her close to nineteen. She flinched and looked away from his gaze, folding her arms defensively over her chest.

He tried to look harmless. It wasn't a look he had practiced very often. He said to the older woman, "He's half you, that child you carry –"

"And half monster!"

"Well, yes," Ezekiel conceded. "But half you, and black dogs don't have to be monsters. To us, he would be a child. He would be a valued member of Dimilioc. You are his mother. We would cherish and respect you. You'll need help with him. You've felt him moving in your belly, haven't you? He's almost ready to be born. But a black dog birth can be difficult. The women of Dimilioc know how to take care of you, and how to take care of him."

Natividad or DeAnn would need to do the *Beschwichtigan,* the Calming, the moment the child was born. Before, if possible. The baby's shadow was a strong one; Ezekiel could feel it from where he stood. Without the *Beschwichtigan,* this woman's son would surely kill her, probably at an age where a human child would still be crawling. And, with a shadow that strong, he would soon be consumed himself. A tragedy from conception to death, that child's life, unless Ezekiel could make this woman listen to him. He said, not loudly but letting his voice gain intensity, "Dimilioc would welcome you and protect you. *I* would protect you—I would stand against any who sought to harm you. And I assure you, I am not the least of the black dogs of Dimilioc. *No one* would dare lay a hand on any I take under my protection."

"Probably true," muttered Ayerson.

Ezekiel raised an eyebrow at him, but gave him a nod of gratitude at this unexpected vote of...partial confidence, perhaps. The women looked at one another. Ezekiel thought they might almost be willing to trust him—at least, a little—at least the woman in blue. He said as persuasively as he knew how, "A black dog child—a human can't safely raise one of us. A child of ours has to be taught to control the monster. We can do that, at Dimilioc. We can raise your child to be a decent man. Not like those." He gestured contemptuously around at the house. "Nothing like those."

"You can't *seriously* expect us to go with you," said the woman in blue, angry and doubtful.

"Certainly I hope *you* will come with me," he told her. "All of you, but particularly you. Your child is unmistakably a black dog, and very near his time. You need our help, and Dimilioc could use his strength. He'll be strong, any child of yours, I know that. You'll be respected at Dimilioc. You'll be a valued guest, not a prisoner. Or a part of our family, if you choose to stay. Either way, if you bring us this child, he'll belong to a civilized house. He'll be taught the control he needs. He'll have a good life –"

"I want an abortion," one of the younger women declared abruptly. "I'm not going to *have* it! I was—I was—it's not mine, it's *nothing* of mine, it's not even human, it's *his*!" She clenched her fists and glared at Ezekiel. Her eyes were an unusual gray-green, her cheekbones high and angular. She seemed to have gained courage from the other woman's example.

"That's certainly another option," Ezekiel agreed. "But you're not far enough along to know whether it's human or not. Do you want to destroy it before you even find that out? Maybe it's a little girl, a daughter as human as you. Even if it's a boy, it might be human." He glanced around at all the women. They were all staring at him. So was Detective Ayerson. But the detective made no move to interrupt this sales pitch. Ezekiel said softly, speaking directly to the angry woman with the greenish eyes, "You can certainly end your pregnancy before it's too far along. That would be safe and easy. But Dimilioc will offer you haven if you choose to bear it. If you want time to decide, we will give you time. If you bear it, we'll be glad to keep a black dog child. Or if it's human, if you don't want it, I promise you, we would value a human child as well. Our human kin are important to us."

"You think we should trust you?" demanded the blonde girl.

"I *know* you should trust me. I realize you can't be so confident."

Ayerson cleared his throat. Ezekiel eyed him sidelong,

but the detective said, his gruff tone apologetic, "My report...I can pass over some details. But some things will come out."

"I don't want people to know!" exclaimed the blonde girl.

"It's worse than that," snapped the woman in blue. "He means everyone will know you were raped by a *werewolf*. Or *some* people will know," she added sharply, as Ayerson made to interrupt. "You'll be lucky if you don't have your baby in a *lab*, whether you planned on an abortion or not, with people in white coats all ready to take it off and experiment on it –"

"That's sick! You're sick!" said one of the other women, one who hadn't spoken before. She looked like she would be pretty if she were happy. At the moment, she looked strained and ill, but not quite as frightened as she had been.

"It'll take some time to get through all the paperwork," said Ayerson. "Days, I expect, for a case this complicated. And it might not leak. Or not too fast."

Ezekiel raised an eyebrow. The detective shrugged.

"He means, if you want to go home and have an abortion, do it immediately, before anyone stops you," said the woman in blue impatiently, when a couple of the other women looked confused.

"Or if you choose otherwise, or if you want time to think of what to do, you will be safe at Dimilioc," Ezekiel promised them. "You will be safe with me. Come with me and your babies will have a family—and so will you, if you choose. I speak for the Master of Dimilioc, and what I say is true." He wished again for DeAnn. She could surely have persuaded these shocked and traumatized women to trust her. But all Ezekiel could do was speak the truth and hope they heard the sincerity in his voice. He was much better at terrifying people, he knew, than reassuring them—not the first time in his life he'd regretted that.

"I'll come," the dark woman said flatly. "I'll come with you. It's illegal to have an abortion this close to term—and I don't want one anyway." She spread hands protectively over her stomach, and looked at Ayerson as though daring him to object. "It's *my* choice! I can choose what to do and where to go!"

"Well, ma'am," Ayerson answered gravely, "you're not a perpetrator here, you're a victim, and you're sure not under arrest, so I guess you can do anything you want." He gave Ezekiel a sidelong glance, wary, undoubtedly wondering if he might be making a terrible mistake by offering this tacit approval.

Ayerson seemed so straightforward. And then he stepped way, way outside official procedures. Ezekiel had not expected that. Ayerson meant to protect the women, of course. White coats and labs were surely in his mind's eye, too. Helping Ezekiel was not the point. Nevertheless, Ezekiel acknowledged both the detective's helpfulness and his wariness with a firm, reassuring nod, trying to indicate that yes, everything he'd told these woman was true. It might have helped that it actually *was* true. In his career, Ayerson had probably learned pretty well how to sort truth from lies. And the man had made his decision earlier, after all, on the stairway.

Ezekiel hadn't expected that moment of carelessness to yield useful dividends of trust. But if it had, he was more than willing to draw on that account.

"I'll come," the woman in blue said again. And again, fiercely, "I'll come, and you'd better be telling the truth!"

Ezekiel said, to her, to all the women, "I've told you nothing but the truth. So come with me. Come with me, all of you, and I'll take you home."

BANK JOB

The call came at a surprisingly convenient time, as Ethan and Thaddeus were just heading out of St. Louis. That was as far west as their circuit took them; more than far enough, in Ethan's opinion. Just the Cleveland-Chicago-Indianapolis-Columbus loop had taken nearly a month, last time he'd drawn that assignment. Even a sharp team just could not do a thorough job in much less, and if anything out of the ordinary came up, well, you might as well write off your downtime, and never mind the unofficial rule that said you were due a couple weeks off between missions. Adding another loop for St. Louis, Nashville, and Louisville was too damn much.

Not that Grayson had asked for Ethan's opinion. Nor was he going to. No, he'd take their report, glance through it, make some pithy comment about the grammar, and order Ethan to get ready for a turn on the eastern loop. Grayson might give Thaddeus a break because he was a family man with a kid, but he would expect Ethan to say *Yes, sir* and pivot right around, with a snap to his step and not even taking time to unpack.

Of course, Grayson had no choice. The Master was trying to ensure that Dimilioc retained absolute dominance over all black dogs in the entire U.S, and that meant making it absolutely dead clear that Dimilioc black wolves were everywhere at once, all the time. Even if Grayson had to wear every remaining Dimilioc black dog to a shadow—hah!—of his former self to do it. But the Master was right. It would be worth it. Eventually. No matter how much of a pain in the neck it was now, taking turn and turn about on one assignment after another.

Ethan didn't know which he disliked more: the new

Midwestern loop or the East Coast loop. The states got big as you got into the Midwest, which, unless you had the plane, meant a damn lot of driving to get from one city to another. That was tedious enough, but just to add excitement to the tedium, they'd also all found out, as Dimilioc reasserted its dominance over the whole continent, that the farther you got from the heart of Dimilioc, the more likely you were to run across some leftover nest of blood kin. Even now, nearly two years since the official end of the war, you had to worry that it might be more than blood kin hiding in the shadows, eating careless hitchhikers and stray dogs. It might be an actual vampire. *Probably* not, but it could be. They'd all sure learned that, last spring. Probably not, but it *could* be. And no one—no one, no matter how crazy or ambitious or tough—wanted to take on another vampire without Ezekiel at hand to take point.

Ethan himself would be perfectly fine if he never in his life so much as glimpsed another vampire. He'd had way, way more than enough of vampires during the war. But if he did have to face one, he definitely wanted Ezekiel right there in the front lines. In fact, if he had to work with anyone on these damned sweeps, against vampires or blood kin or ambitious black curs...if he couldn't team up with his father and cousins, he would rather have worked with Ezekiel. His cousins were gone in the war, along with so many others. His father...Ethan never let himself think about what had happened to his father.

Dimilioc always outmatched the strays because they fought smart and they fought in teams. Now, since the war that had decimated Dimilioc, everyone was having to find ways to fit into new teams, and there just wasn't any black dog Ethan felt right fighting beside. But he was *used* to Ezekiel. There was no shame in giving way to Dimilioc's executioner. Everyone had to. Besides, Ezekiel was a Korte, a true Dimilioc black wolf, with bloodlines that wove their way back to the founding of the house.

But it was God's own truth that Ethan hated working with Thaddeus Williams. He'd done it before, and no doubt he'd do it again, but Ethan hated having to keep his eyes down and his tone careful, and he hated it a whole lot worse when he had to defer to a mongrel like Thaddeus. But Thaddeus was too damn strong to challenge, definitely the strongest of all the strays that had been allowed, or in some cases forced, to join Dimilioc.

But Grayson assigned teams as he saw fit, and there was no arguing. Not even if you were Grayson's nephew and ought to have had a real say.

Six months. Just six months to go until Grayson would allow Ezekiel back. Who would have thought it possible to miss having that supercilious bastard around the place? But then, who would have expected to have to do so much heavy lifting and take out so much trash just because he wasn't?

In the meantime, it was just one damn assignment after another, with one damn uncomfortable partner after another, racking up miles and hours and kills to show the world that Dimilioc was still very much a going concern.

Actually, on balance, the Midwest loop wasn't so bad. More driving than in the east, true, but the East Coast had a whole lot of big towns close together, so running that loop actually took longer. Besides, while there were fewer stray black dogs closer to the heart of Dimilioc territory, any black dogs that did turn up in the east were generally ambitious bastards who'd managed to pull together something like a pack and thought they were such hot stuff they might as well move in against Dimilioc. They had no damn idea, of course. None of them were anything much, not compared to Malvern Vonhausel. Not even compared to Zinaida Kologrivova, the Black Wolf of Russia her own ambitious self, who'd been such a problem last spring.

But every single fool who thought he was hot enough to challenge Dimilioc had to be dealt with, and there hardly seemed any end to them. You cleared out one black-souled would-be pack leader who thought he was Hell's own special pet because he could hold five or ten strays together for two days, but hardly before you'd put him down, here came another. Damned mongrel strays, most of them ignorant as pigs; no decency, no discipline, nearly all of them sure Dimilioc law didn't apply to them.

That was what Ethan thought this was, at first, when he took the call: one or two black dogs determined to challenge Dimilioc, making a lot of noise to be sure of drawing attention. That kind of thing drew attention, all right. You'd think they'd learn better.

But that wasn't what Grayson said was going on, this time.

"Wait," Ethan said, after listening for just a moment. "There's a problem with strays, and *Herrod* called *you*?"

"A policy I believe we may wish to encourage." Grayson's deep voice was dead level, not encouraging argument. "Fortunately, there you are, days behind schedule, but now ideally placed to answer Colonel Herrod's request. I may have led the colonel to believe that Dimilioc has a permanent presence in that general vicinity. I would prefer you did not contradict this impression."

"Yes, all right," said Ethan. "But –"

"The problem is evidently contained within the Federal Reserve Bank of St. Louis. I gather there is more than one such establishment in the vicinity, which might lead to some confusion. However, I understand this specific building stands virtually within the shadow of the Arch. I don't imagine it will be at all difficult to locate, under the circumstances."

"Wait," said Ethan again. "Seriously? Sir," he added belatedly. "I mean, don't you think this could be a *trap*?"

"If it is, don't walk into it," Grayson ordered him, and hung up.

Right. Ethan shoved the phone into his pocket and looked at Thaddeus.

Thaddeus was driving. Any black dog preferred to drive rather than ride along as a passenger, and Thaddeus got to drive on this assignment because he was way, way out of Ethan's league. They'd got that straight between them real fast.

Ethan had never actually tried to fight Thaddeus.

Infuriating as it was, he'd had no choice but to turn his head and step out of the newcomer's way. He'd known, the moment he'd laid eyes on Thaddeus Williams, exactly how any fight would come out. The other black dog might be a mongrel, but he was much bigger and heavier than Ethan even in human form, never mind black dog form. He was also more than ten years older, but his shadow was so strong, it was plain that even if they'd been the same age, Thaddeus would already have been a whole damn lot stronger than Ethan. Dimilioc control and training counted for a lot, but it didn't count for everything, and there was just no way Ethan was ever going to match Thaddeus.

He said sharply, "You hear that? Some damn problem with black dogs and hostages, special forces got involved, and that damned colonel Grayson's such buddies with decided to call *us*."

"I heard," Thaddeus rumbled. "Black dogs, and they took hostages. They didn't just kill all of 'em? Penned up a bunch of people and waited to see how long it would take special forces to get there, is that how it was?" His deep, deep voice held just a hint of the gravelly black dog growl. He didn't believe it either. He might be a mongrel, he might have grown up a stray, but he wasn't actually a fool.

"Doesn't seem likely, does it?" Ethan agreed. "If you take this next exit, I guess we can go find out." He was careful not to make that an order—he still had to be careful. It wasn't automatic, even yet. He, a Lanning—Grayson Lanning's nephew—and *he* had to take orders from a cur stray who couldn't even name his own grandfather.

Oh brave new world, that has such people in't! Yeah, though Ethan wouldn't exactly call any part of mankind *beauteous.* And he doubted Thaddeus had ever read Shakespeare. He wouldn't have laid odds the older black dog could *read.* Strays and street curs...no point in arguing with Grayson about the stray thing, though.

Actually, Thaddeus wasn't so hard to take. Or he wouldn't have been, if he'd been just a little less powerful. Mustn't forget Thaddeus had had the guts or good sense or sheer good luck to marry a Pure woman. Couldn't say that about many strays. Maybe DeAnn had even gotten Thaddeus read Shakespeare; crazier things had certainly happened.

Ethan stared out the window, deliberately not looking at Thaddeus, as the other man took the exit and headed back toward the city. Off in the distance, Ethan could already see the thin silver thread of the Gateway Arch.

The Federal Reserve Bank was a massive building, all limestone or granite or whatever, white stone of some kind. It looked a whole lot like it was all just one huge vault plunked down in the middle of downtown—it had windows, sure, but they were barred. It wasn't actually an ugly building, though. It looked strong. Not damn easy to break into. Or out of, right now, because just at the moment it was surrounded by all the cops in the entire universe. Roadblocks, too, which Thaddeus ignored. That drew attention, but the special forces were right over there, in black body armor marked with no symbols except the American Eagle badge.

Those guys didn't need more than that. Everyone knew who they were. Formed during the latter part of the war, after so many vampires had been killed that their mind-clouding miasma had faded and ordinary people had figured out that all their nightmares were real, the special forces were specifically meant to deal with the monsters. Ethan could feel the silver in their weapons all the way across the street.

Most of the special forces units had been folded back into the regular military since the war had ended. But Colonel Herrod's unit was clearly up to snuff. Which was fine. Because right at the tail end of the war, with Dimilioc's victory looking more and more Pyrrhic every day, Grayson had quite deliberately formed an alliance with Herrod. He'd fed the colonel the information the special forces needed to get at the vampires that were out of Dimilioc's reach. That alliance was tense, everybody knew human and black dog priorities might not turn out to align very well, but it was still in force. Not to mention that after that mess last year, Dimilioc owed Colonel Herrod. Worse, *Ethan* owed him, specifically and personally.

This situation might be Herrod calling in that marker because he was just that desperate. Or it might be the colonel testing the alliance, seeing what he could get from Grayson.

Or it might be a trap.

If it was a trap, Grayson's order notwithstanding, they had already walked into it.

Herrod himself was right there, though. He'd appeared almost before the nearest cop could order Thaddeus to *Turn your car around right now, sir, can't you see we have the street blocked off?* But no problem, there was Colonel Herrod, waving the cop away with curt impatience and then waiting with equal impatience, arms crossed, for the Dimilioc black wolves to get out of their car. That was a good sign. He wasn't wearing body armor. He was wearing a suit, a sharp brown number that certainly hadn't come off the rack, with a cream-colored shirt that perfectly complemented both the suit and his walnut-dark skin. Despite its elegance, the suit didn't make Herrod look like any kind of harmless bureaucrat. Nothing could have made the colonel look harmless. But the suit was probably also a good sign.

Herrod was not a big man, but he was the sort of man who seemed intimidatingly acute, even on a first glance. His eyes were set deep and wide in his dark-skinned face; his hair was iron gray and cropped military short. He was probably no more than five ten, maybe less, and he didn't bulk, either. He commanded attention anyway. It wasn't just the warm tones of that expensive suit. It was the attitude. He was like Grayson that way: you could tell at a glance that Colonel Herrod was always going to be the man in control under any circumstances. Yeah, when those two had met in person last spring, it must have been like the irresistible force meeting the immovable object. Ethan was sorry he hadn't been in good enough shape at the time to enjoy it.

The colonel wasn't wearing a weapon, not that Ethan could see, but he had a cell phone clipped to his belt. He didn't look overly concerned by the police lieutenant talking to him urgently from one side, nor by the man, not a cop, trying to edge in from the other side. He looked impatient, mostly.

"*You* talk to him," Thaddeus growled under his breath as they got out of the car.

Ethan glanced at him, surprised. And then, after a second, not surprised at all. "It's a lot like dealing with the Master of an allied house," he said, keeping his voice low, pitched for black dog hearing. "He's a tough bastard, and we want to be polite and not burn any bridges Grayson might want to cross later, but we don't owe him obedience and we don't trust him too far."

Thaddeus tilted his head to show he understood, but what he said, grimly, in the same low tone, was, "You think it's a trap?"

"If it is, we're in it and Grayson is going to be seriously irritated. But I don't think so. Or he wouldn't let us keep coming, would he?" Because they'd almost reached the colonel, and once they were close enough, all the silver bullets in the world couldn't keep a black dog from ripping the head right off an ordinary human. And they were damned near in arm's reach right now. Thaddeus huffed a laugh, and Ethan stopped, met the colonel's eyes because that was polite when you were talking to a human, and said formally, "Colonel Herrod. We understand you have a little problem here."

"These men are *werewolves*, Colonel," one of the men, not the cop, put in sharply. He glowered at Thaddeus suspiciously. Not at Ethan, unsurprisingly. With his size and attitude, Thaddeus was the one who looked dangerous. And his face was just a little distorted already, which the man must have noticed—his shadow must be fighting to rise, or else he truly did not trust the colonel or the situation one bit. Well, Ethan had already known the other black dog was not a fool.

But Herrod only said, without any particular emphasis, "They are independent consultants." He nodded to Thaddeus, gripped Ethan's arm, and led them both right past the still-protesting man and a whole wave of police officers, into the midst of his own men. The special forces people opened ranks to let their colonel and the black dogs through and closed again behind them, and suddenly no one was anywhere near except Herrod's own men.

Ethan let this happen. He was mainly just glad the colonel hadn't tried to take Thaddeus's arm—though Thaddeus had very good control, for a stray raised outside Dimilioc. Ethan would be embarrassed if his own control wasn't at least that good. He strenuously put down his first impulse to tear off the colonel's hand, instead allowing himself to be guided right into the middle of the special forces group. His shadow, too, was pressing him hard. It knew they were surrounded by enemies—by enemies with silver—by a huge number of enemies and a whole lot of silver. It took the colonel's grip as a threat. As a stupid threat, from an ordinary weak human. It wanted to answer that threat with violence and blood.

Ethan smiled without showing his teeth, drew back half a step when Colonel Herrod let him go in order to discourage the man from trying that again, and said diplomatically, "A hostage situation, I believe? That's very unusual, for black dogs. Perhaps you'd lay out the problem a little more clearly and explain what you'd like us to do."

"Yes," said Herrod. "One moment." He turned to one of his men. "Handle the mayor's aide. Say friendly, reassuring things until he seems happier." Then, to someone else, a woman: "Get with Lieutenant Burke and make certain the police do absolutely nothing without orders from us."

"Harris is already sitting on Burke," said the woman. She didn't look at her commander, but watched Ethan and Thaddeus steadily—sensible, Ethan thought.

"Go help Harris," Herrod told her. Then, as she nodded and vanished, he turned back to his...consultants. Not prisoners, apparently. At least, if this was a trap, he was taking a very roundabout route toward springing it. He said briskly, "What we have here, it seems, is a bank robbery gone...sideways. We have the security feed, so I think I can tell you with some certainty that there were five men in the gang that attempted the robbery. We believe they're all dead. So is a security guard and one of the bank tellers. There are twenty-seven people still in the main lobby area, not including two black dogs. They've been in there for going on three hours now. The black dogs do not seem to be allowing anyone to move. But nor have they killed any of the hostages, yet." He didn't say *werewolves*. He used the correct term as though he knew what it meant. In fact he didn't, quite, or he would never have touched Ethan. This was probably not the time to discuss black dog sensibilities.

"Who killed the guard and the teller?" Ethan asked.

Herrod smiled thinly, not at all surprised by the question. "The bank robbers shot the guard when they made their initial move. They shot the teller to compel everyone else to cooperate with their demands. The black dogs then shifted form and killed the bank robbers Since that time, we have seen a quite astonishing lack of excitement in the lobby. It therefore seemed best to avoid any precipitous action that might...create excitement."

Ethan nodded. "Those aren't ordinary strays. Or you'd already have had an ordinary bloodbath. All right, Colonel, exactly what do you want from us?"

"Our first priority is ensuring the safety of the hostages. Our second priority is getting your people out of the bank. Since the bank is, as you can see, built to withstand attack, and since we have no way to talk to the black dogs, who do not seem inclined to pick up a ringing phone, both objectives present practical difficulties."

Yeah, Ethan wouldn't want to try to storm that building unless he had a tank. The whole thing really did look pretty much like one solid vault. Sure, there were windows, but they were small as well as barred. Probably the glass was bulletproof, too. He studied Herrod, whose dark face was impenetrably calm. If the colonel had a third priority, he clearly wasn't going to mention it to Ethan. Ethan nodded again, soberly, just as though he had no memory of the colonel trying to take him and Alejandro prisoner that other time. Just as though the possibility of a trap had never occurred to him. He said, "From your account, those black dogs are not perpetrators. They've simply defended themselves. In fact, they may have saved everyone in there from your trigger-happy bank robbers. We want custody of them."

"We can agree to that."

No argument, no debate. Right. But Ethan only asked, "Is the mayor's aide going to agree?"

"I have jurisdiction," Colonel Herrod assured him smoothly, and smiled.

Yeah, that was reassuring. Well, it actually was, in some ways. Not so much, in others. Ethan said, striving for his blandest tone, "Then there's no problem. This shouldn't take long. Ten minutes, maybe." Then he said to Thaddeus, "Come on," and led the way toward the bank. The special forces people moved out of the way, and closed again at their backs.

"He said he could agree to that, not that he *did* agree to it," Thaddeus muttered as they crossed the street.

"Yeah, I noticed that." Ethan laid a hand on the bank door and added, "Listen, I'm not going to shift unless I have to. I'm going to deal with the hostages. I want you to handle the black dogs. Don't kill them. Force them into human shape so we can get a look at them. I want to know who they are."

Thaddeus nodded, his face and hands distorting further. He was already bulking up, and if they didn't get through the door pretty damn soon, he wasn't going to fit. Ethan turned, shoved the door open, and just walked into the bank lobby. No hesitation, no pause for reflection, just straight in, except that the very first thing Ethan did once they were inside was look at the door, find the set of quite impressive deadbolts, and lock the door tight behind them. Luckily it didn't take a key, just physically flipping the levers. There. No one would be coming in at their backs now, at least not very damn easily.

Like any bank lobby at a main branch, it was big, mostly empty space broken here and there with pseudo-Greek pillars, small groups of plush chairs around low tables, or higher tables where people could stand for a minute to sign checks or whatever. The floor was marble, or it looked like marble to Ethan's inexpert eye. A high ceiling, dotted with those black glass bubbles that hid security cameras. Undoubtedly the images from those cameras had a rapt audience; that was something to keep in mind. Flowers on the desks, paintings on the walls, all that kind of thing. Semi-private cubicles to one side, the row of teller's windows to the other side, a couple doors leading into the interior of the bank. The doors were closed.

And, at the moment, a lot of scared people, tucked singly or in small groups behind desks and partitions and overturned chairs. The dead ones weren't tucked away, of course; they were mostly sprawled out in the open. There was a whole lot of blood, mostly puddled on the floor, but some of it spattered across walls and cubicle partitions. Guns, too, mostly lying near the dead men, and a damn good thing none of the hostages had tried to get one and shoot the black dogs because Ethan could tell even through the scent of the blood that none of the guns was loaded with silver. Shoot a black dog with normal ammunition and you'd probably just make him mad.

The two black dogs were at the far end of the lobby. They had both pivoted toward the big main doors when Ethan had opened them. Now one of them made a sound between a cough and a roar, and everyone in the room flinched and cowered. The scents of fear and blood were powerful, intoxicating. Ethan's opinion of those two black dogs went up a notch. They must have very good control, or they wouldn't have been able to resist killing everyone in the lobby. Ethan felt the urge to do that himself, and *he* was Dimilioc. These two black dogs had fought back that bloodlust for hours, even when penned up and surrounded by enemies—they had to be aware of all those cops and special forces people out there, that was why they were still in here. No black dog was born with control as good as that. No. This kind of control was the result of rigorous training. And he was almost certain both of those black dogs must also have had the *Beschwichtigung*, the Calming.

He called to them, "Hey, you want to do this the easy way or the hard way? Shift to human, right now, you hear me?" But he was pretty sure neither of the black dogs was going to be able to follow that order. He guessed, just looking at them, that they were scared and furious and had both probably lost language. A lot of black dogs lost human speech when they shifted, especially when they were upset. No matter how good their control was, they were probably going to break –

Then one of them did break, and charged him. The second lunged after the first, joining in or trying to stop his partner, it wasn't clear.

Thaddeus shouldered past him, and Ethan said sharply, "*Don't* kill them!", repeating his earlier order because it was going to be hard to remember when the fun started. Then, affecting nonchalance as Thaddeus met the strangers' attack, he looked around at all the hostages. Ignoring the fight, he said in a loud voice, just as polite as could be, "It's been a tough couple of hours, I know, but if all you ladies and gentlemen will just stay calm and quiet for a few more minutes, we'll get this taken care of and you can all go home and have dinner with your families tonight, okay?"

There, that sounded reassuring, didn't it? If none of the hostages had panicked so far, maybe none would. Most of the ones he could see were peeking around or over furniture. One man, a distinguished-looking older guy in a gray suit with a muted-pink shirt, was sitting in the doorway of a cubicle, blocking the doorway. Ethan could see several young women, probably bank employees, hiding in that cubicle. The guy was a white knight, apparently, but not stupid about it or he'd probably have tried to get one of the guns long before this. That would have been a disaster, but if it hadn't happened yet, probably it'd be okay –

There was a roar and a crash behind him, which Ethan pretended not to notice. A covert glance was reassuring. Thaddeus had bodily picking up one of the other black dogs and thrown him twenty feet—not in the direction of any of the hostages, fortunately—to slam into a big desk. The desk must have been super heavy, or maybe bolted to the floor, because it didn't skid under that blow. Most of the hostages had flinched and gasped at the crash, but none of them broke for the door, so that was all right, for now. Ethan began collecting all the fallen guns, though, because he didn't want to risk anybody trying to grab one now that all the black dogs seemed to be occupied. Letting himself or Thaddeus get shot at the last minute by one of the hostages would be ridiculous. Besides, even ordinary bullets *could* kill a black dog if he was hit just right. Ethan unloaded each gun and set them all aside on one of the tables, keeping half an eye on the fight going on across the lobby.

It wasn't really a fair fight, even though it was two on one. Ethan had seen Thaddeus fight before, but never when he had been in human form himself and staying out of it. Now he had a ringside seat, so he could really see how, compared to the other two black dogs...there just was no comparison. Fully transformed, Thaddeus was bigger than any other black dog Ethan had ever seen—even bigger than Ethan's father had been, and Harrison Lanning had been massive. Thaddeus must be half a ton if he was an ounce, except that he carried a lot of his weight in his shadow, so he was also superbly light on his feet. Superbly fast. Not as fast as Ezekiel, but no one was that fast. Thaddeus was certainly faster than either of those strangers.

On the other hand, the two unknown black dogs fought as a team—Ethan wasn't at all surprised, though working together didn't come naturally to black dogs. Even so, they wouldn't have been any kind of match for Thaddeus, except they were trying to kill him, and he was trying not to kill them. That could be a problem. Ethan thoughtfully looked over the last of the guns, lifted it, and shot one of the two black dogs in the gut when he reared up. Just once. He didn't want to kill him; that would be embarrassing after he'd told Thaddeus to restrain himself.

The gut-shot black dog screamed and lunged toward Ethan, and Thaddeus took the chance to rip claws across his side and belly, and that did it—the black dog was down, contorting helplessly into human form, his shadow taking the injuries that would otherwise have killed him. The other one, silent and furious, got between the first and Thaddeus, who simply bulled forward, drove his opponent down with his overwhelming weight, snapped powerful jaws just once, and flung him aside. That one, too, was already mostly in human form when he smashed into a pillar and collapsed to the floor.

Thaddeus backed away from his two opponents, snarling but not pressing for the kill. Good for him. Ethan watched carefully, but everything looked fine. The two black dogs were trying to get up, but they were both still in human form, unable to shift back yet. If either of them took a serious injury now, their shadows might not be able to take it away. They were vulnerable, desperately vulnerable, and when Thaddeus snarled, a low deadly sound, one of them flattened down in submission. The other gripped a nearby desk and hauled himself up, rubbing a shaking hand across his mouth, probably trying to recover human speech. That one would be the leader of the pair, then.

Ethan was surprised Thaddeus could restrain himself well enough not to smash that one back to the floor, but he tried to look like nothing had ever surprised him in his life. He said briskly, "Good job." Then he glanced around at the hostages, who were still, astonishingly, behaving like good little hostages and not tempting fate. He pointed to the man in the pink shirt, who definitely seemed one of the steadiest. "You," he said. And remembered to add, "Sir."

The man straightened, tensing, his hand moving half an inch before he wisely stopped all movement. He met Ethan's eyes, but he didn't mean anything by it, probably, and anyway he was still sitting on the floor.

"Time for everyone to leave. Get that organized, please," Ethan told him. "One of those doors over there, not the main door, you understand? Fine, then. No screaming, shouting, or running. One little group at a time. Have everyone walk quietly, single file. See to that, please. Not you, though. You're a bank official, aren't you?"

"I'm the manager. Brian McNamara."

"Great. That's perfect. Then you stick around in case we need anything else, okay, Mr. McNamara? Thank you for your cooperation."

The manager didn't ask any questions. He got to his feet slowly, plainly stiff after sitting on the floor that long. He glanced from Ethan to Thaddeus and back again as he moved, and kept an eye on the other two black dogs as well, especially the one on his feet. Thaddeus was the only one in black dog form now, but clearly the man didn't take any of them lightly, which was another reason to respect his good sense.

Then something about the way the man moved and stood struck Ethan, and he asked sharply, "Sir, are you armed?"

At this question, Thaddeus turned his head, so he hadn't lost language after all, or else he'd gotten it back when the situation had started to calm down. His eyes glowed with lambent fire, and he curled a lip to show jet-black fangs.

McNamara stood very still. "Yes," he said, in a voice that was admirably steady.

"Well, you've been very sensible so far," Ethan said calmly. "Let's keep that going, sir. Everyone's safe now. Take your weapon out, unload it, and put it back in your pocket...just drop the clip, if you don't mind...good," he added, as the bank manager obeyed.

It was a small gun and Ethan could tell the bullets weren't silver, but everything was under control now and he definitely did not want to tempt fate by letting anybody get shot unexpectedly. Definitely not. He would never be able to explain to Grayson if he let things go to hell *now*. "Very good. All right. Go on. Those nearest the door first, please. No hurry. Everything's fine. No hurry at all." He shoved his hands in his pockets in order to look more nearly harmless and pretended to pay no attention as McNamara started quietly directing the other hostages out of the lobby through one of the smaller interior doors. He had to unlock it first, but that was no problem, since naturally he had a key. McNamara made no move to get out himself, at least not yet. He'd had been making all the right moves so far. He was clearly a very brave man, and clearly he kept his head in a crisis. So far he seemed exactly what Ethan would have hoped for if he'd thought the scenario through for an hour before walking into this bank.

Pretending to pay no attention to the slow retreat of the hostages, Ethan walked across the lobby toward the nearer black dog, the one on his feet.

The black dog was older than Ethan, but probably not as old as Thaddeus. Early thirties, maybe, somewhere around there. His shadow was fairly dense, moderately strong for a black dog his age. He was a slender man with high, sharp cheekbones and dark hair. There was a familiar look to him, Ethan was almost sure.

The man looked up, meeting Ethan's eyes for a moment. Probably he would be able to shift again by now, and no doubt he could tell as well as Ethan that if he did, he would probably be the stronger. But then his gaze shifted toward Thaddeus and he dropped his eyes again. Yeah, he wasn't going to challenge Thaddeus again, not now, not when he'd already has his ass handed to him. Yeah, not likely.

Ethan tried not to be bitter about his own relative lack of strength. God knew he should be used to it. Anyway, it didn't matter right now. He told the black dog, "I'm Ethan Lanning. Grayson Lanning is my uncle."

The other black dog bowed his head. After a moment, he went to one knee. "We did not deliberately intrude on Dimilioc territory," he said, in precise, accented English. "We beg your pardon. We are Lumondière. We are both Lumondière."

"Yeah." Ethan was not surprised. "Names?"

The man gestured toward his own chest. "Frédéric. I am Frédéric Lumondière. My uncle Fabian was the last Lumondière Master but one." He glanced up, probably to see whether Ethan recognized the name. Ethan pretended he was Grayson, keeping his face still, ungiving. The other black dog dropped his gaze immediately. After a moment he went on quietly, "That is my cousin, Absolon Lumondière. We had hoped...we had hoped to find others of our house. We had heard perhaps some of our house had come to America. We did not mean to intrude. We beg your pardon. We would not have drawn your notice, Ethan Lanning. We would not deliberately have drawn Dimilioc attention."

"That would have been wiser," Ethan told him, still channeling Grayson. "What happened here?" Over to the side, the bank manager was carefully directing another group of hostages toward the door. Ethan kept an eye on him, but so far that whole part of the problem seemed to be working itself out just fine. One more group of hostages after that, the ones farthest from the door, five people, all women, probably bank employees. They were all on their feet, but McNamara had somehow kept them from rushing the door. No panic, no running. That was fairly impressive.

Of course, Thaddeus was still looming in the middle of the room, his massive head swinging slowly back and forth as he watched the hostages and menaced the Lumondière black dogs and kept an eye on all the doors—he was keeping himself together really well in a tough situation, and Ethan was suddenly intensely glad he had Thaddeus at his back and not any of the other new Dimilioc wolves. He would never have trusted Keziah with the Lumondière wolves, nor the Meade brothers to remember the hostages were not to be touched. Alejandro...Alejandro might have done okay, which made sense considering his father had been a Toland, but Thaddeus was older and stronger. Alejandro might not have been able to take the two Lumondière wolves without a lot more help. Though he might have forced one or both of the strangers into human form; there was that. Thaddeus hadn't needed that kind of advantage, though.

Frédéric Lumondière had looked up again, though carefully, not meeting Ethan's eyes. "We did not murder anyone. We keep the law. Our law is the same as Dimilioc law. The ones we killed, they were not good men. We only wanted to change money. But they came in, those men. They were *animaux*." He used the French word, but his meaning was clear—and even more pejorative when a black dog used it that way than an ordinary human. He said harshly, "They shot the other one, and the girl, and when Absolon did not step aside for them, they shot him also. What choice did we have?"

"They shot your cousin first? You both shifted only after that?"

"Of course. Or Absolon would not have shifted. His control is better than that. Mine is far better. Though I know...I know I have not shown good control to you." He bowed his head again, this time a little more deeply. Embarrassed. He should be, was Ethan's opinion. Terrorizing everyone. For hours. He ought to have forced his shadow down, pulled himself together, and worked things out.

Granted, it might be harder to handle yourself in a foreign country, especially once the cops surrounded the building and everything got thoroughly out of your control. Maybe even more when Dimilioc black wolves showed up and you knew you'd stepped in it but good.

"All right. Stay there," Ethan told him. He beckoned to the other one, Absolon. "You, come over here with your cousin." Then, as the younger of the two black dogs crept to join them, he glanced at Thaddeus, meaning, *Keep them right here. Don't let them defy you.* Thaddeus dropped his jaw open in a black dog laugh and made a low, low sound like distant thunder deep underground, and both Lumondière black dogs flinched.

Satisfied, Ethan strode across the lobby to intercept McNamara before the man could slip out with the last of the hostages. Waving the women on out the door, he took the man by the arm and guided him firmly back across the lobby toward the little group of black dogs.

Thaddeus certainly dominated the scene now. He looked even bigger now that everyone else was in human form. Ethan felt the tension in McNamara's arm and let him go, because under the circumstances he could see that even a human might take that kind of grip for a threat. He said in a clear voice, speaking for the cameras, "You've done an excellent job, sir. You're almost done now."

"Almost done, am I?" said McNamara, in a tone that managed to be drily amused and wary and sarcastic all at once.

It was, in a way, very much like black dog humor. Ethan laughed before he caught himself, but the bank manager was so rock-steady he didn't flinch even at that. "You're our token hostage," Ethan told him, this time in a low tone. Clearly the man had already figured that out. "But it's my firm intention to get all of us out of here and on our way home without any more violence. You're just the type of hostage I want. You keep your head. You kept it together for *hours* in here. That's very impressive. You could have got out with the first batch of hostages. I couldn't have stopped you."

"It was obvious you wanted a...token hostage."

"Yeah." The human had guessed that from the beginning, then, and he'd deliberately let himself be stuck with the role, making sure his people got out. Ethan gave him a respectful nod. "Just hang on another moment or two. We'll get this worked out, sir." The 'sir' came out a lot more easily this time. Nudging the man toward a chair, one that was neither broken nor saturated in blood, Ethan said to the Lumondière cousins, "We are all back in control, yes? We are not going to have any more trouble, because if we do, I guarantee Dimilioc will take it personally, understand?"

"We absolutely understand," Frédéric Lumondière said earnestly. "We are grateful for Dimilioc's indulgence."

"Yeah, you should be. Your cousin have a voice?"

Absolon didn't look up. He was on both knees, his head down. Young, just a kid, really; if he was out of his teens Ethan would be surprised. And his shadow wasn't all that strong even for his age. He was overwhelmingly outmatched by Thaddeus, outmatched even by Ethan, and he knew it. But he swallowed and managed to say, in a fairly normal voice, "I understand. I will not let it up again. I...I beg Dimilioc's pardon. I didn't mean to make trouble."

"Not your fault they shot you, kid," Ethan told him.

"But do better now, hear me?" He looked at Thaddeus. "All right. I think we've got this."

Thaddeus dropped his jaw again in violent black dog amusement and reared up...and dwindled into human form, though for him the change didn't seem to make as much of a size difference as it would have for most of them. Once he had shifted, he straightened his back and grinned fiercely at the other two black dogs, and there was *no question* about anybody arguing. Frédéric's eyes had widened, though. He opened his mouth, maybe to make a smart comment about Dimilioc letting strays into their bloodlines—it had to be pretty clear to anyone familiar with Dimilioc bloodlines that Thaddeus must have been born a stray; generally Dimilioc had been fairly priggish about just whom they brought into their pristine bloodlines. Though never as much as Lumondière. If a comment about strays had been on the tip of the Frenchman's tongue, he kept it there, closing his mouth without uttering a word. Wise of him.

"All right," Ethan said again, with a narrow look to emphasize that Lumondière had better not make any comment at all about how Dimilioc chose to arrange its affairs. "Listen up. Étienne Lumondière's establishing a presence in this country, with Dimilioc permission. I expect he'll be delighted to recover some wolves from his own house. You understand?"

They did. Absolon looked up with dawning hope, flinched when he realized he'd met Ethan's eyes, and dropped his gaze. Frédéric said with dignity, "We would be very grateful to have Dimilioc's permission to join our cousin."

"Yeah, I bet," said Ethan. "You have it, and let me just mention that it is a damn good thing you did not kill anyone besides the bad guys. Now. What we need to do next is get clear of this situation, and I think we will be able to do that. But you listen to me, both of you: there are a million cops out there. They are not your problem. Your problem is staying on Dimilioc's good side. The police and special forces and national guard and, hell, just whoever is out there, they are my problem and I will deal with them. You will stay close to me and follow my lead and you will not, repeat not, attack anyone. You got that?" He leaned forward and added, in a much lower voice, "Unless I attack them first and then all bets are off, but that is not what we want, is that clear?"

"Very clear," said Frédéric, and his cousin nodded fervent agreement.

"Good," said Ethan. He took McNamara's arm again, and never mind the man's slight flinch. "Mr. McNamara and I will go first. Then you two. Then Thaddeus at the back. We won't have any trouble."

There were indeed about a million cops out there in the late afternoon sunlight, when Ethan threw the bolts again and opened the lobby door. A million and a half, maybe. Ethan was glad to see the special forces guys in the front, between the black dogs and all the ordinary cops. A solid wall of special forces in front, then a good-sized gap, then the police behind that. With here and there a special forces man among the police; good. And the special forces woman; he picked her out, too, right beside a guy who had to be the chief of police. Even better; he was glad to have someone over there preventing mistakes. Ethan trusted Colonel Herrod...at least, he trusted him not to let his people shoot *accidentally*. And not to let anybody shoot without his order.

In fact, yes, there was Herrod himself, right there in the front in that elegant brown suit, the jacket just two degrees lighter than his skin, highly visible in the sea of black body armor. Yes, and the colonel was just as obviously in control as always. Every single special forces man had his weapon leveled right at the black wolves, but Colonel Herrod didn't even have a gun in his hand. Again, good.

Ethan nudged McNamara and walked with him toward the colonel, feeling the other three black dogs at his back. Sticking close, as he'd ordered them. They made a perfect damn target if all those special forces guys opened up, but there had never been any hope of avoiding that danger. And the colonel must have given some signal, because all the guns were actually going up now, pointing at the sky. That was excellent.

Ethan stopped several feet from Herrod, just far enough back, he hoped, that the special forces people wouldn't be too concerned. He looked ostentatiously at his watch. Then he met the colonel's eyes, trying for human-direct rather than black dog-threat. "Twelve minutes. Not bad, I'd say."

"Indeed," agreed the colonel. "We certainly appreciate your assistance in resolving this situation so expeditiously. We're very grateful." He looked thoughtfully over the two French black dogs. Then his gaze turned, unsurprisingly, toward Thaddeus.

Thaddeus sure did draw the eye: Big and black and bald and absolutely badass. Except it was no laughing matter. He was too damn recognizable. Ethan could see how that was likely to be a significant problem, under the circumstances. "Dimilioc is always glad to assist the special forces in such matters," he assured Herrod, in his blandest tone. What *would* Grayson say at a moment like this? Something formal, even stilted; formality was Grayson's way of making sure everyone knew he was in control and in charge. It worked, too. Ethan said, "Dimilioc believes, in these dangerous days, that it's important to promote a spirit of cooperation and mutual trust." Did that sound too ridiculous?

The colonel didn't crack a smile. "I agree, naturally."

"I'm glad to hear it." And that was enough, surely, so he added more quietly, "So let's tie a bow around this situation, how about it? We can all go home and sleep in our own beds tonight."

Now Herrod did smile, though barely. "I think Mr. McNamara would particularly appreciate that." He hadn't been speaking loudly, but now he lowered his voice even further. "Let him go now, if you please."

"Of course," agreed Ethan, and waited, not loosening his grip on the human's arm by one iota.

There was a little pause. Then the colonel lifted his eyebrows questioningly.

"At the earliest possible opportunity," Ethan added,

putting a little bite into his tone. *Your move, Colonel Herrod, sir. So make it.*

The colonel's smile took on a sardonic edge. "I don't suppose the four of you would simply release Mr. McNamara and agree to surrender yourselves into my custody?"

"That doesn't seem likely, no."

"Unfortunate." The colonel paused. "At the moment, I have a useful working relationship with Grayson Lanning. I wouldn't care to ruin that. Nor do I intend to precipitate a bloodbath. Certainly not on national television. You've no need to be concerned."

Undoubtedly there were cameras everywhere. Ethan didn't look for them. He had already assumed that. He said, "That's great, Colonel. I'm glad to hear it. Why don't I let Mr. McNamara go and you personally walk us to our car? That way we can all part friends. How does that sound?"

"Colonel –" one of his men began.

Herrod held up one hand. "No, I agree." He shook his head slightly to stop a more determined protest before it could be made and repeated, "I agree. We'll do it exactly that way. There's no problem." He stepped forward, putting himself well within Ethan's reach. Then he nodded to McNamara. "Sir, I think you should move aside now."

"You kept things in there from turning into a disaster," Ethan told the bank manager before letting him go. He raised his voice and went on, enunciating clearly, "Dimilioc is grateful for your courage and good sense." Then he finally released his hold on the man's arm.

McNamara had too much pride to move immediately. Maybe he was thinking of the cameras too. He said drily, "I did absolutely nothing."

"Which saved everyone," said Ethan. "Our people as well as yours. Keeping everyone quiet, keeping anyone from doing anything, was essential, and far from easy under the circumstances. We understand that. Dimilioc is in your debt. Lumondière is very seriously in your debt." He continued to enunciate for the cameras, but it was all true. He met the man's eyes to show human-style respect and inclined his head.

After a moment, McNamara nodded back. Then he turned and walked away, not too fast. The special forces men parted for him and closed ranks again behind him, and there went the last civilian hostage. Ethan turned to Colonel Herrod. Who only smiled thinly and tilted his head toward the waiting car. "Your vehicle," he said, and at his gesture, his people all shifted back and aside, leaving a clear path.

"Good," said Ethan. He didn't touch Herrod, but held out a hand, inviting the colonel to walk with them. Herrod turned without haste and led the way, the black dogs close behind him. The car wasn't locked. Ethan opened the driver's-side door and ordered briskly, "Thaddeus behind me, Frédéric beside him, Absolon in the front. Let's go." Then, as he waited for the other three black dogs to get in the car, he studied Herrod.

The colonel did not step back. He said, his tone dry, "It's a nice afternoon for a drive, I suppose."

Ethan thought about it. He didn't want to be unnecessarily stupid, but...there *were* all those cameras, no question. It would look all wrong if he made it *obvious* Herrod was a hostage. But the cameras worked for them, too, because once the black dogs were all in the car and moving, Herrod would have no chance of taking them without highly visible violence. Ethan was almost certain the optics of any such move would not be good for the special forces. Absolon in particular was plainly just a kid. He didn't look at all like a monster *now*. He said at last, "I don't think that will be necessary, Colonel. You're a busy man. I'm sure you have things to do."

Herrod raised one eyebrow. Then he nodded. "A pleasure working with you," he told Ethan. He sounded like he meant it. Maybe he did.

Ethan nodded back. Then he got in the car. The key was in the ignition. He turned it. The engine started without the slightest problem. Herrod had stepped back and was holding up his hand; all his people were shifting to leave the road clear. The police were clearing out of the way, too. All right.

That all looked fine. Ethan eased the car forward and just...drove away. He kept an eye on the rear view mirror, but so far as he could tell, no one followed them.

Thaddeus started to say something. "Shut up," Ethan snapped. "No one say a single damn word." He turned a corner and then another corner, leaving all the flashing lights and guns behind them. Not quite all their problems, not yet, but he could feel some of the tension ease out of his shoulders and back. He turned again, spotted a Walmart, and turned into the parking lot. Drove through it, turned, and drove through it again. There. A woman, by herself, getting out of a dark blue SUV. He said sharply, "We're trading vehicles. No one touch the woman." Then he was out of the car and nodding politely to the woman. "Ma'am, sorry, this is a hijacking. We need your car. You'll get it back."

The woman, obviously surprised, fell back a step. She looked scared, but she didn't scream. She reached into her handbag, but she was human-slow. Ethan took the handbag away from her and tossed it onto the passenger seat of the other car as Absolon got out. Then Thaddeus got out on the other side of the car and the woman immediately took a step back. Yeah, sheer size was a plus sometimes. "Move!" Ethan snapped at all of them, and slid into the driver's seat himself. Then they were rolling and out on the road again.

"She will surely report the theft immediately," Frédéric said after a moment, quietly, the way a weaker black dog would speak to a stronger when he did not want to give offense.

"Yeah, we'll have to trade cars again, but at least this one won't have bugs or tracers. Special forces had our car for twelve whole minutes. What do you figure the odds on that one being clean?" Ethan signaled and turned sedately onto the highway, accelerating smoothly and...they were clear. He thought they were clear. He did think so. They would indeed need to ditch the SUV as soon as possible. But that wouldn't be a problem. Black dogs could perfectly well go across country for quite a distance. He thought that would probably be the best strategy for all of them, in fact. They could try to rent cars, but he bet that after today they would all be too recognizable for some time. Especially Thaddeus, who was definitely going to have to stay out of sight for a while.

He said, "In a few miles, I'll let you two out. Étienne is in Denver."

Absolon, beside Ethan, let out a slow breath, and Frédéric said in a low voice, "That was true, then."

Ethan glanced over his shoulder at the other black dog. "You didn't think so?"

"I hoped...I hoped it was the truth." Frédéric was silent a moment. Then he said quietly, "We are very much in your debt."

"You sure are," Ethan agreed. "Don't think I won't remember, either. Now, listen. I suggest you go straight across country for fifty miles or so, then steal or buy another car. Don't kill anyone, hear me? That would interfere with, how did I put it?"

"Promoting a spirit of cooperation and mutual trust," rumbled Thaddeus.

Ethan blinked, startled. He hadn't expected Thaddeus to pick up his line. But he said smoothly, "Exactly. We are all about promoting a spirit of cooperation and mutual trust these days. So don't kill anyone. Do not get into situations where you can't control your shadows. Or if you do, damn well don't get caught. At the very least, make sure it doesn't look like black dog work. Is that clear?"

"Yes. That is very clear."

"All right, then." Ethan was silent for a moment. Then he added, "Ezekiel Korte is out in Denver, too, at the moment."

"Ah!" murmured Frédéric.

"Yeah. Just so you know. Étienne is in charge out there, but only because Grayson put him in charge. Ezekiel is nominally under his authority, but that can change if Étienne pushes it too far and I'm sure he knows that. Lumondière is not a separate house anymore. Grayson won't stand for it. That isn't going to change. There aren't enough of us left to divide up that way. All of us, Lumondière and Dimilioc, need to support each other. Or we risk men like Colonel Herrod playing divide and conquer. So Lumondière is a sept of Dimilioc now. You understand?"

"*Oui*. Yes. I understand, Ethan Lanning. We understand you very well."

A black dog who felt threatened would agree to anything, but Frédéric Lumondière had no real reason to feel that way any longer. He spoke slowly and thoughtfully, and Ethan was fairly sure he meant what he said.

"Good," Ethan said, and took the next exit, one that led not to a town, but just to some small road or other. Lots of not much out here in the Midwest. Amazing how close to the city you ran out of city.

He pulled off on the shoulder. "Out," he ordered. And added impulsively, "Good luck."

Absolon slid out fast, eyes down, but Frédéric got out of the car more slowly, with a little nod. "Thank you," he said—not usual, from a black dog, but he nodded again, a little more deeply, before he backed away a step and another step, and finally turned to stride after his cousin. Not running, neither of them was running. But walking briskly.

And just like that, the two Lumondière cousins were out of Ethan's hair. Another load off his mind. Ethan stretched, shaking his head, relaxing for the first time in...it seemed like hours and hours. Days. He yawned, hardly able to believe they had got away with...all that. And in pretty decent order, all things considered. He said over his shoulder to Thaddeus, "We'll leave the car here. Remember to lock the doors; the lady might as well get her car back intact. We'll cut across country too, pick up another car someplace where it might not be missed for a couple of days."

"Yeah?" said Thaddeus. "Probably that'll be smart of us. You still giving the orders, huh?"

It took a second. Then Ethan's heart jumped, all his relaxation abruptly gone, every muscle tense. His hands closed hard on the steering wheel. Because it was true. He had been giving the orders. From the time they'd pulled up outside the bank, right through to this moment. He hadn't even noticed he was doing it.

Obviously Thaddeus had noticed.

Clearing his throat, he faced forward, staring out the windshield. Definitely not looking at Thaddeus. He had to clear his throat again before he could be sure of his tone. "Yeah, okay. Will you take an apology?"

There was a pause. It didn't help that Ethan knew the other black dog could hear his rapid heartbeat.

Then Thaddeus said, his voice rough, "No, I don't want an apology."

"Fine!" Ethan said tightly. He flung himself out of the car, looking around to assess this location. As it happened, the spot really did look pretty much ideal. It wasn't a busy exit, not much in sight to draw traffic, not even a gas station, just this little road going off nowhere important.

Then Thaddeus got out of the back seat and straightened to his full height.

Ethan wanted, badly, to back up. But there was just no point in putting it off, so instead he snapped, "How do you want it? Human form or black dog? The former might draw less attention." And it would be better for Ethan; a little safer. He didn't say that, but then it wouldn't make all that much difference anyway; he was sure Thaddeus could do a bang-up job with just his fists and feet, no need for claws. But there was less chance of one black dog killing another accidentally if they stuck to human form. And less chance of drawing too much attention, if Thaddeus would make it quick. *There* was a good reason to do it right here in this semi-public place; Ethan would have suggested it just for that reason if he'd thought of it. He hadn't, though. He hadn't thought of anything much. That was the whole problem, right there.

He met the stronger black dog's eyes for a long moment, deliberately. Then he bowed his head and waited.

"Shit," said Thaddeus.

He sounded seriously pissed off, and again Ethan had to fight the urge to back up. He shoved his hands into his pockets to make it perfectly clear he wasn't going to fight back, but he didn't otherwise move. But...nothing. At last he risked a look up.

Thaddeus was just standing there, scowling at him.

"What?" Ethan snapped, now truly exasperated as well as tense with sheer physical fear. "Damn, *what?"* And realized a heartbeat too late just how out of line that tone was, under the circumstances. He couldn't keep from flinching. "Look, I –"

"I don't want an apology because *I am not angry*," Thaddeus said, coming down heavily on the last words.

He was plainly furious, but Ethan wasn't about to contradict him.

The bigger black dog went on in a low growl, "I'm not mad. *I* wouldn't have known how to handle Herrod. Or those Lumondière black dogs. Hell, I wouldn't even have thought of that thing with the bank guy. How would I know stuff like that?" He stopped, but Ethan didn't know what to say. After a pause, Thaddeus said slowly, "The thing is, I don't know how to figure when I'm in charge and when I'm not. When Grayson's around, it's simple. But out here, I don't understand how you can...just tell when to take over. I don't understand when I'm supposed to step back. How am I supposed to tell about shit like that?"

Thaddeus was still glowering, but...this time Ethan could see what he meant. He opened his mouth, closed it again, and shook his head. But he had to come up with something, clearly. He said finally, "I don't know what to tell you. I didn't think it through. I didn't think about it at all. I...guess I was thinking about Grayson, about what he would do, how he would handle it. I guess I was trying to deal with the whole damned mess like I was the Master of Dimilioc."

He looked away, took a deep breath, and looked back. "But I'm not the Master. I am never going to have half Grayson's strength. I know that. I can't begin to challenge you, and I didn't mean to try. I should absolutely have checked with you before flying wide. It was not your job to figure out I had forgotten you were in charge and accommodate that. It was your job to tell me to take over, or if you didn't, I should have suggested it. I had no business just...pushing in." He hesitated, but he had to say it, so he did. "You have every right to beat the crap out of me. I could not say a word about it."

"Yeah," said Thaddeus. "No." He flexed his big hands and then stuffed them in his pockets. "No," he said again.

Ethan nodded, intensely relieved, yet baffled. "You don't . . ." he stopped. Then he said, "You wouldn't have to worry about Grayson. You know that, right? He'd agree I had it coming."

"It wasn't your fault," Thaddeus said shortly. "You were right to step in. I get what you mean. I should have figured you would know what you were doing better than me. I should have told you to take charge. That was my fault."

"Yeah, well...anyway, I'm sorry I didn't handle it better. I was out of line." Ethan thought about it and winced inwardly. "Not the first time. I've been, look, I've been holding it against you. That you weren't born into Dimilioc. You know that, I expect, I haven't been— well, anyway. But...I knew you had my back today. I knew you were backing me up and I knew I didn't have to worry about you. So, I was wrong. Grayson knew what he was doing when he brought you in, and I know that, and I'm sorry."

Thaddeus heard him out, his broad face expressionless. Then he shrugged. "Shit, kid, you're all right. A stuck-up asshole sometimes, but what kid isn't?" He ran a powerful hand over his bald head and laughed suddenly. "You know what? Since I'm in charge, I'm telling you, you get to write the damn report about this."

Ethan groaned, but he laughed, too. "Right. All right. Yes. Fine."

"Yeah. Well." Thaddeus looked around. No one had stopped yet, though a few cars had gone past. "Somebody's probably called us in by now, you think? Across country, is it?"

"If you agree," Ethan said, not quite smoothly.

Thaddeus chuckled, deep but with real humor. "Yeah, I agree. Look . . ."

Ethan glanced at him.

"The Master of Dimilioc doesn't have to be the strongest," Thaddeus pointed out, his voice a quiet rumble. "Grayson isn't the strongest. Ezekiel backs him up, but even that's not why he's Master. Grayson is the Master of Dimilioc because enough of us agree he should be. If he had only half his strength, he would still be Master." He stopped, gave Ethan a hard look that dared him to say anything, turned off the shoulder of the highway, and strode away toward a distant belt of trees. The sun was low by this time, shadows stretching out. After a moment, Thaddeus shifted to his massive black dog form and loped away toward the setting sun, much faster than a man could run.

It was a little bit of a risk, maybe. But soon it would be dusk and then full dark, and after that two black dogs would be damn near invisible. Ethan stared after Thaddeus for a stretched-out moment. Then he laughed suddenly, and shifted, and leaped away from the cars and highways of ordinary humans, running toward the night along the path of the sun.

A FAMILY VISIT

Justin flipped his phone closed and put it away, frowning.

Keziah glanced at him, sidelong and skeptical. “She said you are not to come,” she observed. “She said she is too busy for you to visit. She said she has duties for her church that will use all the hours of her days, and so she has no time for you, the son of her daughter. She said many foolish things to you, her grandson, who has come so very far to visit her.”

Of course Keziah had heard every word of both sides of the conversation. Everyone had heard. Black dog hearing was death on private phone conversations, even if they hadn’t been in the close confines of a rather small car. “Yeah, kind of a change from last week,” Justin said. He tried to keep his tone neutral, even though he knew he wasn’t fooling anyone. Black dogs could hear your heartbeat speed up, too. They could probably smell your sudden anxiety. He wasn’t sure about that; he’d never asked. Frankly, he didn’t want to know.

“Well, I think you will not wish to turn around and go back to Dimilioc,” Keziah said drily.

Justin knew she was being sarcastic, but he shook his head anyway. “Could you maybe drive a little faster?”

Keziah was driving, of course. Black dogs always wanted to drive. They hated being passengers. They hated not being in control. If Justin had learned one thing over the past eight months, he had learned that. The highest ranking black dog always got to drive, and in this car right now, that was definitely Keziah.

He was okay with that, though. He’d learned to accommodate black dog emotional volatility. Every one of them was like that: fierce-tempered and intolerant of any constraint. They were born that way. He was willing to make allowances. After all, the Dimilioc black dogs did their best not to be monsters. Most of them, anyway.

Besides, not only was Keziah a good driver, this was actually her car. Dimilioc owned a good many big muscle cars, high-slung vehicles with broad tires, the better to handle rough roads and snow, several passengers and plenty of luggage. Keziah's car was shiny silver Jaguar, quick and responsive, with deep bucket seats and plenty of guts to send it slashing down the highway in the fast lane. He didn't know where she'd gotten the money for it. Keziah always seemed to have money; he guessed she'd stolen it from her family when she fled, but he didn't know for sure and had no plans to ask.

However she'd come by it, Keziah's Jaguar wasn't the best choice for Vermont where it was winter practically all year. But Justin had to admit that way out here in the desert, it was just right. Or it would have been just right, for two. The back seat was a little cramped, unfortunately. More than a little, when you were talking about a couple of black dog kids who weren't exactly sure they got along.

Oh, neither of the kids whined *He's touching me* or *Make her stop looking at me.* They weren't five. Besides, Keziah had made her opinion of whining real clear. So Amira and Nicholas ignored each other. But it was the ostentatious kind of *blatant* ignoring only kids in their early teens could pull off.

Keziah's sister Amira was all right, actually. She was an odd combination of timid and bloodthirsty, wistful and violent. It probably made sense if you were a thirteen-year-old black dog girl with a long scar where a silver knife had cut across your face some time in the past. But somewhere in her life she had learned *really solid* control. Maybe that injury had done it, though Justin suspected it was Keziah's influence during her sister's childhood. Whoever had trained her, Amira was deadly in a fight—Keziah said so, and despite the girl's age, Justin was sure it was true. But he trusted that she wasn't likely to kill anybody by accident. Besides, she took Dimilioc's mandate to protect the Pure very seriously. So even before this peculiar conversation with his grandmother Justin hadn't minded having her along. Or not much.

He'd been a lot less happy about having to bring Nicholas along, though. But Grayson had been adamant: three black dogs, a full team, or he wouldn't permit Justin to make this trip at all. That was why Nicholas Hammond was back there with Amira.

Nicholas was a sullen, angry fourteen-year-old, a real pain in the neck sometimes. Not that the kid didn't have reason to be sullen and angry: Last spring, Nicholas and his friends had fallen afoul of a master vampire—hopefully the only master vampire left in the world. Justin didn't like to remember that vampire, or the brief, grim, desperate struggle to destroy it. But it had arguably been worst for Nicholas, who had lost every single one of the remaining black dogs of his sept, including his sister. Worst of all, no one had ever found Carissa's body.

Justin knew all about loss and grief. But not knowing what had really happened to someone you loved...that had to be the worst. So he was sorry for Nicholas. He really was. And he knew from personal experience that the kid was brave and determined and quick-thinking. But even so, he would never have trusted this kid's sense or his temper around Grandmama Leushin, except that there was no question who was in charge of their little team. Keziah was in charge. Nicholas was scared of Keziah, like anyone sensible would be. Justin might not have trusted the kid on his own, but he trusted *that*.

Still, until this phone call, he'd definitely wished neither of those kids was in the back seat; that no one was in the car besides him and Keziah. He had first conceived of this trip as just the two of them, with endless miles between them and Dimilioc. He'd thought of it as a chance to...not get to know each other, exactly, because after all they'd been living in the same house for months. Even if it was a huge house. But he'd definitely thought of it as a chance for them to get to know each other far away from the numerous eyes of all the rest of the Dimilioc black dogs.

And, until now, Justin had looked forward to introducing Keziah to his grandmother. He knew Keziah expected the worst from that meeting, but Grandmama Leushin was just the kind of woman to appreciate a fierce, haughty, beautiful girl like Keziah. He was sure she was. At least, as long as she didn't realize Keziah was a black dog—a werewolf, she would probably say.

Though for all Justin knew, Grandmama Leushin would recognize a black dog right off. If she did—if Grandmama Leushin knew all about the Pure and about black dogs, then Justin had a whole lot of questions for her, starting with why she'd never told him anything, why his *mother* had never told him anything.

Or if Grandmama Leushin *didn't* recognize what Keziah was, then Justin had different questions, but he might not get any answers. He almost hoped for that, because he really didn't want to find out that his grandmother and mother had been deliberately lying to him about everything important all his life. He'd rather get no answers at all than learn that.

That was probably a big part of why he'd put off this visit so long. Why he'd accepted Grayson's order to just send his grandmother a postcard every now and then, nothing important, nothing that would show exactly where he was, or with whom. But now here he was at last, hardly any distance from Roswell, far more tense about a visit with his grandmother than about the fact that he had an escort of three werewolves.

He wished he only had an escort of one. Or he *had* wished that, until Grandmama Leushin said airily, *It turns out this isn't a good time for a visit, dear.* As though he had called her up from across town instead of on the last leg of a two thousand mile drive. Now Justin was glad to have the extra company. He said, "Someone must have been there with her, or she'd have told me what was going on."

"You think?" said Nicholas, leaning forward from the

back seat. “Did you notice she never said your name? She didn’t want whoever was there to know it was you.”

Justin was embarrassed to admit he hadn’t noticed this.

“Don’t be afraid,” Amira told him, reaching forward pat Justin’s arm. “Now I am glad we are here. We will eat the hearts of your grandmother’s enemies.”

“I hope she turns out not to have actual enemies,” Justin told her. “But hold that thought. It’s surprisingly comforting.”

Amira laughed, and even Keziah smiled, a slight tug upward of one side of her mouth.

“I could call her back,” Justin suggested to Keziah.

“If enemies are there with her, it may be better not to distract her.” Keziah paused. “Unless you wish to distract *them*. You could demand to speak to whomever is there. You could warn this person that your grandmother has allies and that we will eat the heart of anyone who harms her.”

It was actually tempting. But Justin reluctantly shook his head. “I guess maybe not, when we don’t know what’s going on.”

“Perhaps discretion is wiser for the moment,” Keziah conceded.

Justin had called from Dimilioc before they’d arranged this visit, and then he’d called from the hotel last night, and both times Grandmama Leushin had sounded fine. Bright, cheerful, asking no questions about where he’d been or with whom or why he’d sent nothing but a couple of postcards since last spring, when he’d walked out of the empty house that echoed with loneliness and grief, away from his old life. He’d assumed she hadn’t wanted to yell at him over the phone. Wait till she got him in her kitchen and sat him down with cherry pastries and gingerbread and couldn’t disappear. *Then* she could yell at him properly, for walking out and worrying everyone.

That’s what he’d assumed. But now he wasn’t sure. Maybe even then she had been in some kind of trouble. If Grandmama Leushin were Pure after all...he didn’t have a clear idea of how much trouble she might be in, or what kind. But it undoubtedly broadened the possibilities.

"I'm sure she's fine," he said to Keziah. "Surely we can get there before...anything happens."

He thought he did a pretty good job of concealing his fear, but Keziah slanted a glance his way and smoothly accelerated. They were already driving well above the speed limit, which was a generous seventy-five out here. Justin didn't comment. It was fine with him if Keziah wanted to drive fast. She wasn't likely to get a ticket, no matter how she punched up her speed, because Justin was pretty good with Pure magic these days, at least some kinds of Pure magic, and that meant Keziah's car was hard for police to notice.

"As long as truckers don't fail to see you," he muttered, but under his breath. Keziah undoubtedly heard him anyway, but she pretended not to.

"She'd just dodge anyway, if a truck started to cut us off," Nicholas said, leaning forward to look at the speedometer. "She's not even going really fast yet. I'd go faster."

"You may practice with one of Grayson's vehicles, if he is foolish enough to lend it to you," Keziah told him, not turning her head. "Not mine."

Nicholas didn't exactly argue—not many black dogs would argue with Keziah. But he said just as though it were a random comment, "These roads are a lot better than anything in Vermont."

Keziah shrugged, *not my problem* coming off her in waves.

The roads *were* a lot better out here, though. Mostly straight and mostly level, visibility outstanding in the clear, dry air. Gritty red soil stretched out in all directions, streaked with snow because they were high enough up for the desert to be pretty chilly in winter. Justin remembered that from childhood visits. Scrubby little trees and tough grasses yellow with winter and the odd jackrabbit out despite the bite in the air. Mountains in front of them, half lost in the distance. The tallest of those would be the Sierra Blanca peak, judging from the navigator's map. There was snow up there, too, glittering in the sunlight. A string of lakes were up there somewhere in those mountains, water bitter with alkali, but lending life to the desert nevertheless.

Roswell was only another twenty miles away, according to the navigator. So close. Justin almost felt he ought to be able to see his grandmother's house right from here: a white southern-style house that might have been picked up in Georgia and set down here in the desert, but with a tamarisk tree in the back yard. He'd spent enough Christmases there as a kid. When his mother had still been alive.

It was so short a time ago. It seemed like so much longer.

This country was so empty. He'd almost forgotten what space was like, in Vermont, where people thought a hundred miles was a long way. The horizon was so much wider out here. Irrigated farms stretched out to the southeast of town; west was all cattle ranches. Justin knew that from childhood visits. But the way they came in this time, crossing the narrow Pecos River from the northeast, they mostly saw the rolling arid wilderness of national parks or other wild areas.

"Not so far now," Amira volunteered in her shy little voice. "Then we will know. Your grandmother will be well, Justin. We will come there and be certain of it. If anyone has harmed her or offended her, we will tear them to pieces and burn them to ash."

Justin's hand twitched, wanting to reach for his phone, flip it open, call again. He resisted the urge. Keziah was right; if Grandmama Leushin was dealing with some kind of problem, better not to interfere until they knew what it was.

Besides, maybe nothing was wrong. Maybe she really was just too busy this week for a visit from her grandson. Her grandson who had disappeared eight months ago and only sent her the occasional postcard since. And she'd just forgotten to mention this urgent church business when he'd called her two weeks ago to tell her he'd see her for Christmas. Sure.

Fifteen miles to Roswell, said a sign they passed. The way Keziah was driving, that wouldn't take more than another ten minutes.

Justin couldn't help but compare the land here to the damp, chilly, greenness they'd left behind. He couldn't quite remember now when they'd driven out of woodland hills into miles and miles of wheat fields, or when they'd left the wheat fields behind for this dry country. But it looked...sparse. Bitter. Though that might be worry for his grandmother. Or grief for his mother. Or the memory of grief. He'd used to find the desert beautiful, he could remember thinking it was beautiful, but those feelings were hard to touch, now. His mother had been gone...not even a year, yet. Driving through New Mexico was like driving into the past. The months seemed both to stretch out infinitely far behind him, and to somehow compress to nothing.

As though she'd read his thoughts, Keziah said, "It is too much like home here, and too little. Both at once."

Justin couldn't quite hide a flinch, but almost at once he realized that she wasn't echoing him after all: she meant it literally. Of course the country around Riyadh must be a lot like this, even if the plants and animals and the architecture of the scattered buildings were not the same. Red soil, red stone, scrubby brush, tough grasses...they probably had jackrabbits in Saudi Arabia, too, for all he knew.

But Amira said, sounding very certain despite her quiet little voice, "No. It is nothing like home."

Keziah glanced over her shoulder, surprised. Then she smiled at her sister, a quick flicker of affection and humor that for just that second altered her expression completely. "No. Perhaps after all it is not so much like home." Then she glanced ahead, at the outskirts of Roswell, and added in a different tone, "No, not so much."

Justin could hardly blame her. Roswell surely couldn't look like much of a town to a girl from Riyadh. After meeting Keziah, he'd looked at pictures—pictures taken before the Saudi people had learned they were ruled by monsters. Once that had happened, the Saudis had risen up in furious defiance against their black dog masters, and half the city was destroyed practically overnight. But he could picture how, not so long ago, Riyadh had stretched out into the lazy golden distance under the Arabian sun.

Roswell wasn't like that at all. In fact, Roswell was hardly a quarter the size of Los Alamos, where Justin had lived with his mother. If fifty thousand people lived in this town, he'd be surprised. It had never had anything to match the top-flight engineering and rocket science labs of Los Alamos. Small and plain, haunted by an indefinable air of age and poverty, Roswell's downtown area wasn't much to look at. A drugstore, a movie theater, both looking pretty much deserted; a mom-n-pop café-type of restaurant with a sadly faded red awning, a couple gas stations...nothing that seemed worth a second glance.

"I wonder where Area Fifty-One is?" Nicholas said. And, when Justin looked at him in bafflement, added, "You know! Area Fifty-One? Where the government is supposed to be hiding the alien ship that crashed in 1947. There was a show about it when I was a kid—dissected aliens on ice, but they weren't *all* dead. Some of them had crazy psychic powers. They kidnapped people and brainwashed them and made them into slaves." He sketched something with his hands, a bit like an upside-down pear. Possibly it was supposed to be an alien.

Amira looked interested in these putative aliens, but Keziah said scornfully, "Aliens!" and her sister ducked her head and didn't ask Nicholas about them.

Before Nicholas could snap back at Keziah, Justin said diplomatically, "I expect, if there ever was an alien ship, the government probably didn't have much time for it once they found out about vampires and werewolves."

Nicholas was glowering, but he nodded reluctantly at this. "Yeah, I guess."

"The house of your grandmother?" asked Keziah. "Where should I turn?"

"Uh, yeah, get off at the next exit." Justin had nearly forgotten she wouldn't know. He tried to remember landmarks from his childhood visits. "You'll want to turn right. It's a few minutes yet. She lives off West Mescalero, just west of an Eastern Orthodox church and a little park."

"Mescalero," Keziah repeated, and smoothly passed a truck, cut back in front of it, and tucked her little silver car neatly into the exit lane.

Grandmama Leushin lived in a big, square white house, wide porch set off by pillars and a steep roof in a northwest part of town. All the houses on her cul-de-sac had that generous southern look, though a couple were brick and one was painted pale yellow instead of white. Yards were big, lawns irrigated in summer but hidden under a couple inches of snow right at the moment. No kids' toys out on driveways or lawns, which was no doubt the season but was probably also because this was a neighborhood for older people. Grandmama Leushin had been a teacher, like Justin's mother, but for high school instead of college. But even though she wasn't so very old, she'd retired years and years ago. When teaching became all about meeting stupid bureaucratic benchmarks and hiding grade inflation, she'd said. Whenever they got together, she and Justin's mother had always tried to top each other's stories about that kind of thing.

The car he remembered from childhood visits was this big old station wagon kind of thing, a tan-colored whale of a car. Maybe Grandmama Leushin had traded it at last for the sporty red number presently occupying the driveway. It seemed possible; he could remember her declaring she was going to go wild and get a fancy car someday. *Hey, I skipped my mid-life crisis, guess I'm* due *a snazzy little car before I'm too old and decrepit to enjoy it.* Besides the red convertible in the driveway, there was a heavy black car parked on the side of the street just a bit up from the house, some kind of big, old-fashioned thing that almost looked like a hearse. It didn't really look like the kind of car Grandmama Leushin would have wanted, and Justin couldn't think of any reason why she would have parked in the street. But it *could* be hers.

Definitely more puzzling than the unfamiliar vehicles was the dim silvery glow around the house. That might belong to Grandmama Leushin, too. It was a sort of rolling, sinuous glimmer, a bit like the light Justin had gotten used to seeing around Natividad and DeAnn, but muffled somehow, or...not quite finished. Or something. It looked almost like Pure magic, but different. Sort of like a function that was only half defined and might yet turn out to be something simple and pretty like a parabola, but might just as well turn out to be something complicated with a lot more back-and-forth movement in it. Justin frowned at the glow, uncomfortable with it, with his own ignorance. He wished Natividad were here. She knew a hell of a lot more about magic than he did.

If this were a kind of Pure magic, though, at least it didn't appear to be a problem for Keziah or her sister or Nicholas. Keziah drove right into the faint glimmer without hesitation, and no one flinched as she guided her car to the curb in front of the truck. Parking in this spot would give them a few more steps to walk. Justin didn't ask Keziah about this decision, partly because he was sure she wouldn't appreciate backseat parking advice, but mostly because he guessed she was thinking about the possibility they might have to peel out quick so she didn't want anybody blocking their way. Paranoid, sure, but then she *was* a black dog. He was uneasy himself even without that excuse.

He didn't ask if it were okay to get out of the car, though. Black dogs were all either control freaks or wanna-be control freaks, and it was hard enough to know exactly where the lines were, but this was, after all, *his* grandmother's house. And that glow didn't look *bad*. It didn't look dangerous or ill-intended. Just...vague and undefined.

"Besides, I've brought the big bad wolf right along with me," Justin muttered under his breath.

Nicholas grunted with amusement. Even Amira smiled. Keziah, swinging her long legs out of the car and strolling around to join him, lazy and sleek as a lioness, gave Justin a look but didn't ask. Maybe she, too, recognized the reference; he couldn't tell. All she said was, "Someone is in the house. An old woman, I think, but also someone else. A man, I think."

"An old woman, though? Good," said Justin, relieved

and impressed by black dog senses. He hadn't realized they were quite that good. Maybe this was actually some sense peculiar to black dogs.

Keziah jerked her head impatiently before he could ask. "Yes. She might be Pure." She frowned, tilting her head. "I am not certain. Maybe she might be Pure. Or human. It is hard to...the feeling here is strange. But I think no black dog is near this place."

Other than them, she meant, obviously. Justin nodded. That was good, at least. *Probably* it was good.

Keziah touched Justin's arm, a light brush with the back of her hand, the way a black dog would offer reassurance. From her, it was a rare gesture. "There is no blood smell," she said.

Justin let his breath out and nodded. That was definitely good.

Amira exchanged a glance with her sister, hopped out of the back seat, and traded a second, longer look with Nicholas. He bailed out, too, and the two of them headed down the street, then trotted across the lawn toward the back of the house. They might have been a couple of kids stretching their legs after a long car ride, except for the more-than-human grace with which they moved and the predatory air with which they circled the house. Justin nodded to himself, because if anybody in there would make trouble for an old woman and then bolt out the back way when her grandson knocked on the front door, he'd deserve to meet those two.

"You should wait in the car," Keziah told him, disapproving of the whole situation but perhaps most of all disliking their exposed position.

"Not likely." Justin rubbed his fingertips nervously together and then sketched a quick mandala in the air, holding the familiar shape in his mind, defining the equations of its circle and straight lines with heart and mind and will. He said out loud, framing his intention the way Natividad had taught him, "Let those of ill intent depart this house!" Then he brought the mandala to life, not the little sketch he'd traced in the air, but a great burning mandala that swept all the way around Grandmama Leushin's house, the quartering lines spearing right through the doors and walls before them. It was a thing of fierce, perfect geometry, its clean lines as different from the amorphous glow as an eagle was from a sparrow. Justin nodded again, this time with conscious satisfaction. He'd learned a lot in the past months.

Pure magic worked best against vampires and blood kin, pretty well against black dogs and moon-bound shifters, and was by far least effective against ordinary people. But *least effective* didn't mean *useless*. Pure magic could draw your friends to you and turn your enemies away, protect your home ground and defend against hostile intent, ease anger and encourage kindness. That kind of thing was what Pure magic was all about. So Justin more than half expected a response of some kind from within, startled or outraged or pained or *something*. He wouldn't have been at all surprised if some human or maybe-human person had come running out of the house, someone who expected trouble but maybe not exactly the kind of trouble that was about to fall on him like a ton of werewolves. But there was nothing.

"Well done," said Keziah, her testy tone suggesting that she had to admit this but didn't actually appreciate him working Pure magic without checking with her first.

"If that guy's still in there, whoever he is, I guess maybe his intent is good after all. So let's see who it is." Justin took the steps to the porch two at a time, and opened the door without knocking.

The door wasn't locked. Sometimes people in small towns didn't lock their doors. Sometimes old people didn't lock their doors, having grown up in a more trusting era and forgetting that times had changed. Justin couldn't remember his grandmother being quite that trusting. But the door opened to his touch, with a little squeak of hinges.

Justin didn't step through the door, though. Because Keziah seized his arm and pulled him firmly back and out of the line of fire, if anyone had fired, which no one did. She gave him a withering look: *Have the basic intelligence to stay behind me*. Then she stalked into the house. Justin hurried after her, trying to see over her shoulder, which he couldn't, very well, because Keziah was a tall girl.

The short hallway was deserted. Keziah strode right down it, past the little alcove where a dozen small framed icons occupied space around and above the small table with its single candle. The candle wasn't lit, a detail which immediately sent a chill down Justin's spine, though he hadn't realized how off and wrong such a small thing could seem.

Keziah didn't let him pause. She pivoted in a clean right-angled turn unhesitatingly to the left, straight into the kitchen.

And there they were, the guy and the old woman that Keziah had known were in this house. Justin crowded into the kitchen after Keziah, stepping quickly to the right to get a clear view, then stared in consternation. "She's not her!" He realized instantly how stupid that sounded, and amended it to, "Who are you?" He edited that down on the fly, barely, from *Who the hell are you* because he had no idea about the woman, but he thought he could guess, if not who, at least what the man was. He touched Keziah's hand just with the tips of two fingers, suggesting restraint without being pushy about it, the way Natividad had shown him. Keziah slanted an ironic look his way, but crossed her arms over her chest and tipped her chin arrogantly in a way that demanded answers.

The man, sitting at the small, square kitchen table, was a big guy, fifty-ish, with a short grizzled beard and the kind of face that suggested he might have once have been a brawler—crooked nose, one cheekbone unmistakably dented. But whatever his early life might have included, he didn't look much like a thug now. He was wearing nice black slacks, a black button-up shirt, and an ornate Orthodox cross—Russian Orthodox, not a surprise in Grandmama Leushin's house. It was definitely the kind of cross a priest would wear, exactly the kind that Orthodox priests *did* wear; it was identical to the one Grandmama Leushin kept in her room, that had once belonged to her father. This man had a priest's air of authority, too. Justin was sure he was an OCA priest. Certainly the very last thing he looked like, as he leaned back in his chair and tilted his head, was a man who'd been caught somewhere he wasn't supposed to be.

The woman was also obviously respectable. She was probably about Grandmama Leushin's age, about twenty years older than the man. She wore a classy-looking ankle-length skirt, a tan blouse, and a tiny wooden three-barred cross, not quite seven-eighths of an inch long. Her silver-blonde hair was up in an old-fashioned knot on the back of her head—Grandmama Leushin wore her hair like that, too, though hers was pure white. Unlike Grandmama Leushin, this woman wore thin-rimmed glasses that gave her a severe, authoritative look. Justin instantly decided she was the kind of older lady who might not be officially in charge of some group or organization, but whom everyone knew actually ran things. She looked like she could organize everyone and everything within an inch of their lives without disarranging a hair of her head.

The man—the priest, Justin was almost certain—had a stack of papers in front of him on the table and a pen in his hand. The kitchen was warm, fragrant with the scent of tea and lemon—there was a pot on the stove, and several of Grandmama Leushin's delicate china cups on the table. Through the open doorway on the other side of the kitchen, Justin could see a lot more papers laid out in neat stacks on the dining room table. But the man certainly seemed to think he had a perfect right to be here in Grandmama Leushin's house, going through her things. His expression as he studied Justin and Keziah was interested, but not hostile.

The woman, on the other hand, was ignoring Justin in favor of glaring at Keziah, and he didn't think it was Keziah's tight jeans or gauzy sapphire blouse that had offended her, nor even her aggressively lazy predator's smile that showed her small white teeth in an expression that wasn't exactly friendly. The lady's spine was straight, her chin up, her eyes narrowed—she looked a lot like a dignified cat seriously offended by a trespassing dog. She'd raised one hand to the little handbag on the table, and Justin would have bet the entire contents of his college savings account that she had a weapon in it—and that she knew that Keziah was a black dog.

"I think the woman is Pure," Keziah told Justin, seeming unimpressed by the possibilities inherent in that handbag. "But she is not bright in the world, as you are—as those Pure I have seen always have been. Even in this room I cannot be entirely certain. This I do not understand. I would say she is half Pure if I had ever heard of such a thing."

Justin studied the old lady. He could see it himself, sort of, once Keziah had pointed it out. He *could* see the complicated Escherian curves of Pure magic folding around the lady, but none of it was nearly as complicated or—*bright* wasn't exactly the right word—vivid, maybe. Not as clearly delineated, either. The magic around this lady was more like wisps of steam on a cloudy day; something you almost thought you might see except then you weren't sure. Justin would have liked to compare what he saw around her to the magic that folded and curved around him, but of course he couldn't. He had never been able to glimpse his own magic.

The woman's stern attitude had become tinged with uncertainty, but she still flicked open the clasp of her handbag.

"Anna –" the priest began, making a movement as though he might restrain her.

"That girl is certainly a werewolf," declared the lady, and whipped a little tiny gun out of her handbag. And Amira slid sideways through the dining room door and took the gun neatly out of her hand without so much as brushing her fingers. The woman twitched back in startlement, saw that Amira was a child and straightened with what looked like both surprise and offended dignity—then flinched in sympathetic horror as she saw Amira's scarred face. And then realized, visibly, that the she was a black dog. Justin saw the lady realize it, and her reaction was surprising considering she'd already pulled a gun: she went still. Not frozen like a rabbit before a fox, but watchfully still, like a woman who might yet have another kind of weapon. Pure, he was certain of it, no matter how faded and diffuse the magic around her might seem.

"That little girl, too?" asked the priest, obviously interpreting the lady's reaction exactly as Justin had. He sounded faintly shocked.

"They're born that way, you know," Justin told him. "And learn to control their dark shadows practically before they can walk, if they're raised right."

Amira ignored this exchange. Grimacing, she set the gun fastidiously aside on a cabinet. "Silver bullets," she warned Keziah, shaking out her hand. Nicholas slouched in the doorway, backing up Amira and also blocking that way out of the kitchen, penning these people up between himself and Keziah. He told Keziah, "The whole house is empty except here, I'm almost sure. I didn't search everywhere, but I walked from front to back and I couldn't hear or feel anybody else."

Keziah nodded thoughtfully, acknowledging them both.

"They are *all* werewolves!" said the lady. She sounded more offended than terrified, which Justin suspected meant she had probably never seen a black dog in the other form, at least not up close and personal. Or else she had a much more impressive weapon stashed away somehow, which was possible, since she was Pure. Though in her place he'd have been pretty well terrified even if he'd had a bazooka or the equivalent tucked away in his back pocket.

Or maybe she had just such a solid habit of gracious dignity that she couldn't look panicked if she tried. Grandmama Leushin was like that. Justin could believe this lady might be his grandmother's friend.

He cleared his throat, pointedly.

The lady peered at him over the tops of her glasses. "True, young man; you aren't," she conceded as though Justin had objected out loud. And then, in a different tone, for the first time seeming shaken, *"Justin?"*

"Do I know you, ma'am?" Justin didn't recognize the lady, but it was perfectly possible he'd met her. No doubt

Grandmama Leushin had plenty of friends. On the occasions he and his mother had come here to Roswell, he'd been just as self-absorbed as the next little kid and hadn't paid any attention to any other adults that his grandmother might have chatted with on Sunday mornings.

"So this is Natalie's Justin?" the priest asked. "Keeping such company."

It was hard to blame him for disapproving. Keziah wasn't merely a black dog: she was dangerous, ruthless, ambitious, and indifferent to practically everyone outside Dimilioc—nor was she very concerned about the well-being of most of the people *in* Dimilioc, either. And all that showed, pretty much, because that was the part of herself she wanted people to see.

Justin nodded to him. "Father –?"

"Stepan." The priest rose to his feet at last, facing Keziah squarely. "I am Father Stepan Ivanovich, and I call upon the grace of God to dispel evil from this house."

"Yeah, I already did that," Justin told him, deliberately casual. "And no one ran out screaming, so I guess that's something. These aren't werewolves, they're black dogs, and they're my friends."

"Your *friends*. Is that what they are?" Now Father Stepan looked Justin up and down. "Sometimes it's all too easy to compromise with evil—"

"It's really not," Justin told him. "It takes constant struggle, but black dogs from decent houses never give up." He eyed the priest, whose frown had both deepened and become more thoughtful. "You might keep in mind that I'm the one who knows these people. Do you really think I'd deliberately bring werewolves along to eat my grandmother? That'd be a new twist on the fairy tale, I suppose."

"A red cape is okay, but it's stupid to wear a hood," commented Nicholas. "They block too much of your vision and hearing."

Father Stepan, somewhat surprisingly, snorted. He eyed Nicholas with penetrating interest.

Nicholas straightened up, shoved his hands in his

pockets, and demanded, "So where is she?" When the priest didn't immediately answer, he went on in an aggrieved tone, "Justin *finally* gets permission to drive out here and see his grandmother, dragging all of us along for three whole days in Keziah's little bitty car, which believe me does not make for a joyride, and something happens to his grandmother an hour before we get here? I don't believe it. And then she says she's too busy and he shouldn't visit, when she knew he'd come thousands of miles and was less than an hour away? I don't believe that, either. I wonder why, when she made up lies to tell Justin why he shouldn't come, she said it was *church* business?"

"Now, look," Justin protested. "It has to be coincidence. I mean, us arriving just now. And I'm sure my grandmother didn't mean *Father Stepan* was planning anything, um, nefarious." He really was sure about that last, or nearly; the priest just didn't seem to him like that sort of person. Whatever sort of person he was thinking of.

"Yeah, you Pure are way too trusting," Nicholas told him. "I'm sure I'll never understand it. Your grandmother *said* it was church stuff –"

"Maybe she meant us to find Father Stepan when we couldn't find her."

The priest said quietly, "I hope she would have thought of me."

Nicholas rolled his eyes. "Sure."

"You actually spoke to Natalia Leushina?" the lady demanded of Justin. She used the Russian feminine *Leushina,* which as far as Justin knew his determinedly Americanized grandmother used only among her friends from her parish. Not only that, but this woman must be an intimate friend of his grandmother's to call her *Natalia*. Justin relaxed a little, but the lady went on urgently without pausing, "An hour ago, you say?"

"Not quite an hour," Keziah said smoothly before he could answer. "And when did *you* last speak with her?"

"You're Justin's *friend*, are you?" The lady inspected Keziah, then raised her eyebrows at Justin. "Your grandmother was so very relieved when you finally sent her a postcard, young man. Plainly she ought to have worried about what company you'd gotten into, but she always said her grandson had good sense. I hardly like to think what she'd have said about these *friends* of yours."

She picked up her handbag. Amira took it away from her and set it down next to the gun, and Justin tapped the table with one finger, framed the equations for a pentagram in his head, and said firmly, "*Que haya paz en esta casa.*" He'd learned magic mostly from Natividad and couldn't help but think of Spanish as the right language for magic, but these people might not understand what he'd said, so he repeated it in English: "May there be peace in this house."

The pentagram had glimmered to life, no wider than his hand, the star bounded by the pentagon. Justin, watching carefully, was almost sure that Father Stepan didn't see it, but that the older lady did. But they should both feel its effect. Justin certainly could: the tension in the room, despite everything, eased back a notch.

"Hmm," said Father Stepan, studying Justin with a different kind of interest.

"Can you do that?" Justin asked the lady. And, when she didn't answer, he asked the priest, "Could my grandmother?"

"I have no idea," admitted Father Stepan. "I can certainly think of occasions when she would have certainly wished to. But she is a righteous woman. You, on the other hand...I must admit to doubts about a young man who associates with werewolves."

Well, noncommittal was definitely better than ringing denunciations. Justin said patiently, "Black dogs. These particular black dogs, who are my friends. We're all friends here, or I think we are, or at least I think we ought to be. Nicky, is there more tea? Ma'am, can you tell me when you last spoke with my grandmother, and what she said, and where she is now, and what you're doing here going through her things?" He could see her thinking about whether to answer all these questions, and added, "You're Pure, of course. Have you deliberately masked yourself somehow?"

"I don't know what you mean," declared the lady.

"Of course not," Keziah said drily. "Such a skill would be most useful, so probably it is not a skill at all, but something this woman does with instinct."

"Or else it's something that was done to her," Nicholas put in.

Justin had to admit this wouldn't surprise him a bit, but he couldn't tell whether the lady meant she didn't understand his question about masking herself or whether she also didn't know what he'd meant by Pure. He started to try to frame that question better, but before he could, the lady added haughtily to Justin, "I cannot say I think much of your friends, young man."

Justin let out his breath, counted rapidly to approximately 3.16227766 by square roots, and said to Nicholas, "Tea?"

Nicholas poured a cup of tea, set the cup on a saucer, and handed the tea to Justin with an ironic flourish that said plainly, *Don't get the idea you're the boss of me*. But what he said out loud was more to the point: "Maybe it's all one thing, whatever's going on with your grandmother and whatever's muffling the Pure magic here. Except you've still got your knack, obviously, Justin."

Which instantly made Justin wonder if his own magic might suddenly dwindle and fade to the muted kind of half-present magic around his grandmother's friend. This was not a comfortable idea. To distract himself from that thought, he sipped too-hot tea, pulled out a chair, sat down at the table, and picked up the top paper from the stack in front of Father Stepan. Letting all questions about the Pure go for the moment, he asked, "What are these? Letters? What are you looking for, evidence of . . ." he hesitated, not quite sure what to ask. Evidence of foul play, of kidnapping, of Grandmama Leushin's involvement in...what? He folded his hands on the table and gazed at his mother's friend, trying to look as expectant as possible.

The lady looked at Father Stepan. Who, after a short pause, lowered himself back into his own chair, nodded at the woman, and told Justin, "This is your grandmother's friend, Anna Farris. Anna, why don't you tell Natalie's grandson what you told me."

It took a moment, but eventually Mrs. Farris also took a seat at the table. She picked up her cup, sipped, put it down, and said, her tone guarded but precise, "Natalia called me last night. She told me she'd found out about something. Something like vampires and werewolves, she said, but different. She said, 'It could be anyone, Anya, and we'd never be able to tell.'"

"That isn't very much like either vampires or werewolves," observed Keziah.

Justin considered this. "It's like vampires before the miasma faded, isn't it? It's worse, in a way, if whatever this is still can't be recognized for what they are even now the miasma's gone."

"Nothing's worse than vampires," Nicholas said, his tone flattening on the last word.

Father Stepan slapped the table, not hard, but everyone except Keziah jumped. Keziah raised her eyebrows, sardonically amused, but when Anna Farris went on, she didn't interrupt.

"I told her I wouldn't be surprised at anything anymore, and she said 'That's just what we all thought five years ago, didn't we? And look at us now.' But she didn't tell me exactly what she'd discovered. She was going to join me for breakfast today—there's this nice little bakery with quite acceptable croissants. She was supposed to come to my house at eight." Mrs. Farris looked around the table. "You know your grandmother is always so punctual, Justin."

He nodded, though he didn't remember one way or the other.

"She didn't show up. But someone else did. A young man, no one I would care to know. Grungy." Mrs. Farris pronounced this verdict with a slight sniff. "His hair needed a good washing. He had a bag over his shoulder. I thought he was probably selling something, and I thought he'd do much better at it if he took some decent pains with his appearance, but you can't tell young people anything these days. I said, 'Whatever you're selling, I'm not buying.' And he looked at me with this funny expression, reached into his bag, took out a handful of dust, and blew it at me. I could *not* believe it," Mrs. Farris added. "As though we don't get plenty of dust without that sort of thing! I sweep my front steps every day, even this time of year. Then he said, 'Anna Farris, come with me,' and beckoned, like this." Mrs. Farris crooked a preemptory finger.

"Of course I said, 'Young man, I can't imagine why you'd think I would go anywhere with you, but I think it would be best if you'd leave immediately.' And he laughed, not a nice laugh at all. He said, 'You're a white witch. I thought so. Your power isn't much, but it'll do.' Then he turned out to have a knife."

The whole story was peculiar, but Justin definitely hadn't seen that particular twist coming. He leaned forward. Everyone did, even Father Stepan, who had undoubtedly heard it before.

"So I said, 'Young man, whatever you've been taking, I hope it doesn't make you believe you're invincible.' And I showed him my gun and told him again to leave. He didn't expect that, evidently, because he did go away." She added to Father Stepan, who was looking pained, "I would merely have shoot him in the foot, of course, since he was human. Or he seemed to be human. But the bullets were silver, just in case he turned out to be something else."

"Good for you," whispered Amira, who was listening wide-eyed. "But you should have shot him. You should never leave an enemy alive behind you."

Mrs. Farris gave her a gracious little nod. "Quite right in a tactical sense, child, but murder is a terrible sin."

"It would have been self-defense," Justin pointed out.

"Killing a child of God is a very serious matter, even if one has no better choice," Father Stepan said gravely.

"Yes, yes," agreed Mrs. Farris. "Still, these days you never know when you might discover your enemy is actually a monster, and then it's just practical to make sure you have an extra little ace in your hand. Either way, the young man did scoot off. But then, while I was sweeping off my steps, I thought of Natalia, who was very late by that time, and what she'd said. Here's this young man babbling about witches. And aren't witches like vampires and werewolves, but different? Mightn't witches look like normal people so you can't tell who they are? And you know, Justin, your grandmother is a very capable woman, but she never would carry a gun, not this year, she said the vampires and ghouls were all gone and why should she weigh herself down with silver bullets?"

"Now, wait," Nicholas objected. "There's no such thing as witches. Witches are like elves and fairies and things, they're not *real*." He looked at Keziah for support.

Keziah inclined her head. "Nor have I heard of true witches. Girls in my family were taught little of the world, but I recall nothing of witches."

"I assure you, young woman, I am not inventing this conversation –"

Justin cleared his throat. "Miguel mentioned witches. Not black dogs and not vampires, he said. I don't remember the details." He wished Miguel were here now. That kid was like a walking reference library.

"Either way, Anna very sensibly called me," Father Stepan said. "We came directly here. The door was standing open, but Natalie was not here." He tapped the papers stacked in front of him. "Your grandmother is a great one for writing letters, Justin. We hoped she might have written one to Anna, or to me, or to *someone*." He turned up a broad hand. "A long shot. But we couldn't think what else to do."

Justin stared at the heaps of letters, mostly hand-written. This was all worse than anything he'd expected. Even when Grandmama Leushin told him she was too busy and not to visit, he'd thought...he didn't know what he'd thought. But not this. "She didn't keep a journal, did she?"

"Not so far as we know," the priest said regretfully.

"Useless," Keziah pronounced. "All these letters are worthless. Justin, you will find your grandmother yourself.

This will be far more efficient than examining many letters."

"It would be, but I don't know how!" Justin protested. "Mandalas I can do; if you want a pentagram, I'm your guy; spirals I can manage. But finding people? I don't know how."

"The Pure can totally do finding magic," Nicholas objected. "They used to do it all the time when I was a kid, before the war. A Pure woman would go out with a team of black dogs, help them clean the strays out of a city –"

"You see? We are certain this is something the Pure can do," Keziah told Justin. "Therefore, you will do this."

Justin ran a hand through his hair, frustrated. "Natividad can make this thing using a mirror, she calls it a *trouvez*, it's a tool for finding things. People. You know, whatever you're looking for. But there's no geometry in those. I always concentrated on circles and things. Natividad's the one who made a *trouvez* when we needed one. Which we hardly ever did, since Grayson doesn't let the Pure go out on circuits anymore." Which he'd always been glad of, actually; weeks-long missions to kill violent, ignorant, dangerous black dogs might be necessary, but that didn't mean he wanted to have anything to do with that kind of thing himself. Now he regretted that he lacked that experience. Well, he sort of regretted it.

"She never showed you how?" Nicholas asked, skeptical.

Justin glared at him, exasperated. "Sure she did. Once, months ago! Even if I could make one, I don't know how to get it to find a particular person. The one I made let me find Natividad, and I don't think it'd be terribly useful to know where *she* is right this minute!"

Amira slipped up beside Justin and leaned against him, a rare gesture from any black dog, but she was so much better with the Pure than with ordinary people or other black dogs. She said softly, "This is your grandmother. She is important to you. You have come all this way to find her. You will find her, and we will eat the hearts and lungs of her enemies."

"Oh, the lungs too, huh?" Justin couldn't help but smile down at the top of the girl's head. For a black dog, Amira was just really sweet. In a bloodthirsty-killer kind of way.

"Charming," murmured Mrs. Farris.

"What do you suppose that grungy young man of yours is doing to my grandmother right now?" Justin asked her. "I think I'd be willing to let Amira eat someone's heart and lungs, if it were the right someone. All right, fine, I need a mirror. A small one, if possible." He cupped his hand to show how small he meant.

"No one is eating anyone," Father Stepan stated. "However...I believe a mirror might be possible. Anna?" He gestured politely toward Mrs. Farris's handbag, perched on the counter next to her gun.

"I might have a mirror," the lady murmured. "Let me just look –"

"I shall look." Keziah picked up the handbag before Mrs. Farris could reach for it.

Justin caught Keziah's wrist. "Silver," he reminded her. "Or who knows what might be in there? Let me." He was pleased he remembered to wait for her to nod before upending the handbag on the table.

No second little gun, no silver knife or letter opener—a *lot* of people carried pocketknives with silver blades these days, for exactly the same reason that silver jewelry was now a hundred times more popular than gold. Justin had a pocketknife himself, tucked in a back pocket, a nifty little number Grayson had given him. He'd blooded it for both Keziah and Amira, just in case. Blooding silver was one thing Natividad had made sure he knew how to do, even though there was no geometry to it, either. There wasn't anything like that in Mrs. Farris's handbag. But an extra cross, much bigger than the one the lady wore, was tucked in its own little pocket. A silver cross, on a silver chain, heavy enough to swing at anything demonic and make sure they'd feel it.

Justin gave Mrs. Farris a look.

"Oh, yes, I had forgotten about that," Mrs. Farris said blandly, not in the least abashed. "You never know what might come in handy these days, do you?"

"Right," said Justin. But he had also found a compact

with a small round mirror set in the lid, so there didn't seem much point in arguing about silver chains and who might have intended to do what with this one. He dropped the cross and chain on the table, handed the bag back to Mrs. Farris, and tilted the mirror to catch the light. At least there was plenty of natural light from the kitchen windows.

Making a *trouvez* had to do with light. Capturing and holding light, getting it to show you what you were looking for...light and intention and will, like so much Pure magic...Justin tilted the mirror back and forth. "A light in the dark," he muttered. That was what Natividad had said. A guiding light when you had lost your way, something like that. But he didn't think Natividad had ever explained how to make that kind of *trouvez*. He said out loud, "Finding what you seek...moonlight for the Pure, I remember that. Mrs. Farris, *are* you Pure? Is my grandmother?"

"Young man, no one who gets to be our age remains *entirely* pure."

"So you aren't familiar with the term the way we use it." Justin tipped the mirror again, watching the light flash. "Moonlight for the Pure," he repeated. "Twilight for the half-Pure, maybe. I wonder, could this kind of witch person stifle Pure magic, kind of like the vampire miasma stifling ordinary sight?"

"There's a nice thought," muttered Nicholas. "Let's not have anything at all like vampire magic, huh? But it doesn't follow, Justin. Pure magic was always completely resistant to vampire magic, that was the whole point –"

Keziah flicked a glance the boy's way. "Hush!"

Justin barely heard either of them. He was thinking about Grandmama Leushin, about the straight-backed certainty with which she'd strode through life. He had no idea whether she were Pure, he didn't know whether the dim silvery magic that curved around Anna Farris was a kind of muffled Pure magic, but his grandmother had loved life and living. He remembered other Christmases in his childhood, this same kitchen filled with warmth, Christmas carols on the radio and the scent of gingerbread...real gingerbread, dense and moist, topped with lemon sauce and a swoop of whipped cream. Mistletoe hanging in the doorway, where Grandmama Leushin had always hung it before Grandpapa Leushin passed away, and still did for his memory. Gingerbread and mistletoe, and oranges stuck all over with cloves, and the same carved wooden decorations on the tree every single year...if he went through the house to the parlor, he was sure the tree would be there with those same wooden decorations...she would have hung each one with its own bit of different-colored yarn...Justin swallowed and closed his eyes, unable to believe she wasn't here. Where had that grungy punk with the knife taken Grandmama Leushin? Where was she?

"There!" whispered Amira, leaning against his side.

Justin opened his eyes. He'd done *something*, because the mirror in his hand had become opaque, filled with heavy light. Not moonlight. This was an opalescent shimmer like the sky before the sunrise. Pearl gray, dove gray, dawn gray; like moonlight shining through fog or mist.

He turned the mirror in his hand, watching at it dimmed and brightened. Streaks of shimmering light slid across the glass from left to right.

"West," murmured Keziah, peering over his shoulder. "West of this house. What lies west?" She glanced from Father Stepan to Anna Farris.

"We're already near the west edge of town," Mrs. Farris observed, frowning in thought.

"The military base," said Father Stepan.

Justin looked at him. His head felt stuffed with shimmering fog. He scrubbed his hands hard across his face.

"It's an abandoned military base," Father Stepan explained. "There's still a fence around the underground bunkers or whatever they are, to keep out the young and the adventurous. The army did tests of some sort out there; mines or new kinds of artillery or something, I don't know, but I suppose it's probably still dangerous to poke around, even though they locked it up and left it behind a long time ago –"

"It's Area 51!" said Nicolas, with more than a little

satisfaction. “Underground bunkers, yes! Where they hid the alien ship –”

“Yeah, pretty sure we aren’t going to find aliens out there today,” Justin interrupted him. “But underground bunkers and a fence must be handy if you get up to...whatever a witch gets up to when he kidnaps old ladies.” Putting it like that made the whole thing seem even more urgent. He got to his feet, staggering a little, and stole another glance at the mirror, wary in case the light had faded away. But the mirror still glimmered. Streaks still ran through it. When he tilted it to the west, the light didn’t exactly brighten, but it intensified.

“A hunt!” whispered Amira. “A hunt, with blood and death at the end! We will protect your grandmother or avenge her!”

“We are not murdering anyone,” Father Stepan said firmly. “Not even a murderer, witch or not, even if we find one –”

“We have the *trouvez,”* Keziah said drily. “You need not involve yourself, priest.”

“We know where the military base is, and the way to get around the part where the road’s washed out. You won’t get a car through by the route Google maps suggests, I promise you that.”

Anna Farris put in, “And *I* am the one who has a gun with silver bullets, young lady. A gun which I don’t believe any of you can even pick up.”

“What was that about not killing anybody?” Nicholas asked. “And we could too pick it up. It’d sting, that’s all.” He picked it up, demonstratively, but his mouth tightened after a moment, which lessened the effect.

Mrs. Farris sniffed. “And can you hit what you aim at, young man? You may be quite confident that *I* can. And if *I* shoot someone,” she added with some severity, this time to Father Stepan, “you may also be quite confident it will be a monster, or else dire necessity.”

Justin ignored this argument because none of that mattered. He looked at Keziah and found her eyes meeting his. He knew the black dogs didn't need a car; they could go straight across country. She knew he couldn't. They both knew Keziah wouldn't leave him unguarded—and they both knew he wouldn't forgive her if she refused to rescue his grandmother to keep him safe. None of that needed to be put into words.

"Besides," Justin said, "we have to find out what this is about so we can tell Grayson and the rest. Witch or something else, we have to find out, especially if this guy is interfering somehow with Pure magic."

"If any harm comes to you, Grayson will be...beyond angry. I will also be very angry."

Justin nodded. "But you don't really think we're going to find something that you and Amira and Nicholas can't handle? Anyway, I'll promise not to take unnecessary chances—I do promise—but we don't know what this guy is or what he can do. You might need me. You know that. Think about last time and how that would have worked out if it hadn't been for me and Natividad!"

"None of that would have happened at all if not for you and Natividad," Keziah muttered.

"Yeah, and then that master vampire would still be out there, and how would that be better? I'm not fragile, I'm not helpless, and I'm definitely not staying behind, Keziah! We'll all go. Keziah, listen, you know it makes sense." He met her eyes, willing her to agree. "They can help, and besides that we *can't* leave them behind, they know where we're going. We can all go together—Father Stepan, is that your car outside, the big black one? We could all fit in that, plus my grandmother when we find her –"

"Very well!" Keziah snapped. "Justin, *you* will keep the gun. You will protect yourself, do you hear? You are most definitely fragile, all you human people, and you Pure most of all." But she also swept an encompassing gesture around the kitchen, turned on her heel, and stalked out the door.

Five minutes later they were heading west, in Father Stepan's car. With Keziah driving. That had probably surprised the priest, but he had lost that argument without a word being spoken, as Keziah had simply taken the key out of his hand before he'd even unlocked the driver's side door.

So Keziah drove, Father Stepan riding shotgun beside her, and the rest of them in the back. Justin sat behind Keziah; no one had to tell him she wouldn't want anybody behind her but him or her sister. Amira crowded against him, with Mrs. Farris beside her and Nicholas in the far back behind the seat. There was indeed a lot of room back there, even if the car wasn't actually a hearse.

"How far, priest?" Keziah asked.

"At this speed, not long, young lady, unless you cause an accident with your reckless –"

"She won't," muttered Justin, and finished the *telaraña* he was making. He rolled down the window of the car and threw it out. Then he patted Amira's shoulder apologetically, she handed him some more hairs from her head, and he began to make another one. Tangled webs, Natividad called them. Tangled webs to tangle sight, *telarañas* to distract the eye and prevent your enemies from spotting you even when you were in full sight. You left them along your back trail to confuse pursuit, or draped them over your car so you could drive straight up to a bad guy who'd kidnapped your grandmother and he'd never know till you were right up in his face. If you did it right, and it worked the way it was supposed to, and this guy's witchcraft, whatever that turned out to be, didn't make the whole effort worthless.

Light slid through the *trouvez*, and they left town and headed into the desert. The road got rougher, the way little-used desert roads would, eroded by rain and wind. A barbed wire fence appeared to their left, and then changed into a high chain-link fence with barbed wire across the top.

"Area 51," said Nicholas, nodding.

"Miles to go before we get to the entrance," Father Stepan told him. "Longer because we have to go around where the road's washed out. Turn here, please." He indicated a secondary road that was little more than the faint impression of tire tracks. Keziah turned, the car skidding a little on loose grit and gravel as they left the main road.

"North and then west again," Father Stepan said. "Then we'll cut back south and come out a little too far west. We'll have to backtrack a mile or so." He paused. "If we want to go in by the main entrance."

"We do not," Keziah said firmly. "We will go in there at that place where you say the road will bring us."

"There's the fence," Father Stepan pointed out.

"Well, that's a problem," Nicholas said. "A fence, wow. Whatever shall we do."

Justin sighed. "Nicky, please be polite. Father, a chain link fence is not a problem, but is this car going to be able to get to the main buildings or bunkers or whatever cross-country?"

Father Stepan hesitated. "I'm afraid I don't have a clear idea of just how the land lies in that area. If there are no arroyos, probably."

"If we cannot take the car, we will run," Keziah said. Her tone was calm, but flecks of gold burned in her dark eyes. "It does not matter. We may well wish to leave the car before we have come all the way. It is always better to surprise one's enemies. Justin, the *trouvez?"*

"Yeah, we're going the wrong way, but it's still showing us which way we ought to go –"

"Turn west up there, by that old oil drum."

It was a battered, rusted oil drum, but it did indeed sit next to another barely visible track.

"Used to be a ranch out here," said Father Stepan. "The Thompson place. It was never good country for a ranch. The well wasn't reliable enough. But old Thompson was a stubborn man. Took him years to give up, but early this fall he finally packed up and disappeared."

"He did not *disappear*," Mrs. Farris corrected sternly. "He went to his daughter in Albuquerque. Ever since her husband passed away, she'd been after him to sell this place and move in with her and the children. Eugenia told me all about it at the ladies' luncheon back in May."

"Probably the aliens made him leave," said Nicholas. "They probably drove him off with their crazy psychic powers."

Somewhat to Justin's surprise, Father Stepan added thoughtfully. "Or a witch, with some kind of curse."

Nicholas shrugged, but Mrs. Farris said, "I wouldn't be a bit surprised. Eugenia's impression was that he didn't mean to go, until suddenly he changed his mind. She was quite surprised. We all were. Not one to change his mind about anything, that old man."

They drove past the faded homestead: a battered mobile home and an equally battered lean-to shed, fences with sad, leaning posts and a half-dry pond surrounded by cracked earth. The whole property looked as though it had been abandoned a long time ago rather than just a few months previously. A feral cat, black and thin and looking exactly like it ought to be a witch's familiar, glared at them from the mobile home's porch as they drove past. Other than that, there was no sign of life.

Shortly after passing the Thompson place, before Justin had really expected to, they came back to the fence. Without a word Amira flowed out of the car and into her black dog form. She was so young that her other form was not much larger than a big dog—granted, a *really* big dog; she probably weighed twice as much in her black dog form than she did as a girl. But she was more than strong enough to peel back the heavy steel wire and leave a twelve-foot length of the fence in a tangled heap at the side of the road, while Father Stepan and Mrs. Farris stared. The priest crossed himself, murmuring in Latin. Mrs. Farris said, not quite under her breath, "That poor little girl!"

"She would not understand you," Keziah said, but with more irony than offense. "I assure you, she would not wish to be a soft, helpless human girl. The world is sufficiently unkind to black dog girls."

Justin reached forward to touch her shoulder. "Not in Dimilioc, surely."

After a moment, the stiffness under his palm eased. "Not in Dimilioc," Keziah conceded. "But neither Amira nor I would wish to be merely human."

Amira certainly showed no sign of wanting to shift back to her human form. She glared around at the empty desert, the shaggy black pelt bristling over her heavy shoulders and down her spine. Then she loped away, not too fast, not quite parallel with the road, but at a slant that would take her deeper into the forbidden area.

"Good," said Keziah. "She will go ahead of us. Carefully, for we do not know what we may find. Nicholas, go out and stay by Amira. Be careful."

"Yeah, I was going to be careless," Nicholas muttered. "I'm not stupid, you know." But he got out of the car, shifting not quite as smoothly as Amira had. His other form was larger than hers, but Justin was accustomed enough to black dogs to notice the way he averted his gaze from Amira's when he came up with her, and understood that Keziah's sister was the more dominant of the two. He wasn't surprised, either. Nicholas might be Dimilioc-bred and a Hammond, but Amira was Keziah's sister.

Then there was a long, slow, careful progress, following whatever sense the black dogs were using to tell them *this way to our enemies*. As far as Justin could tell from the light sliding through the *trouvez*, they were still going the right way. Whatever they found waiting up ahead, surely his grandmother must be there. The light was not exactly brightening, but it was growing more intense and the streaks were moving faster, and Justin felt they were getting close. He was starting to think they must be right on top of his grandmother, that they probably ought to slow down and look around for something like underground bunkers—if they could even find them, underground bunkers might be pretty hard to find, something they ought to have thought of earlier—

Then the light flickered and dimmed. Between one breath and the next, the magic invested into the *trouvez* faded. The mirror misted over and then cleared, and Justin was left staring, shaken, at a blank bit of glass.

"Well, that does feel a trifle peculiar," murmured Mrs. Farris next to him.

Keziah took her foot off the accelerator and allowed the car to coast to a gentle, near-silent halt in the middle of what seemed a vast stretch of flat, dry nothing. She said, her voice tight, "Justin. Your magic has faded. If I did not know you were Pure...I would not know you were Pure."

Justin had already figured that out, at least the part about his magic fading. He hadn't even known that magic was like an extra sense, but he felt like he had suddenly gone blind and deaf. Or not really. More as though he had unexpectedly walked into a bank of heavy fog that muffled sight and hearing. He drew a slow breath and let it out again. "How do *you* feel?"

"I?" Keziah considered this question. "Well enough," she concluded. "Well enough." She held out one hand, all its bones shortening and thickening, jet-black claws sliding out of distorted fingers. Then the change reversed itself until her hand was hers again, right down to the cobalt polish on her long, smooth fingernails.

Even at this moment, Justin had a moment's realization that this was finer control than she'd been capable of earlier in the year and that she must have been practicing in private. But mostly he was just relieved black dog magic didn't seem to have been affected by...whatever this was. Witchcraft. Whatever.

"Witchcraft," he said out loud, experimentally. "Witches." It still sounded ridiculous.

Father Stepan was studying Justin and the now-useless mirror. He told Keziah, "Back up immediately."

This was so plainly a good idea that Keziah didn't even glare at the priest for his temerity in giving her an order. She simply put the car into reverse and eased backward, gently, not too fast. Outside, Amira and Nicholas were loping back to join them. But Keziah waved them off, a sharp jerk of one hand, and they melted away into the desert instead, surprisingly thoroughly for large shaggy black monsters. Justin only hoped that was a good idea; he had to admit he would have felt considerably safer with the two younger black dogs near at hand.

Especially when the muffling effect did not reverse itself.

"Of course it couldn't be that simple," he muttered. Then he said to Keziah, "Okay, maybe we should go on, then. Or I should. Maybe this witch or whatever he is felt me coming. Or maybe he had some kind of spell set up to zap Pure magic if any of us got too close. But since you're not affected, you should get clear away and Father Stepan should take the wheel. No, listen, we'll be perfectly safe –"

Keziah cast her eyes up to the heavens, but waited, with unusual patience, for him to finish.

Justin shrugged. "Okay, not *safe*, but even if this witch expects me, even if he's set up to handle human visitors like Father Stepan and Mrs. Farris, I bet he won't expect *you*. So you get away from the car and join the others. The three of you can see what's up and then figure out what to do, and we'll just see –"

"Too late," muttered Father Stepan, and nodded off to their left, where a young man with a narrow, sly face and long greasy blond hair had suddenly appeared about fifty feet away, from, yes, an underground bunker. Or so Justin assumed from the camouflaged door he'd pushed up, which had been invisible until he opened it. Stepping out, the man scattered a handful of what looked like elongated dice or little white sticks before him on the ground, spun three times in a tight circle to his left, blew a handful of gray dust toward the car, and made several broad gestures in the air like he meant to start a game of charades. Only after all that did he stroll toward them. With, in fact, disturbing confidence. Justin wondered exactly what the guy had done—what they'd let him get away with doing. And how much they'd regret not just shooting him before that thing with the spinning and the dust.

"Grungy, as you see," pronounced Mrs. Farris. "A quite unprepossessing young man. Justin, you had better let me have my gun."

Justin glanced at Keziah, but he gave Mrs. Farris the gun without waiting for her nod. Keziah didn't say a word.

Her eyes were narrowed; her expression in profile coldly hostile, but she was watching the approaching man, not anybody in the car. Mrs. Farris tucked the gun beneath a fold of her skirt and sat up straight, looking dignified and very much as though she'd never dreamed of touching anything more dangerous than a nail file in her life.

"We'll have to play it by ear," Justin said in a low voice. "Keziah, if you can pass for human...until it's time for you *not* to pass for human . . ."

Keziah didn't answer. She had both hands on the wheel, her fingers long and graceful and completely human. Justin hoped her eyes were human dark rather than burning with black dog fire, but couldn't see her face from his place at her back.

Then the young man was at the car, leaning down to look in Keziah's window. His glance took in Keziah and Father Stepan, skimmed across Justin, and settled on Mrs. Farris, who coolly pointed her gun at his face. Justin hadn't see that coming and froze. Keziah raised one elegant eyebrow. Father Stepan let out a slow breath, but appeared willing to let Mrs. Farris take the lead.

The man was probably no more than five or six years old than Justin, but looked older, with the dark tan and broad shoulders and ropy muscles of someone who'd spent a lot of time working hard out of doors. Dirt was ground into his palms and around his fingernails, the way it got when someone had been working with his hands without wearing gloves. He held no obvious weapon, but he had a cell phone clipped to his belt and, despite the gun pointed at him, he was grinning. It was not a very nice expression.

Keziah was staring at the young man—they all were, of course. But Justin could see nothing of the anger he would have expected in Keziah's expression. If anything, Keziah looked faintly surprised. When Justin reached forward to touch her arm, she didn't seem to notice, even when he gripped her wrist pretty hard.

"Hey, look at this!" the young man said to Mrs. Farris. "You found me. And you've brought friends! Including, yes, a black dog!" He seemed disturbingly happy about this, and not the least bit worried about standing well within Keziah's reach. "Anna—can I call you Anna?—how *did* you find one of *these?* And a smokin' hot *babe,* too. That was real clever of you."

Keziah didn't gut the punk, even then. Justin sat back, glancing from her to the bad guy. A witch, yeah, or something. He'd done *something* to Keziah, too fast for anybody to even realize he was doing it—maybe that stuff with turning in circles and the handful of dust. And none of them had even tried to stop him. When Justin figured this out, he would fix it. He'd find a way. And when Keziah tore this guy's head off, he would *cheer.*

The young man didn't seem worried about anybody tearing his head off. He said happily, "Listen, Anna, don't threaten me, *that* wouldn't be clever. That was one thing this morning, but you can't shoot me now, you know. Just put the safety on before somebody gets hurt. Natalie Leushin, for example." He took out his cell phone and flourished it dramatically. It didn't take a rocket scientist to figure someone at the other end was probably listening.

Her expression stony, Mrs. Farris continued to point her gun at the young man's face. "Young man, I believe it's most likely Natalia is already dead. Unless you prove otherwise, shooting you would be only sensible."

Justin held his breath. Everything had gotten so crazy so fast, but he thought Mrs. Farris was probably right not to let this guy have everything his own way. Except Justin was afraid of what might happen if she actually shot him.

The young man was still grinning. "No, no! Not *yet,"* he protested. "She's fine. A little pissy, maybe. I bet she'll last a lot longer now you've brought us a black dog for a pet, especially a black dog that's already got a leash on it. Kristoff really wanted one and now he doesn't have to catch his own. Yeah, you've been real helpful." He thought he was just terribly funny, Justin could tell. That sly tone—he really did think he was in control, despite the gun pointed at him. Mrs. Farris didn't impress him at all.

Justin said quickly, before anyone could do anything hasty, "You say you've got my grandmother, whoever the hell you are. I want to talk to her, or else as far as I'm concerned Mrs. Farris is right and she can just shoot you right now."

"Oh, ho!" said the young man, really paying attention to Justin for first time. "Look at *you,* kid! You're Natalie Leushin's grandson, are you? That's great! You can call me Crowley, how's that?"

Father Stepan snorted, though the name meant nothing to Justin.

Crowley ignored the priest, concentrating on Justin. "What's *your* name, kid? You a white witch like the old lady? You *are,* aren't you?" He stared at Justin, disturbingly avaricious. "Well, how about that? Kristoff says white witches are always girls, but just look at you."

If Justin had been holding the gun, he definitely would have been tempted to pull the trigger. "Why should it matter to you?" he asked, concentrating on keeping his voice even. "What do you and this Kristoff want with...white witches? What have you done with my grandmother? Listen, let me talk to her, or Mrs. Farris *will* shoot you."

"Sure, she'll *try,"* said Crowley, but he also said into the phone, "Put the old lady on. Come on, Kristoff. No, c'mon, listen, I've got this, but it'll be easier if the kid talks to her." He listened for a moment and then rolled his eyes. "I bet you can *make* her," he said.

"Put her on!" Justin snapped, alarmed. "Nobody needs to make her do anything!"

Crowley laughed, but he held the phone out—tauntingly just out of reach.

Justin wouldn't give this guy the satisfaction of reaching for it. He raised his voice. "Grandmama?"

"Justin?" said his grandmother's voice barely audible. But it was clearly her. Justin clenched his teeth.

"There, you see? The old lady's fine," Crowley said cheerfully. "Come on out here, kid, and I'll take you right to her, I promise."

Staying in the car offered no protection at all. Especially with Keziah frozen in the driver's seat. But Justin wasn't at all sure getting out would improve anything. He stayed where he was.

"Black witches gain power by making a deal with the Devil," Father Stepan said abruptly. "So it's said. Is that true, young man? You can't imagine it will work out well for you in the end. It never does." He was studying Crowley, his eyes narrowed. He didn't look intimidated. He looked like a guy who'd been in a tight spot once or twice before and knew all about how to get into and—more importantly—out of trouble. Justin was suddenly glad he was here, even if he couldn't see any obvious way for Father Stepan to fix things.

"Well, lookie here, this other guy's a priest!" Crowley exclaimed in evident delight, looking Father Stepan ostentatiously up and down. "Don't you worry about us, Father—worry about yourself. Come on out here and I'll introduce you to Kristoff. He'll be real glad to meet you. Oh, this is perfect, it really is. Totally makes up for Anna being such a bitch this morning." Stepping back, he beckoned to them all. "Come on. Come here." And he added, directly to Keziah, "Come *here,* pet—and bring me that gun."

Justin caught his breath, because Keziah twisted around with smooth speed and took the gun away from Mrs. Farris. Then, her face blank, she got out of the car and handed it to Crowley.

"Oh, yeah," the young man said, grinning. He put the cell phone back on his belt, stuck the gun in the waistband of his jeans and set his hands on his hips. "Yeah, that's what I'm talking about." He gave Keziah a lazily admiring look and added to Justin, "You the one who got the leash on her? *Damn,* kid, good job. She is *nice*. Gotta admit, Kristoff was right about setting up a hook for black dogs. Worth the graveyard dust and burning the bones and all that shit. I gotta learn how to do that."

Keziah didn't react, but Justin set his teeth and stared longingly at the gun Crowley now held.

Crowley laughed at him and said smugly, "The rest of

you, come on, out of there, let's go. You want to see your granny, don't you, Justin?" He rapped impatiently on the hood of the car. "Come on, or I'll tell my pet here to fetch the lot of you. She'd be pretty rough about it, I bet—except for you, right, Justin?"

Justin longed to punch this guy in the face. He couldn't remember ever wanting to punch someone before in his life.

"Let's go, Justin," Father Stepan said quietly. It was a calming, easy tone: *Come on, I've got this*. He got out of the car and walked around it to face Crowley, quietly confident even now. Mrs. Farris followed him, clutching her handbag. She looked elderly and frail and helpless, not at all like the kind of woman who might carry a gun. So that was another possible asset, because the old lady sure hadn't looked like that before.

Moving slowly, Justin got out of the car, too He didn't believe it, he didn't believe for a second that Father Stepan had anything under control, but he couldn't see anything else to do and maybe he was wrong, maybe Father Stepan did have some kind of plan. Some better plan that just going along to see what happened. He was pretty sure the priest had been military, once. Or something. Maybe he had a plan. Maybe he did, or Mrs. Farris did, or they both did together, since they were friends.

Besides, Justin couldn't bear letting that punk *order* Keziah to drag him out of the car. There *had* to be a way to free her. He thought about circles and pentagrams and mandalas...if he drew a circle around Keziah, maybe he could knock out Crowley's influence, whatever it exactly was. *If* he could draw a circle. Only he couldn't. Not the fast way, at least. He tried. He opened and closed his hands, and he could *see* the geometry of what he wanted to do, but he couldn't *do* it. Trying to get a circle to leap to life around Keziah felt like...it felt like trying to pick up a needle through a handful of cotton wool. He *couldn't do it*. If he had a chance to walk it, trace the full circle the way Natividad did...he wasn't sure he could do that, either. If Natividad were here, he bet *she* would come up with something.

"Let's see, let's see . . ." Crowley looked them over. "All right, get rid of his cross," he told Keziah, pointing at Father Stepan.

Blank-faced, Keziah walked forward and reached for the chain, touching it gingerly with the tips of her fingers, hissing at the burn of the silver. Without a word, Father Stepan ducked his head and slipped the chain off over his head. Rather than force Keziah to touch it, he set the crucifix aside on the hood of the car. "It's not the crucifix that makes the priest, you know," he said quietly.

"That's what you think," Crowley said, offensively smug. "You're not the first priest to come after Kristoff, you know. You priests, you're even more vulnerable than a normal person. You'll find that out."

Father Stepan still didn't look afraid. He looked angry, but more than that, he looked *grieved.* Like he'd heard more in this than Crowley had maybe meant to say. Justin tried to draw a mandala on the dusty earth with his toe, but the circle wasn't straight and nothing happened that he could tell. When Crowley waved them all toward the open door, he set his teeth and followed.

The little white objects Crowley had scattered by the camouflaged door turned out to be small bones; finger bones, maybe. Justin wasn't even surprised. The bones were dry and cracked, or etched with writing of some kind, he couldn't quite tell. He thought of ducking to pick one up, but couldn't quite bring himself to touch any of them, and in the end just made sure to step carefully around them. No one else stepped on the bones either, he noticed, except for Crowley, who seemed to do it on purpose.

The camouflaged door led to a metal stairway that clanged underfoot, unnervingly loud, and from there to a dusty hallway that looked way too ordinary to belong to a secret government complex. The hall, all cheap institutional paneling and linoleum, looked like it belonged in a not very impressive office building somewhere. Except for the door at the end of the hallway which was kind of like a vault door and not much like anything you'd find in an office building anywhere.

Crowley slammed this door closed behind them just as he had the first, but when the young man waved them all forward, Justin took a second and set his hand on the door, trying to lay a spiral on it and around it. A spiral would draw your friends in and help them find you. He knew how to make a spiral, for God's sake, he could hold the indefinite equations in his head and open a spiral right up...but not here. Not through all the gray, diffuse fog these...black witches, or whatever they were, had laid down.

So Justin drew a spiral on the wall with the tip of his finger, he held the equations in his head and drew it blindly, even though he couldn't *see* it, and hoped that he'd done something.

Probably he hadn't done anything useful. Keziah was still trapped somehow, and Crowley had Mrs. Farris's gun, and Father Stepan had no cross, if that would have made any difference...Justin couldn't imagine anything the priest could do.

This was completely ridiculous. The whole thing was completely *ridiculous*.

The bunker looked a lot more like a bunker once Crowley led them down another stairway, with dim lights along the ceiling and a musty smell, and through yet another vault-like door, and finally into an enormous concrete-walled room. Machinery growled somewhere, the sound echoing off the distant walls. Two rows of big metal pillars marching into the distance, and a kind of low stage or dais or something, raised maybe three feet above the surrounding floor, took up a lot of the foreground. An unidentifiable heap of something, maybe a bundle of cloth, lay up on the platform, close by the nearest edge. All around this bundle stood a ring of fat white candles in black bowls, the candle flames tall and wavering. A bonfire burned inside the ring of candles, near one end of the bundle. Black smoke rose up, heavy and unpleasant. Not woodsmoke. More like burning plastic, but with an undertone of charring bone. The stench of the smoke mingled with the heavy odor of gasoline and the musty, unused smell of the bunker itself. Justin thought this smell would come back to him in his nightmares, if he lived through this.

Metal boxes and platforms bolted to the floor around the stage had probably once held some kind of machinery, but they were mostly empty now, bare clamps and the cut ends of wires protruding here and there. It was surprisingly easy to imagine an alien spaceship lying up on that stage, surrounded by scientists and military people and God knew what kinds of equipment. Nicholas would have gotten a kick out of exploring this place...for a moment Justin had nearly forgotten about Nicholas and Amira. He made himself not look at the heavy door, which Crowley had left standing open behind them. He hadn't managed to draw a spiral on that one. But it was open. Surely that was good.

Then he spotted Grandmama Leushin. She was below the near edge of the stage, half hidden by the flickering shadows from the fire. She was sitting on a straight-backed chair, surrounded by a tangle of wires and a black powdery circle that had nothing to do with high-tech equipment, a circle that looked to Justin like it had been made of something soft and powdery that absorbed light. Graveyard dust and the ashes of burned bones, he assumed.

His grandmother didn't seem to have been hurt, not as far as he could tell. He couldn't see any ropes or cords or anything tying her to the chair, but he guessed the circle was doing the job of keeping her confined. He wondered what would happen if somebody rubbed out part of that circle—what would happen if *he* did. Hard to guess how this kind of black witchcraft might interact with Pure magic. Easy to guess that the ash circle had been specifically made to counter Pure magic.

Grandmama Leushin looked older than Justin remembered. A lot older. If he hadn't known she was in her seventies, he'd have guessed she was twenty years older. Her face was thinner than he remembered, and her hair—he remembered it as almost pure white, but the light down here gave everything a grayish, yellowish tinge. Maybe that was why she looked so old and kind of sick. She had turned her head and leaned forward, but she hadn't gotten to her feet—maybe she *couldn't* get up, maybe she really was sick—or hurt—Justin couldn't tell; he was still too far away. They were heading in that direction, at least.

Someone—Crowley and his buddy Kristoff, no doubt—had brought in a generator, wired it up and turned it on. That was the machinery Justin had heard. It wasn't far away, but the room was so big and the generator so small that even with the echoes the racket wasn't actually deafening. And at least the generator meant they weren't stuck in the dark, with nothing but that unpleasant fire and those nasty candles to light up this place.

Though that...that was actually a mixed blessing, because as they got closer, Justin gradually made out more details of the scene up on that stage. He supposed he'd known from the first that the heap lying in the circle of candles must really be a body. He would have been glad not to see the specifics. He hadn't really wanted to know that it had been another old lady, at least as old as his grandmother; or that all her fingers had been cut off. He tried not to wonder whether that had been done before or after her throat had been cut. He tried even harder not to imagine his grandmother sitting in that chair, watching while these people killed her. Maybe she'd known her. He hoped they hadn't been friends.

He could see the same kind of muffled almost-Pure silvery magic around Grandmama Leushin, exactly the same as the half visible glow around Mrs. Farris. It was appallingly easy to imagine a whole circle of old ladies with some kind of peculiar magic, like the Pure but different, and these nasty black witches or whatever they were murdering one old lady at a time. A bargain with the Devil, maybe; Justin didn't know and wasn't sure it mattered. Whatever this was, it was definitely a way to gain power—power over black dogs, maybe over regular people. Maybe not over the Pure, judging from this Crowley's first approach to Mrs. Farris.

Not that that would mean the Pure were safe. As always,

the Pure appeared to be special targets. Justin couldn't help but glance at Mrs. Farris. Her mouth was a thin line, her eyes pointed straight ahead, her handbag clutched in both hands. She looked timid and old. Father Stepan, a supportive hand under her elbow didn't look afraid. He looked angry.

Keziah...Keziah didn't look like anything. Her face was still, masklike. But her eyes had gone bright, pale, fiery yellow. And her shadow was blacker and sharper edged than it had any right to be, in this artificial light. As though she stood a lot closer to that bonfire than she actually did.

Keziah wouldn't be afraid, Justin knew. She would be *furious*.

He was scared enough for all of them. This was not how he'd pictured this scene, when he'd declared they had to rescue his grandmother. Somehow they'd gone from facing a punk kid who backed down from the ordinary threat of a gun, to facing a black witch who didn't seem at all worried about being shot and who could put a leash of some kind on a black dog as strong and angry as Keziah.

Then it got worse. Because a man who had to be Crowley's friend Kristoff walked around the generator and stopped, waiting for them.

Justin had expected a guy a lot like Crowley—young, cocky, maybe not too smart. He saw at once that this guy was not like that. Kristoff was a lot older, probably closer to Father Stepan's age. He was bigger, too; not big like a guy who worked outdoors or with his hands, but bulky and soft, with round arms and plump hands. He was pale, like he never set foot outside in the sunlight if he could help it. The light down here gave his skin an unhealthy yellowish tinge. His face was round, his eyes pouchy, his mouth pursed. He looked like somebody who worked in an office somewhere. Like a lawyer, maybe. A senior partner, who sat behind a big desk and gave orders to legions of flunkies. The way he tilted his head and crossed his arms and waited for the rest of them to come up to him suggested that he thought he was better than all of them put together. The contempt in his attitude wasn't subtle. Yeah, Justin had no trouble imagining this man sitting in some office somewhere, casting spells on his business rivals to make their clients walk away or the IRS audit them or whatever the modern equivalent might be to making their cows go dry.

Crowley ushered the rest of them forward and showed them off to Kristoff with a proud wave of his hand. "Look, a black dog and everything. Nice piece, isn't she? That dust is good stuff, you should show me how to make it, we need more if we're gonna find black dogs working with white witches, and now we've got plenty of white witches. Not just a bunch of old dried-up bitches; look at this kid. I thought you said white witches were always –"

"Shut up," Kristoff said. His voice was heavy, unemotional, inexpressive. Crowley shut his mouth, and Kristoff spent a long stretched-out moment studying them all, one at a time, starting with Keziah and ending with Father Stepan. He didn't seem very interested in Mrs. Farris—Justin supposed that once you started murdering old ladies, they might all blur together—and only marginally more interested in Justin himself. But his gaze lingered on Father Stepan. "A priest, I see. You've never seen a true black mass," Kristoff said to Crowley. "I'll show you one."

And without a word, Father Stepan shot him four times. He aimed twice for his right foot and leg. Then, as Kristoff staggered in surprise but, obviously unhurt, did not fall, Father Stepan took a sharp breath and shot him twice more in the chest.

Justin, taken perfectly by surprise—he'd never once guessed the priest might be armed, and hadn't seen him draw his gun—nevertheless left Father Stepan to it, seized Keziah by the arms and, moved by a sudden impulse that came out of nowhere, reached up and drew a pentagram on her forehead, tracing the five-pointed star with his fingertip. "Be free," he told her. "Be free of it!" He tried to draw a pentagram around her the other way, the fast way, by defining it mathematically and so bringing it to life; but he couldn't do that, not through the muffling fog of black magic that filled this place.

Keziah shuddered and blinked, but her eyes stayed fiery

and when she turned, her hands broadening and distorting, it was away from Justin, toward Father Stepan. She was going to kill him, she was already half in her black dog form, and though Justin put himself in her way, she only shouldered impatiently past him, toward the priest. His grandmother was shouting in a high voice, cracked and terrified and furious, urgent words Justin couldn't understand, about opening or approaching or releasing something. Her hands were together as though she were praying.

But Justin lost track of her, Kristoff was still on his feet and still a threat—deformed silver bullets were scattered around the black witch—Mrs. Farris threw the crucifix she'd had in her handbag to Father Stepan, who caught it and started toward Kristoff, his gun in his left hand, but holding the crucifix in his right like it was the true weapon. At this, Kristoff backed away, his hands held up as though to shield himself. A nasty snaky solid kind of blackness writhed before him, between him and Father Stepan, but at least Kristoff was no longer smiling.

Mrs. Farris had also drawn yet another gun from some hidden holster and was now shooting at Crowley, but with no better results. Crowley first ducked back, but then rushed forward and knocked the gun out of Mrs. Farris's hands, though she tried at the last moment to duck away. He slapped her, contemptuously, the kind of slap he might have aimed at a misbehaving child. Mrs. Farris stumbled and fell to her knees, and Crowley aimed the gun *he* still held—he was going to shoot her, he was going to shoot her right now, but Keziah had nearly reached Father Stepan. Justin, torn, flung himself after Keziah—it wasn't a considered decision, he wasn't thinking at all, he just *couldn't* let Keziah kill Father Stepan -- though he didn't have any way to stop her, apparently –

Amira flowed out of the shadows and tore Crowley apart, and Nicholas leaped up on the stage, scattered the candles with two swift blows, tore right through the horrible bonfire, leaped down again, and raked his claws across the ashen circle surrounding Grandmama Leushin. And Father

Stepan turned his back on Kristoff, who had turned and was now walking away, not quite running, but walking fast. Father Stepan let him go, slamming his heavy silver Orthodox crucifix against Keziah's shaggy throat as she reared over him. He shouted, "May the Lord rebuke thee, Devil! Depart from this servant of God, from her mind, from her soul, from her heart –"

And Keziah whirled away from the priest and slammed a blow instead against the generator that tumbled it over and tore it free of all its wires and connections. All around them, the lights went out, but Justin instantly made another kind of circle around himself and around Father Stepan, and another around his grandmother, and another around Mrs. Farris, light blooming in one protective circle after another. Only after he'd done that did he realize the muffling effect of the witches' magic had disappeared.

Even in the dark, Justin was aware of Keziah leaping away, fully in her black dog form now, after Kristoff.

The silvery light of the Pure was not very useful to see by, unless you happened to be Pure. All but two of the candles had been extinguished, and what Grandmama Leushin called the banefire had been scattered and mostly put out. But Nicholas was good with fire, especially when he was upset, which he definitely was right now. He tumbled various chairs and a small table together and set them alight, and although Justin wouldn't have wanted to toast marshmallows over that kind of fire, even black dog fire wasn't as horrible as what the black witches had made. And after all, they only needed enough light to get out.

Somehow it seemed farther on the way out than it had coming in: the darkness seemed to press down harder and the stairs seemed longer and the vault-like doors seemed heavier, and likely to slam in their faces...Kristoff had gotten away. Keziah had lost him, somehow. That should have been impossible, but who knew what a black witch might be able to do? Justin had been relieved beyond measure when Keziah had come back, and relieved again when no one tried to shoot her even though she was still in her black dog form. But he had been terrified when she'd taken back her human form and told them bitterly that Kristoff had gotten away from her. Justin had immediately felt a terrible certainty that the black witch would somehow get out first and shut the doors and seal the rest of them down here with horror and death and the lingering miasma of black magic.

Even if that happened, they'd get the doors open again. Justin knew that. But the idea of those doors slamming shut still sent cold shudders running down his spine until they were through each one and hurrying at last through the desert sunlight spilling down the last flight of stairs, and...out into the light.

Justin stopped, blinking through dazzling light. It seemed like they'd been down there in the dark for a lot longer than a few minutes. The sun was still high overhead, the brilliant winter sunlight pouring down around them. It seemed like it should be midnight. He was so glad it wasn't.

He stood with his arm around Grandmama Leushin, and behind him Father Stepan was assisting Mrs. Farris, who was showing her age at last, and probably not as an act this time. The three black dogs had gone up first. Justin knew why, though he would never have put it into words. If he'd feared the black witch getting ahead of them and locking them down in the dark, the black dogs must have been terrified at the far more rational idea that Kristoff might come up behind them and put his will on them, the way he'd done on Keziah.

She had a vivid cross-shaped mark on her throat where that big silver crucifix had burned her. It had burned right through her shaggy black-dog pelt, leaving a red, raw mark on her human skin when she shifted back. It looked even worse in bright sunlight than it had underground. Silver-burned, that mark would take weeks to heal, probably. Keziah was pretending it didn't hurt, though her jaw had set tight and her eyes were narrow with anger and—Justin was sure—pain. She hadn't said a word about it, not to Justin and certainly not to Father Stepan.

Father Stepan hadn't said a word about that mark, either.

He and Keziah were now standing several yards apart, on opposite sides of the small group, carefully not looking at each other. Justin imagined neither one was going to be very comfortable with what had happened; neither Keziah who had been so briefly enslaved, nor the priest who had, apparently successfully, called on God to free a girl who still, inarguably, harbored a different kind of demon. It probably raised all kinds of questions about black dogs and demonic forces and God and everything. Justin was just as glad he didn't have to offer an opinion about any of that.

"Well," Grandmama Leushin said, interrupting these thoughts. She pushed away from Justin, turning to gaze up into his face. She was shivering a little, even out here in the sunlight, but her voice was just as he remembered, firm and confident. "Well. Justin. I *did* tell you not to come. I honestly don't know *what* I would have said to your mother if anything had happened to you. Heaven knows if I'd have had the nerve to visit her grave ever again."

Justin didn't point out that, first, he could hardly have turned around and just left her in trouble; and second, that if he hadn't come, his grandmother would have been lucky to wind up in a decent grave of her own. He said, keeping his voice mild, "I didn't expect quite that much trouble. I figured my friends could handle anything. I thought probably some mundane problem, or just possibly a black dog was threatening you, something normal like that." He paused, because it did sound a little odd when he put it that way. But he didn't pause to think about it. He said instead, firmly, "I figured my friends and I could handle anything except finding you *dead.*"

"Um." His grandmother studied Keziah, who was looking very nearly as arrogant and assured as ever, but...not quite. And not like she would welcome anybody noticing any new trace of uncertainty that might be affecting her, either.

After a second, Grandmama Leushin gave her a provisional nod of approval and nodded to Amira, who had tucked herself against Keziah's side as though she needed comfort, which to Justin was pretty obviously a pretext for offering it. His grandmother's gaze softened. She said to Justin, "I *am* sorry about that, Justin, but when you said you were bringing *friends*, this is not exactly what I imagined. Perhaps if you'd *explained* –"

Keziah crossed her arms over her chest and tilted her head, her eyes narrowing dangerously. Justin said quickly, "Well, I don't know, Grandmama, maybe if you'd warned me *witches* were after you, we'd have been a little better prepared. Did you *know* about that, Grandmama?" The silvery Escheresque curves of Pure magic were a lot brighter around her now. And around Mrs. Farris. Still not as clear as around Natividad or the other Pure girls and women he'd met, but...better. Like the muffling fog was still present, but thinning. "Did you know...what *do* you know? About me? About...my mother?"

"Not as much as I thought, probably," his grandmother admitted. "Not enough to expect you to make...this kind of friend. You needed my friends as well, I gather." She didn't glance toward Keziah, nor the cross-shaped burn on her throat. She only added, "I'm so glad they were there for you, Justin. Father Stepan, it was so kind of you to help my grandson, but it was a terrible risk for you. What if you'd killed that man? He *was* human, you know."

"After the first two bullets bounced off, I was fairly certain shooting him wasn't likely to be very effective," Father Stepan said mildly. "I was willing to take the risk. I'm not quite certain what my confessor will say about this…incident, I admit."

"Demonic entities are properly a priest's concern; that was settled years ago when the monsters appeared. And that man was definitely harboring a demonic entity." Grandmama Leushin shook her head. "I must admit, you and Anya were quite right about carrying a gun with silver bullets. But I was right, too. Silver's not enough, not by itself. That was poor little Yelena, you know. They fed her to their . . ." she paused.

"Pet?" Keziah suggested, her tone soft and dry and bitter as ashes.

"Well, that imprudent ass Kristoff certainly seems to think so," Grandmama Leushin said tartly. "Chains break, don't they? All chains break, in the end. It'll be his master one of these days, and I don't imagine he'll enjoy that."

"Neither will anyone else, I fear," Father Stepan murmured.

"No, probably not," Grandmama Leushin conceded. She sighed. She was looking better, though still not well. The glance she sent around the wide desert and camouflaged door and waiting car was indecisive.

Nicholas looked up, got to his feet, and walked over to join them. "I can seal that door, probably," he said without preamble. "Heat it up, melt it shut. The door's metal, so's the frame. But there have to be other doors."

"Young man, we must certainly recover Yelena's body," stated Mrs. Farris. "And inform the proper authorities. If we are to find ourselves facing witches –" her lip curled slightly on the term—"we had best be certain everyone knows it."

Father Stepan inclined his head. "Corruption prospers best in secret, whether it involves black magic or the old-fashioned venality of ordinary sin."

"Well," said Justin, looking at Keziah, "Somebody can call the police; that's fine. But I'm pretty sure I know who else ought to be informed about...all this. As soon as possible."

"Yes," Keziah agreed, not very happily.

"Hot chocolate," Justin told her. "My grandmother makes it so thick you can almost stand a spoon up in it. We all need hot chocolate, in a nice comfortable kitchen where the house is surrounded by a really strong mandala. And then you can call Grayson. Or I will."

"I will call him," Keziah said, and sighed. "He will be pleased you are safe, at least. Perhaps Natividad will know something to do, to protect us all against that kind of witchcraft." She was still trying not to let anybody see her horror at what had happened to her, but nevertheless she came and put an arm around Justin's shoulders, and let him put his own arm around her waist and hold her. "Why do these terrible things always happen when I go somewhere with you?"

"Hey, as long as we always have friends to help us survive them," Justin told her, and tightened his arm around Keziah, trying not to think of what might have happened.

"Hot chocolate?" Amira reminded them all, hopefully.

"Thick enough to stand a spoon up in it," Grandmama Leushin promised, and patted Amira on the shoulder exactly like she was an ordinary grandmother, and Amira an ordinary little girl. Justin couldn't help but laugh at that, and at the sheer pleasure and relief of being alive and out in the sunlight. It had been a terrible beginning for this visit...but maybe not a terrible introduction of his friends to his grandmother.

These days, there aren't any vampires left in the natural world. Or not many. Or we hope not. But we know that vampires had a tremendous influence on human affairs for thousands of years, spinning webs of corruption and despair within human communities wherever they established a power base.

We know, of course, that the demonic entities we call vampires invade the human world by inhabiting corrupted corpses. How exactly the corpse becomes corrupted...that's less well known. We know that the bite of a master vampire allows the demon to infect and corrupt an ordinary person, creating lesser vampires (if the infected person dies) or blood kin (if the infected person lives). But how did the whole thing get started? How did the first vampire gain access to a human corpse in the first place?

Black dogs and vampires have been enemies, or at least rivals, practically forever. Naturally we know that a person is born a black dog, with a demonic entity bound to him or her. When you think about it, you may not think this seems like something which is likely to happen spontaneously, even in a world filled with demonic influences and other kinds of magic.

We know that if a black dog bites someone, the unfortunate person is at dire risk of becoming a moon-bound shifter: infected by a demon that forces its way up through the corrupted soul when the moon is full, manifesting in a monstrous form. All this is obviously grossly similar to what happens with vampires, but quite different in detail.

The two kinds of entities are not the same. Where a vampire strives to corrupt and ruin mortal people and institutions and cities, black dogs love power and want to rule. Black dogs are vicious and sadistic and enjoy inflicting pain and fear, and societies where they gain power become brutal, but even that isn't as bad as the slow rot and decay that afflict cities where vampires take control. We know all that, yes, but how and when did the first black dogs appear?

The answer to both questions is the same: witches did it.

In our world, the popular view of witchcraft has gradually changed from dire evil that involves a deal with the Devil to the modern conception of Wicca and so forth. In the world of *Black Dog,* there is no such thing as Wicca, and witchcraft actually *does* involve a deal with the Devil. Or at least with demonic entities. In exchange for power in this world, the ambitious witch allows a demon to establish a foothold in his (or her) soul.

As you might imagine, this carries certain intrinsic risks.

Many thousands of years ago, in southern and central regions of Africa, spiteful witches were already working secretly to harm others. Other kinds of people worked to balk them with other kinds of ceremonial magic, of course. But from the earliest days of humanity, witchcraft spread across the continent and then outward to other regions of the world, though the exact methods used by witches differed from one area to the next.

Most witchcraft was petty stuff: curses and ill-wishes. In the Black Dog world, pettiness is in fact intrinsic to witchcraft, for two reasons. First, anybody drawn to witchcraft is probably not very good at long-term planning, a personality flaw which is highly exploitable by demonic influence. And second, the practice of witchcraft inherently tends to focus the mind and attention on day-to-day selfish concerns, rarely leaving room for large-scale ambition. However, as witches experimented and practiced and gathered knowledge, witchcraft, though still generally focused on narrow personal concerns, became stronger and darker and harder to thwart.

There were at this time hundreds of words for witches and witchcraft; as many as there were languages. But one thing was common to all conceptions of witchcraft—that witches were always evil, and that the power of witchcraft came through possession by evil spirits, which endowed the witch with supernatural power to do harm. As humanity spread out of Africa into other continents, people carried with them their understanding of the supernatural, and of course they also carried with them all the normal human inclinations toward ill and toward healing.

Civilizations rose and fell. Some are remembered now, though faintly; and some are entirely forgotten. In all of them, witches worked their curses and ill-wishes. Sometimes, here or there, a witch learned enough and became powerful enough to cause real harm. Every now and then, such a witch stretched that little bit too far, reached for power that was not really understood or could not be entirely controlled.

Inviting an evil spirit to possess you, while sometimes an effective pathway to power, turned out not to be entirely safe. Somewhere, thousands of years ago—no doubt on various different occasions in various different places—a witch summoned an evil spirit, was possessed by it, lost control of the witchcraft, and became a black dog. Each time this happened, it was bad, but not end-of-the-world bad. We all know that the curse turned out to be transmissible through the generations, and transmissible in a weaker form by contagion. Nevertheless, though black dogs were certainly dangerous, they weren't much more so than any ordinary thug. Black dogs had trouble concealing themselves among ordinary people. They tended to flee society, and when they caused too much trouble, they could be hunted down and killed. Everyone knew that silver could kill a black dog, and everywhere there were priests or shamans or other holy people who could face down black dogs. In general terms, ordinary people could cope with black dogs.

Or they could, until a witch somewhere—maybe more than one—made a much worse mistake.

Somewhere a witch decided that it was too dangerous to call an evil spirit to possess him (or her). Somewhere a learned and careful and ambitious witch decided it would be far better if the evil spirit was called instead to possess a corpse. Or perhaps a witch tried to prolong his own existence after death, using the demon bound to his soul to magically keep his body functioning after death. Maybe that even worked, here and there, now and then.

Eventually, two or three thousand years ago, such an experiment created the first vampire.

It might have happened in Egypt. Or Assyria. (Not China—there were always dragons in China, and dragons are proof against all things demonic.) But in some land where there were no natural protections against demonic influence, a corpse opened its eyes and a vampire rose.

Once it defeated the control of its summoning witch, the first vampire made others, of course. Perhaps it forced the witch to make others. Certainly it quickly learned to make living people look away from it, look somewhere else, see something else: from the beginning, vampires could influence the minds of ordinary people. It also learned how to turn living people into blood kin—slaves it controlled by the force of its will.

No one now knows whether the first vampire already knew or

guessed that if enough vampires could be made, their ability to cloud minds and turn away the eyes of their enemies and force obedience would spread out…and out…and finally settle as a permanent miasma across the minds of ordinary people everywhere. Perhaps the vampires worked purposefully for this, or perhaps they just made the miasma as bees make honey: mindlessly following some instinct peculiar to their kind.

But vampires had another effect on the world, perhaps less obvious: in much of the world, they suppressed witchcraft. For hundreds—thousands—of years, the miasma prevented most people from even thinking about magic and demons. Often, the vampire miasma prevented people who might have become witches from noticing grimoires, even if one was already on a shelf in someone's library.

Of course some potential witches were less affected by the miasma—you will recall from the essay on black dog genetics that some people are naturally resistant to all kinds of demonic influence. In some parts of Africa and in Polynesia, witches were more common or the type of witchcraft practiced was particularly difficult for vampires to suppress, and in those regions vampires never established themselves and witchcraft continued to be practiced on a wider scale (along with many different methods of resisting and countering witchcraft).

But in much of the world, if someone began practicing witchcraft, he would most likely bring himself to the notice of vampires long before he realized his danger. In areas where they became established, vampires were always watching for witches, presumably because witches pose a special threat to vampires. Quite possibly vampires sometimes left grimoires on shelves specifically to bait potential witches into revealing themselves. Whether purposefully or instinctively, vampires hunted the holy—and later the Pure. But for their entire history, whenever they could, they also actively hunted witches.

Thus, by the time the miasma was broken, there were only a few practicing witches in Europe, the Middle East, the Mediterranean region, or the Americas. And in those regions, all the witches left were *profoundly* paranoid. That was why they survived, and why they took several years to begin making themselves visible after the black dog/vampire war destroyed the miasma.

In our own world, belief in various kinds of witchcraft was widespread in many, perhaps most, cultures. Today in our world, not only has Wicca developed in some areas, but a belief in evil witchcraft has surged in other regions. In recent years, in a (real) ongoing tragedy, tens of thousands of children in Nigeria, Congo, Angola, and other parts of Africa have been abused or thrown out of their homes for being witches. Reasons for this vary. In some areas, accusations of witchcraft are the only acceptable excuse not to take in a relative; in others, exorcists identify child-witches (for a fee) and perform the exorcism (for another fee).

Much of this is not true in the world of *Black Dog.* As is often the case, the world of *Black Dog* is both better and worse, kinder and crueler, than the real world. In the Black Dog world, there were no medieval witch hunts, no Salem witch trials, no Wicca. *The Wizard of Oz* exists, but Glenda the Good is not a character in the movie. In all cultures, fairy tales and folk tales feature evil witches, almost never good ones. But in the modern day, particularly where vampires were most influential, there is far, far less belief in witchcraft and witches of all sorts.

Even those who are more aware of the supernatural—for example, black dogs and their human kin—know at most only that some kind of demonically influenced witchcraft exists in some areas where vampires have been less powerful—that is, of course, primarily in some parts of

Africa and Polynesia. Only in those regions have ordinary people retained not only belief in, but also defenses against, witchcraft. Ironically, because witchcraft was never thoroughly suppressed in Africa, effective methods of dealing with witches were also retained, and thus Sub-Saharan African countries are not plagued with the witchcraft-accusation tragedy seen in our world today, even though they do have other problems with real witchcraft.

All this came about because of vampiric influence. Both the miasma that prevented people from seeing and understanding the supernatural, and because vampires always hunted witches in every region they ever had under their sway.

Now, of course, the vampires are all gone. Now anyone who fancies himself or herself a practitioner, anyone who encounters the right kind of very old book in some dusty library, anyone who happens to think that summoning evil spirits sounds like a great way to wreak harm on an enemy...well, in most regions of the world, there's now no one hunting witches and no folk memory of how to guard against witchcraft.

Really, that's just bound to lead to trouble.

I hope you enjoyed these stories! All of them are set either before *Black Dog* or in between *Black Dog* and *Pure Magic*.

The third novel in the series is *Shadow Twin*. Read on for a preview.

A preview of *Tuyo*, a high fantasy novel in a completely different setting and world, follows the preview of *Shadow Twin.*

If you enjoyed this or any other book of mine, I'd appreciate it if you would leave a review at **Goodreads** or **Amazon**.

For news about the Black Dog series and about my other fantasy novels, please visit www.rachelneumeier.com.

To stay informed about upcoming releases and giveaways, subscribe to my newsletter when you drop by my website.

SHADOW TWIN

-1-

Natividad began to feel strange during the last part of the service. The choir led the congregation in "Holy, Holy, Holy," but she found herself unable to listen.

She knew all the words, even in English. She had learned them over the past year. *Maker of Heaven and Earth*...she knew the words, but she couldn't voice them. She found she couldn't quite hear the organ or the choir or the congregation, nor even DeAnn, who had a beautiful alto voice and was standing right next to her. Not even Grayson, whose gritty bass laid down the deep foundation of the melody.

She heard something else. Or not exactly *heard*. It wasn't a real sound. In fact, it wasn't actually much like sound at all. It was more like...it was like a lingering silence where sound ought to have been. It was as though some long note of music, a humming she felt in her bones and her blood, had suddenly stopped.

She didn't understand what it was, that stiff, empty silence that was both like and unlike sound. But she knew it frightened her. She blinked, gripping the back of the pew in front of her, dizzy. Or not exactly *dizzy*, her balance was all right, but *something* was off.

Alejandro took her elbow, always the attentive older brother. Sometimes she found his close attention a tiny bit *asfixiante*, but this time she was grateful for his concern. She wondered if she had actually swayed after all.

But then the strange sensation ebbed, and the music came back, all the massed voices: *Heaven and Earth are filled with your glory*. Straightening her shoulders, Natividad took a breath and smiled reassuringly at her brother, though she did not yet try to sing. He was studying her, his concern edged with anger because for a black dog almost everything was tinted with anger. He tilted his head at her smile, clearly doubting her reassurance. She offered him a firm little nod and shaped words under her breath: *Estoy bien.*

Alejandro didn't believe her; she could tell. But he returned her nod, pretending he accepted her assurance. He would ask later what had happened to her, though. And she did not know.

She looked for Grayson. The Master of Dimilioc was blocked from her view by the massive form of Thaddeus, who was on the other side of DeAnn. DeAnn had one arm around each of her children—her black dog son Conway, and the little Pure girl they called Paloma. Paloma still did not talk, only a word now and then, but she followed Conway around, a little blonde shadow. Con pretended he didn't care, but he had kind of started looking over his shoulder to make sure she was there. Of course a Pure sister was a very good thing for a black dog boy.

Beyond Thaddeus and DeAnn and the children, Grayson stood right by the aisle at the left-hand side of the pew, here at the back of the church, in the rearmost pew of the three reserved, unofficially, for the Dimilioc wolves.

Black dogs didn't like people behind them. Black dogs never liked people behind them. Not even their own people in their own town. These *were* their own people: the whole town was practically part of Dimilioc. Many of the people here were Dimilioc connections: cousins of one degree or another. The church, the new one, built on consecrated ground across town from where the old church had stood, had protections layered into its foundation and set into every stone of its walls. It did not seem a likely place for violence. But even here, the Dimilioc wolves did not like to have anyone behind them. So these pews in the back were theirs, by long custom unspoken but understood. The people of the town knew it and made sure that not even occasional visitors trespassed.

Grayson Lanning, Master of Dimilioc, did not actually *insist* that all the black dogs of Dimilioc attend services every week. He permitted alternatives, all of which were also designed to build patience, self-control, and tolerance of the human community. A Dimilioc black wolf might choose instead to attend the local town hall meetings, or join the school board, or even hold an actual job like an ordinary person—though it was understood that Dimilioc duties came first.

In practice, everyone came to mass. It was simple and not too demanding, and there were doughnuts afterward. Even Keziah and Amira usually came, though they weren't Christian. Keziah was allowing Father McClanahan to teach her about Christ and the church, in pure spite of the memory of her family—Natividad was almost sure about that motivation—and Amira, as always, followed her sister's lead. Except both Keziah and Amira were away right now, guarding Justin as he visited his *grandmamá* for Christmas. Keziah and Amira and Nicholas Hammond, so that Justin would have a team of three black dogs to protect him while he was away from Dimilioc, even if two of them were kids.

Nicholas had lost his older sister to a really horrifying

master vampire, and almost worse, they still didn't know absolutely for *sure* whether his sister Carissa had truly been killed by the vampire. She *might* have gotten away. Probably she was dead, but they couldn't be *sure*. Nicholas was kind of hard to get along with, but Natividad couldn't blame him. That kind of uncertainty must be almost worse than *knowing* that someone you loved was dead.

Natividad missed Justin a lot more than Nicholas. He was so *restful,* a Pure boy among all these black dogs. She missed Amira, too. She'd grown kind of used to telling the younger girl bedtime stories. She even missed Keziah. Keziah could be hard to get along with, arrogant and sarcastic and with a cutting sense of humor, but Natividad had kind of learned to get along with her. Besides, she trusted Keziah, in a way that she didn't trust most of the newer black dogs of Dimilioc.

Russell and Andrew Meade probably didn't truly accept Dimilioc law, but at least they had a human sister, Liz. She'd told Natividad that she'd never imagined living somewhere among normal people who knew about black dogs so that she didn't have to hide everything about her life. So Andrew and Russell were probably all right, because of their sister.

But the other newer wolves, Carter Lethridge and Max Smith and Don and Rip Jacobs—Rip was really Richard, though only Grayson called him that. *Naturalmente* Grayson would never use a nickname like *Rip*. Natividad didn't trust any of them a bit.

Grayson had brought them all into Dimilioc from a small shadow pack in Tennessee. Carter Lethridge had ruled that little pack. He'd held no fewer than eight other black dogs together and establishing a territory that encompassed parts of three states before Grayson had personally broken up his pack and brought him in, and the others that had survived.

So now they all had to deal with Carter. Natividad was almost certain he was going to be trouble. She thought he was going to challenge Grayson eventually. She didn't trust him. She would have been even more worried except she *did* trust Grayson to handle whatever Carter eventually tried.

Natividad guessed, though she did not *know*, that Grayson mostly wanted his wolves to attend mass because so many of the Dimilioc black wolves *were* new—new to Dimilioc, new to being around ordinary people. He probably thought all his wolves needed structure and ceremony and reasons to really feel like they had joined something bigger than themselves. He was probably right. He usually was.

So every Sunday morning, all the wolves of Dimilioc who were at home came to services and then joined the townspeople for doughnuts and *café* in the parish hall. It wasn't only doughnuts, although that was what people said. Natividad made *besos* and *cuernos* and cinnamon rolls. DeAnn made pies, with canned pie filling. Until coming to Dimilioc, Natividad had never imagined pie filling in *cans*, but it was actually pretty good, especially the cherry kind. Miguel, who could sometimes surprise even his twin, made scones. Before coming to Dimilioc, Natividad had not imagined her twin learning to bake, but he said it was nice to stop thinking about big things and just think about whether to make scones with chocolate chips or coconut or lemon.

Miguel wasn't next to Natividad this morning; he was up in the front, with Cassie Pearson and her father. Natividad knew Alejandro was uneasy having their brother *pasa tiempo,* hang out with, Cassie Pearson, who was a *cambiadora,* a moon-bound shifter, and dangerous when the moon forced her into the *cambio de cuerpo.* The moon-bound could not control their shadows, and when the shadow came up, it always first tried to kill those the shifter loved most. That was all true, and Cassie really was dangerous when she shifted, but Natividad had been working and working to figure out ways to help her control her shadow better. Eventually she was sure Cassie would truly master her shadow and prove that *cambiadors* could learn to do that and didn't have to be killed. That would be wonderful.

Besides, Natividad just liked Cassie, and she was glad Miguel liked her, too. Cassie was the right kind of girl for her twin: Miguel thought he knew everything and he did know a lot, and he could sometimes *pasa por encima...*walk all over, an excellent phrase...yes, her twin could *walk all over* someone without even noticing he was doing it. But it was impossible for him to do that to Cassie Pearson, who was just as smart as he was and just as used to being right about everything.

But right now, she kind of wished her twin was right next to her, instead of Alejandro. Miguel would have noticed that something was wrong, too, but he would help her try to figure it out, not just get all suspicious and protective.

In the pew in front of them stood James Mallory, now the only remaining black dog to carry the Mallory name. James had lost his younger brother in that terrible fight with Vonhausel. He had changed after that. He had been loud and effusive, but Natividad had barely known him at all before his brother had died. He was quieter now. Or maybe it was because Grayson had lost Zachariah and Harrison and now had so little support; maybe that was why James had become serious and quiet.

Next to James Mallory stood Ethan Lanning—Ethan stood with his arms crossed, only *marginalmente* more patient than Conway for all he was more than twenty instead of just six. But Ethan was Grayson's nephew. Natividad knew he probably thought he shouldn't have to follow the rules as closely as the new black wolves.

Theodora and Maddie and Rebecca, the three women Ezekiel had brought to Dimilioc a month ago, were all over there with Liz, surrounded by ordinary people. They had only been at Dimilioc for a little while and preferred to stay in town.

Those women had very good reason to hate black dogs. But despite his father, Theodora loved her son. Soon she would have to move into the Dimilioc house. Even that she would do for her *bebé*. It was too hard for a human woman to raise a black dog child without help, even a child who had had the *Aplacando* done for him before he was born and again when he was a day old so that he would have better control over his shadow.

No one could tell about Maddie's *bebé* yet, but everyone could tell Rebecca's would be a black dog also. That was why Ezekiel had brought the three women to Dimilioc, of course, and why Grayson had accepted them. But Grayson hadn't let Ezekiel stay even a single night. Natividad hadn't seen him at all. In a way it had been good just to know he was so near. In another way, it had been very hard, so she had been almost glad he had gone away again so quickly. Except that she would have felt completely safe from all the newer black dogs if Ezekiel had been nearby.

But it wasn't any of the newer black dogs who had made her feel suddenly uneasy a minute ago. Black dog magic couldn't make sound fade out and come back. That hadn't been anything familiar from Pure magic, either. She didn't understand what had happened. Whatever it was, she thought it was actually still going on, too, because there was still that feeling of something missing, something that should have been there. She didn't remember ever feeling anything quite like this, except at the same time it seemed almost like she *did* remember feeling this way before. She frowned, puzzled.

Grayson's phone vibrated. Natividad couldn't hear it, but despite the last dwindling notes of the organ music, every black dog turned his head. Grayson took his phone out and held it up, frowning, to look at the number. Then, instead of rejecting the call, he stepped quietly out of the pew and left the church. And he didn't come back.

Of course, the service was nearly over, so it made sense that Grayson wouldn't want to disturb everyone by coming and going. There was no reason at all to *para preocuparse...*to fret. To fidget and wish Father McClanahan would hurry through his closing. Natividad tried to wait patiently, but she was surrounded by all these impatient black dogs, so it wasn't her fault that she kept catching herself shifting her weight and twisting the reminder sheet and trying to look over her shoulder without being too obvious about it. And she definitely didn't suggest going over to the parish hall for doughnuts. No one did, not even Miguel, who usually liked that part of Sunday services best. Even though he'd been close to the front, her twin almost beat her out the door and into the chilly sunshine.

Grayson was standing a little way from the church, listening to someone on his phone. Natividad could see nothing of the ordinary give and take of conversation. It looked more like he was listening to someone report. He wasn't saying anything himself, just occasionally nodding, the way you did on the phone even though the other person couldn't see you. And he was frowning. Grayson seldom looked *cheerful*. But surely his expression now was more forbidding than usual?

The feeling came back to her, or maybe just the memory of the feeling. Of something missing, a spreading silence where there ought to be...she didn't know. Not exactly sound. But something sort of like sound. She took a step toward Grayson, found her balance uncertain, and caught Alejandro's arm quickly. Her brother steadied her. "Natividad—"

"Espera," she said to him. "Wait."

Andrew had gone to join Liz and her *novio*, and Alejandro was paying more attention to Natividad than to Grayson, but most of the other black dogs were gathering, moving slowly, giving each other plenty of space but all watching Grayson attentively. They knew something was wrong, too. Thaddeus had his back straight and his arms crossed over his broad chest; a dominant posture that sent all the other black dogs wide of him. He was scowling, as always when he felt uncertain. DeAnn had her hand on her husband's back, rubbing gently, nudging him and everyone else toward calm and peace. She'd let Con and Paloma run away to burn off the impatient tension of staying still for an hour, which was probably as well, but she'd stayed by Thaddeus and Natividad was glad of it. Just having the other Pure woman nearby made Natividad feel better. Especially when she saw how intently Carter was watching the Master.

Miguel, as curious as any of them and probably more than most, had edged forward, bringing Cassie with him. Plainly aware that something was happening, Cassie's father, Sheriff Pearson, also joined them.

Grayson said finally, in a flat tone that did not invite argument, "Yes, I understand. I will come myself." Then he thumbed the phone off. He stood still for a long moment, looking at nothing. At last he turned, scanned the gathered Dimilioc wolves and everyone else, and met Natividad's gaze.

"Oh," said Natividad, somehow surprised and not

surprised, both at once. “Something’s happened to Ezekiel.” She knew it was true. Something was wrong with Ezekiel. Since they’d fought the vampire together, she’d held a tiny bit of his shadow, just a trace, less even than she’d kept of Alejandro’s. But it was enough to spin a thread of awareness between them. It wasn’t much. She hadn’t even realized it was there until Grayson had sent Ezekiel away, and then she’d found it was just enough to let her kind of tell where he was, even when he was a thousand miles away. It also let her know, even more vaguely, that he was all right. That thread of awareness was a comfort to her, even though she also worried about it sometimes—about what that trace of black dog magic might be doing to her own proper Pure magic.

At least, it had been a comfort until now all of a sudden it wasn’t.

A sharp silence had spread out around her, around all of them. Natividad blinked, becoming aware of it, realizing only when it was too late that it was a silence that had teeth in it. Then suddenly half the black dogs in the gathering were moving, aggression flaring in the air. She froze, understanding what she’d said.

Grayson himself only lifted his head and squared his shoulders, but Ethan and James both swung around to put their backs to him, facing the rest of the black dogs. Ethan’s attention was on Russell Meade, and, as though they’d sorted out their priorities by some unspoken black dog telepathy, James was staring straight at Carter Lethridge.

The other black dogs realized this, too. Russell’s lip curled in silent contempt: he knew he was stronger than Ethan. But he glanced away despite this, declining any challenge. His brother stood behind him, but he stood still, he wasn’t moving either, at least not yet.

But Carter stared back at James, deliberately holding his

gaze. He was a light-skinned black man of thirty or so, trim and good looking. More importantly, he had, for his age, a dense, powerful shadow and surprisingly good control. When he glanced around at the rest of the newer black dogs, the ones who hadn't been born into Dimilioc, they all looked away, wary and deferential.

Max backed away, not strong enough to put himself into the middle of a challenge, if there was going to be a fight. Alejandro, stronger and with better control than most of the other newcomers, stared at Carter, his eyes taking on a fiery tinge. Of course Alejandro would understand that Carter was the most dangerous of the new ones. Natividad gripped her brother's wrist, not that she could stop him if he moved, but she thought she'd better remind him she was here, and Miguel, and lots of other people. This would be a terrible place for a fight.

Sheriff Pearson had backed away, too. His hand rested on the butt of his gun, but he didn't draw it, being too sensible to step unthinkingly into this situation, though Natividad seriously suspected the sheriff would get involved if he thought it would help and never mind Dimilioc law that said ordinary humans weren't to involve themselves in black dog quarrels.

Then Thaddeus caught Carter's eye, raised his eyebrows, and said in his deep, deep voice, "Well, that's too bad, something happening to Ezekiel."

Suddenly everyone's attention was focused on Thaddeus, who was unquestionably the strongest black dog here, except just possibly for Grayson himself.

Thaddeus took one step toward the Master, and turned, putting Grayson at his back, the clearest possible statement of his allegiance. Immediately Natividad was ashamed of the instant of doubt she'd felt, because *of course* Thaddeus would side with the Master, she should have known he would—she *had* known, really, because obviously DeAnn would never even think of siding with a *cabrón* like Carter Lethridge.

"Ah," said Carter, and shrugged. "Well, that is too bad. About Ezekiel, I mean."

"Indeed," said Grayson, his tone dry.

Carter turned his head to the side, a gesture of submission, but not a very strong one. Natividad didn't always understand how black dogs worked out all their dominance issues, but she couldn't see how that would be enough, especially when Carter said, in a light, easy tone, "Master."

Grayson walked forward. Carter tensed...and stepped aside. The Master brushed past him and came to Natividad. He said to her, ignoring the rest of them, "That was Étienne Lumondière. He has encountered something peculiar, it seems. Peculiar and troubling. He has evidently not been able to determine precisely what has happened to Ezekiel. It appears that Ezekiel has been out of touch for some days. Yet you only just now felt something happen?"

Natividad stared at him. She said after a moment, "I don't know if I'd have felt anything until it became serious. But whatever's happened, he's alive. I know that."

"You are confident?"

Natividad nodded.

Grayson's eyes half closed. Other than that, he didn't show any visible reaction, but she knew she'd better be right. She nodded again. The connection might be thin and the feeling it gave her might be hard to interpret, but she was positive she could tell that much. She looked away, west. "He's...something's happened. He's not...right. Or...maybe it's not him. Maybe it's the..." she gestured helplessly. "The *connection*. It's like it's...faded. No, that isn't right, not faded. *Muffled.*"

"Muffled," said Miguel, coming up beside her.

Natividad nodded. "*Sí.* Yes, muffled. It's like hearing something, only there's a wall in the way. Or like you're down a well, or buried in blankets, or something." She made a frustrated gesture. "It's not like any of those things, really. I know he's alive. I don't even think he's hurt, exactly. I don't *think* so! But there's something wrong anyway. Something strange. I think—I think he's angry. Very angry. But that is muffled also."

Grayson considered this. After a moment he glanced around. "I shall see all of you back at the house," he told them. "James, if you would join me?" He walked away, without, so far as Natividad could tell, even a flicker of extra attention for Carter Lethridge.

Natividad stared after him. He was going to Colorado. He'd said that, to Étienne. The Master of Dimilioc was going to leave Dimilioc. That idea gave Natividad a thoroughly uneasy feeling in the pit of her stomach.

Even so, she was determined he would take her, too. If Ezekiel was in trouble, she was not going to be left behind.

TUYO

-1-

Beside the coals of a dying fire, within the trampled borders of our abandoned camp, surrounded by the great forest of the winter country, I waited for a terrible death.

I had been waiting since midday. Before long, dusk would fold itself across the land. The Lau must surely come soon. I faced south, so that my death would not ride up behind me on his tall horse and see my back and think that I was afraid to face him. Also, I did not want to look north because I did not want to see that trodden snow and remember my brother leaving me behind. That might have been a different kind of cowardice. But I could only face one direction. So I faced south.

The fire burned low. My brother had built it up with his own hands before he led our defeated warriors away. Now it was only embers, and the cold pressed against my back. I wished I could build the fire up again. Mostly that was what I thought about. That was as close to thinking about nothing as I could come. It was better than thinking about the Lau. I hoped they came before the fire burned out, or I might freeze to death before they found me. Even an Ugaro will die of the cold eventually, without fire or shelter.

I tried not to hope that I would die before they found me.

Then I heard them, the hoofbeats of their horses, and there was no more time for hope. I held very still, though stillness would not protect me now. Nothing would protect me. I was not here to be protected.

They came riding between the great spruces and firs,

tall dark men on tall dark horses, with the Sun device of their banner snapping overhead in the wind. Ten, twenty. Twice twenty. And even this was only the vanguard. I stood up to meet them, raising my hands to show that I was bound to a stake driven into the frozen earth—to show that I was tuyo, left here for them. They looked at me, but they rode past, down the trail my brother and our warriors had left. They rode through the remnants of our camp, around the fire and around me, and a little distance more. At first I thought they meant to leave me to die alone in this place while they went on to pursue a broader vengeance against my people. That would have been a death even more terrible than the one a tuyo should face. But then they came back and circled around me, not many paces away, looking down at me. My relief was so great that for the time it pushed away fear.

I knew immediately which must be their warleader. My people prefer silver, which is the metal that belongs to the Moon. The Lau decorate their warleaders with gold, as befits the people of the Sun. This man had gold thread worked into the collar of his coat and the backs of his gloves and the tops of his boots. He did not carry a sword or any weapon, only a polished black stick as long as a man's arm, with gold wire spiraling around its length. I had seen illustrations, so after a moment of puzzlement I recognized this as a scepter. This man was not only a warleader, but a scepter-holder, carrying the authority of the summer king. I had not known any such had come to the borderlands. At least my death would come at the hands of a worthy enemy.

The scepter-holder's horse was the color the Lau call fire bay and we call blood bay, which is common for their animals and very rare for ours. It was a fine animal. The Lau breed beautiful horses, but they belong to the summer country. They are too long-legged and too thin-skinned for the cold of Ugaro lands.

Like their horses, the Lau are long-legged and thin-skinned, and they like the cold no better. They are a graceful people, with elegant features and smooth brown skin. Lau men often grow beards, rare for Ugaro men, but they shave them short, just to outline the jaw and mouth. The warleader had a beard like that. He had cut his hair short to match. No Ugaro man would do such a thing; for us, cropped hair is a mark of shame. We tie our hair back or leave it loose, but we do not cut it.

For a moment, while the warleader gazed down at me, the silence was almost complete. A horse picked up one foot and set it down again, and the wind blew across the snow, and leather creaked as a man shifted his weight in the saddle. Other than that, there was no sound. At last the warleader dismounted. He was far taller than I; even taller than most of his own people. He looked cruel to me, with a hard set to his mouth. I knelt and bowed my head to show the proper respect the one defeated owes to the victor.

He looked at me and then at one of his people who had come up beside him. He said to that man, "We must have pressed them even harder than we knew, if they've left a tuyo for us. I suppose this must be the son of an important Ugaro lord, but he seems merely a boy."

I must have jerked in outrage, for he turned quickly to look at me again. I said, speaking carefully in darau, "Lord, I have nineteen winters, so I am not a boy either by your law or ours. You should accept me as tuyo. No one could set any fault against you for it."

He tilted his head in surprise, perhaps at my words, or perhaps because I spoke darau at all. He asked, "What is your name? What is your father's name?"

I answered, "Lord, it is a son of Sinowa, lord of the

inGara, who kneels before you in defeat. It is a brother of Garoyo, warleader of the inGara, whom you hold in your hand. My name, if you wish to know it, is Ryo. In leaving me for you, my brother acknowledges defeat. Accept me as tuyo, permit my brother and our warriors to withdraw, and my people will not challenge you again."

He nodded. But he said, "I understand that giving you to me constitutes a promise to cease hostilities. I might have trusted the efficacy of that custom when your people raided mine more rarely. Today, I don't believe I can expect much of a check in your people's aggression."

I could not protest. He was right. The war was too important for the inGara to step away from it. But I said, "Yet my people will not wish to face *you* a second time, lord, for to do so would be an offense against the gods. My father and my brother will take care to stay out of *your* way. Is that not enough?" I took a breath, making sure I could speak steadily. Then I said, "Please, lord. Let that be enough. Whatever vengeance you desire for every blow my people have struck against yours, take that vengeance on me and be satisfied."

Again a pause stretched out. The warleader looked into the forest, the way my brother had gone. Then he looked around at the long shadows and the deep forest that spread out all around that place. At last he turned back to me. He said, "Well, this is the first time anyone has ever offered me a tuyo. No doubt it will be a novelty."

"My lord, surely—" began the soldier beside him, but the warleader lifted his hand and the man fell silent.

The warleader tucked the scepter under his arm, drew a knife, and stepped toward me. I set my mind at a distance so that I would not disgrace myself or my people by flinching at the first touch of the blade. But he did not begin my death. Instead, he cut the thong that bound me to the stake. So I understood he would take me back into the summer lands and kill me there. It meant he intended to take his vengeance at greater leisure than was possible here in the winter country, but even though I knew I should wish to have my death over and not waiting ahead of me, I could not help but be relieved at any delay.

He put the knife away and said to the man beside him, "Take him to my tent and hold him there." Then he walked away.

I had known many Lau had pursued us, but I had not guessed how very many until I saw their camp.

The Lau are not a brave people, but they are so many they do not need to be brave. When they fight, they stand in close formations that Ugaro cannot break. When we attack their lands, we are quick, striking at undefended farms, then disappearing into our forests. Sometimes they pursue us across the river that marks the border between their country and ours, but not often, for we have taught them better. In the winter country we can evade them and stay out of their reach, and harass them by shooting from a distance their bows cannot match. During the long cold, they must be especially cautious, for our land itself becomes deadly to them. Yet this time they had come in force, disregarding the risk that snow might begin to fall heavily enough to weaken them and hinder their retreat. This scepter-holder was braver or more reckless than most of his people.

The camp was taking shape quickly and quietly, with no arguments about where any tent should be set or who should do which of the waiting tasks. The warleader's tent was the same as the rest: plain canvas with pegs to fasten the entry. The Sun banner stood beside it; otherwise I would not have been able to pick it out. The Lau soldier took me into the tent and pushed me to sit down. I might have stared at him to show that I was not afraid. But I did not wish to be insolent, only proud. I lowered my gaze and knelt down where he had indicated.

Three lamps, made of fine, clear glass set into bright copper, hung from hooks. In the middle of the tent, a brazier smoldered, taking the edge off the chill. At the back of the tent stood a small table and one chair. A pitcher and some cups, glazed pottery rather than the pewter one might expect in a camp, rested on another table. The pitcher drew my eye more than any of the other things. I was thirsty, though I had eaten a little snow during the afternoon. I did not ask the warrior for water. No such kindness was due an enemy, far less a tuyo. I tried to think about nothing.

After a time, not long, the warleader came into the tent. Two more soldiers came with him, but they stayed by the entry. The warleader turned the chair to face me, dropped into it, and beckoned to me. I got to my feet, came forward the few steps necessary, and knelt again. The soldier who had brought me to the tent moved to stand behind the warleader's chair. The warleader gazed at me, frowning. "Tuyo," he said.

I bowed before him. "Lord."

"I'm not entirely familiar with the nuances of the tuyo custom. Sit up and look at me, Ryo inGara, and tell me: what is the usual manner of death for a tuyo?"

Straightening, I looked him in the face as he had ordered. "Anything," I told him. "A tuyo might be stoned." If he were lucky. "Or flayed alive." If otherwise. "With so many men as are here in this camp, it could be hard to make a tuyo live long enough to satisfy them all. Small cuts, little burns, fingers taken—" I raised my bound hands illustratively. "A little at a time. Such a death can be made to last a long time if you are careful."

"Yes, I see," said the warleader, and I thought for an instant that he meant to begin immediately. Instead, he leaned his chin against his fist and regarded me for a little while. I could not guess what he was thinking. Perhaps about the war, about the Lau we had driven away from the borderlands or killed, the farms we had burned, the grain and cattle we had taken for our own. Perhaps about the men of his own he had lost in the short, sharp battle that had occurred when he had closed his trap, before we understood we had to run.

Perhaps he was thinking about vengeance. About the uglier kinds of death.

At length, he asked me, "How many sons does your father have?"

I answered, "Four that walk the land of the living, lord, and four that walk the land of the shades."

"In which of those categories do you count yourself?"

"The second, lord."

He nodded as though he had expected that answer. "Even with four sons remaining to him, your father will surely be angry when he understands what happened to you."

I hesitated because I did not know how to answer. Finally I said, "My father will indeed be angry, lord. But he will agree that it was better to lose a son than to lose all the warriors who fell into your trap. He will have no choice but to agree my brother was right to leave me for you rather than risk your men coming against the camp of our families. He will not set any fault against my brother for leaving me, nor against you for my death."

He looked at me for some time. His expression was impossible for me to read. Finally, he asked, "Is there any limit to what I can do to you? To how long I can make your death last?"

I answered as steadily and clearly as I could. "There are no limits at all. The manner of my death may be any that pleases you." I tried not to imagine what that might be. I knew something of the Lau and their customs, but I did not know very much about the cruelties they might prefer.

The warleader stood up, drawing his knife. It seemed unlikely he would begin it here, inside his tent where the blood would go everywhere, but I was not sure. I set the fear aside, breathing slowly and deeply so that I would not flinch.

He cut the thong that bound my wrists. Then he sheathed the knife and walked away. He poured himself a cup of water, standing with his back to me while he drank it. He took his time, and by the time he faced me again, I had recovered. I sat back on my heels as I knelt, keeping my back straight so that I could look at him as he preferred. I did not know why he had cut my bonds. I did not know what he would do next.

He said briskly, "I shall have to consider your fate. As the custom is unfamiliar to me, it may take me some time to settle upon appropriate ... measures."

While I was trying to understand this, the warleader turned to the soldier by his chair. "Bread and salt, Lucas," he said. The man drew in his breath, but the warleader raised his eyebrows and the other Lau closed his mouth without speaking, turned, and went out.

The warleader poured more water into his cup and brought it to me. I hesitated, but he commanded me, "If you're thirsty, drink."

I took the cup from his hand. The water settled my stomach a little. I wanted to ask what he would do. But he had said he would have to think about this, that he did not know himself what vengeance to take. I wanted to ask when he would decide. More than that, I wanted to creep out of his sight and hope he forgot all about me. Such fools men are made by fear. I managed, with an effort, not to move or speak.

The soldier came back with a round loaf of bread and a little packet of salt. These things he presented to the warleader with a flourish, the way a man might offer his lord a weapon or a prize. Something with heft; or something fragile. Something that mattered.

The warleader tore off a piece of the bread, sprinkled it with salt, and faced me. "My name is Aras Eren Samaura," he told me. "I am lord of Gaur—that is a county in the northeast of the summer country. You may address me as Lord Aras or my lord. Stand up and take this. Eat it." He held the bread out to me.

I got to my feet and took the bread from his hand. I thought of the way the soldier had given the bread to him, with that showy little gesture. "This is not only bread," I said. "It means something. What does it mean?"

His eyes narrowed, and I thought he would hit me for my insolence in questioning him. I bowed my head in apology and braced myself for a blow.

But the soldier laughed. He said to me, "Bread and salt is *guest-right,* and a more ill-considered, reckless gesture the gods have never seen in this world! But there's no dissuading him, you know. Raise your chin and stand up straight! Lord Gaur's *guest* should never cower like a beaten dog."

I think I have never been more astonished in my life.

"Lucas, please," the warleader said to the man, his tone sharp. But he spoke to me more gently. "But he's not wrong. I will treat you honorably if I can. Among other things, once I give you guest-right, I'm not likely to flay you alive or remove your fingers one joint at a time. Now eat the bread."

I ate it. The bread tasted of wheat and barley and salt, and of the ashes of the hearth where it had baked.

"Good," said the warleader. Lord Aras. "Now, I will expect you to obey whatever orders I—or Lucas—may give you." He indicated the other man with a little tip of his chin. "Talon Commander Lucas Terion Samaura. Call him by his title, or sir. You will obey him or anyone I set in authority over you. Do you understand?"

I hesitated. Then I said, "Forgive me, lord. I do not wish to be insolent. But you said you accepted me as tuyo. You said you would consider my fate. I understand your words, but I do not understand anything."

Lord Aras tapped the scepter gently against the side of his boot. It made a quiet sound. He said, "I *have* accepted you as tuyo. I do indeed intend to consider your fate. As you inform me there is no limit to how long I may draw out your death, I see no reason to rush my deliberations. Giving you guest-right seemed the simplest way to make certain I have no need to hurry the matter. I'm likely to come under some pressure to surrender you to one civil authority or another. Guest-right takes care of that. Not even my king could require me to give you up now, not that he would be likely to try. Do you need to sit down?"

Taking this as permission, I knelt quickly. I rested my hands on my thighs, breathing deeply. I knew now—it was obvious—that he did not intend to put me to death. Not right away. Perhaps not at all. I did not understand this, and it was surprisingly hard to accept, but I thought it was true.

Other Work By Rachel Neumeier

The *Black Dog* series:

1. BLACK DOG
2. BLACK DOG SHORT STORIES
3. PURE MAGIC
4. BLACK DOG SHORT STORIES II
5. SHADOW TWIN
6. BLACK DOG SHORT STORIES III
7. COPPER MOUNTAIN
8. BLACK DOG SHORT STORIES IV (forthcoming)
9. UNTITLED FIFTH NOVEL (forthcoming)

Young Adult Fantasy titles

THE CITY IN THE LAKE
Booklist starred review
For fans of Juliet Marillier, Patricia McKillip, Robin McKinley, and Sharon Shinn, looking for that next fix of luscious, romantic, flawless fantasy – Thea, The Book Smugglers Blog

THE FLOATING ISLANDS
Selected as one of the ALA 2012 Best Fiction for Young Adults
Amelia Bloomer 2012 List for recommended feminist literature
A Junior Library Guild Selection
A *Kirkus* Best-of-2011 selection

THE KEEPER OF THE MIST
Neumeier delivers intriguing political problems, complicated and charming personal relationships, and magic running the gamut from the domestic hominess of Nimmira to the terrifyingly gorgeous enchantments of Eschalion – Publishers Weekly

THE WHITE ROAD OF THE MOON
Neumeier firmly establishes the laws and rules of this medievallike fantasy's reality early on, but she also gives Meridy's world a romantic tinge, from the colors of a couture gown to the gnashing tusks of a fire horse. – Kirkus, starred review

Adult Fantasy titles

THE GRIFFIN MAGE TRILOGY
Lord of the Changing Winds
Land of the Burning Sands
Law of the Broken Earth

If you like your Fantasy to be subtle and complex, this could be the trilogy for you. – Geraldine, Fantasy Reads

HOUSE OF SHADOWS DUOLOGY
House of Shadows
Door Into Light

A beautifully realized tale of three young lives intersecting in a magical city where the shadows of the past threaten the tenuous peace of the present … Especially and whole-heartedly recommended to fans of Patricia McKillip."– Charlotte's Library

THE MOUNTAIN OF KEPT MEMORY
This isn't the kind of story to race through. It's one to linger over, and a world to get lost in. – Jason Heller, NPR 2016

WINTER OF ICE AND IRON
The story is tense throughout, with attention focused on its characters and the implications of its worldbuilding. – Publishers Weekly, starred review

THE TUYO SERIES
Tuyo
Nikoles
Tarashana (Forthcoming)

Read this novel if you like character-based action stories, if you love it when conversations are more intense than sword fights, if you like war stories because of the opportunities for heroism, if you have a fondness for winter landscapes, if you like families and friendship, if you enjoy lovely, assured writing. – Kim Aippersback, Goodreads reviewer

Collections:

Extremely well written and fun... Includes stories with Neill from City in the Lake, Bertaud from the Griffin Mage trilogy, and many more. I love the fact that Neumeier's short fiction always advances the main story line, but also works by itself. If you enjoy books by Robin McKinley or Susan Dexter, you'll also like Rachel Neumeier. – Amazon reviewer

Made in the USA
Middletown, DE
27 March 2021